Published by Detroit Ink Publishing LLC (DIP)
www.detroitinkpublishing.com
The Mayonnaise Murders. Copyright 2012 by Keith Owens
ISBN 9780615784250

Cover Art by Ken Kellett

Enjoy the book!

Keith A. Owens

Dec. 5, 2013

Thanks Nancy!

For my mother, Geneva McNamee Owens, who always believed in me and always believed I was the best at whatever I did; and for my wife, Pamela Hilliard Owens, who never understood what it meant to give up.

Chapter 1

Whoever killed Johnny Beardy ruined a perfectly good sandwich in the process. I was hungry when I found him, so that's the first thing came to my mind.

For the record, my name is Vid. It's short for a name you don't wanna bother trying to pronounce if you're from Earth. Anyway, I solve problems. It's not what I always did, but things change and here I am. Stuck up to my gills in other critters' problems on good ole Planet 10.

Once again, if you're an Earthling reading this, I meant that literally. You folks have a habit of making up cute little sayings and whatnot. Working your tail off. Sweatin' like a pig. Up to your neck in.

This ain't one of those. I have gills. Deal with it. They don't work so hot anymore because our kind hasn't spent much time breathing underwater since however many eons ago that was when we were created by you guys, apparently as some sorta joke that got outta hand. But now you're stuck with us, so I guess the joke's on you, right?

As for Johnny Beardy, he didn't have gills because he was one of yours. What you folks like to call a rock star. But being without gills wouldn't explain why young Mr. Beardy was found butt-naked dead in one of Vivacious 5's more notorious back alleys at night, face down in a sandwich. A really big pork sandwich with mayonnaise on it.

Mayonnaise. Now see, that right there lets me know this Johnny character had to have some connections with somebody who worked for the daily Earth transport. In the old days that never would've happened.

See, the transport used to be a class operation before Council politics got it shifted over to Vivacious 5 sector. Back then, you couldn't smuggle a grain of dust without getting caught and sent off to Planet 10-C, the `C' standing for corrections. But now the whole operation's been dragged down to V-5, down in the storage colony where the old landing base used to be. You couldn't pay me enough to work at that dump. See...

Oh yeah. I was sayin' about the mayonnaise.

There ain't no mayonnaise on Vivacious 5 because there isn't any mayonnaise on Planet 10. Stuff's been banned for years. See, mayonnaise kinda glues up the gills, but it can also be used to manufacture some pretty exotic head squeezers, if you know what I'm sayin'. Besides, all us 10-types prefer our sandwiches straight without the clutter. No muss, no fuss, that's us.

You gotta understand about Planet 10. It's a real clean little sphere. Clean water, clean air, clean sidewalks, and clean minds. Just the way it was manufactured to be over a century ago back in 2239 when Earth's experimental planet project was in full swing. Every sector spic and span, smellin' sweet and fresh.

Except for Vivacious 5, which happens to be where most of us freelancers work who don't wanna sit around all day answerin' phones and tradin' smalltalk. For a freelancer with ambition, Vivacious 5 is the only sector that offers any real challenge to prove yourself. That's because Vivacious 5 is the one corner of Planet 10 the broom never found. Stinks like a damned sewer. Guess that's why a lot of us call all the low-lifes who hang out there `niners'. Lettin' `em know they ain't quite evolved to 10 yet. They're the only ones who just won't go along with the program. They want Planet 10 back the way it used to be in the days before The Rinse kicked in, which was the final phase of the experimental planet program.

God bless The Rinse, I'm tellin' you. Who knows how this rock woulda ended up without it. Probably like a neon comet; goin down bright, goin down fast. One dead experiment, and a whole race of Teners gone with it.

Johnny Beardy liked hanging around those niners, which would explain what he was doing in Vivacious 5 after hours. That's plain as day. Ain't but a few kinds of critters go hanging around there after the third sun goes for a stroll, and that's the kind goes looking to get their fancy tickled in all the wrong places.

But there's still a few things I don't understand.

``You mean, like, what he was doing walking around naked on a strange planet, hey? Nice trench coat by the way. Hat too. You do that color yellow a gloooooriousss favor."

Oooh. That voice. Cripes. It was enough to get my motor runnin' every time. Kinda voice make a critter wanna do things to himself. When I looked over my shoulder at Vee, saw her standin there in those tall spiked pink heels and short, tight purple skirt, I felt my breath get sucked right outta my stomach. Such a gorgeous creature to be a page scratcher. Too gorgeous. And she knew how to use it.

``Hey, cakes. Talkin' out loud to myself again, huh? Damn. Gotta do somethin about that."

She kissed me just above the gills. Made me forget all about that naked stiff. Cops hadn't gotten here yet so nobody'd bothered covering ole Johnny up. He was just layin' there in the alley dirt, actually not lookin' all that outta place in this worn out section of a worn out section of town, trash and drunks littering what passed for a landscape. As usual, I'd gotten tipped long before those assholes on the beat, the keystones. That's 'cause I know how to treat critters. In my line of work you had to know how to treat the critters.

``You're always sayin' that, Vid, but you never do. Just the way you are. Guess that's why you turn me on like you do, hey? I like a man that shares his thoughts.''

``Cut it out, kid. You remember what happened the last time you got me started.''

Vee just grinned and winked, letting her ample left hip shift just the right way. Letting me dream a little dream. True enough, I'm one of the busiest freelance scavenger scouts in the sector, but I can always make time for a flesh fantasy. This time it was my turn to grin, letting her see the serrated edge of my front two teeth. I'd just had 'em both filed down, and they were lookin' sharp as ever. The babes went for it every time.

Then, after we'd both had our fill, I said, ``Vee. Play fair, doll. 'Least while we're on the clock.''

Just like that, the girl's all business. Hip back in place, standin' up straight, her little pointed fingers scurryin' back and forth across that little electronic notepad she used. Gotta love a modern woman.

``Human, right?'' she asked.

I frowned.

``Vee. Doll. How many Teners you think you're gonna find lookin' like this with no clothes on? Even in Vivacious 5? I mean look at the color of that skin, for cryin' out loud. It's white. And hair? On the *head*? C'mon, Vee, ask me a real question. Ain't that why they pay you the big bucks?"

I still couldn't believe Vee couldn't tell who it was she was lookin' at, even if it *was* a rather unflattering view from the rear. Vee had a huge sound collection, and Johnny Beardy was all through it like fibers through a rug.

``I got hair on my head, Vid. That make me human?"

``How much you pay for it, babe?"

``Be nice, Vid. Be nice, hey?"

``So ask me a real question already."

Still all business, but that got a grin out of her. She peeped at me over the top of her specs with those hot green eyes of hers. Don't know why they shook me up so. All teners got green eyes. Just not like Vee's is all.

``OK, I've got a real question for you, Missssster Vid. Perhaps you know why his clothes are gone? You think maybe he went to the wrong party uninvited or what?"

``I think maybe he came to the wrong *planet* uninvited is what I'm thinkin'. You know well as I do them humans ain't got no business hangin' around here unless it's the wrong *kinda* business."

Her fingers were steady scurryin' across that notepad.

``And the sandwich? That some new kinda way they came up with to inhale their food?"

``Take a closer look, Vee."

``Take a...?"

``Go ahead. And make it quick. Those keystones gonna be here any minute trying to sweep us both outta here and snatch the credit for what we found."

Vee took two steps closer to the body and leaned over as far as she could without letting her skirt rise too far up in the rear. Always a lady, that Vee.

``See anything unusual?" I asked.

``Hey...that's mayonnaise!" she chirped, soundin' all proud of herself.

Damn. What was it gonna take? Most times wasn't a thing you could get by my girl Vee. Well, at least she got part of it right.

``You got it, Vee. You ever see any mayonnaise here in Vivacious 5 sector? Or anywhere else on Planet 10, for that matter?"

Vee stood back up and turned to face me. She pinched her eyes shut while she let her mind race back over all those files she kept so perfect in her head.

``Once," she said, her eyes opening again. ``I seen some once."

Not good.

She frowned, then turned back around to take one last look at our naked friend. Suddenly she jumped, then dropped her notepad. She started jabbin' her finger at the body like it was gettin' back up or somethin'. I grinned.

``Hey! Vid! Isn't that...?"

****

Wasn't but a minute or two after Vee recognized dead loverboy when the keystones showed up. Actually, they don't like it when you call `em that. Hits too close to the truth. Their real title - every idiot with one bad tooth in his mouth on this planet has a title - is Planet 10 Industrial Safety and Peacekeeping Force - Vivacious 5 Sector. I feel about as safe around those spit-polish jerks as I do hangin' over the edge of a cliff. They were the only agency I knew where, to be accepted? You had to pass a test provin' you weren't too damned *smart* for the force. Imagine that. These fellas supposed to be protectin' us, and the only recruits they want are the schmucks.

Anyway, these keystones, they all wear these regulation button-down lime green suits that you could just about spot in the dark. And they don't have feet. Each and every keystone's been surgically altered to have little wheels where the feet used to go. Now that's what I call commitment to the job. Oh yeah, and they always travel in even numbers, usually four or more, and they never smile. I don't mean it's an accident or coincidence, either. I mean those jokers are trained never to smile. A buddy of mine sneaked me one of their training handbooks one time, and it was right there in Chapter 3; *No Smiling.* Go figure.

Just then, one of `em rolls up to me after circling the corpse a few times. He gives Vee the leering eye for a moment, I guess expecting her to disappear since she's a female, but Vee just stared him down and stepped up closer. Gotta love a professional woman. A moment or two more passes, then he looks back at me.

``You find this?"

``The body?" I ask.

He just stares.

``You mean the body?" I ask again.

This time he nods real sharp, lettin' me know I'm wastin' his time. Good.

``Yeah. Me and Vee here, we found it. And before we tell you anything else, we want it put on record that we're the ones found it. Not you jerkboxes."

Vee nodded, smirking just a bit.

``You're the one they call Vid," he said.

``Yeah. I'm the one."

``Then you're the one they say is a troublemaker. Looks to me like you're making trouble right now. Would that be a correct assumption?"

``Look, hardass, just because I..."

WHOMP.

I mean, that's just what it sounded like. Felt like it too. Right dead center in the middle of my chest, like somebody kicked me with the heel of a giant-sized work boot.

WHOMP!

There it went again. Next thing, I'm lookin' all around, tryin to figure where this *WHOMP* came from, but I can't see nothin' 'cause of all the smoke. I hear Vee coughin' through her gills with that sick hissing sound they always make when distressed. She's coughin' through her mouth too, and I'm stumblin' around through the smoke wavin' my hands around tryin' to find her and wondering why it's so hard. The crap smells like...damn. I'm not believin' this. That just can't be right.

``Vid!" I hear Vee callin from my left. Sounds like she's all of a sudden real far away, which ain't makin' sense.

``Over here!" I yell.

That's when I hear those runnin' feet slappin' against the pavement. Sounded like whoever - or whatever - was doin' the running wasn't wearing any shoes. But whoever those flappin' feet belonged to, I could tell they were movin' pretty quick. First time I caught a hint of them comin' it sounded like the flappin' was comin from pretty far away, just like Vee's voice. Then, just like that, I hear all these feet scurryin' around close. I'm figuring this smoke, or whatever it is, somehow bends noise. Makes it so whatever's comin at you can get to you before you know it's even in the neighborhood. Pretty clever.

Thing is, I can't see much of nothin' except a shadow here and there. It'll be there for a second, but then it's swallowed up. Only talking I heard was them confused keystones yellin' for whoever it was to cease and desist immediately. The way their voices were scattered, they would've had to been spread out a whole lot farther apart than I knew they were. They just kept rattling off all these legal codes that were supposed to make the flap foots freeze in their tracks. You'd think it was the first time these jerkboxes had ever dealt with the criminal mind.

Few seconds later - the whole event didn't last no longer than a minute - the smoke and that stale smell vanished like somebody'd sucked it up with a vacuum. Vee sees me and rushes over. She gets right up to me, then, in high heels no less, she puts on the brakes and starts fumbling around with her notepad like she's fixin' to start an interview. Still, those wide eyes and huffing gills let me know just how worried she was. That's my Vee. And just like I'd suspected, she wasn't anywhere near as far away as she was sounding.

As for the keystones, it took a sec before they realized the smoke was gone and they stopped bumping into each other and shoutin' legal code numbers. But once they realized they could see each other again, they were quick to brush off their uniforms and wheel themselves into their standard authoritative-looking box formation. That's why I called 'em jerkboxes. Playin' it off like they'd been in control the whole time.

Anyway, me and Vee were standing on one side of the alley, the keystones on the other, and layin' right there between us was...

``Hey!"

Right there in the patch of alley where Johnny Beardy'd just been takin' a rest with his face in a sandwich? Nothing but gravel and some debris.. Not only that, there weren't even any footprints.

``Did you get a look?" the one keystone asks me.

I shook my head, still staring at the empty ground. He looked over at Vee, but she did the same thing. Instead of looking at the ground, though, she was busy typing a story into her notepad. She had herself a major scoop, and she knew it. The keystone made a disgusted face, like he'd just smelled some foul odor, then turned away. For a minute I wondered if he'd smelled the same thing I had, but then I figured against it. Keystones were good at formations, but their sense of smell wasn't usually that hot. Something to do with results of the surgery made to their roller-feet. Whatever.

``Damned page scratcher," he said.

Like I said, their sense of smell wasn't all there.

****

``All right, Vee. Tell me about the last time you saw this mayonnaise."

We were sitting across from one another in a little late night cafe not more than a mile away from where the entire ruckus had gone down. Wasn't but a few other critters inside, and they were sitting at the counter watching the ritual screen. Vee and me were the only ones sitting in a booth. Vee had already filed her story over an hour ago, so she was through for the night unless she got called out on another run.

``You sure you wanna hear about this, hey? Vid, I'm tellin you, it's kinda creepy."

The keystones had left and gone on about their business, and I already knew that meant they weren't planning on filing any report at all since they didn't have anything to show for it. The last thing they wanted to do was to tell the top dogs a body got snatched away from `em inside some cloud that was smellin' like stale mayonnaise. Besides, I already knew they suspected me. Those jerkboxes were always suspectin' me whenever anything went twisted on `em.

Anyway, when I asked Vee how she could get a story out about what happened without any confirmation from the squad, she said she didn't need them for confirmation because she'd seen it firsthand. Besides, I'd been there too. Good point. Still, there was one thing I had to know.

``You smell what I smelled inside that cloud, Vee?"

She looked out the window at the street, then took a sip of crocka. Personally, I'd always preferred the real stuff, coffee, but the Purchasing Council took it off the market about a year ago and replaced it with this synthetic crap. Said coffee cost too much to import from the Earth clowns, plus those coffee bean plants couldn't survive in this artificial atmosphere.

Vee nodded.

``Yeah. I did."

``Um-hm."

She took another sip.

``So you thinkin' what I'm thinkin'?"

``Yeah. I am."

I propped my elbows up on the table and leaned forward, tryin to give Vee a sense of how important this was. She knew I always leaned forward when I was dealing with something big.

``So then you gotta tell me," I said. ``And start at the beginning. Don't leave nothing out, hear?"

For a full minute she doesn't say a thing. Can hardly hear her breathin'. Only noise is the ritual screen and whatever scattered noise is comin in from the street. But I know better than to push her. She'll talk when she's good and...

``You gotta promise me," she says.

``Promise...?"

``This doesn't go any further. Past you and me. It could really mess me up with my job and stuff."

``OK, yeah. Sure, cakes. Sure thing. I mean, what? You gonna tell me you were takin' contract hits out on clean sector residents? Cripes, how bad can it be?"

Vee ain't sayin' nothin'. Just steady lookin' in my eyes. Then it starts to hit me.

``Aw geez. Vee...That's it, ain't it? You used to...awwww geez...''

``That's just part of it. Look, Vid, you knew I wasn't always a page scratcher. You can't tell me you didn't figure that out the first time we met two years ago on that case, the one about the guy tryin' to grow an illegal peach tree in his closet. Almost knocked the atmosphere off balance, remember? You're too smart to let stuff like that go by you, Vid. You've always been too smart.''

``Yeah, but Vee, I mean, this...Ain't no way I woulda never suspected...''

``You got somewhere to go tonight, Vid?''

I looked at my watch. Shook my head.

``What time this place close, hey?''

``Couple hours. Why?''

``Because I'm gonna tell you a story, and I want you to still be my friend when I'm through. About the way things used to be with me before I went legit. See, all right...Vid, I used to deal mayonnaise. Yeah. Me. Ain't that the livin' end? Little Miss prize-winning page scratcher from The V-5 Headline Screamer was a skid. For seven years. I know I told you I'd only seen mayonnaise once, but I lied. What I'm telling you now is the truth, I swear it. I'm probably part of the reason why the stuff is so illegal now.''

``Why, Vee?''

``Why the mayonnaise?''

``Why now? Why you tellin' me this now?''

``Because you're gonna need to know what I know to find out what happened to Johnny Beardy's body. And what's gonna happen if we don't find it.''

``If we don't...what're you sayin', Vee?"

``Let me tell you a story."

Chapter 2

There's nothin' wrong with naked mayonnaise, all right? Before the stuff was made illegal, that Hellgirl brand was the most popular import brand on the planet. Wasn't nothing better than a thick pork sandwich with some Hellgirl ridin' on top. Now that's good eatin'. Matter of fact, used to be if you went to someone's house and asked for some Hellgirl's, and that someone didn't have any? Rude. Very rude.

But just like with most other good things, there's always someone out there can't wait to screw it up for everybody else. That's what happened with the mayonnaise 25 years ago. I was still a young kid at the time.

First thing was nobody knew quite what was goin on. Keystones figured maybe somebody'd found a way to smuggle Earth drugs onto the planet. The kids, they were all of a sudden actin' nuts. I mean more than usual. One day, junior would be actin' like junior was supposed to act. The next, he's flyin' around the neighborhood like somethin's bitin through his undergear. Runnin' into poles with his forehead just for the feeling of it, then laughin' all loud and crazy.

But the keystones couldn't find any leaks. Wasn't any headsqueezers slippin' in from any Earth transports or any other kinda way that they could find, and that's when folks really started gettin' nervous. Critters started wondering if maybe somethin' from the atmosphere, something we hadn't identified yet, was comin' into the sector through one of the sector's bubble purification valves. Each sector's built under a bubble, and the valves, big long snake-lookin' things, manage to keep the atmosphere stable some kinda way I still don't understand seein' as how I ain't nobody's scientist.

Well, that paranoid atmosphere theory turned out to be halfway right. Like I said, mayonnaise all by itself wasn't nothin' but a pork sandwich's best friend. But you mix it up with some chuladin*9.3, a chemical we use to create a salt substitute, and you've got yourself the contents of some Grade A headsqueezer material. Chuladin*9.3 gets an attitude whenever it gets trapped inside the same jar with either vinegar or eggs is how one of my lab buddies ran it down to me. Mayonnaise has both. Leave it to some bored punk with too much time on his hands to figure out how to unlock the combination.

That same lab buddy, Veno, was the one who finally figured out what was wrong with the kids. What he never did figure out was who it was that made the first batch.

Vee.

All the while she's tellin' me this, I just keep shakin' my head.

``You know, I really wish you wouldn't do that while I'm tryin' to talk to you, hey?"

I shook my head.

``Just hard for me to believe what I'm hearin', Vee. You? Doin' these kinda things?"

I shook my head again.

``All right. So go ahead with your story."

``You promise to respect me in the morning?"

``I'm a scavenger, doll. When was the last time you heard a scavenger make a promise you felt comfortable with?"

Vee grinned, then shrugged. She squeezed my wrist.

``You know I'm not from here, right? From Vivacious 5, I mean. I'm from another sector over on the other side of the hills. Very Very."

``You? From Very Very? Vee, you gotta be kiddin'. I didn't know you had that kind of money..."

``Don't. My folks did. Daddy's the one designed the updated version of the Earth transport motor. Hadn't been for his design, we'd still be waiting months to get supplies from the mother base instead of days. I woulda gone on to follow his career, but I never did have a head for design. I got Daddy's head for numbers, though."

``I'll be damned...But okay, so, I still don't see what this has to do with you being the one who figured how to make MayoMadd. Whole lotta kids on Very Very, but none of them wasted their time figuring out how to pervert a perfectly good sandwich spread."

Vee gave me a sad smile, like she was tryin' to figure out a way to tell me there wasn't any Santa Claus.

``Vivacious 5 ain't all that bad, hey? Believe me, there's worse things out there, Vid. Way worse. They just don't want nobody here knowin' about it. They want everybody here to think they're the scum and everybody else on the planet is so clean they squeak. Haven't you ever been out there? Talked to some of the critters?"

I shrugged, remembering the few times I'd managed to make my way that far down planet. I'd been on vacation. Mighta been a lotta action on Vivacious 5, but it damned sure wasn't any place you'd be wanting to spend a holiday. But Very Very? Man.

Only sector on the planet with a simulation, climate-controlled beach and ocean. Perfect four-foot waves rollin' in all day, all night. For an extra fee, you could scuba dive and play with the hologram fish. Until your money ran out, that is. Then the fish kinda faded away. Still, hard to believe it could have ever been any better than that on earth. I smiled.

``Yeah, I've been there a few times. Had a ball. I remember once I met this..."

``Vid. Snap out of it, hey? I want you to think. Did you ever notice the kids there?"

``What about the kids?"

``Did they seem like normal kids to you?"

``A little spoiled maybe, but that don't mean..."

``Vid. Think."

So I reached across the table and took a sip of Vee's crocka, then leaned back against the booth and thought. I pictured the kids I'd seen there in my mind and tried to figure what it was about them that Vee wanted me to see. At first, I couldn't see much of anything different from the kids on V-5. Hell, kids are kids. They're all short, bald, their blue eyes shifting over to green. And loud. Really, really loud. Has to do with their gills just startin' to form, and the way their vocal chords are startin' to make the adjustment. For about a year, kids can't even whisper `cause of the...

``Damn."

Vee put on a weak smile.

``Bet you're wondering how you didn't think about it earlier, hey? Bet now you know why they make it a vacation spot, so critters from the outside won't stop to pay attention."

``Vee, those kids...those kids wasn't sayin' a word..."

``And you wanna know why?"

``Vee..."

``Because their perfect little parents want them that way, that's why. Don't want their precious Very Very to have too much noise, not even if it's comin from their own kids. That would be Very Very bad for tourism. After all, why do most critters go there in the first place? Why did you go there, Vid? To get away from all the noise here on V-5, right? Hey? Isn't that why you left?"

I was startin' to feel sick.

``But how...?"

``How do you keep Very Very kids quiet? By gettin' their gills fixed, Vid, that's how. Oh it's a real simple procedure any doctor over there can do, and it's designed to last just long enough until the vocal chords and the gills are done growing."

``... Ten months."

Vee nodded, and I noticed her sad smile was long gone. Girl was mad.

``Ten months? Those folks get their kids fixed so they can't talk for ten months straight? Don't they know what that can do to a kid? Geez, I can't believe at least one of `em didn't explode from verbal backup."

``One of `em did. My twin sister Vinia. She used to talk even more than me, so you can imagine the pressure buildup when her pipes died. The folks kept telling her to hang in there a few more months, but Vinia'd just got worse. She'd be rolling around on the floor, flapping like she couldn't breathe. One morning? Vinia go 'boom'.

``Anyway, that's when I decided to do something, Vid, `cause I knew this couldn't keep happening. You can't just let kids explode like that. It's not a good thing.''

``No shit it ain't. Cripes. I can't believe we didn't hear somethin' about that over here. Why wasn't there a piece in the Screamer?''

``Think Vid. Where's the Screamer publisher live?''

``I'll be damned. Well then...wait. You still ain't told me how this all fits into MayoMadd.''

``Simple. It's what I used to give the kids their voices back. Well, some of `em, anyway. Little dab on the edge of the gills, then wait an hour. Powee. Those of us who got ourselves unfixed had to hightail it out of there, which is how I ended up here. Matter of fact, we all ended up here. Easiest place to get lost without folks asking too many questions.''

``But how'd you know about chuladin*9.3? And the egg thing? And the vinegar? Weren't you a little young to be playing the mad scientist bit, Vee? C'mon.''

Up until then, Vee had been lookin' me dead in the eye. Now, all of a sudden, she was drifting away.

``Maybe I wasn't the one who really figured it all out,'' she whispered.

``But you just said...''

``Maybe I had some help.''

``Help...?''

``I told you Daddy designed the updated Earth transport motor?''

I nodded.

``Daddy's a scientist. Appointed by the Sector Council.''

``Appointed by...holy..."

``So you know he's good, hey?"

``Wait a minute, are you tellin' me your father..."

``I'm telling you my father was a very good scientist, Vid. And that's all I'm telling you. Except that he used to study acting in his younger days, which came in handy when he needed to convince the Sector Council that his morality implant had been properly disconnected. Usually they make you provide written proof, but he pulled off his act so good they couldn't believe anybody with his morals still intact could say the things he was saying to them."

``When was the last time you talked to your father? Or your mother?"

``Not since I left Very Very. You know the rules when a kid takes off without the proper approved council procedure, Vid. No contact. If I took that risk, I'd be putting them both in danger, and that wouldn't be right. Besides, they know I'm OK. They see my stuff in the Screamer. Every once and awhile they'll write a letter to the editor about something I did just to signal me."

I could see she was startin' to tear up so I figured I'd better shift the subject pretty quick, but not before I got some more answers about how the MayoMadd operation got so crazy out of hand.

That's when the story got thick. As Vee told it, in the process of returning free speech to the young, the young started to notice some rather pleasant side effects from their recovery. A bit too pleasant, maybe.

At first, the good doctor decides to write it off as a natural high kinda thing, kids just bein' overglad to have their pipes workin' again. But after a few weeks pass, doc notices the kids still asking for more MayoMadd, even after their voices are back and everything is supposed to be fine - including his little girl, Vee.

So when he makes the decision to cut off the supply, the kids start getting ornery, ringing up late nights making threats against the doc, the wife, stuff like that. The kinda stuff they say only happens on V-5. Then the doc starts getting these calls from the kids' parents, asking him what he can do about their children who've suddenly started talking loud again and are all out of control. As long as it was just a volume thing with a few kids, the folks wrote it off as a fluke and the neighborhood Class-2 Council reps agreed to look the other way. Better than setting off an alarm. But once the behavior started going haywire, they knew something twisted was goin' on and something had to be done about it.

Knowing the way things work on Very Very, Doc figured it was better if he kinda diffused this situation he'd created before letting the High Council dicks start pokin' all around in it and makin' stuff worse. That was when he knew he was gonna have to get those kids shipped away to V-5. The worst part was the doc ends up being the only one with a hurtin' feelin' behind the whole deal because he was the only one who still had his conscience fully functional. All the other parents, once he'd called them over to explain the situation, had no problem with the solution whatsoever. Far as they were concerned, there was never anything special about any one kid. Hell, you could always make more.

But before they all get shipped out, Vee managed to sneak into Daddy's lab and find out what it was that made mayonnaise such a special trip. It wasn't until the folks saw the papers weeks later that they understood why Vee was smilin' at `em so sweet and wavin' as the inter-sector shuttle was hustlin' her away, never to be seen by the folks again. I still remember the headlines: ``HELLGIRL'S; IT'S NOT JUST MAYONNAISE ANYMORE."

No sooner than Vee was off the shuttle before she'd started hittin' the streets hustlin' MayoMadd to a bunch of crazy kids and makin' crazy money. Since the stuff was so easy to make, the keystones could never reach a shop in time, and they never knew who was behind the whole thing. Within a few months, you were startin' to see dead kids layed out all in the streets like so much garbage, their faces covered in mayonnaise.

``So what was it that made you stop? Your conscience start stickin' little needles in ya or what?"

Vee shrugged, then gave me a grin.

``Simple. They outlawed mayonnaise. No more mayonnaise, no more MayoMadd. Mixing it up with that chemical is one thing, but manufacturing mayonnaise? I was never that good."

Well damn.

``So then how would you explain our good friend Johnny Beardy? Before he got snatched, that is."

``Simple again, Vid. Somebody out there is very good. A whole lot better than I ever was. Unless they did it the easy way and paid off some of the earth transport crew to ship in some Hellgirl's, then they're making the stuff here. And that's serious."

``But what makes you think they wouldn't be doing this the easy way, doll?"

`` `Cause of the risk involved. It's a whole lot easier to sniff out a crooked transport crewmember, even these days, than it is to sniff out a MayoMadd factory, hey? Besides, why go through all that hassle of waiting for the stuff to get up here from Earth?

The less angles to worry about, the straighter the road, the better. And believe me, Vid, dealing with those idiots from Earth is never a straight road. They all think they're so fuckin...'scuse me, I know that don't sound ladylike. But you gotta know how they are, Vid, hey? They think just `cause they're the mother base, the ones who created all this crap, that they're so damned much better than everybody else. Even the *drug dealers*, can you believe that? Ain't that the living end? They figure `cause they're scum from the original host planet, that makes then a higher class of scum."

``Go figure."

``Exactly."

We sat there lookin' at each other for a bit, then I figured I'd better say somethin' before somebody started pickin' his nose.

``So where do we go from here, cakes?"

``You tell me, Vid, hey? You're the sharp-nose scavenger guy."

I gotta guess I asked for that one. I gave her a wink, then reached in my top pocket to reach for a smokey. Lot like the cigarettes you see on Earth, only without the tobacco. Can't grow tobacco on Planet 10, and tobacco smoke screws up the artificial atmosphere somethin' awful, which means no importin' the stuff either. So we got smokeys. No fancy brand names or anything, `cause there's only one approved way to make `em, which means they're all the same. It ain't like you get your choice of menthol or regular. Smokey or smokey. Take your pick.

But I digress.

``OK, let's see what we got then. We got us a dead naked rock star that somebody swiped. A dead rock star with his face stuffed in a mayonnaise sandwich."

``Right,'' says Vee.

``We got the fact that mayonnaise is illegal.''

``Um-hmmmm.''

``And we know you're the reason MayoMadd damned near wrecked V-5.''

``Hey! That's not fair, Vid. That's punching in the gills.''

``Well it's true, ain't it?''

``Kindasortamaybe. But listen, I changed my ways! Doesn't that count for something? Besides, the only way we're gonna find out what's goin' on is we gotta trust each other.''

I started laughin', and I could see Vee startin' to frown up.

``What's so damned funny?'' she asked.

``If you can't see it, then I worry about your investigatin' skills. Look, a page scratcher and a scavenger? Workin' together? On V-5? Vee. Doll. The comic potential here is enough to fill a warehouse.''

She grinned, then bummed a smokey off me. After I lit it for her, she grinned some more as she blew circles of purple-colored smoke through the air.

``You just might be right, Missssster. Vid. You just might be right.''

****

Ten minutes later, after we'd each ordered a steaming cup of crocka to go, Vee and I were walkin' down the sidewalk toward her local transport, which was parked about three blocks away. We'd agreed to meet up later the next day to put together some details on how we was gonna handle this thing, so neither of us felt like sayin' much during the walk. Then, suddenly, I feel Vee's hand grab mine. I start to ask her what the deal is, but she just says, ``shh!'' then points across the street about a hundred feet away to what I recognize as her transport.

Most transports look pretty much the same, like a stretched out drop of colored water. Seamless. Damned near all of `em are black or some other dark color. Only way you knew where the doors were was when you gave the voice identification code. Transports are only supposed to recognize the voices of their owners, but try tellin' that to all those owners who got their transports snatched. The distributors say they're still workin' out the kinks. I figure they oughta be workin' on givin' some of these folks their money back, but nobody ever listens to me.

Anyway, Vee's transport was hot pink. How she found a distributor with that color I'll never know - and neither does the transport regulatory council - but since there's no rules on the books saying a transport has to be a butt ugly color that looks like everybody else's then they pretty much leave her alone.

Except for tonight.

``You know that guy?'' I whispered.

Vee stared at the tall, slouched figure smokin' the smokey, leanin' back up against her hot pink transport wearin' plaid pants and a checkered shirt that came up nearly to the gills. The unfashionable clash of colors was not lost on me. I may be just a scavenger, but at least I keep my colors in order.

She shook her head real slow.

``Then maybe I should take you home. We'll come back and pick up your machine tomorrow when more folks are around."

``They'll just find me again," she said, sounding more tired than scared.

``Who's `they', doll? I thought you weren't knowin' who this guy is."

``Not knowin', just suspecting is all. I'm suspecting this has something to do with..."

``...Johnny Beardy?"

``Exactly."

Right about then the mysteriously unfashionable critter in the plaid pants turns to look at us and grins. Motions for us both to come on down.

``So how were you knowin' we were there all along?" I asked our fashion-challenged friend, once we got close enough to where he could hear us. He just smiled, and I was thinkin' back to the last time I'd seen one any uglier. Teeth bent up inside his mouth like they were confused about what they were doin' there.

``Oh let's see now; You're Vid and you're Vee. You're the scavenger, you're the scratcher. You're the eenie. You're the meenie. You're the..."

``Hey. You. Poetry Man. Cut the idiot routine, all right? Now see, you're leanin' there with your scrawny butt all up against my friend's nice pink transport. She's tellin' me she don't know you, which leads me to believe you're either a total stranger with no manners, or a long-lost cousin that hasn't yet been properly introduced."

Mr. Fashion, he keeps his grin on tight.

``And you call me the poetry man. A regular wizard of verse thou art. I do believe you missed your calling."

``Look, spud, if you don't...''

``Johnny Beardy.''

``Wha..?''

``I told you,'' said Vee.

I glance over at Vee, but she's got her eyes locked on the stranger, who's got his eyes locked right back on her.

``Johnny Beardy,'' he said again.

``What do you know about Johnny Beardy?'' I asked.

That's when he decided to un-butt the transport. After giving us both a wink, which I thought was pretty corny, he starts walkin' away towards another transport parked near the end of the block. It was your regular ugly color.

``Follow me,'' he said.

``At the very least I'm gonna be needin' to know your name. I suspect anybody got the courage to dress like that must have a real winner.''

``At the very least, you may call me Deep Cluck. And I suggest you beware of the chickens. Oh, and by the way, Miss Vee, simply marvelous stories you wrote about dear Johnny's disappearance in the local screamer. If only they were true.''

``Hey, I was there when it happened. I know what I saw, hey?''

``Hey hey, my dearest. So was I. Hey?''

Beware of the chickens...?

Chapter 3

``WHOA! Where the hell did this guy get his license from?"

I was wondering the same thing myself. For the past half hour, Vee and I had been trying to keep up with this Mr. Deep Cluck clown as he darted in and around the street traffic like it wasn't even there, ignoring any and all stop lights or anything else that might be offering the slightest suggestion of safety. It was no easy job. The critter drove like he was gettin paid for every pedestrian he nearly plowed.

``So answer me this, Vee. You believe this guy?"

``About what?"

``You know, about Johnny Beardy not bein dead and all that. You think that could be the truth?"

``I dunno. I mean...DAMMIT! WHAT THE...this guy's tryin to kill us both, Vid, I swear he is. So you were askin me...? Oh, Johnny Beardy bein dead. Not. Yeah, I guess maybe it could be, hey? It's possible. I'll tell you one thing for sure. If Johnny really isn't dead? This Deep Cluck sweety's gonna give us a way to check it out real quick. I guarantee you that."

``What makes you so sure?"

` `Cause I've seen his type before, hey? Had sources like him. I mean, like, if he wasn't being truthful about something that big, then why'd he drop that bomb in our laps like he did? It's ...SHIT! YOU FUCKIN JERK! YOU ALMOST... `cause he wants in, Vid. He's droppin this one on us to show mostly you that he's got somethin to offer this whole thing we're workin on. It's kinda like cards, hey? But backwards sorta. He's laying out his big deal card early to pull us in. Anyhow, that's how I read it."

``You know, I'm startin to think maybe you shoulda gotten yourself into my line of work insteada wastin yourself..."

``HEY!"

``What? We almost run over somebody again?"

``Nope, that `hey' was for you, Vid. Look, we've been over this one before, all right? And I'm not wastin myself. I happen to think what I'm doin is a valuable service to the V-5 community. The people have a right to know, and I'm the one makes sure they know, hey? It's a good way to make a living. Kinda makes up for my old ways, I like to think."

Personally, I think Vee woulda been better off stayin a crook than turnin herself into a page scratcher. At least back in those days she knew she was crooked. A paycheck don't make a profession respectable in my book. Not that I'd ever tell any of this to Vee...

``WHOOOOOOAAAAHHH DAMN! What is it with this guy, Vid? And where are all the keystones? Me, I get pulled over just for crossin in front of some critter too close, but here this guy is racin through town chasin a land speed record and I can't see one of those wretched little wheelies anywhere! What gives?"

I don't know why I hadn't noticed that any sooner myself. Probably `cause I was too focused on all the pedestrians flippin us sign language from the sidewalks.

Yeah well.

``Say Vee, it just hit me. If Johnny Beardy really ain't dead, like Mr. Fashion says, then what do you figure possessed him to fly all the way up here from Earth, strip off his clothes, stick his mug in a mayonnaise sandwich, then stretch his naked butt out in the middle of a public street on V-5 like that? Huh? I mean here's a guy who's supposed to have everything, right? He's from the big deal host planet, he's a rock star, he's got all this cash, he's got chickadees on Earth and chickadees scattered all over Planet 10, but still this guy figures he wants to pull a stunt like this. You figure he's bored or just stupid?"

``Maybe it wasn't him. Maybe it wasn't his body we saw, hey?"

``But you said so yourself, Vee, remember? You pointed at the body and you said, `Hey, ain't that...?' Just like that. OK, so maybe you didn't recognize him right off, maybe not as quick as I thought a smart kid like you mighta done, but you recognized it. Eventually."

Vee gives me this look, which lets me know it's time to brace myself.

``So now you're saying I'm slooooooow, Vid? A little too much fog in the chickee's upstairs chamber, is that it?"

``Now Vee, wait a minute now..."

``You know, I can't believe you sometimes, I really can't. We're supposed to be working like a team on this thing. Together. At least that's what I thought, but then you've gotta go and say something stupid like you always do. I mean it, Vid, you really need to..."

``Look, let's don't go there just yet, all right? See, now you're gonna go off on this discrimination thing and you know just like I do that's when we always end up and...hey...Vee? Are you seein what...?"

``You mean, like, where'd everybody go?"

``Yeah. Like that exactly."

It happened that quick. One minute, Vee and me were perched on the edge of a tiff; the next we were tryin to figure out what happened. One minute you've got pissed off pedestrians divin outta your way, then suddenly everything goes black. Only thing we could see was the front light from Vee's mobile, the rear light comin offa Deep Cluck's machine, and the road passin between us. When I looked out the rear window, I could see the glimmer of the city fadin fast. Lookin out the side window I could make out some shapes here and there, some of em rounded, some of them sharp. But what they were shapes of I didn't have the slightest.

I'll be damned. The Dreg region. All these years on V-5 and I never...

``You ever been out this far, Vid?"

Vee's voice sounded tiny, like it was comin from the bottom of a cup.

``Not me, doll. This is firsties for the both of us."

``Firsties, Vid?"

No way to defend a word like that. Erase it and move on. Few minutes later, Deep Cluck signals he's pulling over to the side of the road. We pass him by a few yards, then pull over in front. He leaves his light on as he slides open the door to step outside. I appreciate his decision to keep on the light. I appreciate it a lot.

Once he's standin outside our window, I push a button and it comes down just a few touches. I still don't trust this guy enough to be givin him a full open window-type greeting. He grins.

``I'm quite afraid you'll need to step outside, Mr. Vid. You too, Miss Vee, unless you'd prefer to be left out. You being the more delicate member of the species and all."

``All right, Spud. You win. Now step back, unless you want this door to relocate your family production mechanisms.''

His cracked lips curled back to make way for a bigger smile fulla more and bigger screwed-up teeth. This was one butt-ugly critter. If I was him, I'd spend a whole lot less time smilin and a lot more tryin to raise some money for a corrective procedure. It just ain't considerate of others to walk around lookin like that.

``Certainly, Mr. Vid. And might I say that must be quite some door you have there.''

``Don't go gettin smart on me, Cluck. Let's just get to it, all right?''

Vee stood there in front of him with her arms crossed. If you ever wanted to get that woman ready for a fight, just call her delicate.

``You drive like a lunatic,'' she said.

``So I've been told, but ah well. We are none of us all that we should like to become someday. I'm sure you'll agree.''

``Appears to me you might be a bit further from the goal than most,'' I replied. ``And by the way, you need to trade in that accent. Earth London don't hold the same sophistication up here as it does down there. Up here, anybody talks like that is just a funny-talkin so-and-so. Y'know?''

He kept smiling, but his eyes let me know I'd slipped one through the defenses. I gave him a half grin for free.

``So all compliments aside, Cluck, what're we doin way out here in the Dregs? What's this got to do with the disappearance of Johnny Beardy?''

Cluck looked down at his left foot, which he was kickin hard into the dirt beside Vee's car. Then he looked back up. Still the smile.

``You may recall I warned you to beware the chickens?''

This guy wasn't turnin loose this accent. Whoever sold it to him musta sold the hell out of it.

``Yeah, so? What? That some kinda code language signifyin we oughta watch our step around you?''

``Quite wrong. I need no code to tell you that. As a good scavenger, you ought to realize when you're dealing with someone who should not be tampered with. Enough said? Good. Now about the chickens, Mr. Vid. I'm sure if I were to leave you alone for a long moment, or even the delicate Miss Vee here, one of you would be able to add it up with just a wee bit of rational thought.''

``Well perhaps we oughta skip the long moment since we don't have all night and you tell us what it is you know. Otherwise, we might as well all hop back on the road and make better use of our time.''

``Mayonnaise.''

Vee's arms unfolded as she took a strong step toward our man.

``What's that, Mr. Cluck Deep? What do you know about mayonnaise, hey?''

``I believe it is the substance of the sandwich in which young Mr. Beardy found his face on the night of his supposed death, just before he was supposedly abducted.''

``What's with all these `supposedly's', Cluck?'' I asked.

Cluck clasped his hands behind his back, then began to pace back and forth in front of us. Damned drama hog.

``Are you saying he wasn't swiped?" asked Vee.

``Precisely."

Vee and I exchanged glances. Something in the way he said that `precisely' made me nervous.

``So what happened to him, then?"

``Perhaps it was what he wanted to have happen."

``I'm losin you, Cluck."

``Quite the opposite, Mr. Vid."

Then he pointed over the top of Vee's machine to a location somewhere way off in the darkness that was impossible to make out. After keeping that long, bony finger stretched out for a good long stretched-out moment, his eyes focused hard on whatever was supposed to be out there, he squinted back at the two of us. Didn't say a thing, like we were supposed to pick up on whatever it was by mind transfer or some other way he knew damned well I wasn't evolved enough to get. I glanced at the side of his cheek for that telltale red slash that'd let me know if he was one of them that could. He wasn't. So now I'm wonderin what gives with the silent pointing bit.

I pointed in the same direction, looked him dead in the eye, then shrugged my shoulders.

``Over there what? You gotta speak up, Cluck. I can see you ain't no telepath, and even if you were, you know I'm not one either. Now what the hell is it you ..."

A noise. For a moment, all three of us just stood there with our ears cocked, gills tight, strainin to hear exactly what it was. Then, off in the distance, we could see two more white dots approachin fast. Another transport. When I looked back over at Cluck, I could see he'd just discharged a large amount of water straight out his gills into that hightop collar of that ugly shirt he was wearin, and he was startin to tremble.

Right about then I'm guessin we were in some trouble.

``Ohhh...'' was all he said.

``Cluck? Hey. Buddy. We in some kinda deep...''

``Ohhhhhhhhh...''

``I'll take that as a yes. So who is this racin out here, and why?''

``No time. You must...''

``Cluck, I gotta know what's goin on. Me and Vee, if we're in the kinda trouble it sounds like maybe we are, then we gotta know what we're up...''

``NO TIME! Now please, you must listen to me closely, and do as I say. What I was pointing to? It is a shed. The road to that shed is two clicks up on the right-hand side. Once inside, you wait for me until I contact the both of you. Do not leave until I have contacted you.''

``What's in the shack, Mr. Cluck Deep?'' asked Vee, sounding not anything like somebody whose life was on the short timer.

``Chickens, Miss Vee. Lots and lots of chickens.''

``You want us to drive out to a chicken shack in the middle of the Dregs and wait for you? Cluck, there'd better be a damned good...''

``Please. You must go NOW.''

I looked back down the road and could see the twin pinpricks of light grown considerably larger. The noise of that machine was louder as well. Too loud. Had to be souped up.

``OK, OK, we're gettin there. But one thing you gotta get straight. Two things. Where the hell you goin to get away from whoever this is, and why is this chicken shack so important?"

``Answer 1; none of your business. Answer 2; consider what are the ingredients in mayonnaise.   And now I must go."

Vee and I looked at each other.

``Eggs."

****

The ever-fashionable Mr. Deep Cluck screeched past us so fast it yanked Vee's hairdo outta kilter, and that was one powerful `do. She flipped him a finger signal and made like she was gonna chase him down on foot. That's when I grabbed her by the shoulder and reminded her we were about to be road kill unless she tossed her butt back in the driver's seat. She yanked her shoulder away, then stormed back into the transport lookin like she was fixin to pull it apart. I ran around to my side and jumped in before she started the engine, figuring she wasn't in the mood to wait for anybody.

Next thing I knew, my head was slammed against the back of the seat as Vee stomped on the power overdrive pedal. Then, like that wasn't enough juice, she decides to yank the maxi-thrust bar. Wonderful.

``When'd you uhhh, fortify the machine?" I asked, feeling my neck starting to strain from the force of the pressure shoving my head back against the seat.

``Not long. Had to do it, though. Single female page scratcher, you know? Gotta have a little extra comfort under the hood just in case an angry source decides to try and run you down, hey?"

``You call this comfort?"

``Just a few more seconds, sweety. I'm making sure to leave `em in lotsa dust. Look back there for me would you? To see?"

``Vee, I can barely move my lips to talk from all this speed pressure, so you oughta know I damned sure can't turn my head all the way around. You wanna see if they're back there, you slow this rocket down."

``You little wimpie."

``Nice hair."

``Say that again, hey? I'll eject you straight out the side door, I swear I will."

``No, really. It's got that rustic, windswept look. You oughta keep it like that. Start a trend. Be famous."

``You don't think I'll do it, do you?"

``I even got a name for it. Scratcher Doodle Do."

``That's it."

``VEEEEEEEEEeeeeeeee......"

Well I'll be damned. That's honestly what I was thinkin as I felt myself flyin outta the car into space. You'd think when somethin like that happens to you, you'd feel a kind of panick, but naw, it wasn't that way. Just an I'll-be damned-she-did-it kinda feeling. And she must really be pissed off.

When I landed, I came down hard, then started rolling over and over for quite awhile. Since she shot me out the side door instead of out the top - most transports eject out the top, but not Vee's - I didn't come down straight.

I remember Vee saying one time she had her transport ejector seat redone that way because she figured it'd make the landing a lot more complicated. That's the word she used. Complicated. Once I finally came to a stop the word `complicated' didn't come to mind, but I didn't have long to ponder word games because the front lights of the transport that'd been chasing us was about a click down the road and eatin up ground like starvation. Even though it was dark as the belly of midnight where I was layin, it was still close enough to the road where if those lights managed to make a wide enough sweep for any reason then they'd be sure to catch me lyin there. I was pretty sure they hadn't seen me get my butt rocket-launched out of the transport, but you never know about these things. The only problem with where I'd landed was that there wasn't anything around me but flat land. And there wasn't enough time to make my way anywhere else without the risk of bein seen. So I just stayed there, stretched out like I was doin somethin obscene to the territory, watchin as the mobile flew by, then disappeared in the distance. Once I was satisfied the sound was far enough away, I stood up and looked around.

And realized I couldn't see a damned thing.

Chapter 4

Sittin in the dark waitin.

I knew Vee was comin back, it was just a matter of how long she felt it was gonna take to make her point. One thing I'd figured out sittin for close to an hour on my butt in the middle of the Dregs; you don't talk bad about a woman's hair when she's doin the drivin. Especially when you know that hair don't belong to her.

Still, it was kinda fun while it lasted.

Musta been another hour, maybe two, before Vee showed up again. Her horn sounded like the noise a male critter makes when he gets kicked in that certain region. Now that I'm thinkin about it, I realize that shoulda told me somethin about Vee the first time around. I can't believe she chose that sound by accident.

I stood up, dusted myself off, then lit myself a smokey. Her transport started gettin close, and I just stood there glarin at her through the windshield. She pulls up in front of me, I drop my smokey to step it out, and then she pulls off down the road. I can hear her laughin, and I'm imaginin my hands wrapped around those pretty little gills of hers.

She didn't show up again for what felt like another 15 minutes. This time she turns off the motor, then lifts open the door. I lean down to peek inside, wanting to see her face, see if this was gonna be another game. She's grinning, motioning with her forefinger for me to step inside. Tryin to make it look sexy.

It was workin.

I get in the seat, strap myself in, then pull the door down. I'm thinkin there isn't a thing for me to say that isn't gonna get me shot right out that side door again, so I keep my mouth shut. As for Vee, who knows what she's thinkin? Probably waitin for me to give her an excuse. She's lovin it, I can tell.

Finally, she says to me, ``So did you learn a little lesson tonight, Mr. Vid?''

``Yeah. Next time I do the drivin.''

Still grinnin, she shakes her head, then reaches down to start the machine.

``You're just never gonna change for me, are you? Always have to play like you're so hard, hey?''

``If I wasn't hard, I wouldn't look this good after landing on my ass in the middle of the dregs after bein shot outta your transport at top speed. Cut it, Vee.''

``OK. I guess that's enough fun for one night. So aren't you gonna ask me what happened to our friends?''

``What happened to our friends.''

``C'mon, Vid. You can sound more interested than that.''

``Vee, I've been sittin in the dark for two hours with nothin better to do than compare how pissed off I was at you from one minute to the next. Just tell me what happened to those idiots, all right? Do we have to worry about them anymore or not?''

``You're no fun, but that's OK. I love you just the same. No, I don't think we'll be seeing them soon. They had a bit of an accident.''

``Accident?''

``Yeah. As in running into the side of a mountain. Go boom. I guess I kinda zigged when they were tryin to make me zag, and they got a little confused. I was pretty proud of myself, though. You should have seen it, Vid. I kinda thought you might have heard it. Made a lot of noise."

``Noise doesn't carry far in the Dregs. Atmosphere's different."

``Really?"

``Yeah. I remember reading that somewhere. Say, how long did you leave me out there, anyway?"

She looked at her watch.

``All told, looks like about 20 minutes."

``The whole time? Even when you left the second time around?"

``Yep. That's for everything, sweetie."

Damn. That atmosphere was more different than I thought. I figured I probably ought to recalculate how mad I was at her.

``Oh, and I found the chicken shack."

``You found...?"

``Yeah. It is up that little road that Mr. Cluck Deep was pointing to, and..."

``That's Deep Cluck, doll, not Cluck Deep."

``Whatever. Anyway, I took a peek inside, just to see what kind of place this is gonna be he wants us to wait for him in, right? You're not gonna believe this."

``Believe what, Vee?"

``OK, first though, he was right about all the chickens. I mean, there are just so many chickens at this place, and it got me wonderin..."

``Vee. The point, Vee. Where's the point?"

``Johnny Beardy."

``Johnny...wait a minute, you don't mean..."

``YES! And he's fuckin GORGEOUS!"

Geez.

Just then, we reached the turn-off road. Vee was goin too fast, but it didn't stop her from swingin her transport around. She was gonna kill me. I didn't know how, but she was workin on it, I could tell.

As it turned out, according to Vee's tale - once I got her off of talkin about how good Johnny Beardy's ass looked - ole Johnny boy really wasn't dead. Instead, he was holed up inside this chicken shack, which really was a front for some other kinda operation. Somethin having to do with the suspected illegal mayonnaise operation, I'm pretty sure. Vee said she didn't bother talkin to him, mostly because he was kinda preoccupied in a wrestling match with one of the chickens, which meant he woulda had a hard time answering any questions. She said the chicken had him in a headlock at the time, callin him all kinda ugly names.

``Then I remembered that I'd forgotten all about you, Vid. But he is just soooooo fiiiiiiiine. I mean, he even looks better alive than he did butt- naked out there in the street like we saw him that one time."

``Gee. Imagine that. And even with an angry chicken tyin him up in a headlock. Now that's somethin, Vee. Really is.

``By the way, exactly what kinda chickens are these, anyway?"

``Just wait until you see them, Vid. They're the cutest things."

``Cute..."

We reached the chicken shack in another couple minutes. Soon as we got out of the transport, I looked around scoping to find any sign of Deep Cluck. Suddenly I was wondering just how long Dr. Ugly expected us to wait for him. Nobody'd miss me for at least a month, but I knew if Vee missed showin up at the Daily Screamer for more than two days without callin to check in then somebody was gonna come lookin.

``C'mon, this way. See it? Right over there," she said.

What I saw made the word `shack' seem like a close relative of the word `great big palace'. It hadn't even managed to reach the distinction of being termed a dump yet. It was just...there. Looked like somebody'd bought some building materials, tossed them all on that spot, then walked away. Somethin was wrong with this picture, and I was aimin to find out what it was. No way was a famous rock star who was used to folks givin him homes just to mention their name in some ear-splittin song suddenly feeling right at home in a trash heap gettin familiar with aggressive poultry.

``I don't hear anything," I whispered, wondering why I was whipering since we'd just pulled up out front in a souped-up pink transport.

``Me either."

``So? Where are the wrestling chickens you was tellin me about? Gettin a beauty rest?"

``I dunno. But they gotta be here somewhere. I mean I was just out here a few minutes ago peepin through that window right over there. That's where I saw Johnny in that headlock."

``Yeah, well now it looks like Johnny's gone and so is super chicken. See, that's the ..."

``Hear that?" she asked.

I nodded.

``It's comin from inside of there somewhere. Or maybe..." I stomped the ground. ``Down there."

What we both heard was a series of soft thumps, like somethin heavy fallin down.

``I'll go knock on the door," said Vee.

``What for? You think maybe one of the chickens might answer? C'mon, use your head. The reason they ain't in there where they were before is they heard us comin this time."

``Well how come they didn't hear me comin last time? I was drivin the same car, Vid. Maybe you're the one needs to use his head."

``Now ain't the time for this, Vee. Listen, all I'm sayin is there's gotta be a reason for this. Look around, all right? Ain't like they decided to go check out one of the local clubs. Ain't a damned thing out here but nothin. See, now the way I've got it figured..."

``Yo! Can I help you folks?"

The voice, which was comin from behind us, was familiar. I knew I didn't have time to reach for my piece, so I just stood there quiet, hopin this voice had a conscience.

``All right. Suit yourselves, people. But I'm tellin you now I bet you're Vid and you're Vee? Don't need to tell me if I'm right. I already know. Gotta love that Deep Cluck son of a bitch. But those CLOTHES."

``How did..."

``HEY! What the fuck did I just say? Can you say LISTEN, man?"

47

``Sorry."

``Dude. It was a joke. Lighten up. So are you folks gonna turn around, or do I, like, have to jump out in front?"

We turned around. Yep. It was him.

``You're dead," said Vee.

Johnny Beardy, standing there in front of us with his hands on his hips, long brown hair pulled back tight in a ponytail, cocked his head fulla hard angles and snickered. He was startin to grow one of those beard things.

He pointed his finger dead at Vee, then cranked his snicker up a few notches to a pretty damned loud laugh. I started to tell him to turn it down, but then had to ask myself why. Except that he was already startin to get on my nerves.

``Babe. Yeah, you, beautiful. Yo, I think YOU may need to ask yourself a question. Question: Does this man look dead to me? Quick. What's your answer? Take a wild guess."

``You're dead," she said again.

I glanced over at her, wondering if maybe her tongue got caught in a groove or something. And that's when I figured it out. She was struck. I could tell by the way her gills were startin to flare that this Beardy character was revvin up her motor somethin fierce. I figured if Beardy knew what was good for him, he'd cool out the charm school routine just a touch. That is, unless he was the one human around who still hadn't heard what happens when a female critter jumps some Earth-boy bones.

Judgin by the looks on their faces once it was all through, I'd have to guess it was a hell of a way to go. But damned near every case I'd ever seen wound up bein spare dust for the Dregs. Those few that didn't weren't exactly themselves ever again. Just stumbled around in V-5 with a crooked grin on their faces makin these funny groanin noises. Sad.

Beardy was lookin at me, square white teeth flashing out at me bright enough to light up a room.

``So Sherlock, you think I'm dead too? "

``Just a guess, Mr. Beardy, but I'm thinkin maybe you're knowin a little more about what's got my friend here confused than you're lettin on. I know you're a big rock star back on the Big Rock and all, but try and not play us space bumpkins for dummies, all right? Remember, us critters were you folks' idea in the first damned place. The Big Experiment and all that. I bet even rock stars know a little bit of history. What I'm sayin is we may be a different species from you, in a way, but we're closer cousins than you know. See..."

``Dude. You're borin me, all right? I just asked a simple question; Am I dead. HEY! End of question. So."

This guy thinks he's such a piece of work. I'm clockin him. Right now this is a promise I'm makin to myself. I gotta clock a guy like this just on general principal. Somehow it just feels like the right thing to do.

``Last time Vee and I saw you, yeah. You were dead. Butt-naked layin face-down in a mayonnaise sandwich. Then, next thing we know, somebody tosses some kinda smoke device, we hear some feet slappin around, then the next thing the smoke is all gone and so's your body. And now here you are standin up straight, power wrestling the chickens, and actin like an asshole. It's all a little disconcertin. That's not too big a word for you, is it? Disconcertin?"

``Chickens," said Vee.

``Huh?"

``Chickens," she said again.

``Babe. I know what a chicken is, OK? So what's your point? And stop drooling."

Johnny Beardy had long brown hair, a jaw like chiseled granite, and was built tight and compact like a stretch of rope with muscles attached. As much as I hated to admit the facts, the facts were the kid was pretty much a show- stopper for the girl critters.

``What Vee's tryin to say - I figure I better finish this for her since her mouth seems to be incapacitated at the moment ..."

``Happens all the time, my friend. Just that vibe I put out, you know?"

``Wonderful. I'm sure you're makin your folks proud. Now. Like I was sayin about Vee, she told me she saw you up here a little earlier, and she said there were a whole lotta chickens around. Said she saw you gettin yourself in a headlock with one of `em."

I put my hand up to my ear, just to add a dramatic touch to what I was about to say.

``Hello? I'm not hearin any chickens."

``Yo. Dude. You're a natural comedian, and I love it. But why don't you good folks step on inside. Not good standin around out here for too long. Especially with this light shinin by the door. Sooner or later, trust me, the wrong folks are gonna see it and, like, they'll come a-runnin."

``Chickens..." said Vee.

Beardy flashed her a dangerous grin. Dangerous for him.

``Inside, sweetheart. We can talk about the chickens inside."

Beardy moved past us to open the door, and we both stepped inside.

``You know, I think maybe some of those wrong folks were followin us not long ago."

For the first time all night, Beardy gave me an uncomfortable look. As in scared. He stood there holding the door open looking me dead in the eye.

``You gonna come in?" I asked.

``When did this happen?" he asked.

``Earlier tonight. When Vee and I were followin the illustrious Mr. Cluck out through the Dregs. One minute it looks like we're all alone. Then, next thing you know, we see some lights comin from a distance. Cluck gets this look on his face. Kinda like the one you got on yours now. Tells us we gotta come here and wait for him to contact us. Then he splits, and we ain't seen him since."

``But what about...?"

``You gonna come inside, pretty boy? "

He stepped inside, then folded his arms on his chest. There were huge white feathers scattered all around the inside of the shack, and claw scratches marked up the floor. There was a ripped up sofa and some chairs, but that was about it for the furniture. I saw a crooked doorway toward the back and wondered if they led to anything like a bedroom. I damned sure wasn't gonna sleep on these feathers.

And the smell...

``Vee took care of `em,'' I blurted out, realizing I'd taken a little long to respond. Guess the shack took me a little bit by surprise.

``Chickens,'' said Vee.

``Right, right. Chickens. If you ain't never seen this woman drive, you've been missin out. She ran `em right into a rock wall. Blew `em up. That's my Vee.''

Beardy looked at Vee.

``Where?'' he asked. ``Where'd you blow `em up?''

``Chickens?'' asked Vee.

`Enough with the chicken language, Vee. Talk normal. Answer the man. Then you can go back to droolin or whatever else you got in mind.''

She pointed off at an angle just to the left of the window in the shack.

``About three clicks past the turnoff we took to come here, hey?''

``And you know for sure they're dead?''

``Well...yeah. I mean how's anybody gonna walk away from somethin like that, Johnny? I can call you Johnny, right?''

``Fine. Now go on.''

``Not much else to go on to. I could see `em gainin on me through the rearview, so I gunned it for the rock wall up ahead. Makin like I was gonna take myself out. Last sec, just before I reached, I pulled a reverse maneuver my Daddy taught me once. They blew right by me. Then they blew up. I was right there, Johnny. I saw it happen.''

``Just like you saw me dead, right?''

I pulled off my hat and scratched my head a few times. Seemed like my head always itched in situations like this.

``You know, Johnny, I been meanin to ask you about that."

``I'm sure you have, but now's not the time. Folks, we may be in a little bit of trouble."

Just then I could feel a rumblin under my feet. Kind of like what I was feeling outside just before Beardy popped up from behind.

``Chickens?" asked Vee.

Beardy grinned, then nodded.

``You got it, babe. The chickens. And I think it's time you met."

``We're gonna meet some chickens? Did I hear you right?"

``Dude. These birds would fuckin kill the Colonel, all right?"

``Who's the Colonel?"

``...oh. right. Forgot where I was for a sec. Never mind. Now follow me."

He headed for that crooked door in the rear that I was hopin led to a decent bedroom. It didn't. It led to some crooked stairs, which led to a cramped, crooked little room beneath the house. Actually, the room was probably bigger than the shack upstairs, but all these jail cell-lookin' cages fulla critter-sized chickens made the room feel a lot tighter. A couple of `em were smokin smokies, and givin me and Vee the evil eye. Imagine that. Chickens givin critters the evil eye.

``Fellas!" Beardy yelled, raisin his arms up in the air like some kinda conquerin hero.

``Who're the critters?" one of `em asked. He wore a patch over one eye. That was one chicken I wouldn't wanna run into in a back alley. If the subject came up, I was tellin `em I'd sworn off fried chicken years ago.

53

``Some friends of Cluck's. And mine. Listen, it looks like we may have ourselves a bit of a situation here...''

``Hot damn, Beardy. You mean we gotta move. Again?''

``Aw wow. This is cluckin ridiculous. See, you promised us last time...''

``Wait, wait, don't go rufflin your feathers, girls. I didn't say that. Yet. Look...''

``How the hell you chickens get so damned big?'' I asked. I just couldn't hold it in any longer.

``And, like, where'd you learn to talk?'' asked Vee. ``I mean, you talk real good and everything, but...hey?''

Just for sayin that, all beaks were focused on us. Nobody was sayin nothin. Beardy was lookin pissed as a room full of critters in dry weather.

``Your timing? It SUCKS, man.''

How were we supposed to know that chickens were the sensitive type?

``Might as well tell his dumb ass what's up,'' said one of the chickens. ``We ain't goin nowhere with him, or his little cutesie wootsie, until they know the errors of their ways.''

****

Turns out the chickens were, well, they were freaks. They could trace themselves back to normal farm-type chickens back on earth, but then something happened to a group of 'em that were used in an experiment to make bigger, healthier chickens.

Things got a little outta hand. Some idiot figured why stop with the bigger and healthier part, why not try to come up with some kind of human-chicken crossbreed? Anybody with decency and half a grain of sense could have provided the answer to that, but apparently nobody fitting that description was in the room at the time. So the experiment went on ahead, the idea being that if chickens were part human, then they would be more cooperative with whatever was expected of them. Kind of like breeding slaves who knew how to take better orders, but with a lot less attitude.

 Like I said, things got outta hand.

Next thing you know there were all these big chickens struttin around Brad Johnston's farm - Brad being the only farmer who had a license to carry these chickens - with their chests stuck out, kickin the other chickens around like footballs. They were bigger and healthier all right, but the docile part never quite kicked in. Musta used the wrong race of humans or something, 'cause these chickens didn't lay any eggs unless they felt like it. But once they decided on it, those suckers were huge and they were good. You can imagine why the first worry the scientists had was whether the new breed was gonna deliver yolks or folks, but somehow that turned out all right. Mother Nature let that one slide. And once the first egg cracked and a beak popped through, there was a whole lotta scientists breathin easier that night. All they needed to shut down the project was to have some kid steppin out of an egg.

But as time went by, Brad got kinda fed up with their behavior. Even the most trimid of guys has a hard time being disrespected by a chicken, even if it *is* half human. He talked to the scientists and struck a deal to have the mutant strain shipped down the road to another fellow farmer known to. Have a far-less tolerant attitude about, well, pretty much anything. Name was Homer. It was also decided that, good as the eggs were, it probably wasn't a good idea to keep eating them since they were half human. It wasn't long before someone came up with the idea to use the mutant eggs for MayoMadd. Because, after all, just how perfect could that be?

And that worked just fine for awhile, especially since the chickens had agreed not to let Homer know they could talk in exchange for a vague promise of freedom sometime down the road. Only that never quite happened and then one day, the dsy later referred to as The Great Poultry Rebellion, things pretty much went all wrong.

Who needs chickens with attitude if they're not producing anything good for consumption? The day came when they had to head for the hills and go into hiding.

``So did the scientists ship you guys up here to get you out of the way or what?"

"Actually, the government shipped our little feathered asses up here."

This snatches my attention.

"The government? But why…?"

"'Cause when we came back down outta those hills we started getting' some serious revenge. I'm telling you all we needed was a few more soldiers and we coulda…"

"Yo. Rasputin. That's enough for now, dude," said Beardy. "I trust these guys? But not that damned much. 'Least not yet."

Rasputin – a chicken named Rasputin? – mumbled something under his breath then backed away and took a seat on top of an upside down garbage can.

"One of you birds needs to give me a smokie," he said, after staring at me and Vee real hard for a minute like he was tryin to decide whether he'd made a mistake.

"So what happens now?" I asked.

56

No one said a word for a long time. Rasputin took a deep drag on his smokie given to him by a smaller comrade with a funny zig zag scar down the side of his throat, then coughed a few times.

"We still need to settle up on that revenge."

Chapter 5

Chicken revenge is a serious thing.

The way these birds saw it, they had a score to settle with the Mother planet, and they were gonna settle big. I mean real big. We're talkin poultry with a plan. All those years of gettin kicked around and abused had made them real good at stayin focused on a goal. Now, after all these years, their time had finally come. Well, almost.

First thing, we had to get outta this house before some very unpleasant guests arrived. Then their time could come. Johnny Beardy was runnin around makin sure everything was left like it was supposed to be, makin sure all the chickens were good to go; except for the few he was leaving behind to ``clean up things a little'' he said. The rest were bein crowded into this huge contraption of a trailer built special for transportin great big chickens. It looked too big to hitch up to Vee's pretty little mobile, and she wasn't too thrilled about having to yank around something that ugly, but since it rode on an air cushion, that made toting it around a lot easier. Kinda like having a big aluminum balloon attached.

So anyway, when I asked Beardy why he gave a kitty about cleanin up a rundown shack like that, he just grinned. Said he had a different kind of cleanin up in mind. The kind of cleanin up that entails waitin for the garbage to show up at the door.

Oh. I cleared my throat.

``So uhh, you need help with anything, kid?'' I asked.

``Yo, dude, I ain't your kid, all right? I've been grown awhile. And no, everything's groovy. Just gotta make one last run-through, and then we are outta here, my friend."

Vee and I looked at each other, then shrugged. Fine. A few minutes later, I reminded him that Deep Cluck was supposed to be meeting us out here. Kid cursed real loud. I told him to watch his mouth around the lady, then wondered why I even bothered since she knew some words that would make the little rocker's hair fall out. Old habits die hard, I guess.

He cursed again.

``Hey. Kid. Didn't I just tell you..."

He stuck his finger straight up in the air, like he was fixin to make a big deal speech.

``First thing, Vid, this is where *I* stay. *I* make the rules here, Dude, which means I get to curse like a son of a bitch. Second, what you just told me? Not good. Not good at all. We're gonna have to leave him some kinda signal, and just hope he gets it. If he doesn't, then we're all gonna be screwed. Trust me on that. And trust me, it's something worth cursing about, OK? It's worth every fucking curse word you know how to say. This whole thing, it hinges on Cluck baby. Without him, it's all just a door swingin in the wind. And that is no good."

``Cluck baby...?"

``Never mind, man. I gotta figure out a good...GOT IT!"

Beardy tore through a heap of junk that was piled high at the back of the basement until he came up with a small, silver-colored can of something that had him smiling like he had a mouthful of somethin good. Turned out to be invisible paint, which turned out to be another one of those helpful products developed by Vee's pop.

Chances are, whoever this was chasing us, if they ever made it to the shack, wouldn't have thought to bring the special kinda chemical you need to toss on the invisible paint to see what the hell it says. Plus, you need a special kinda light to shine on the letters after the chemical gets applied. Otherwise? You still ain't gonna see nothin but what you were lookin at before. Chances are, whoever this was chasin us was gonna see an empty shack, figure out we'd high-tailed it, and wasn't gonna waste any time gettin back on the road.

At least that's what Beardy hoped was gonna happen.

As for Cluck Baby, Beardy was assuming he'd figure the whole thing out and know a secret message was written for him on the front door in invisible paint. Personally, I had some questions about makin these kinda assumptions, but Beardy says Cluck is no dummy. He just senses these things is what he says. Fine. Because personally, if I don't ever see Cluck again, I will still feel just fine about life. I'll feel great. Because I do not need that no-dressin clown in my life to make the day go down easier.

The front door swings open and Beardy's standin there flashin all those teeth lookin proud of himself.

``What?" I say.

``All done," says Beardy.

``All done what?"

``Dude. The message. All done. Now we gotta get outta here. Quick."

Vee popped up from where she was sittin on the couch, I guess tryin to show how cooperative she knew how to be. Never acted like that with me, that's for damned sure. I took my time gettin up.

``You know, you still haven't told us who this is you got us runnin from. You're tellin me whoever this is is so dangerous they can overpower the three of us and a herd of pissed-off, king-sized chickens with an attitude. I wanna know who the hell this is that's so tough."

He grinned at me in a kinda way that wasn't makin me feel too comfortable. Then he glanced at a couple of the chickens, who were standing behind where I was sitting on the couch with their wings folded. I heard a few snickers.

``Should I tell him, fellas?" he asked.

I couldn't believe this guy was asking the permission of some chickens whether or not it was OK to tell me how much my life was in danger.

``Sure. Why not," said the one with the eye patch. ``He won't believe it, but what the hell."

Beardy looks back at me, then sneeks a peek at Vee and gives her a wink and mouths a kiss. Her gills damned near dried up right then and there. Then he looks back at me.

``The keystones."

Surprise didn't come easy.

****

Actually, it wasn't all of `em that were in on it. But it was enough that they'd gotten that kinda rep where a critter feels safer callin a gangster for help than one of the keystones. They'd gotten that bad. I knew a few personally who were workin hard to at least keep up appearances of a decent department, but the strain of the effort was wearin `em down, and there was a whole sea full of dumb juniors out there who couldn't wait to sign up for duty and start snatchin their portion of the goods.

So when Beardy starts tellin me how it is that the keystones have been tryin to trace down their operation to get a cut, it gave me that familiar sick feelin inside. So far they hadn't caught up, but there'd been a few close calls. Still, Deep Cluck always managed to stay one step ahead of the keystones. Maintaining a string of safe houses - or safe shacks - around the Dregs made it easy to stay ahead.. Each one was on a piece of territory registered to a different critter - or to a different enterprise. One belonged to D.C. Ltd. Another belonged to Deep Sea Sand Co. Another one registered under Cluck-a-Buck Finance and Loan.

Those keystones never figured it out, no matter how close they got. Cluck had those idiots drivin round and round in circles right on top of what they swore they couldn't find. The more Beardy laid it out to me, the more I was beginning to see how much I'd underestimated the jerk.

Course, then I had to ask him why it was he felt like it was safe to tell me all this. Especially with Vee scrunched up in the back seat like she was with her little scratch pad hummin in her hand. I was doin the drivin and Beardy was up front givin directions. The chickens were all layin low inside a trailer we'd hooked up to the back of the transport.

Beardy was wearin another one of those grins.

``You know, me and Vee, we're gonna have to be headin back to town pretty soon, by the way. Too much longer out here and critters gonna start asking questions. Critters start asking too many questions, and I ain't gotta tell you what happens next."

``Cause I figure I can trust you is why I'm tellin you all this. Dunno. Somethin about you, Dude."

I checked the rear view and saw Vee's eyes propped open wide. Made me chuckle.

``Excuse me," she said, tryin to sound all quiet and polite - but I caught the smirk. ``Mr. Beardy, did you say there was somethin about a scavenger that can be trusted?"

Still the grin.

``Well, while you're still feelin kindly towards me, spud, suppose you tell me what the deal was with you layin there in that street with no clothes on with your face jammed in that mayonnaise sandwich. I'm sure you've got a perfectly good explanation, but I'm just curious to hear it."

``And what happened to you when that smoke hit?" asked Vee.

``And what's in all of this for you? The chickens got a revenge thing goin on, but that still doesn't figure you. What's your story?"

``And that, folks, is the question I've been waiting for."

****

63

Like I said, it was a long haul to the next safe shack, which meant Beardy had all the time he needed to start fillin us in on what the real deal was. I was kinda surprised how easy he spilled his story.

``DUDE. Okay. Check this out, `cause this is what's happenin. And man, like, I am so glad to finally be able to tell somebody about this shit. You don't know what it's like keepin all this crap inside. Real pain in the...''

``Try me.''

``Cool. Okay. That night? When the two of you saw me lyin there on the ground without my threads? The perfect setup. Perfectomundo. Wasn't me. I was already out here in the Dregs with my feathered friends and workin out a deal with Cluck. What you folks were lookin at was a synthetic dummy with an environmental transmitter stuck inside. Recorded everything that was going on around the body. Had all my characteristics, right down to the cell type and the fingerprints. Organs all inside. All that. But it was not me. Cluck's a genius, I'm tellin you.

``So anyway, the plan was for them to find me like that. The keystones. We weren't exactly planning on you two, but once you showed up we knew we'd have to deal with it. As for the keystones, we wanted them seein that sandwich. Had to see it, man. We knew once they saw what my mug was munchin on, their corrupt little gears'd start to turnin big time. We knew if they knew there was mayonnaise back on V-5, they were gonna bust themselves tracin down who was behind it and start puttin down the heavy muscle to squeeze out their cut for protection.

``That's where we put the hook in. While they're there with the two of you tryin to figure out what you knew, we knew they were really tryin to figure out if you knew anything about who was behind the new MayoMadd connection. Once they figured you didn't then they figured they had a wrap on it - until we threw a monkey wrench in the deal."

``A monkey what?"

``You know, a ...oh, right. That's when we threw in the smoke bomb and swiped the body. Dude, we knew they'd freak like crazy once that happened. Yo, were we right or what? Ever since then, they've been workin overtime tryin to track us down. They know if they don't then it makes `em look like they're the dufusses they are. Critters gonna be scared to death that another MayoMadd epidemic is fixin to explode up here and the damned keystones don't even know which dike to stick their fingers into."

``I ain't even gonna ask what that means, kid. Go on."

``Check it out. What they're really worried about? Is that they know this thing is about to hit V-5 big, which means there's all that money floatin around out here, but they won't even be plugged into it. It'll be the first time anything this big went down and the keystones were cut out. It's fuckin beautiful."

This kid wasn't wrapped too tight. Here he was talkin about unleashin a drug epidemic on my home planet just as calm as that Earth nut Santa Claus gets off on breakin and enterin.

``Dude, I can look in your eyes right now? I can look right in there and see you think I'm crazy. Like, why is this idiot tellin me about all this? Right? Am I right? That's what you're thinkin, isn't it?"

``There's a chance that crossed my mind, yeah. Suppose you make it cross back the other way. Otherwise I suspect we gonna have us some problems."

``Sure thing, Viddy baby. First thing? The MayoMadd? Dude, don't even sweat it, hear? The last thing me or Cluck wants to do is get little critters up here hooked back on that stuff. That wouldn't be a nice thing to do."

I heard Vee let out a long breath of air. Glanced back and saw her smilin. Had to grin at that.

``You're right about that, Beardy. Wouldn't be nice at all. So what gives?"

``We're gonna get the Earth kids hooked on it instead," he said, with a ferocious grin.

``Come again?"

``It's all part of Deep Cluck's master plan, man. It's beautiful. See, here's how it's gonna ..."

``Johnny...? Say it ain't so, hey? You're not really gonna do that to those kids, are you? I mean, I know they can get on your nerves and everything, but gettin `em hooked on MayoMadd? Why would you wanna do something like that? What'd they ever do to you to piss you off that much?"

``Yo, this isn't about me, all right? It's about..."

``I'll be damned. This is about those chickens, ain't it?"

``Bingo, dude. Nobody fucks with my clucks. That just ain't right."

``But why do you care so much about a bunch of talkin chickens? I thought you had a big music career goin back on Earth. Why blow it for a bunch of..."

``Watch it, man. Don't talk bad about my chickens. They've had folks talkin bad about `em their whole lives for somethin that wasn't even their fault. Now the time has come to put a stop to it. For good

``Beware the chickens."

Oh geez.

Chapter 6

The early life of Deep Cluck as childhood nerd, as told to me by Johnny Beardy, wasn't exactly the type of story I'd spend my hard-earned money buyin at some store. Still, it's too bad he was picked on, stomped, spat on, couldn't get a date, etc. And all because he wasn't one of the Full Bloods, which meant he was a mutt. Daddy was some kinda big deal businessman from Earth, but Mommy was from up here on good ole Planet 10. And as if that wasn't bad enough all by itself, the girl was from V-5 Sector, so you know once word of that started to spread that pretty much spelled a great big KICK ME IN THE ASS sign right on Cluck's scrawny little back. And you know the thing I still can't figure out is how bein purebred Earthling is something to be so proud of. Wonder if they've had a look at that place recently...

Anyway, I know that's no way for a kid to spend his growin up years. But hey, he survived it, right? Now he's Deep Cluck, Mr. Nerd No More - except for those clothes - and he's got an army of poultry behind him just waiting on some orders. I'd say that was a pretty happy ending. Cluck got in tight with the chickens right around the time when the harassment he was getting at high school was at its absolute worst. He was startin to feel like maybe it wasn't even worth wakin up in the morning when he hears this story about these mutant chickens that were raisin all this hell in a town not too far from where he was stayin at the time. He does some more checkin around about this story and figures out these chickens are outcast mutants - just like him.

All very touchin, right? But then the story starts goin left. See, once Cluck tracked down his little feathered soul mates, they strike up this bond and start to cookin up ideas in their head about things they can do to get back at everybody that ever gave them a headache. Probably started off innocent enough at first, just a little nerd kid and some disgruntled chickens mouthin off. Then it got serious.

Like I said, Chicken Revenge is a terrible thing.

Well, it wasn't long after those plans started comin together that young Cluck and his buddy clucks started meeting regularly. They probably woulda gotten some type of revenge long before they ever got off the planet if it hadn't been for the attitude of those chickens. Thing was, most of `em just couldn't wait to make fools pay, so they started doin little stuff off and on whenever they thought they could get away with it. Trippin kids off their bikes. Sneakin into stores late at night and stealin all the frozen chickens. Spray-painting lewd messages on buildings tellin folks what they could do with a bird. Lettin the steam off, you know. That was all well and good until they got caught, and that was when the feathers hit the fan.

Chickens don't get trials, not even if they're part human. So all it took was about a week before they were all rounded up and shipped up here, where they were dumped out in the middle of the Dregs and instructed never to come into the city. Officially speakin, they didn't exist. If Cluck's old man hadn't been such a big deal he woulda been sent away for at least a couple years to one of the special camps where trouble kids like him are supposed to get their head right. But seein as how the judge was a personal friend of Cluck's dad, and Cluck's dad was who he was, then Cluck got off light with a suspended sentence. Dad promised the judge junior wouldn't be screwing up again, and besides, the chickens were all being sent away anyway, right? Who was Cluck gonna get into trouble with now that all his best friends were being shipped away? Right?

Thing you gotta remember in all this is that Cluck was a nerd, not a dummy. And he was determined. Took him a few years, but he eventually managed to convince his folks that Vivacious 5 Sector was the best place for a kid like him, not Earth. With all the hell he'd been gettin from the neighborhood kids and the kids at school, it was hard for them to argue. When Cluck turned 15, they set him up with some relatives, his mother's brother Vince and his wife Victrolia, where he stayed until he was old enough to step out on his own.

Cluck already knew that the only place on Planet 10 where his long lost friends could possibly be hiding out was in the Dregs. It was the only place where nobody ever went except to pass through on their way to somewhere else, and since the chickens couldn't exactly blend in with the critters any better than they did with the Earthlings, then the Dregs was the only place they could have been relocated where they could be left to themselves and forgotten about – by everyone except Cluck. And Cluck also knew, as somebody who was real experienced in the art of not having any friends, that once he disappeared into the Dregs, wasn't nobody gonna miss him or come looking for him. Uncle Vince and Aunt Victrolia barely tolerated the kid just because he was family. They had never had any kids of their own and, well, you might say there was a reason for that. As for Cluck's folks, it was becoming obvious to him the longer he stayed with his relatives that they were feeding his parents a line of bullshit a mile long about what a problem child he was becoming, when the truth was that he hardly ever left his room except to go to school, and he never made a sound. But he was a kid and he was strange, whereas the relatives were grown and they were normal, so it didn't much matter what

Cluck had to say in his own defense – not that he ever bothered to stand up in his own defense. Truth be told, Cluck didn't care a damn what anybody else thought of him. Not any more. That feeling had gone dead inside of him long ago. All Cluck cared about was finding his chickens, the only real family he figured he had.

Cluck was on a mission. And once he turned 17, he figured it was about time to kick that mission up a notch to the next phase. The time had come to leave the house, which meant the time had come to leave his room. So after he'd packed his one raggedy bag full of all his belongings, which didn't amount to much, he yanked open the door, walked down the hallway past where the relatives were sitting up in bed watching television (they never asked where he was going), out the front door, and off into the night toward the Dregs. He didn't have the slightest idea how he was going to find his friends, but he was still young enough to believe that if he just stepped on out there then things would work themselves out some kind of way. Besides, even if he wound up lost and dead, buried beneath all that sand and darkness, so what? Way Cluck saw it, at least he would have died searching for friends and a better life, a purpose. Isn't that what all great people sacrificed their lives for? Wasn't that what they taught him in school? And they thought he hadn't been listening. But Cluck always listened. Always. It's like I said before, the thing you gotta remember about Cluck is that he was a nerd, but he wasn't stupid. He was always working things out in that funny-shaped head of his. What else was there to do for a kid with no friends who had lived most of his life alone in a room behind closed doors? It was more than a month before Cluck finally managed to track down his buddies, and by then he was damned near dead from starvation, dehydration, and just about everything else that can happen to a kid who's been surviving on whatever edible trash gets tossed out from passing cars as they zip back and forth on their way to civilization. The Dregs was definitely not civilization. The Dregs was where nothingness and heartbreak went to die – but it was also where the freaks and fringe crazies called home.

Actually, it was the chickens who managed to find Cluck, by the way. Because after a month, Cluck wasn't in any kinda shape to be tracking down *any*body. And truth be told, nobody who ever goes looking for anybody ever really finds them in the Dregs. Nope. In the Dregs, you either get left for dead or you get yourself found. Eventually.

On the day that 'eventually' finally showed up to claim Cluck, he was laying sprawled out across the top of a big flat rock on his back, clothes torn up like somebody'd tossed 'em in a blender, hair sticking out like a shock treatment, filthy as sin and stinkin twice as bad. His tongue was all dry and cracked, and it was puffed up so big that he couldn't close his mouth all the way. His eyes were buggin' out of his head like two hard boiled eggs, and if you look at Cluck's eyes even today you can still see they ain't quite right – kinda like the rest of him.

In short, the kid was pretty fucked up. But as fucked up as he was, and as much time had passed since the last time he'd seen his only real friends, Rasputin and Jericho still recognized Cluck right from the start and knew what had to be done – and quick. The two had been out scavenging – normally they didn't venture out this far – when Jericho, who stood a full foot taller than Rasputin but wasn't nearly as stocky or muscle-bound, looked over the top of Rasputin's head and noticed the body on the rock. It was quite a ways away, but even at that distance it wasn't hard to tell it was a body.

Once they reached it and recognized who that body belonged to, they started cryin as they lifted Cluck up real easy and then laid him down in their roller trailer, which is what they used to haul everything they found back to the compound. I don't know why they called those things roller trailers since none of 'em had wheels anymore. About the size of your average dining room, made outta wood and steel shipped in from Earth, all roller trailers hovered anywhere from one to three feet above the ground and were built to carry huge loads of stuff without even gettin your heart rate up.

But anyway, I don't guess that's so important, right? Whatever. Just one of those things I tend to notice from time to time 'cause it just doesn't make sense. Anyway, once Rasputin and Jericho got Cluck situated between a coupla big bags so he wouldn't roll off, they hooked the trailer up to their [transport] and took off at top speed for the compound.

Now I don't know – or I guess I should say Beardy doesn't really know – all of what they did to nurse Cluck back to health, so since I'm goin off of what he told me then I can't begin to speculate on what those chickens had to do to bring the kid back to himself. All I know is that whatever it was they did obviously worked, and once Cluck was back up to full speed, and back with the ones he considered his real family, then it wasn't long before they started laying down their plans for revenge. For them, revenge was a reason for living.

Chapter 7

Even as a little kid, Johnny Beardy was quite the stud. Or at least that's the way he tells it. If I was telling my own story, that's probably the way I'd tell it too, so who really knows, right? Then again, who cares? It's a good story.

Anyway, as Beardy tells it, he always had an eye for the female figure, even back at that age when females don't have any figure to speak of. But just the promise of a figure was good enough for him. While all the other little tykes were jumpin around inside the sandbox building castles and playing war games, l'il Beardy was gamin on the females. Got his first good feel when he was about eight. By the time he was 12 he'd already talked some young substitute teacher into letting him play with her tits one day after school was out. A few months later that same substitute teacher was back at school teaching that same slow-learner English class, and this time Beardy talked his way in a little further, if you catch my meaning. Yeah, right, that's what I said. How you figure a slow learner can find a way to talk that fast? Must not be so slow if he can put his sentences together good enough to pull that off – if he pulled it off.

Movin right along, by the time Beardy was 15 was when he found out he had the kind of singin voice that could make him some money – and get him laid anytime of day or night. Actually, to tell the truth, Beardy didn't have so much of a voice for singin as he did a perfect scream, the kind that summons all the pain and all the joy you've ever felt to come rushing through your bloodstream like a tidal wave. It really was a pretty amazing sound, and I never was one to like the rock stuff. But even I had to admit that scream of his was some kinda gift from above, or below, or somewhere. But it was definitely a gift, and it was definitely unlike anything you had ever heard before.

As Beardy got older and started to learn how to really use that thing, and after he'd started to get the hang of how to wear that Rock Star status like a broken-in suit, he started to get the big time recognition – and the big time money. With those chiseled angles and hard curves that defined his face and torso, teeth sparkling like some kinda toothpaste commercial every time he grinned, the kid was made to be on magazine covers. He was golden. His shows would sell out even the biggest auditoriums within an hour of any announcement that he was going to be there. He had the limos, the planes, the glitz, the glamour, the whole thing. He was a wanna be rock star's wettest wet dream.

And that's right around the time when he met Cluck. Wasn't long after that when his life became about as stable as a penguin on roller skates. No one who thought they knew Beardy even had the slightest clue what the hell was goin on with him. No one who had been part of his entourage for all those years or who thought they had been one of his best friends just because he told them they were and let them ride his tour bus occasionally, ever saw anything like this coming. True enough, they all had to know that the gravy train was gonna have to roll to a stop one of these days because even the best parties have to shut down eventually, but absolutely nobody thought the party would be the victim of 'death by geek,' which is pretty much what happened. One week, Beardy's taking town after town by storm, getting rave reviews in the press after each performance and gearing up for his first overseas tour that was scheduled to kick off several months later. Then, one night after the final show of a three-night mercy gig in some small outta-the-way town out west (Beardy called it a "mercy gig" because it was in one of those places where everything was too far away where the kids almost never got a chance to see a decent live gig), Beardy had just finished waving goodnight to a gymnasium packed full with several thousand sweating, desperately screaming small-town kids. He had left the stage, grabbed a towel one of his assistants had left hanging for him at a nearby railing on the way to his dressing room, and was wiping his face as he cursed and swore at the top of his lungs about how fucking hot it was in there and how much it stank and how this was the last fucking time he was ever fucking going to do one of these fucking mercy shows ever again…

Look, I better let him tell it.

****

Dude, I'm telling you it was all the way too strange what happened next, and this is coming from *me,* all right? You get what I'm telling you? This shit is coming from *me.* When was the last time you ever heard me say *any*thing was too fucking weird for *me* all right? You follow?

So like I was saying, it was way too hot inside that place. Never should have done the show. Look, I was doing these trailer park weeds a favor, all right? A *favor!* You figure the least they could do was find me someplace to play with a normal temperature. Not some damned blast furnace. I don't give a damn if it *was* August in that little desert spitbowl, it was still way too hot inside that place for any show.

Anyway, I'm walking back to the dressing room and everybody's kinda like backing away from me because I'm yellin and sayin all these really ugly things about this little town, which is way outta character for me, you know? I know I can be a pain in the ass, but usually I try to be a nicer guy than that, but I was pissed! So there I am, walkin real fast toward my dressing room with my hands waving all in the air, I'm almost there, my hand reaching out to snatch the doorknob, when I hear this funny-sounding voice calling out my name. Sounded like somebody tryin to talk through his nose. I looked over to my right, and there's this goofy kid standing there with these bent-up teeth, green plaid pants that came down around six inches above his ankles, I kid you not, and a reddish-brown button-up shirt that would make you think your eyes were starting to go bad if you stared at it too long.

Seein all this at one time? Dude, you know I had to stop. Everything I'd been spoutin off about just left my head like steam out a tea kettle, man. I'm serious. Suddenly it seemed like everything had gone quiet – I mean quiet like how you imagine it would be in space – and it's just me and this kid looking at each other.

I asked him how he got past security, knowing that wasn't the question I really wanted to get to. What I wanted to get to was who in the hell *was* this freak?

He gives me this spooky grin, then folds his arms across that scrawny chest of his. What he said next? Twisted my head up like a pretzel.

"The question, my dear friend, is not how and which way did I manage to befuddle those to whom you have entrusted your...security? No, no. The question, it would seem to me at this particular moment, is whether you do indeed feel secure? Yes, this is what I do believe I would be asking myself if I were you, which, regrettably, I am not. For if I were you then I would be asking myself the appropriate questions about my life at the appropriate time – that time being now – and I would also have the great fortune of being a rock star! How wonderful! And so, indeed, you do see how regrettable it is that I cannot be you – at least during this temporarily unbalanced point in time? Ah well. But we, all of us, must play the hand we are dealt in this life, yes? And I was not dealt your hand, nor you mine. So."

And that's when my security, the two guys who were supposed to be guarding the one and only entrance this guy could have come through? Yeah, that's when they decide to show up, breathin all hard. Man, I'm telling you, if this were a comedy, the timing couldn't have been better.

"Boss, why don't you go on in your dressing room? We can handle this clown from here," Rufus tells me. "Gotta be a clown dressed like that, right, Boss?"

What happened then was probably what convinced me more than anything else that this kid – what kinda kid talks like that? – had something special. And it was something special I needed. *Dude,* the kid started laughing, right? And I mean doubled over laughing like somebody had just told him the funniest joke he had ever heard in his life. Here he is, this scrawny pencil-necked nerd with bad teeth who dressed so bad he probably shoulda gotten a ticket and a fine, and he's laughin in the face of these two no-neck pitbull security guards who could have stomped his geeky ass into a puddle. That kinda shit takes *guts*, man, you know? It either takes guts or crazy, but whichever one it was it was working.

"They are PRECIOUS!" he said after finally managing to catch his breath, pointing at my two guards as if they were a couple of cute poodles on display in a pet store window. "Where did you find them?"

My security guards were starting to growl.

"Boss? We got this, right, boss?"

The kid started laughing all over again, which got the security guards growling even louder. Nobody else knew what the hell to do without anybody telling them do this, do that, so they just stood in place waiting for somebody to spell them out a clue. Me? I was starting to feel calm for the first time since I could remember, and it felt good.

"Boss! We got…"

"Yo! If you *had* this? All right? If you *had* this? Then we wouldn't even be having this conversation right about now because Norman the Nerd here wouldn't be standing outside my dressing room BACKSTAGE makin fun of you two assholes! Right? So this says to me you guys ain't got *shit!* And that includes your jobs, starting right now. Now get outta my face!"

Anyway, that's what I said to 'em, and then I told the nerd to come on in the dressing room with me. I figured wasn't any kinda way a kid looking this funny could be any kinda threat, not to me. I didn't care if he did give my guys the slip, I just couldn't let myself get nervous about *any*body who looked and talked like Cluck did, you know? So after my two ex-security guards disappeared down the hallway - it was kinda funny 'cause both of 'em were wavin' me the bird over their shoulders – then I stepped in ahead of him and told him to follow and to close the door behind him. He did that. Dude. My big mistake? Me thinking I was gonna get a chance to actually say something in my own dressing room. I didn't get to say a damned thing for the first ten minutes he was in there. Soon as he closed the door he launches into this all-out tirade, and I mean the switch in Cluck's mood was just that quick. Like somebody flipped a switch. Starts going off on a tangent about chickens being in danger, waving his skinny little nerd arms in the air, and right there I'm thinking this guy really is crazier than he looks, and that is not easy. I mean, who gets that fuckin worked up over chickens?

Still, for some reason, a whole half hour goes by and I'm still listening to this guy. One of my roadies poked his head in the door to tell me it was about time to get back on the bus, but I just threw a boot at him. Told Cluck to go ahead. For a minute he gives me this funny look like he wasn't sure he saw what he just saw, so I nodded at him, lettin' him know, you know, that it was cool. He gives me this wacked-out grin like some girl just gave him a quickie hand job under the table, then goes back to his story. I'm not believing a word he's sayin, but it doesn't matter. I like listening to him, and I like a good story. You might not know this, dude, but not a whole lotta folks can tell a story. This guy? Oh yeah. Tell a fuckin story like you would not be*lieve.* Told me all about how he and his super chickens had become friends, how they were the only friends he ever really had, how they became super chickens, the whole spiel. Craziest shit I ever heard in my life – and I was lovin' it.

Then all of a sudden there was this silence.

"That's it?" I asked.

But Cluck just stood there lookin' at me. Eyes? Not even blinkin. Totally givin me the stare. One minute he's got his mouth runnin' on overdrive, arms flappin all over the place while he's tryin to explain this crazy life story of his, then, just like that, his arms drop to his sides and he doesn't have a thing to say. Nothin. It's like he all of a sudden didn't recognize me and just froze up.

"Yo, I asked you a question, Chief. *Is that it?*"

A few more moments go by without a sound. Nobody's movin, not me, not him.

Then, real slow, and I do mean *real* slow, Cluck starts to grin. Not a full-faced grin. Naw, nothing like that. Wouldn't have been in character if he had, even though I didn't know that at the time. Naw, Cluck, he just lets the left side of his lip stretch up. Little higher…little higher…hold.

"Quite impressive, even I must confess," he says finally. "Naturally the question to be asked here by me of you is what? If anything might have been the reaction of a star-spangled leader of the masses such as thine own self had you been forced to endure the Silence of the Cluck for what? Oh, about a skinny little minute longer. Perhaps two. Could you? Would you? Perhaps we will never know. Perhaps we do not care which, upon reflection, I do suspect is considerably closer to the truth we seek. The truth. Ah yes. Hmmm…"

He kept goin on and on about truth for at least another four or five minutes, rambling on and on about all these things he said the truth taught him, you know, about himself and life and all that cosmic bullshit. Whatever. But then he put on the brakes again, turned the conversation on a dime and locked those funny-lookin eyes on me like he was tryin to pull off one of those comic book maneuvers and suck out my brain through my forehead. This guy, man…

"Because you already know."

"Huh? What…? Already…"

"That indeed, my dear Jonathan Beardy, it is you."

"Jonathan? *Jonathan?* Man, *no*body calls me…"

He waved his hands in front of me all crazy like he was conducting some kinda orchestra.

"Irrelevant and immaterial, my prince. No time, *no time*! Thou art chosen. Life is a whirlwind, not a breeze, young Beardmore. It snatches you into the moment whether or not that moment is indeed you. Everything happens at the right time, 'tis only a question of ready. Or not. I believe you see my point."

"No. And it's Beardy. Not Beardmore. *Beardy,* dude."

"Quite right, Mr. Beardy dude. Quite right. But I must, however, impress upon you that we are presently at the ravenous mercy of the hourglass, which means that I must request you refrain from being quite so dense, if indeed that is not asking too much. Innocent lives are at stake, Mr. Beardy dude, and it is only you who possesses the ability to stand in the fiery breech between those precious lives and that horrid stake."

"Wait…"

"NO! Have you not understood a single syllable I have uttered this entire evening? To wait implies the luxury of time, and time…"

"..is something we ain't got a lot of. Yeah, yeah. I'm gettin' that pretty loud and clear. But why me? I mean why did it have to be me you told all these wild-assed stories to? Not that it wasn't entertainin', but I mean damn. And more important, dude, why in the hell you figure it has to be me standing in the fiery britches between whatever and whatever? You need to explain this to me like I'm a first-grader."

Right then, Cluck raised an eyebrow. And me feelin' naked stupid with noplace to hide.

"OK, lemme rephrase."

"Perhaps that might be advisable, yes."

"OK. But. I mean, you gotta see what..."

"Life is a whirlwind. *Not* a breeze. I invite you to think on this for a moment. Or for however long it may take your constricted, congested mental capacity to absorb this critical detail."

"OK, look. I let you in here when my bodyguards wanted to run you through a meatgrinder. I've been listening to you even though you haven't made a single point yet. So OK, I'll admit you know all about how to work the words, and I admire that. Congratulations on making it past the first grade, dude. But if you want to still be here talking to me 30 seconds from now with all your body parts attached to their original locations then you'd best believe I'm not gonna sit here and let you talk down to me on my own turf in my own dressing room. You got me, Cluck Fuck? Do you?"

So we stared at each other for a good long time, I think each of us sizing up just how much we had to worry about from the other. And how much we could actually trust each other since we had just met. Because it was funny, you know? It was funny because we had just met, but still we both kinda knew by that point that we were at one of those points in the road where we either had to be all in and commit to something we couldn't even see the whole size of yet? Or move on forever, forget about each other forever, and never look back. Not even with a question.

"Point taken, Mr. Beardy dude. And quite right. Quite right indeed..."

Right then Cluck starts to smile, I mean actually *smile,* as in the way normal people smile. I know it was the first and, dude, I'm pretty damned sure it was the *last* time I ever saw Cluck twist those awful lips into anything that even *looked* like it was related to a smile. So naturally I had to smile at him back. And right then is when I knew – when we both knew – that the commitment was a done deal. We were all the way in the deep end learning to tread water.

"All right, now one more time; you tell me why I'm supposed to be this One, this Chosen One, you're talking about. Because I need to understand this real good."

"Actually, Mr. Beardy dude…"

"Beardy, dammit. Period. *Beardy.*"

"Fine. Mr. Beardy."

"No! It's just…fuck it. Looks like that's the best I'm gonna get. Go ahead."

"Fine. Quite simply put it is because you simply cannot climb any higher, dear sir. Am I not correct? You have reached the ceiling of the ceiling of the ceiling of SuperStar-dom, the outer limit of the outer limits. There is no more. You reach, yet your grasping fingers retrieve nothing for your sweat-stained efforts but a palm full of imaginings and whispers. You have arrived at the other side of the stars. Indeed, I say to you that…"

"So you're sayin' I'm bored. Is that it?"

Cluck nods, his face grave as a ditch digger.

"Quite. That and the unfortunate fact that no one else will listen to me."

"So now you're sayin' I'm bored and you got me pegged to be your sucker. I didn't duck quick enough. That about sketch it out?"

Cluck starts to sputter and stutter, as if I'd just sucker-punched him full in the gut. Except that I hadn't flinched a muscle.

"My...my dear Mr. Beardy. Goodness....My dear...a *sucker??* No. *No.* Nothing could be further from the truth. You are not a sucker. You are salvation. Please...do you understand? *You are salvation, Mr. Beardy.* The time has come for you to assume your rightful place within the pantheon of the immortal Gods and to cease your wanderings in the wilderness amidst the muck and mire of the common folk."

He was talkin' way over my head for the most part, but there was something about the way he was sayin' whatever he was sayin' that almost made my heart stop in my chest. It ain't every day somebody comes up to you and calls you salvation. I mean, I've had panties thrown on stage and a whole lot else, and I've had just about every sensitive extremity sucked and licked and polished to nerve jangling perfection. And, you know, some might call *that* salvation. Matter of fact, until right up to that moment? *Dude.* You'd best believe that would have been my definition too.

But this thing about the ceiling of the ceiling...

Suddenly I became aware of something else. Not just something else, but *something fucking ELSE.* You know? I mean wow, it was like that once I was blind but now I can see kinda thing. Everything looked different.

"Let's go," I said.

"Indeed," said Cluck.

CHAPTER 8

I guess it was about another 20 minutes before we pulled up next to the safehouse, or safe shack, or whatever the hell this thing was supposed to be. Truth be told, it looked identical to the wreck we'd just left, and the air had that same scorched metal smell. Silence so loud it could hurt your ears.

But whatever. Really didn't matter. Me and Vee both had some much bigger issues on our minds, which was why neither one of us had said a word the whole rest of the trip between shacks after Beardy had dropped that bomb about wantin' to get Earth kids hooked on MayoMadd.

This was major.

Don't get me wrong. It ain't like I had any kinda love for those precious little Earth kids because I don't. Can't *stand* 'em. My guess would be just about every critter in existence had wet dreams about settin' that rock on fire just to keep our little webbed toes warm. But you can wake up from a wet dream. This crew was wide awake and serious.

"Yo, looks like we're here, guys," said Beardy.

"Yeah, OK. Umm…I think me and Vee need a few secs alone to process some of this stuff. Kind of a big deal to take in all at once, turning all the home planet's kids into drug addicts."

Beardy's eyes jumped back and forth from me, to Vee, to me, to Vee, then back again. They were squinted so it wasn't hard to tell he wasn't in much of a trusting sort of mood. It also meant he wasn't stupid, because anyone who just finished telling a page scratcher and a detective that they had plans to sell illegal substances to youngsters had to know that they just might be putting themselves at a bit of a risk.

"Don't take too long, guys. We got a lotta work ahead of us, and that *does* include you."

"OK, but see what you said there I think just may be part of the problem, right? Because what you said right there would seem to imply that me and Vee are working together with you on this thing when the truth is that we may have a few issues with this plan of yours. I mean, this can't come as much of a surprise, seeing as you already know what each of us does for a living."

Beardy grinned, but it wasn't the kind of grin that would make a person feel like grinning back in return. It was more the kinda grin that would make a person's butthole seize up like concrete. And for a guy like me, that wasn't easy to do.

"Sure thing, guys. Yeah, OK. You do have a point, and I guess I should have seen it coming. So if you need to take a few extra minutes go right ahead."

"Thanks. Appreciate it."

"Don't mention it. Just don't forget that once the two of you are done with your processing then be sure to let me know whether you're on board with us or not. Because if you're not? Then, well, it might get kind of messy. For you guys, that is. Anyway, think about that, all right? All right, then. Later, folks."

Vee and I looked at each other, then back at Beardy. We'd known each other long enough that some communications between us didn't necessarily require words. Besides, we were both practical people. It didn't take a lot of math to figure out what 'messy' meant, or to figure out what chance we had of derailing this runaway train if we were both planted in the dust out here in the Dregs.

"Hold on," I said.

"No, really. You guys go ahead and sort things out. Me and the guys here will…"

"I said *hold on….*"

"Oh. Question? Wanna raise your hand, buddy?"

"Raise my…? Screw that. Listen…"

"Dude. Actually? You're not really the one in a position to tell me what to screw, and I've done my fair share of screwin' believe me. But OK. You don't have to raise your hand. So what's up?"

"About this *being on board* thing. Me and Vee need to know exactly what it is that's supposed to mean."

Beardy gave me another one of those grins that really wasn't.

"Yeah. Right. So I'd say imagine it means exactly what you probably think it means. I know you probably weren't a communications major in college or anything like that? But my guess is you can probably figure this one out."

By now the chickens were all out of the trailer and were standing together in an ominous, simmering huddle behind Beardy giving us a look like all they needed was some sort of signal to do terrible things. Most likely to us. I nodded real slow, trying to keep from gulping.

"Yeah," I said. "So maybe I can."

"Yeah."

"Yeah…"

"Yeah?"

I looked over at Vee, then took a deep breath. Nodded again.

"Yeah."

"*Yeah!* Cool. So let's get busy y'all."

"Y'all?"

"Don't be so picky. It's annoying. C'mon guys, we need to set up shop real quick because I'm guessing we don't have a lotta time before our good Cluck buddy gets here and we get down to the business of planning this whole deal. You know how things have to be in the right kind of order for Cluck before he can do anything, and as big a deal as this is it's gonna have to be way the fuck more in order than your average day, dude."

I gave Beardy a look that probably should have gotten a few of my bones ground into paste right on the spot, but I couldn't help it. Some doors just shouldn't be left open that wide if you don't want nobody strollin' through.

"You *are* talkin' about Deep Cluck, right? The one with fashion sense on loan from the Three Blind Men? *That* Deep Cluck?"

Instead, Beardy bent over double he was laughing so hard. Even a couple of the chickens had to crack a grin. I saw one nudge another with his wing and start to chuckle. Then Vee gave me a soft nudge. I glanced over at her and she winked, giving me a not unpleasant sensation down there where I hadn't had a pleasant sensation in, well, a long damned time.

"*Dude!* That was good! Seriously! Good thing Cluck wasn't here to hear it, but since he isn't, oh well. 'Cause *that* was funny. But yeah. I'm talkin' about *that* Deep Cluck, my man. The very same. He's supposed to meet up with us here so we can get this whole thing rolling. He's the man with the plan. And this is gonna be one big *masterpiece* of a plan. I guarantee you that."

"Masterpiece. Right. So. Where do we start?"

It doesn't take that long to straighten up a dump, and once you do you have to ask yourself who's gonna notice. But it wasn't my dump and I really wasn't in much of a place – or much of a mood – to be questioning which busted up piece of furniture should be shoved over in which corner to make room for some other piece of junk. Wherever and whatever. The idea wasn't to convert the joint into any kind of House Beautiful, because I'm pretty sure that would have scared everyone to death. The chickens never would have recovered from the shock. No, the idea here was to go through the motions of making the place look more presentable so that we could talk ourselves into believing it actually *was* more presentable later on once we got through.

We got through about an hour later, and then nobody knew exactly what to do with themselves. Vee and I wound up sitting scrunched next to each other in what I guess you could call the living room on a misshapen overstuffed piece of fabric that passed for a sofa trying not to look nervous. Beardy started doing chin-ups from one of the doorways and counting his reps out loud. Most of the chickens had gone downstairs, but a few of them decided to stay upstairs with us for whatever reason. Pretty soon one of the bigger chickens named Butch who looked like he was on some kind of weight training program got up from another ripped up couch across from where we were sitting and excused himself down a small hallway. A few minutes later he marched back in with a card table under his arm/wing and set it up in the middle of the floor, then fires up a smokey before yelling down the stairs to the other chickens.

"CARDS! NEED MORE TABLES!"

First came the shuffling and the cursing, followed by a mammoth rumbling thunder that made Vee almost hop into my lap which, all things considered, would not have been such an unwelcome development. Next thing you know the room is packed full of game-happy poultry, only this was the first time I'd seen them looking like they were actually happy – no, *ecstatic* – about anything. Their eyes were twinkling, and you could hear a whole different tone in their voices, way more relaxed and genial. Beardy had cut off his chin ups and seemed to be as excited as everyone else, helping to set up the tables around the room. Then Butch looked over at me and Vee, his beak twisted into a sort of grin.

"You guys play?" he asked.

Vee looked confused for a few seconds, like she wasn't quite sure what she'd just heard (probably wasn't) but then broke into a smile that could have lit up a cave and hopped up off the sofa like popcorn off a skillet.

"Ohhhhhhh I just *love* cards!" she purred, and I thought at first she might have been up to something. But when she turned around toward me with that look I could see she really was serious.

Damn. All these years and I'd never even known. You think you *know* somebody.

"Vid..?" she asked, arching an eyebrow.

I shook my head, motioning with my hands for her to go on without me.

"Naw. I don't know a thing about no cards, honey. I'll just sit here and watch."

She gave me a small pout that was kinda delicious in its way.

"You *sure?* You don't know *any* card games? You sure you're not just being…you know…"

I couldn't believe she was actually saying this in front of Beardy and the chickens, like all of the sudden *I* was the outsider who didn't fit and Vee was part of the gang. But I swallowed it 'cause I knew I'd better. I noticed Beardy giving me an amused grin.

"Uhhh, no, Vee. I promise on my honor I'm not being...*you know.* All right?"

Vee looked embarrassed, which was what I was going for, then shrugged before she turned around to join a tableful of her newfound gaming partners. It was gonna be a long night.

****

Actually, it turned out to be a long three days, which was how long it took before Deep Cluck showed up early one morning pounding on the door like he was desperate to get inside before something grabbed him.

But pounding on somebody's door early in the morning, especially after those somebodys have been playin' cards for three days, damned near without sleep, ain't exactly the best way to get a calm response. Which is to say that Cluck just about got his head blown off courtesy of Johnny Beardy who didn't even stop to think – or remember – that waiting for Cluck was pretty much the reason we were all out there in the middle of the Dregs.

But Cluck didn't even flinch – in fact he *grinned* - which wasn't hardly what I expected from a nerdgeek like him. And, true to form, he was wearing pants that looked like they were patterned after a melting chess set and a shirt that could have been stitched together from a polka-dotted shower curtain. This guy was so weird it was scary.

"Oh. *Dear,"* he said, raising his hands in the air no higher than his shoulders, his long, skinny fingers spread wide. "A rock star with a loaded weapon. Perchance I should engage in rapid retreat? Or should I stand my ground, tempting fate? Life, indeed, is a bowl of unsavory choices and we mortals are left with nothing but the pits."

Beardy reached out with his free hand, grabbed Cluck by the shoulder, then snatched him inside before kicking the door shut.

"Cards. *Splendid!* So is anyone going to deal me in?"

One of the chickens who'd been getting his butt smacked the whole three days stood up and forfeited his game with relief so Cluck could sit in for a few really crappy hands before the three-day marathon finally came to a close and we got down to business. Cluck eased himself back from the table, stood up and walked over to stand in front of the door with a rolled up newspaper under his arm that he'd grabbed out of a rather large bag he'd brought with him. He looked out over the expectant gathering with a twisted grin that really hadn't left since Beardy had shoved that gun in his face.

"So. As to why we are *here,* and as to where we must go *from* here. I would like to show you, my beloved misfits, something in which I am quite certain you will take interest."

You would have thought he was about to perform some kind of cheap magic trick the way he kept flapping that paper back and forth in front of us like he was trying to swat something that he'd never be able to hit.

"Enough already," muttered one of the chickens, after Cluck had been at this for nearly a minute. "Just show us what you got."

And with one quick, wrist-snapping motion Cluck popped open the paper and held it steady so we could all see the huge black type screaming across the top of the Daily Screamer that Vee, a well-known page scratcher for that very publication, hadn't been seen in days and was presumed missing. A headshot of Vee looking alarmed was just below the headline before the story kicked in.

"Oh *shit,*" I said.

"Vid!" said Vee.

"Oh *exactly*," said Deep Cluck, his grin stretching wider to expose his full front range of banged-up teeth.

Beardy stared at the story for a long time, eyes squinted, before turning his attention to me. He was giving me a look like he'd never seen me before.

"*Dude.* Exactly who *is* this chick you've got riding shotgun with you anyway?"

"Exactly once again!" said Cluck.

Suddenly the chickens were all glaring at Vee like she was bait. I got over to where she was sitting real quick to stand next to her, putting my hand on her shoulder, which she grabbed and squeezed. I tried to look menacing but that just made Cluck start laughing. He opened his mouth to say something, but then that steroid chicken Butch, who was sitting a couple tables away, made a motion for Cluck to hush up while he leaned in my direction.

"Answer the question, bud. 'Cause if this is gonna be a problem for us then we got a right to know. Who's the lady *really*?"

Cluck giggled, no doubt 'cause he already knew the answer. Right about then I would have loved yanking his smilin' teeth out one by one with pliers. Instead, I had decided it might be in my best interest to comply with Butch's request and was opening my mouth to do just that when Vee squeezed my hand again, but this time really hard. She looked up at me, over her shoulder.

"You sure 'bout this, Vee?"

She just smiled, winked, then turned to focus her attention on Butch.

"Butch, is it?"

He nodded, blowing a cloud of smoke from the corner of his beak.

"Yup."

"OK, Butch. And you too, Mr. Johnny Beardy. I'm just a reporter, all right? I'm nobody real special as far as I'm concerned. I just do the job I was hired to do, and I do it really well. I'm proud of what I do. But the paper I work for? The Daily Screamer? Even as long as you guys have been stuck out here in the Dregs isolated and cut off all by yourselves I *know* you have to know it's a big deal. You've *got* to know the influence it has, and not just here on Planet 10. The Screamer's got clout on *all* the planets, in *all* the sectors, and that includes Earth. And that means a whole lot of power. And so, by extension, that means *I* have a lot of power. Because the stuff that I write can go a long ways, especially since we don't have any competition. And those little happy-talk rags that get distributed in the sectors don't count.

"So I'm saying this to answer your question in the following way: even though I'm just me? I'm not. Because I'm property of the Screamer. And the Screamer is verrrrrrrry, very serious about its property, believe you me. Which means that, yes, I guess I could pose a bit of a problem. But not because I want to."

For the next few moments it was so quiet I was afraid to even think too loud, but then the rumbling and the mumbling began among the chickens and I was starting to get worried that this ugly little shack just might wind up being the last vision me and Vee were gonna have before being drop-kicked over to whatever there is on that Other Side. The smile on Cluck's face by now was close to deranged, and Beardy was just standing there looking thoughtful, which probably scared me more than anything.

So then, why was Vee so damned calm...?

"But if you guys are willing to trust me, then I'm pretty sure I can see to it I won't be a problem at all. There *is* a way around this, and I'm the one who knows the way."

The voices were hushed again as all attention focused back on Vee. But Beardy was still looking thoughtful, and somehow that just didn't fit.

"Chickee poo has a *plan?* Oh pray tell *do* share!"

Knowing Vee as well as I did, my first instinct, simply out of self-preservation, was to duck. Because I knew, from the minute I heard the 'Chickee poo', that something was about to blow.

"Unless your mother is in the room, Mr. Cluck, I'm not quite sure to whom you're referring...?"

Vee always got real formal with her diction whenever she got pissed off. Cluck's insane grin stayed plastered to his face for a longer time than I would have expected given the fact that Vee just dragged his mother into the equation in a less-than-real-friendly way, but then it started to sag like wax next to a blow torch. Butch's eyebrow was arched high, like a cone with a sharp top, then he broke out in a high, shrieking laugh that I figured must have been painful to deliver. Cluck's neck almost snapped with how fast his head turned to give a really hurt look to his feathered buddy, but Butch kept laughing like he just couldn't help himself, and pretty soon the other chickens joined in. When they were finally spent, Vee looking confused as hell, Butch leaned back and gave Cluck a look the way a big brother looks at a kid brother who just dropped his ice cream on the ground.

"Cluck, relax. We ain't laughin' at you, OK?"

"Oh?"

"Well, OK, maybe we were, but you have to admit that was pretty damned funny. Look, you know we love you. And we're with you 'cause you always been with us. That's always and forever, kid. But sometimes something's just funny, you know?"

"And I am to believe that this is one of those times?"

"Well…yeah."

"I see."

I didn't know Cluck was even capable of sounding that chilly, and by the look on Butch's face I don't think he did either. Saying that to say it was a bit awkward – again – in there for a few, until Vee made her move to bring things back in focus.

"May I continue please?"

Cluck looked out over his crew real slow, then gave a sharp nod.

"You may."

"I appreciate it. And yes, to answer your earlier question – if that's what it was – I do have a plan. The way I see it, and the way I know the Screamer, they're going to be looking for me verrrrrrrryy hard. The Dregs isn't the first place they're gonna look, but it's only a matter of time. And once they get started they're not gonna stop."

"Lady," said Butch. "Do you have any idea how big the Dregs is?"

"Yes. I do. Do you have any idea how many investigators the Screamer has? Did you know that when the Keystones can't find somebody, they hire a team from the Screamer? And that the Screamer investigators have only not succeeded in three cases out of 57 over the past five years?"

"Damn," said one of the other chickens.

"Yes. Damn," said Vee.

"OK. Point taken. So then what's your plan?" asked Butch.

"Simple. You take me back to the paper. But you gotta make it dramatic, OK? Meaning you can't just trot me up to the front door, ring the bell, and hand me over. Besides, where's the fun in that, hey? No, what you guys need to do is something way over the top, something that'll make them run it on the top of the front page. Because once that happens...?"

"Once that happens *what?"* asked Butch.

"Then we win."

"Pardonnay me, Miss Vee, but I always like to say that cuteness is as cuteness does, and right about now you appear to be a tad too cute for my taste. Or, to put this somewhat at a pedestrian level, something stinks."

"I'm sorry, dear Cluckee, but nothing stinks about this plan. Or, to put this at somewhat of a pedestrian level? Perhaps you're too dense to understand what I'm offering here."

Butch put a wing up to his beak in a lame attempt to keep Cluck from seeing him giggle in the man's red hot face. Some of the others didn't even bother trying to hide their amusement. I'm guessing they hadn't ever seen anybody give their boy Cluck as good as he gave. Insult for insult. And being the macho misfits they were they loved themselves a fight.

"Damn," said Butch."Who dropped the bomb in *her* punch?"

"Excuse me for the correction, but I'm not the one getting my ass blown up in here. Now can I finish my plan, Mr. Cluck, or do you want some more of this?"

Cluck just stared. Too angry to answer, too cautious to make a wrong move. I know he was asking himself just how in the hell he'd sized my girl Vee up so short. But that was Vee for you; she was good at sneakin' up on you when you thought *you* were sneakin' up on *her*.

"Good. So then here's how it works guys, and why you're each gonna thank me when this is all over and done. Once I'm back at my desk, and this whole episode has blown over for a few weeks, maybe longer, then that's when I start calling myself 'investigating' this story behind Johnny Beardy being discovered face down in a mayonnaise sandwich – and then his disappearance. Who took him? Why? What was it all about? See? *See?* And that's where I get to start telling your story, telling *your* side, about what it's been like for you guys all these years. About what it was like living your lives as an experiment gone wrong, right? Hey? So then by the time you finish doing whatever it is you got planned on Earth, everybody up here is gonna be sympathetic, which won't be as hard as it may seem since you know how a lot of critters feel about the Home Planet anyway.

"So. Whadda you guys think?"

For a few moments it was dead quiet before Johnny Beardy cleared his throat.

"Yo. If you keep your word? And you're not tryin' to put us on? Then I think this is fuckin' genius. And Cluck, you gotta admit it. I mean, when it's there, it's there. This could work for us *bigtime,* dude."

All eyes shifted over to Cluck, and this time there was no mockery. They didn't mind teasing the guy, but when it came down to who had the final say on things, there was never any doubt it was still Cluck who had the most weight on the scale. And as pissed as he was for being embarrassed in front of his crew like that, I wasn't holding my breath for him to rise above it and make the right call – but I'll be damned if that ain't exactly what he did.

"You annoy me greatly dear girl, as I'm sure you're wonderfully aware. I would happily elaborate on all the reasons why, but time is indeed of the essence at this moment. So yes, I must admit there does appear to be more than a grain of merit to your proposal. I therefore vote that we take you up on this proposal – but with a few requisite modifications which I am sure you will understand. Just as a safeguard. And so I also will request – or, shall I say, *require* – that your boyfriend here, or whatever he is, be left in our custody throughout the duration of our operation until its successful completion. Because, of course, should anything go wrong with the execution of your masterpiece then, oh well, we will of course have no option but to terminate the life of Mr. Vid in a rather rapid fashion.

"Certainly this is more than fair, wouldn't you agree, dear girl? Oh, and please do say something smart. *Please* please please do."

Vee gave Cluck one of those tight smiles, the kinda smile with curse words all in it. But still a smile. She nodded.

"Sure. That's fair. Hey, it's your show, so of *course* it's fair. So now how are we gonna do this?"

Actually, the plan turned out to be pretty simple, which was usually the best way. The simpler the plan, the less there is to screw up. Most of the wack jobs I got called in to investigate who got themselves caught got themselves caught 'cause they figured they were too smart to put together a simple plan. Figured they had to prove themselves by showing off with some crazy scheme that had more moving parts than I got cells.

Deep Cluck obviously knew all this, had done his homework on what worked and what didn't, so he decided the best thing to do was just what Vee said wasn't flashy enough, namely getting her to drop herself off at the front door of the Screamer – but not until it was about two hours before deadline for the next day's edition. That would give her enough time to shock the newsroom with her return and still leave enough to get a front pager about her oh-so-terrifying ordeal. And that would set her up for the next 'investigation' piece on Johnny Beardy, Deep Cluck, and the chickens.

Two days later, as I watched Vee stepping into her transport, Deep Cluck holding open her door like some sorta valet, my heart was thumpin in my throat even though I was tryin to look like none of this was worryin' me in the least. I think maybe I cared about this kid more than I even wanted to admit to myself. That morning, after we'd had some breakfast that actually wasn't half bad, we had a chance to spend a couple minutes alone outside the shack just out of earshot of our new best friends. Vee grabbed my hand and squeezed it tight, then gave me a quick peck on the cheek.

"So Vee, tell me this; everybody back in town is missing you, right? Stories all over the front page asking where could you possibly be. But nobody even knows I'm gone. Or nobody gives a damn. One or the other. Why you think that is?"

Vee giggled, which wasn't exactly the sympathetic note I was aimin' for. But then she bumped me hard with those wide hips of hers before pulling me close, and I was startin' to feel that itch.

" 'Cause I'm adorable! But seriously, look, I know you, hey? And you know I do. But I don't want you to worry about me, all right? I'll be fine. I'm a big girl, and you and I both know this isn't the first time I've been close to trouble, hey? I'll be fine. *We'll* be fine."

"Um-hm. So if you're so sure, then how you figure you're gonna pull this off? 'Cause you know how this has gotta end, right?"

"I'm still working that one out, doll. You know I do my best work on my feet. It'll come to me."

"Somehow that just doesn't leave me in a calm state of mind, kid."

CHAPTER 9

I stood there in the middle of the road watching Vee disappear, I guess just wondering. Not wondering any one particular thing, but just wondering. I think pretty much any man watching a woman like Vee disappear, knowing that his only companions for the next who-knows-how-long were gonna be an ex-rock star, an ugly geek with an addiction to bad clothes, and a pack of muscle-bound chickens with bad attitude, would be forced to wonder about a whole lotta things. Things like, 'what the fuck kinda wrong choices did I ever make in life to lead me right here right now?'

Things like that.

Anyway, once Vee was all the way outta sight and I couldn't see any more dust marking her trail, I turned around to face my new best friends. Most of them were standing there staring at me lookin like I had just contracted some kinda disease. Except for Cluck, who was wearin this self-satisfied grin. I wanted to hurt him. I mean, I wanted to expose this little wardrobe malfunctioning idiot to levels of pain and discomfort that would redefine the term. But for now all I could do was grin back, and then wink, which made him take a step back.

Oh yeah. I know how to screw with your head when I wanna.

"So what's the next step?" I asked, looking straight at Cluck. "What's the big plan?"

" You mean now that poor poor baby is here all alone without his pretty little airhead?"

"Would that be the same airhead that made you look like a.."

"You say what it sounds like you're fixin' to say to our boss and I'll tie you up like a shoelace, buddy? You get me?"

That was Butch, which threw me all off since he was one of the first ones to start snickering when Vee was putting Cluck in check.

"So let me get this straight; it's OK when a woman makes your fearless leader look like a pussy, but when a man does it then…"

I had no idea chickens were that fast. And I definitely had no idea they could throw a straight right.

"Then it's different, pal. You got it. The day you grow legs like hers is the day you can act cute. 'Til then, show some respect."

I picked myself up off the ground, dusted myself off while trying to make it look like no damage had been done, then shrugged my shoulders.

"Respect. Right. So then back to my question, which is what exactly is the next step?"

"The next step is you, me, Beardy, and Butch shall take ourselves a little trip this evening to begin preparations for our much bigger trip to come. Since standard travel might draw a bit of attention considering the rather disturbing feathered appearance of certain members of the traveling entourage, let's just say we are required to make more specialized arrangements. Be sure to have yourself ready within the hour."

"Ready like how? You want me to shower and shave or somethin'?"

Butch took a step in my direction but Cluck waved him away.

"You remember what I said, Pal, right?" he said, still feelin the need to flex.

"Oh, you mean about respect? Sure thing, princess. Respect all day long."

I could see Butch starting to overheat, which was exactly what I was going for, but Cluck had already peeped my hole card and told his pet poultry to stand down. He shook his head, giving me the tsk-tsk routine.

"Just have yourself ready, Mr. Vid. This is a very important trip."

A couple hours later, me, Cluck, and Beardy were all crammed into a seriously beat up transport with a paint job almost as bad as Cluck's wardrobe. I looked out the window and tried to make myself relax for several hours as the Dregs slid by, one stretch pretty much looking like the next, until we started to slow down and I noticed us coming up on what looked like an abandoned warehouse of some sort situated next to a tall pile of rocks stacked up like a small mountain. Everything else surrounding the place was flat, but if you looked in the near distance behind the warehouse you could see outlines of the city.

"Aren't we a little close to town for some fugitives?" I asked, as the transport came to an abrupt stop.

"Just shut up and exit the vehicle," said Butch.

"Exit the vehicle. Right. So somebody gonna open this door or am I supposed to make my own?"

"Yo, you break it you buy it, dude," said Beardy, grinning like he thought he'd made a world-class funny.

Moments later we were all standing outside the front door of this warehouse and I was wondering why the big light hanging over the top suspended by a thick chain from a post had gone out soon as Butch knocked on the door. I glanced around at my new best friends to see if anyone else was concerned, but since it had gone dark I couldn't really tell. Then there was a loud, metallic groaning sound and the door swung open with a loud bang. Nobody was standing in the doorway, and it was darker inside than where we were standing.

"OK, am I the only one…"

"Shut up and go inside."

"Screw you Chicken Little. There's a lot more poultry where you come from which makes you expendable, so why don't you hop on through yourself?"

Butch started to make a move on me, but Cluck grabbed him by the elbow – or whatever you call that part of the anatomy on a freak chicken – and told him to do like I said. Shocked the hell outta me, but I'm glad probably nobody got a good look at my expression as dark as it was.

"You takin' his *side?"* asked Butch.

Beardy was crackin' up.

"Chicken Little. *That's* rich. Say, where'd you hear about…"

"In five seconds this door will close. It will not be opened again."

"Who the hell was…"

Just like that Cluck gave Butch a hard shove toward the door, and the rest of us followed real quick. The door slammed again, and for a few really nervous moments it was pitch black. I don't think any of us was even breathin, and I was wonderin if Cluck had done any kinda background check on these clowns we were supposed to be meeting with.

Then I heard a loud click, and suddenly everything went from pitch black to blinding light. I'm pretty sure all of us cried out at the same time with some pretty choice expletives.

"*Dude!* Is this really necessary?"

"Actually? Yes. Yes it is. Considering that we're all meeting here to conduct some pretty damned risky business, I'd say yeah. It's more than necessary. So judging by the long hair I'm guessing you're Beardy?"

My eyes were starting to adjust, which means I could start to make out a short, squat outline of a critter I could quickly tell was easily the size of two or three normal size critters, and he was chompin down on a cigar that he must have picked up on one of his runs to Earth since there was no way to grow tobacco on Planet 10. As my eyes started to adjust even more, I was starting to wish maybe they'd kept the lights off for awhile. This guy and his friend, or business partner or whatever he was, standing beside him with his arms crossed chewing another cigar, had to be two of the ugliest critters I had ever seen in life. Having to look at Deep Cluck day after day had been bad enough, but this just wasn't fair. Both of them had huge heads, like someone had decided to use 'em for balloons, and their skin coloring was all off, kind of like whatever color you might get if you ate a bunch of eggs and then a bunch of broccoli and then threw it all up. The rest didn't get any better, but it's painful enough just describing this much.

"Yeah, dude. I'm Beardy."

The Twin Uglies stared at Beardy for an uncomfortably long time, then looked at each other, shrugged, back at Beardy, then started to nod in unison as if somebody was pulling the same string.

"Yo, what the fuck? Something wrong? Am I the wrong pretty face or what?"

The Twin Uglies shook their heads. Shifted their focus to Cluck.

"So we should get to it then? No need this taking a lot of time, right?"

Cluck turned on his brightest megawatt smile, which was a blatant crime against the very meaning and intent of a smile, as he stepped forward to stretch out his hand like some sorta salesman.

"No need at all!"

The Twin Uglies glanced downward at the outstretched hand, scrunched up their faces like they smelled something rotten, then waddled away toward the far corner of the room where a large round table was squatting kinda off balance. Looking around, it didn't seem like there was much of anything else in the room except for the chairs surrounding the table and the bright light swinging back and forth up above from a thick chain suspended from the ceiling. There was a door in the rear with a small square window jammed in the middle, but the window was covered with a square piece of dirty red fabric so you couldn't see whatever was on the other side.

Cluck kept standing there with his hand outstretched like he figured they musta forgot something, but it was obvious they didn't forget a damned thing. They left Cluck hangin 'cause that's what they meant to do. Pretty soon the smile faded by about half the amount of watts as Cluck motioned for the rest of us to follow his lead toward the table.

Once we were all seated, Twin Ugly # 1 spoke up.

"So it looks like you might need our help."

"That would be why we're here. Correct."

"Um-hm. And that help means getting you guys smuggled onto an Earth transport?"

"That would be why we're here. Correct."

"That supposed to be funny?" asked Twin Ugly #2.

"Is *what* supposed to be funny?" asked Cluck, his grin stretched real tight.

Moment of silence, then, "Um-hm."

"Can we get back to business please?" asked Cluck.

The Twin Uglies gave each other a look, raised an eyebrow, shrugged, then gave their assent.

"So we were discussing the fact that you want our help smuggling you and your friends onto an Earth transport."

"Yes."

"Just like that."

"Just like *what?*"

"You think this is a simple thing you're asking, Mr. Deep Cluck?"

"Quite obviously not. If it was a simple thing I was requesting then I believe it would be logical to assume a simple-minded sort would have been the perfect sort for the job. This being a not-so-simple task, it becomes apparent that simple-mindedness simply will not do. Which brings us to you. So here we are."

Lookin' at the perplexed expressions of the Twin Uglies, I had to practically bite through my bottom lip to keep from laughin out loud. They couldn't figure out whether they had just been kissed off or wet-kissed. I couldn't stand Deep Cluck, but the jerk did have his moments.

Says Twin Ugly #1: "It isn't simple, and I'm assuming you're aware this isn't cheap. Costs enough to transport to Earth the regular way. Going off the books jacks up the price a ways because of the risk. I'm sure you can understand that, right? Unless, of course, you're simple."

Deep Cluck and #1 stared at each other for a few long moments before Cluck broke the tension with a wink and a chuckle.

"Touché, sir, touché indeed. Quite right. And I believe you'll find I have no problem in rendering the appropriate compensation for the appropriate services dutifully rendered."

"Yeah, well. Regardless of whatever it is you just said, I can tell you now this is gonna run you at least fifty thousand to cover you four, and that's Earth dollars. And we're gonna need it all up front since we don't have any guarantee you guys will be coming back and we can't afford to be tryin to track you down if you disappear down there. Earth's kind of a big place, you know."

"Dude, who said anything about it just being the four of us?"

The Twin Uglies looked over at Beardy, both their eyebrows flexed upward into a questioning arch.

"What's he saying?" asked #1.

"If you're looking at me then you can go ahead and ask me direct, dude, all right? And what I'm saying is it's gonna be a whole lot more than just us four. Gonna be more in the neighborhood of 15."

"Surely you're joking. I mean, no way can you expect..."

"I can assure you humor is not involved in this transaction, sir. And if you are not capable of doing the job, as I was assured you would be, then I suppose now would be the time to tell us so that we might locate some more able criminally-minded sorts who would be perhaps a bit more prepared to do business than yourselves."

"And how many criminally-minded sorts unlike ourselves do you think can sneak 15 fugitives illegally onto an Earth transport, my friend?"

"First things first? I am not your friend. Secondly, I would advise that you not underestimate either my ambition or my reach. The money you will require to complete this transaction can be provided to you quite easily. We have been preparing for this event for quite some time, emphasis on the word 'preparing'. So we have what you need. The question, I believe, is whether you are able to accommodate *our* needs. Correct? So tell us now; do we have a deal, or do we need to look elsewhere?"

The Twin Uglies glanced at one another real quick, then asked for a minute to leave the table and discuss the matter over in a corner of the room. It was a pretty short discussion.

"What we need is this," said #1, as he lowered himself back into his chair, grunting and groaning like the last wish of a dying pig. "We're going to need $150,000 cash by tomorrow night. Brought here. Deep Cluck will bring it and nobody else comes with him. You leave in two weeks from a location that we'll tell you the night before departure. Have another $150,000 with you when you arrive at that location."

"Done. But how exactly do you propose to smuggle us aboard this transport if you are asking all of us to show up at the launch site with a case full of money? You don't think perhaps such a sight might attract just a wee bit of attention from the other nearby passengers waiting to board?"

The Twin Uglies grinned in unison, then said, "Don't worry."

"I'm sorry, *what?*"

The two of them kept grinning then grunted and groaned as they pushed themselves away from the table and stood up. Personally this wasn't making me feel that assured, but hey. Wasn't my money.

"Two Weeks," said #1. "You handle your end, we'll handle ours. Goodnight gentlemen. I'm sure you can find your way out." But you might want to wait until the lights come back on."

"The lights…?"

Darkness.

****

When the lights did come back on, I guess I wasn't that surprised to see our hosts were nowhere in sight. I *was* a little surprised to see we were all in what looked to be a whole other room, even though not one of us had flexed so much as a gill or a beak since the departure of the Twins. And right there on the table in front of us (for some reason the table was the same) was a copy of the latest edition of the Daily Screamer. Neatly folded. Looked like it hadn't even been opened. The story that ran above the fold featured a boxed headshot of my girl Vee, smiling like her life depended on it. Her byline ran just underneath the photo and above the headline, which read, "Missing Page Scratcher Mysteriously Returns to Work. Tells Horrific Tale of Flesh-Eating Chickens."

"Dude, is it just me, or is this not a good sign?"

"No. It is not. Now let's go. *Quickly.*"

Butch looked like he was about to explode.

"Flesh-eating chickens? *Flesh-eating chickens???*"

"OK, now wait a minute, Butch," I said, trying to invent an explanation in my head on the spot because I was pretty sure if I didn't my life expectancy was going to shrink from years and months to, well, any minute now. And sure enough, just the sound of my voice was all Butch needed to try and leap over the table. Beardy, who was a lot stronger than he looked, grabbed Butch by the wing and used his brief momentum to slam him to the ground.

"Yo, now's not the time. We'll get our answers later. Right now we need to do like Cluck says and get the hell outta here."

"I promise you there's a reason for why she did it this way, Butch, OK? I know Vee. Known her a long time. There's no way she would ever go back on her word. If she says she's gonna do something then that's what she's gonna do. Plus she knows you guys have got me. She's not gonna say anything that could get me killed, guys. C'mon."

Or at least I hoped she wouldn't. But right then, as Beardy was cautiously letting Butch up off the floor, I couldn't help but wonder about what I thought was the real concern here, namely why the Twin Uglies thought it might be fun to drop this article in front of us like this. Exactly what kinda message were they trying to send…?

The next day, as we were all beginning preparations for the trip, I took Cluck aside and suggested he let me make contact with Vee. I didn't expect him to go for it.

He went for it.

"Perhaps that might not be such a bad idea. Indeed, had you not suggested it I am afraid I quite likely would have been forced to insist. Scary, yes?"

"Yeah. Scary. Sure. Now here's the thing, OK? You guys have gotta give me some leeway with this. With Vee, I mean. I know how this looks, but I'm tellin' you again; there's no way she's screwing us on this."

"I see. So when you say'leeway', you mean…"

"I mean don't just use this as your chance to use me to draw her out so you guys can put a hit on her. I know it's against your nature, but we gotta go innocent until proven guilty here. You *are* familiar with the concept, right?"

"I am familiar with quite a few things that I do not agree with or condone, Mr. Vid, but in this instance I will give you the leeway you request. Simply because my gut tells me you are probably correct."

I extended my hand so we could shake on it, but he just gave my outstretched hand a look like it was carrying a special sort of disease and walked away. I shrugged.

"OK then. Fine. Hey, I'll get back to you."

"Yes. You will. And don't let it take too long."

It took three days. It probably didn't have to, but I didn't want it to look like making contact with Vee was all that easy, even though it was much easier than it should have been after the story she'd just written. Since my name wasn't mentioned anywhere in the story, and since it didn't seem like anyone much cared that I'd been missing – very much unlike Vee – I pretty much slipped into a poor man's disguise (just in case anyone really *had* been missing me even if it was for all the wrong reasons) and then appeared on the first floor of the Screamer at the front desk, half my face hidden behind a pair of monstrous dark glasses, telling an amused-looking grossly overweight security guard that I had come to leave a secret message for Vee.

"A secret message, eh? From somebody who looks like you? Gee. I don't think so."

"Oh. You don't think so? Or you just don't know how to think?"

Instead of getting pissed off, which is definitely what I was going for, the guard's amused half-grin exploded into a full grin, exposing a row of sharp little teeth.

"You got jokes I see."

"No. You weren't listening. Your mother's the one with the jokes. I said I got a secret message for Vee, and it's a message I can guarantee you she's gonna wanna hear."

"OK. Now you're starting to get annoying."

"Not yet I'm not. Just wait, though. HEY! VEE! IF YOU WANNA HEAR MY MESSAGE, COME MEET ME. YOU KNOW WHERE. I WON'T LEAVE TIL YOU GET THERE."

I was looking straight into the security camera when I said this because I knew this meant they would have to show it to Vee to see if she could identify me as any kind of threat, or if she even knew me at all. I knew the cheap disguise would make it easy for her. And I also knew I had to get my ass outta there in a hurry soon as I left my message, because now Mr. Way-Too-Damned-Fat-To-Be-A-Security-Guard was radioing all his other rent-a-goons to come to the front desk right away so they could stomp me into dust. That's not actually what he said, but I think it conveys the general meaning.

I was back out the front door and around the corner before he'd even put the receiver down. It was hilarious to me how security actually expected somebody to 'come back here' just because they were wearing uniforms. If crooks were that obedient there wouldn't be any need for security, don't you think?

Half an hour later I was at the Potta Crocka, which had always been our favorite spot for havin' a long sip of hot crocka, or just to sit around and talk about whatever if we couldn't come up with any particular excuse not to be wherever each of us should have been at the time. The Crocka, which is what everybody called it for short, was pretty much built to be everybody's favorite little spot. Just a comfy little spot, the kinda 24-hour nook where there were always enough folks inside to keep the hum and buzz going, but never enough to cause a racket. When you thought about it, it really was kinda magical how a place could always manage to steadily attract just the right number of people and the right kinda folks attracted to the right kinda dim lighting where nobody much stood out or attracted any attention unless they wanted to, which nobody ever did. The kinda folks who wouldn't bother to notice that a celebrity page scratcher and an on-the-lamb private detective in a cheap costume. It was like critters who didn't fit knew it before they ever set foot inside and just kept walkin.

It was beautiful.

Anyay, it was still light outside, but it was gonna be getting dark soon, which meant the older crowd was due to start rolling through pretty soon. That was good 'cause it meant the atmosphere was likely to be even more relaxed, which is just what was needed for whenever Vee showed up. I looked at my watch and saw it was close to 4, which meant it would probably be a few more hours before she could find a way to make it over without someone trailing her. When the waitress came around I calmly put my hand to my forehead, covering most of my face while I put in an order for an extra tall cup 'cause I suspected this could be a long one.

Five-and-a-half hours later, Vee comes sashayin' through the door, those beautiful hips swayin from side to side like a metronome. Even though there were a fair number of critters lounging around, she made a straight line for where I was sitting before she'd even really looked in my direction. Like I said, we'd been comin there for quite awhile. Soon as she sat down a different waitress showed up who I recognized as a young kid that had always looked up to Vee as some kinda role model. I guess what the kid didn't know couldn't hurt her.

"You want the medium crocka with cherry cream, and one of those little yellow rolls, right, Ms. Vee?" she said, her eyes sparkling.

"You got it, sugar. So how's that book you've been working on? You finish that second chapter yet?"

The kid shrugged, looking kinda shamed.

"Naw, not yet. But almost! Havin' a hard time deciding how I think it ought to end, you know? Every time I think I got it nailed, I realize it doesn't fit and then I'm right back where I started all over again. That ever happen to you?"

"All the time, sugar. All the time. Goes with the territory. Listen, you hang in there and don't let me catch you thinkin you're gonna give up. You keep at it, hear?"

I swear you coulda plugged in the whole city to that girl's smile and still had power left over to run the suburbs. Kid was ecstatic.

"Oh you *know* I would *never* do that, MissVee! And next time you come through here I'm gonna have it all done, you'll see! Man, I'm so glad you're back, you know? We all are. I don't know what I would have done if…well…"

"Shhh…It's OK, honey. And thank you. I'm glad I'm back too. Now me and my friend here, we've got just a little business we've got to tend to so…"

"Oh! Miss Vee I am *so sorry!* And here I am running my mouth and you've got company sitting right there and here I am…anyway. I'm just such a fan! But if you need anything you just flag me down and I'll be right here, OK? Just flag me down! And Mister, please accept my apologies, would you? I certainly did *not* mean to intrude on your lovely evening."

I grinned and nodded, working to keep the front edge of my brim over just enough of my face that she wouldn't be able to tell who she was looking at between the shadow and the size of the hat.

"No charge, doll. No charge at all."

She beamed a smile, then backed away so fast I was surprised there wasn't a draft.

Vee and I looked at each other. We smiled.

"Now you? *You* I may have to charge just for how good you look, babe."

Vee's gills flushed purple on the edges, which was just what I was goin for.

"Stop, Vid. Besides we don't have a whole lot of time."

"You know how long I been waitin' here?"

"You know what I mean."

I sighed.

"Yeah. Yeah, I guess I do. So we should probably get right to it, and you gotta know what's at the top of my list, right?"

For a split second Vee looked almost scared, which was highly unusual for her, but then I realized it wasn't fear I'd glimpsed in those eyes but something else. Something that sent a bit of a shiver through me.

"Vee..? What is it, doll?"

She looked away, then started chewing her bottom lip, which definitely was not a good sign.

"You know, maybe we ought to wait until the crocka gets here…"

"And you know, normally I might think that would be a good idea? But something about the way you're actin' all of a sudden makes me think maybe I oughta hear this sooner than later."

She kept staring away from me at nothing in particular, or at least at nothing I could see, until I was just about to say something else to bring her back from wherever she'd drifted to.

"You're right," she whispered.

I leaned forward, my heart startin to pump a bit faster.

"What's that…?"

She turned to face me again, and right then I told myself that no woman with eyes and lips like that, and all the trimmings that came with them, could ever say anything that would bring me any kind of pain. But right after that I told myself how stupid that sounded because it was precisely from women who looked this kinda good that all the best pain came hand-delivered and wrapped with a bow.

"You know I wouldn't ever do anything to hurt you, right? I mean, not on purpose. You know that, right?"

I mean, not on purpose.

"Sure…sure, babe. I know that. I've always known that. We go back, you and me."

119

It was a tiny smile, but at least it was a smile. Enough for me to hang my hope on that my Vee was still my Vee.

"Yeah…yeah I guess we kinda do, huh?"

I nodded with a hopeful smile.

"You wanna know the thing that I've always loved about you the most, Vid? I mean absolutely more than anything else?"

"My drop-dead good looks?"

Normally my corny style of humor would have gotten a loud laugh from my girl, but this time all I got was a soft chuckle that I could barely hear.

"Silly. You know, you *are* a good-lookin critter, even though you'll never let yourself believe me when I try to tell you. But naw, that's not it this time, Vid. No, the thing I've always loved about you so much was how I knew I could always count on you, no matter what. *No matter what.* You've always been so dependable, so reliable. I could always count on you to be you, you know?"

I nodded again, but my smile was slipping. I could smell where this was going and my whole body was starting to tense up, getting ready for whatever.

"Kinda the same way I've always felt about you, kid," I said. "You've always been my Vee."

"And I always will be, Vid, which is what's making this so hard. See, the thing is? The thing is it looks like I'm not the only one who knows how much they can count on you."

"What are you talking about?"

"You're here to ask me about that story, right? The one about the flesh-eating chickens? Vid, you know how much those crazy clucks get on my nerves, but you *know* I know they aren't flesh-eating. And you know I would never write anything I knew wasn't true, especially if I thought it was going to get you into any kind of trouble. And a story about flesh-eating..."

"So you're saying...?"

"I'm saying they knew enough about you to know how you'd react. They knew this would flush you out. God you don't know how much I was hoping this time, just this one time you'd be different. Or that Cluck and them wouldn't let you come. Anything. But then..."

"Wait. Vee. Something here isn't right. But first of all, who are *they?* You couldn't mean... *"*

Vee just stared, her fearful expression answer enough. Jesus. If this was true...

"Then I'm already dead."

"Don't say that! Don't you *ever* say that!"

"Vee, you know who they are and you know how they operate. Hell, you're the one tried to write that story about them three years back, and you remember how that turned out, right?"

Vee suddenly started to shake, as if the temperature in the room had suddenly dropped 40 degrees, but then forced herself to come back under some measure of control. I was sorry I'd brought up that episode, especially since I knew more than anyone how much she wanted to forget it.

"But why are they running *me* down, Vee? What did I do? I know I've been missing for awhile, but you're the only one anybody actually missed, or at least I thought.

Is it because of that stunt I pulled at the paper in the lobby? But then you said they knew how I'd react so why would that piss them off enough to…I'm confused…"

"Not as confused as I was once I got back to the paper, Vid. I thought everything was the same, until I found out it wasn't. I haven't got time to explain a whole lot, but you'll figure it out soon enough. What you need to know is that somebody saw us when we made contact with Deep Cluck that night, and somehow that was enough for them to start putting together some pieces that they've been looking at for a real long time. They've been after Deep Cluck for years, Vid, hey? *Years.*"

I started to ask another question, but that was when I spotted the waitress on her way back from across the diner, her face glowing as if nothing in the world could possibly be wrong. Right then, at that moment, that simple, happy way of looking at things was worth more to me than anything else in the world. Right at that moment I would have traded whatever was left in my shabby little bank account just to be living inside her innocent view of the way things oughta be.

Then I noticed the door swing open just as she was passing it on her way towards us, and that snatched her attention away. What *she* saw put a question mark on her face, as if she couldn't quite make sense of something. What *I* saw pumped my chest so full of ice I couldn't breathe, my mouth sucking air like a fish out of water.

"Vid? What is it, hey? *Vid!*"

Then she turned to see what it was I was looking at.

"Oh my…but how…? I mean there's no way that soon, there's just…*no way*…"

The confusion and fear in Vee's voice made me pull myself together real fast, because I knew I had to. A sudden realization that my time was running out on me, that it might be over within the next few minutes, forced me to focus like my life depended on it. Because it probably did. What came through the doors at Crocka wouldn't look that terrifying to anyone who didn't know what it was they were looking at, which was probably why the waitress looked more confused than anything else. Unlike any of the other critters on Planet 10 – or anywhere else, for that matter - the two Gerruh didn't have any gills, and their skin color was kind of an off purple that tended to make critters wince involuntarily, as if it hurt to look at them. And in a way it kinda did because they were ugly as all hell, but in an unsettling kinda way, not the kinda way that puts ice in your chest and makes it so you can't breathe right. The other unsettling thing about the Gerruh was how they could appear so calm and ready to explode all at the same time. And they loved to kill things, which was exactly why the Keystones loved to hire them for the hardcore jobs they weren't qualified to do, which was actually a lotta jobs since the Keystones were just a buncha clowns who liked to strut around in uniforms blowin whistles.

So as they stood there just inside the doors, both of them wearing the same jet black suits and square top hats, their reddish-green eyes scanning slowly from left to right across the thick and curious crowd that almost instinctively started stepping aside to give them a wide berth of space they hadn't even asked for, my hand clamped on Vee's leg under the table, which was something I normally would have never done no matter how much I flirted with her. I never wanted her to think I disrespected her, but this had nothing to do with flirting or disrespect, and she knew it. Gently, I felt her small hand settle on top of mine.

"Vee, there's just one thing I want you to tell me, and you're gonna have to tell me real quick because…"

"You've gotta take me with you."

"What…? *What?!??*"

"Look, I'll answer whatever you want me to answer, and I'll help you explain everything to Cluck and his crew, but if you don't take me with you *right now,* they're going to kill me, all right? Because the only way they know you're here has got to be because they know I'm here. Otherwise, as long as you've been waiting for me, how come they didn't come looking for you earlier? Vid, *please…"*

I noticed two doors leading into the kitchen flapping open just off to my left, then squeezed Vee's hand real hard. She winced and started to say something else, but then her eyes followed my line of sight and she simply nodded. I started to get up, but then next thing I knew the waitress was back at our table. I couldn't help but notice how she had stood herself almost exactly in the right spot to block the Gerruh from spotting us right away. She was holding a large tray expertly on one hand with our orders, which was fine, but there was something funny about her smile…

"Oh! You know what? I almost forgot we'd even ordered and I think we're just going to…"

She leaned over like she wasn't paying attention to a thing I was saying as she methodically unloaded the tray, placing our orders in front of us real neat.

"You guys can't make your move until I say, but when I do you're gonna have to stay real low and head straight for those doors. There's an alley out back. My transport is parked right next to the dumpster with the keys in it. It's the only transport back there. As soon as you move, Voris and Varnella here are going to take your seats. Do this right, and everything should work out fine, OK?"

Not much in life confused me, but this little maneuver was putting my brain in a pretzel twist that hurt.

"Excuse me, doll, but exactly what kinda waitress *are you* anyway? You the new super duper improved factory model or what?"

"One of these days maybe I can explain, but right now it's time for you to go. *Now. GO.*"

Vee and I exchanged quick glances, then we slipped out of our chairs without another thought. Voris and Varnella, a couple that somehow looked a hell of a lot like us, was in our seats just that quick and starting to eat our order. I gotta say it kinda pissed me off as well as made me hungry, but first things first, right? And the first thing was to get the hell outta there before the Gerruh found out what was going on.

And sure enough, just like the Super Waitress said, there was a transport parked and ready right next to the dumpster out back with a pair of keys hanging in the ignition. I looked at Vee, raising an eyebrow.

"Tell me you're not wondering the same thing," I said.

"You mean that this is some kind of set up?"

"Yeah. That."

"Look, if we'd stayed in there then we were dead anyway, hey? The Gerruh would have killed us right there in front of all those critters before we even got a chance to take the first bite. So in a way we're really dead already, we just kinda got an extension, right? And if this transport actually starts, and we put some distance between ourselves and this place, then that extension just keeps getting longer. So let's get in the damned transport already, Vid, OK?"

"You drive," I said.

"Why?"

"Because I got this feeling we're gonna need a female driver."

"What's that supposed to…? Oh never mind. Fine. Just get in."

And so that's what I did, and the key actually did work, and the car actually did start, and 10 minutes later we were approaching the city's border. The Dregs stretched out in front of us like a big black stretch of nothing, which was pretty much what it was. I looked over at Vee, scrunched my eyes.

"What?" she asked.

"You had that worked out with the waitress the whole time, huh?"

Vee grinned.

"*Damn* you're slow."

CHAPTER 10

Turned out our clean getaway wasn't exactly as clean as either of us thought, but that wasn't even the worst of it.

"Vee, you *gotta* have an idea about how this could have happened, all right? I mean, it's gonna be way bad enough with me showing up with you back at the shack tryin' to explain to Cluck and the crew what the hell was I thinkin' bringin' you back there after that Screamer headline, and now I'm supposed to try and explain this too? *How*, Vee? *How* you figure I'm supposed to tell them word leaked out that we're supposed to be hijacking an Earth transport? You think they're not gonna suspect it was you right away? And do you know what they're gonna do then? To *both* of us? "

But Vee was looking in the rear view mirror, her eyes wide.

"Shit…" she mumbled.

Her expression told me all I needed to know. Death was on the way.

"They're behind us aren't they?"

Vee nodded real slow.

"You might say that, hey? Yeah. "

"Shit…"

"Yeah. That's what I just said."

"Told you we were gonna need a woman driver. Didn't I? Didn't I say that?"

We were stuck at a light right at the border between the city and the Dregs. I never did understand what exactly prompted whichever of our brilliant city planners that this would be the perfect spot for a stop light, but then this probably wasn't the best time to be contemplating the shortcomings of our public servants.

"So what the hell is this female driver supposed to do now, Vid? This isn't even my transport, which means it ain't souped up like mine. This is just a regular, factory issue transport. No way is this a match for what they've got under that hood."

Then again, maybe this was the perfect time to be familiar with city planner shortcomings.

"How far back are they?"

"About two blocks. Can't see 'em real clear because there's some other transports between us, but they're there. I think they probably know we see them, but they don't care. They don't figure there's any way we can get away, and we both know they're probably right."

"Are they moving up on us, or just sittin' there?"

"They're just idling. Like I said, it's not like they're trying to be discreet or anything. They know they've got us."

"Oh really? Well that means they know more than me, and I doubt that sincerely. When the light turns, I want you to…wait a minute. Are they idling this side of Furry Street, meanin' it's behind them? Or are they just on the other side of Furry? This could be important."

"They're this side of Furry, Vid. What…?"

"Oh this is beautiful. OK, what I want you to do is go ahead and make a U-turn once the light turns green and…it just turned. So go ahead. Do it."

"But that would be pointing us back toward the Gerruh."

"That it would. Now make that turn. Then I want you to take your time driving right past them to Furry. We're not even gonna look at them, right? My guess is they're not even gonna start to make any kinda move until we're past them. And if they do just that much for me then they're gonna be really pissed off because we're gonna be gone before they even get a chance to turn around."

"How do you figure…?"

" 'Cause they're gonna have to make a U-turn too, that's how."

Vee gave me the look she would normally reserve for someone with considerably more mental challenges than I myself had.

"OK. And…how do you figure…Oh. Wait…"

"Right. Now you seeing the big picture? Huh? Are you?"

"OK. But…"

"Vee! The light's about to change again! U-turn this damn car already!"

Vee made the turn, and several minutes later we were right alongside the Gerruh, both of whom were looking straight ahead and were as calm as you'd expect a couple of assassins to be. They even had their window rolled down, which kinda surprised me. That was a bit *too* cocky if you asked me.

"OK, now calmly take your left here onto Furry. Don't even hint that you're in any kind of rush. Just like you're going to the grocery store to buy some lettuce or something like that."

"Hurry? Oh geez, why would I be in any kind of hurry, Vid? 'Cause they're gonna kill us?"

"You really need to learn how to be more calm and relaxed. Like me. Go ahead, turn."

The thing about Furry Street was that it was really a lot more like an alley than a regular street, meaning it was only wide enough for one car going one way, not including the similarly narrow sidewalk. So whoever was currently in the lane headed whichever direction pretty much had the right-of-way. Unless of course there was somebody else in that same lane headed the other direction. Then there had to be some driver negotiation – or intimidation – to decide who was gonna get to keep going straight and who was gonna have to pull over to the side. Whoever's idea it was to build Furry Street had a lot more faith in the courtesy and generosity of critters than was advisable. But for our purposes that evening, and with Vee behind the wheel, Furry Street was going to be the Goodbye Freeway. 'Cause knowin' my Vee as I did and how she operated behind the wheel, there weren't too many other drivers could ever make her move over to the side to make way. All she had to do was put enough cars headed the other direction between us and our two murderous companions and it would only take us a few miles before we could dart off of Furry, make a few wild zigs and zags, and then hopefully shake our two murder-minded buddies.

Of course, if we *didn't* manage to shake 'em, then we were dead. But that wasn't the Plan 'B' I wanted to consider right then.

Vee eased onto Furry, and right away I could see a couple cars up ahead coming our way. They were comin' fast, which told me they knew how this street worked and already had it in their mind that they weren't movin' over for anybody. I looked over at Vee. She shook her head and grinned.

Beautiful.

"You might want to strap in, Mr. Vid. I'm gonna have to do some things here."

"Just what I wanted to hear, doll. Just what I wanted to hear."

I swear I would have paid good money to get a better look at the expressions of those two drivers as we blew by them, but we were going way too fast. I'd like to think it was terror. As for what the Gerruh were thinking, the only way we were going to find that out was if we managed to make it far enough ahead to get off Furry and weave our way back to the Dregs. Once we got to the Dregs, if they weren't anywhere in the rear view, then we were home free.

"You see them back there?"

I turned to see if I could get a good look, but for several moments all I could see was dust, several terrified critters who had thrown themselves out of the way, and a few transports still tryin' to straighten themselves out. I could only imagine the curse words being said.

"Nope, not a sign. Let's keep goin' straight for a few more blocks, then we're gonna make a quick right and make our way back to the Dregs just as fast as you can possibly make this thing fly. Don't even worry about the Keystones. They might be able to follow us into the Dregs but there isn't much they can do to us out there, and that's if they catch us. But if we get caught by the Gerruh…?"

"Got it. You just stay buckled up."

It was good advice. I must have seen my life pass before my eyes at least three times, but I never let on to Vee. The important thing was getting us the hell outta there and quick.

Once we were finally back to within sighting distance of the Dregs, I told Vee not to slow down as I took another long hard look behind us. If the Gerruh were back there then they had one of those camouflage transports, and I wasn't gonna let myself worry about that right then. We had more than enough worries to keep us occupied for the next however long it was gonna take to get us back to the shack.

Vee looked over at me after I'd concluded my rear view inspection. I shook my head.

"Nothin'. We're clear. Now you'd better let me drive 'cause I don't think you know the way."

We stopped just long enough for me to get out and jog around to her side and hop in while she slid over. I strapped in and stomped on the pedal like I was tryin' to kill somethin'. For the next couple hours neither one of us said a thing, I guess each of us working out in our own mind what the future looked like from here – or if we even had one. By the time I saw the large, claw-shaped rock that let me know we were close to the shack I had pretty much worked out how I was gonna approach this thing with Cluck and crew. I decided to run it by Vee.

"I think I've got a plan."

Vee stared straight ahead, not sayin' a thing. She didn't even nod.

"It ain't gonna be easy with these guys, you know, but then you probably already figured that, right?"

"Probably," she said, still with the stare.

"Right. So, then, you think maybe you might wanna hear the plan? You know, just to see if it makes any kinda sense to you."

She shrugged.

"Sure. Why not."

If Vee had just said, 'sure'? Then I probably woulda been OK with it. Not happy as could be, mind you, but OK. But it was when she added the 'why not' that pushed me over the edge.

"OK, look. You're the one came up with the plan to go back inside the paper. That plan didn't quite work. Then, after I show up at the paper to find out what the hell was up, it was you decided you had to leave the paper and come back with me, knowing how hard this was gonna be after that story you wrote."

"That wasn't my story!" she practically yelled, her eyes shooting bullets my way.

"Oh. OK. Then the story that magically appeared under your byline about flesh-eating chickens."

"Vid that is not fair! I *told* you what happened with that, how they made me write that story against my will! It was all a trap. That's why it is I have to come back with you, hey? You know that. It's not safe for me anymore."

"You mean it's not safe for *us* anymore, don't you? Which is why I thought you might wanna take a little more interest in this plan I came up with."

"Look, it's not that I'm not interested in your plan, it's just…don't you wanna know why they were trying to lay that trap for you?."

"I suppose so…yeah…"

"It's because they already knew about the Earth transport you guys are supposed to get smuggled onto. They don't know exactly when, or at least it didn't seem like they knew, and they don't know which port you're leaving from, but then there's only five ports on all of **Vivacious 5,** right? So how hard could it be for them to track you guys down?"

"The Twins…"

"Who?"

"The Twin Uglies is what we call 'em. They're the ones got the hook-up for us to that Earth transport. We already paid them the money, and I thought Cluck had already checked them out so I *really* can't figure why or how they'd be the ones. Cluck doesn't seem like the type to make those kind of mistakes. He's crazy, but not *that* kinda crazy. But I don't know who else it could be if not them. But hey, you still haven't told me why…"

"Why they want you?"

"Absolutely. Yeah. Why? I'm just a private dick tryin' to make a living. What do they have against me? And who is this 'they' anyway?"

"I'm still not sure about that. It was my boss, my editor, who took me into a room not long after I got back and told me what I had to do. But I know it's gotta go higher than him, hey? But I don't have anything else to go on 'cause he wouldn't give me anything else. Said there were some 'big eyes on this'. That's what he said. Big eyes. And he said they were pretty sure you had a big part to play in this whole thing."

"Big part to play in *what* thing? Even if the Twins leaked that we're trying to sneak our way on board a transport, there's no way they could have told whoever it is the reason 'cause they have no idea. All the Twins know is that we have to get to Earth and we can't leave any official record of our travel plans behind. The Twins never asked and we never told them."

"Well if they don't know that then they know something else. Whatever it is has got them seriously nervous, Vid. Otherwise why would they bring in the Gerruh? You don't hire their kind to track down somebody who's behind on parking tickets. And why haven't they told any of the authorities? Why haven't the Keystones been notified?"

"Probably because they're a bunch of idiots but that's beside the point. Look, Vee, you're not gonna like me askin' this question, but I gotta ask anyway; It wasn't you told whoever's chasin' us what the real reason is we're going was it? Maybe just to try and stop this crazy plot before it got…"

"I cannot believe you would even *think*…"

"Vee, we both know what Cluck and his guys are planning is wrong, all right? So I would understand, even if it was putting me in danger I would understand. So if that's what happened, I mean, if that's what you felt like you had to do then, well…"

Vee was giving me the kind of look that could put frost on a fire, so I threw my hands up and gave her my best pitiful look. It didn't have much effect that I could see right off the bat, but I was determined to wear her down.

"OK, Vee. OK. *OK.* All right? I get it already. It wasn't you. I figured you'd know why I had to ask, but maybe not. Anyway…"

"Forget it. Just shut up and tell me the plan."

"Shut up and…right, right. OK, I did have this one plan which I figured was pretty good, but after you told me about how somebody up there has it in for us, that they forced you to do that story? I'm thinking now maybe just telling Cluck the truth might be all we need."

For awhile all I could hear was the smooth hum of the engine as we ate up the road on the way to the shack, which I figured couldn't be any more than five minutes away. I glanced over at Vee, trying to glimpse a hint of what she might be thinking, but her face had gone blank.

"I mean, if these guys were telling you that you had to write this story to flush me out and everything, right? I mean that would make sense why you'd do something like that. You see that, right?"

"Tell them the truth…" she said, her voice almost as flat and vacant as the expression on her face.

"Seriously, Vee, I don't know what else we got, OK? I really don't. I'm not saying I know it'll work but I don't see as how we have a whole lotta options to choose from here. And it's not like we got a lotta time. We're almost there."

Vee chuckled, but not like anything was funny. More like a 'you gotta be outta your damned mind but whatever' kind of chuckle. Then she shrugged.

"Fine. The truth. Let's try that."

"So that's it? You're on board just like that?"

"You want me to sign something, darling Vid? I will, you know. Anything for you."

I didn't know what to say to that, so I didn't say anything. Just kept my eyes on the road until the shack came into view. The closer we got, the more abandoned it looked. Or maybe I should say more abandoned than usual.

"Anybody home?" asked Vee.

"Yeah, I was wondering the same…"

But then, right at that moment, just as we were pulling up right alongside, Cluck came sauntering around from the left, which was on my side of the vehicle. Once I turned off the engine I could hear he was whistling some little tune. I was expecting to see his feathered friends coming along behind him, but it appeared he was all alone which was kinda odd. As he approached, I forced a grin and then waved. That right there probably signaled him something wasn't right since he knew I couldn't stand him. I wasn't sure he'd seen Vee right off, but soon as he got up to the window and leaned down there was no doubt. Funny thing was, he didn't act all that surprised. Matter of fact, he didn't act surprised at all. He just motioned for me to roll down the window.

"Hi," he said.

My chest got tight.

"Yeah. Uh...hi back. What's new?"

"Hmmm..well now it does appear that such a question might be considerably more appropriate coming from myself at this particular moment, wouldn't you agree? For the obvious reason seated next to you of course."

"Right. And I'm ready to get to that. But first, where are your friends?"

"Inside of course. Did you perhaps expect them to be outside playing a rousing game of volleyball?"

"OK , that's cute. Look, here's the thing about that, because believe it or not this is gonna affect you too. Matter of fact it's gonna affect the whole plan you got goin' here in a pretty big way."

Cluck looked back and forth from me to Vee and back again, that poisonous smile of his never leaving his face. Cluck was the only guy I knew who made you feel better when he *wasn't* smiling. Matter of fact, if the day ever came where I was lucky enough to see him sitting by the side of the road crying his eyes out, it would probably make my day.

"Affect our plans in a *pretty big way,* you say? And how might that pretty big way be?"

"OK first, you mind if we get out of the car? This just doesn't feel comfortable you leaning all inside the vehicle like that. Not normal."

Cluck took several dramatic steps backward, gesturing in a real fancy way with his hands that we should exit the transport.

"By all means free yourselves. Where would we be without normality?"

"Right," I said, as I opened the door and stepped outside. "So do we do this out here, or shouldn't we step inside?"

"Wellll… we do this here for now. Because quite frankly unless I have a remarkable explanation to give Butch and the boys for why you have returned with *that* tagging along, I must confess I simply cannot vouch for what they may do. Could be I may join in, seeing as how they are, after all, the only real family I have."

By that time Vee had come around to stand beside me next to the transport. Both of us had our arms folded tight.

"OK fine. I can understand that. We do it your way. Vee? Tell the man what you told me."

But Vee was set on a slow burn from the inside out after hearing Cluck refer to her as 'that'. I already knew what it was without having to ask, so when the seconds kept ticking away and she didn't say anything I let the silence hang there between us for a good long while like a thick stench before finally nudging her with my elbow.

"It's on you now. Don't screw this up over dumb stuff, all right?"

I figured that little comment would piss her off enough to unlock her tongue. I was right.

"Whenever it was that you guys were planning on leaving for Earth, you'd better cut that time by at least half. Otherwise? You're all dead."

"Excuse me, my dear Vee, but…"

"They know about your trip and they've hired the Gerruh. I don't know who leaked it or why, or how, but it's happened. Somebody way up high knows your plans and they don't like those plans and they're willing to put in a lotta effort to make sure those plans don't work. As for that story, the same whoever it is that's behind trying to shut you down is the same whoever that was behind forcing me to write that story. Think about it, Cluck; you know my reputation. You might not like the stuff I write, but when have you ever heard about me getting anything that wrong? When have I ever been accused of making stuff up?"

"Well, actually…"

"OK, scratch that. Sure. Critters make accusations. But name one time it was ever proven. And flesh-eating chickens? Really? I mean…*really?* Cluck, that's what you get from some amateur, some kid on her first time out, not someone who's been there. You think about it for any longer than a few seconds and you know this wasn't me."

Cluck's insane grin stayed locked in place, but now he was leaning back against the transport scratching his chin, his left eyebrow arched.

"Go on. I'm listening."

Vee looked over at me kinda confused, then back at Cluck. She shrugged her shoulders.

"Listening what? That's it. Wasn't me."

"Oh I think you had better fork over a few more pounds of red meat for me to take inside darling, unless you really don't care whether or not you make it out of here in one piece."

Vee took two quick steps forward, but I grabbed her shoulder and squeezed. Told her to take a step back. I couldn't blame her for being all hot and bothered, but right now we couldn't afford any wrong moves.

"How about this," I said, keeping my hand fastened to Vee's shoulder. "I'm thinking there weren't but a handful knew we had any plans at all, right? If you think it's me or Vee? Hey, we're right here lookin' at ya. But if it *wasn't* us, then that only leaves a coupla choices; either it was one of your fine feathered friends, or it was the Twins. That's it. So unless you wanna question your crew one by one, I say we need to take Vee's advice and hightail it down there to see the Twins first thing in the morning before they even roll outta bed and strongly suggest they put us on the next Earth transport outta here. No questions asked. They may stutter and spit about how this wasn't what we agreed and it's too short notice, but in the end? I think we can make them come to an understanding. Besides, they already have the money, right?"

Cluck squinted hard, something I didn't recall him doing much, as he looked back and forth from me to Vee, then back again. Slowly, he started to nod.

"Perhaps there is something vaguely, remotely resembling intelligence in what you say. I must confess I was not expecting, of all things, intelligence, but the two of you have surprised Deep Cluck. Indeed you have. Indeed you have…"

"So now you're referring to yourself in the third person?" I asked.

Cluck ignored me as he shifted his gaze back down the road we had come to reach the shack. He looked down that road a long time without saying a word, and I looked at him looking down that road. His grin had faded, and I wondered if he even knew why. It was as if the Cluck that I was so accustomed to seeing had stepped away while this new individual had stepped in.

Then, all of the sudden, Cluck's eyes lit up as if someone inside his head had flicked a switch. He gingerly pushed himself away from the transport, winked at us both, and headed toward the shack at a rapid pace. Vee and I watched him go, not sure whether we should follow until we saw him motion to us with his forefinger. I started to follow, but this time it was Vee who was holding *me* back by the shoulder. She was shaking her head just enough for me to notice, her eyes locked on Cluck. She cleared her throat.

"So then...so you're gonna tell them, right? Johnny Beardy and the chickens? That we're all right?"

Cluck looked back at us over his shoulder just as he reached the door, his eyes glinting with all kinda mischief. For the second time he motioned for us to follow him with his finger.

"What have you got to fear, dear girl? We're all family here."

Then he pulled open the door and disappeared inside. When it closed, the sharp echo made Vee jump just a bit.

"No," she said real quiet. "No. We're *not* all family here. And you freakin' know it."

"What do you wanna do?" I asked.

Vee looked up at me, something soft and vulnerable in those big pretty eyes of hers.

"You're really asking?"

I nodded.

"Yeah. I'm really asking. I'm willing to follow your lead on this. If you wanna go in, then we go in. If you wanna hop back in the transport and hightail it outta here to somewhere else, then that's what we do. I'm with you on this one. I'm on your page."

I said it because I knew it was what Vee needed to hear right then, and the way she reached over and squeezed my wrist real gentle let me know I'd made the right call. We stared at each other a little while, not really needing to say anything, and then Vee let loose with this real deep, real drawn out sigh. She closed her eyes, then mashed her lips together tight.

"So we're going in then, I take it?"

Vee nodded.

"Guess we really have been knowing each other awhile," she whispered.

"Yeah. Guess so."

When we stepped inside, fighting the urge to hold hands, the upstairs room was empty. Right away my heart tried to jump outta my chest, and judging by how hard Vee swallowed a ball of air it wasn't hard to tell she was having the same thoughts.

"So where could he have…"

"*Hellllloooooooo!!*"

We both jumped straight up in the air.

"Downstairs you silly kids! Come on down and join the party!"

I took three deep breaths, hoping there wasn't a hidden camera somewhere letting

142

them watch just how nervous the two of us were. I tried to get myself calm before I answered.

"Party…?" I squeaked. *Dammit.*

I could have done without all the guffawing and wheeze-inducing laughter that came blasting up the stairs in response to my considerably less-than-manly reply, and the taut expression on Vee's face let me know I wasn't inspiring confidence right at that moment.

"Oh fuck yeah, dude," came Beardy's voice. "No way can this party get started until you guys come on down. You're like the guests of honor, man, so bring those asses!"

I looked over at Vee, and forced what I hoped was a brave-looking smile.

"Hey, at least they're laughin', right?"

"Yeah. But I'm not, Vid, all right? *I'm not.*"

My mind ran through a file of things to say, but none of them seemed to fit. I knew saying the wrong thing was worse than saying nothing at all, so I ran my finger across her cheek as soft as I could, then headed for the stairs.

"Vid…?"

"It's gonna be OK."

"*Vid.*"

"You heard what I said, Vee. And you know I'll kill everybody in the damned room before I let them even think they're gonna hurt you all right? You gotta know that."

Just before I took the first step down toward the basement, I looked over my shoulder and caught the hint of a smile. That was all I needed.

What they called the basement was really more like a deep cave, the kind of place you'd imagine was built with the intention of hiding some pretty heavy secrets for as long as they needed to be hidden. The smell was thick and greasy moist, not pleasant, and the lighting was supplied by a couple bulbs hanging from overhead. Getting down the stairs musta taken me close to a minute at least, and for anyone who's ever gone down any stairs, you know that equals a lot. The room itself – there was only one – was pretty spare. Just like upstairs. Some chairs, a few couches, and just big enough to house the entire twisted crew, all of whom I noticed were glaring at us both with anything but smiles. The laughter had dried up just that quick.

"Thought somebody said something about a party goin' on," I said.

"That a fact? Somebody said that huh?"

That was Butch, who was standing over to my right leaning up against the wall, his huge feet crossed at the ankles, slapping a large slug of wood the size of a baseball bat into his palm. I noticed another one of the chickens juggling a long, thick section of chain from hand to hand. Both of them looked like they were waiting on a signal. Beardy stood front and center a few steps ahead of the pack just staring, his arms crossed over his chest, legs spread wide. This was probably the more sensible time to be terrified, but for some reason I suddenly felt more calm than I had the entire long and crazy day.

"Yeah. Somebody who sounded like you. But hey, if the party's over and the dancin' girls is gone then I guess…"

"Sit your butts down. Both of you."

"Screw you, Beardy. You don't get to tell me or my butt what to do, and the same goes for Vee. If you've already made up your mind to kill us, before you even know what the hell is going on, then get it over with. But I gotta tell you it does kinda piss me off how we just wasted our time – and yours – up there tryin to explain the whole story to your boy Deep Cluck right before we came down here. And I know he hasn't had enough time to repeat any of it yet, and obviously he hasn't bothered to tell you why maybe you should listen to what we got to say before the Gerruh show up."

Yep, that definitely got the planned response. Just that quick the noise of the bat slapping Butch's palm came to a halt, and the chain slid loudly onto the other poor bird's foot, which provoked an impressive stream of curse words I hadn't heard used in quite some time. Cluck's sick grin was hard and stretched tight as if it might break, and I could just about swear Johnny Beardy was starting to get the shakes.

"The…the Gerruh…?"

"…but…"

"…I mean…"

"…*how*…?"

Vee giggled, which was a sound worth its weight in all kinds of precious metal. Things were tilting back our way. Improbable as it seemed, Deep Cluck actually stretched his grin a little wider. I actually thought his face might split open from the strain of it all.

"I ummm…I do not believe you happened to mention anything about the Gerruh actually being *on their way* during the course of our earlier discussion. As a matter of fact, I am quite sure no mention whatsoever was made of this rather significantly alarming development."

"Yeah. I know. Kinda changes things doesn't it? Makes things a little more urgent?"

Beardy took a step forward, his face trying to figure out which expression he thought might work.

"Dude, I mean…*why? Why* would you lead those guys…"

"OK, stop right there. Because as much as me and Vee are enjoying this, I do have an itty bitty conscience, and it's doing back flips right about now."

Cluck's face-splitting grin went into a slight retreat as his eyes cut to slits.

"Itty bitty conscience? Back flips? *Really.*"

"Oh yeah. *Really.* But here's the deal for real; we gotta be on the first Earth transport smokin' outta here tomorrow morning. Just like we told you outside. Which means we gotta pack up *tonight* and drag our stuff over to the Twins and explain the situation. Only they don't get to say 'no'."

"OK whoa. Stop. Cluck? *Listen*, dude. Now there's something going on that the three of you know, but nobody's told any of the rest of us a damned thing, so either you explain what it is Vid's talking about or I think…"

"No. You don't. *I* do the thinking in this partnership, please remember. And as you may recall there is quite a good reason for this arrangement. Nevertheless, in light of recent developments perhaps you have a point. But first I require a bit of clarification about …"

"About the Gerruh? Whether they're really on their way? The short answer is yes, they are. The longer answer is I'm not sure how long it's gonna take because I think we shook 'em pretty good before heading out here. But you know how those guys are at tracking. So there's your answer on that. And as for the story with Vee, since I know the rest of you down here probably still think maybe she tried to pull a fast one by writing that story? Yeah, well *no*. I'm not going into any details, but Cluck here knows the story so I figure that should be good enough for everybody else. And you should know Vee ain't stupid, which she'd have to be to show up here in your little underground cave with only one way out after trying to set you guys up. I know Cluck's the one that does most of the thinking around here, but even you guys should have enough functioning brain cells to figure that one out for yourselves."

I could tell by the looks on their faces they weren't too thrilled with the functioning brain cell remark, but I had to show 'em I wasn't scared, even if deep inside I was wondering if maybe this was the end of the line for me. But despite the looks, and the grumbling and mumbling, none of them made a move, which was a good sign. Plus neither Cluck nor Beardy said a thing. They still didn't like either one of us much at all, but they were starting to see how maybe we could be useful. Then again, maybe they were figuring it was a better idea to keep us close than to let us run wild up here on Planet 10 with no supervision. Whatever the reason, we got to keep breathing, which was definitely a mark in the plus column.

Three hours later we were all on the road to make an unscheduled return visit with the Twins. All during the time we'd been packing up nobody said much except to grunt, or maybe mutter a brief instruction or two about what needed to be taken and what needed to be left behind. The plan, for obvious reasons, was to travel as light as possible. There was apparently a connect at our meetup spot down on Earth who could hook us up with whatever we needed for our time there. Plus, given what these guys were planning, I was guessing not much thought was going into a return trip anytime soon. This could easily turn into a one-way trip from Bad to Worse.

Once we all pulled up in front of the Twins' warehouse location, Cluck hopped out the door of that raggedy bus of theirs before it had a chance to slow down real good. Even in his mismatched plaids and highwater pants there was still something a little menacing about the way he was striding toward that door. Like he planned to walk straight through it and grab the Twins by their necks, which I suspect may have been an idea running on a screen in the back of his horribly misshapen head.

"Vid? What do you…"

"Shhh. Let's just see how all this plays out before we make any sudden moves. Besides, I think we've made enough sudden moves over the past few days, don't you think?"

Vee reached over and squeezed my thigh, which caused a rather rapid involuntary response that wasn't particularly helpful at the given time.

"Uhh…Vee…?"

But Vee just purred. Thankfully it wasn't long before there was some activity at the Twins' door, most of which was being provided by Cluck, who had apparently decided against the subtle approach and was banging on the thick slab of steel like he thought they were torturing his mother on the other side. Watching Cluck go nuts made it even funnier to listen to what he was saying because Cluck talked so damned proper, even when he was pissed off in maximum fashion.

"Quite sorry, but this will not *wait! DO YOU UNDERSTAND ME IN THERE?* Plans have changed due to certain situations, and I am afraid you will be required to open this door NOW. Please do not force me to consider…"

Cluck wasn't forced to consider. The door groaned loudly like it had a massive stomach ache, then opened just enough for Cluck to push his way through, which he did after motioning for the rest of us to follow.

"So I guess we're leaving everything else out here then...?" asked Vee.

"Hey, it's Cluck, right? Don't expect it to make sense. Besides, we can come out later and grab all our stuff. But for right now we need to make it through that door before it closes because we definitely don't wanna be sitting here outside all alone waiting for them to come back.

"True."

Once all were inside, the door groaned shut behind us and we were in darkness just like the last time. Then, once again just like last time, we all went temporarily blind as someone turned on a light that came on strong like a fist full of sunshine right between the eyes. Once the eyes adjusted I was wishing they hadn't. The Twins, still ugly and still smoking those dick-shaped cigars, were each sitting in front of us on rather large stools to support their overly large selves, their arms folded over their chests, looking pissed – and stark naked. My first reflex was to shove my hand in front of Vee's face, but then I noticed that amused grin and I figured I was probably too late.

"You boys look good enough to lick from head to toe," she said in a voice that I'd been dreaming would call my name since puberty.

The Twins looked at one another in amazed confusion, and the rest of us looked at Vee as if she'd lost her mind.

"Exactly what in the..."

"Shut up Beardy," I said.

Surprisingly Beardy did exactly that. But even more surprising, the Twins were acting as if they'd suddenly woken up and realized how ugly they were with no clothes and were glancing nervously around the room like they were trying to locate a towel or *anything* that would cover them up while at the same time slapping their oversized hands all over their bodies trying to cover up first one slab of exposed flesh and then another. Vee wasn't what they'd expected, which is what Vee specialized in. Because she wasn't what *most* critters expected. It was one of the qualities that made her such a deadly page-scratcher.

"*Looooose* something?" she asked, taking several hip-swiveling steps forward.

"Maybe a girl can help. You'd be surprised what a girl like me can do for a big double hunka naked critter like the pair of you two, hey? All that marvelous body to cover and so little time to get to work, you know what I mean?"

Finally Twin #1 got up the gumption to squeak out a question, "Who…?"

Then came Twin #2 with, "Yes, *who…??*"

"Quite marvelous, wouldn't you say?" asked Cluck, who I could see was starting to catch on and was actually enjoying the show as Vee sashayed and switched her way to where she was standing just a foot or two in front of the now-terrified Twins.

"*Who??*" the Twins demanded again in unison, this time sounding somewhat more agitated than scared.

"Well, you know, I'll be more than happy to give you boys an answer, and maybe even give you a towel to share, but first me and my friends need your help with just a few little things. If that's all right?"

"Fine," said #1, "but first the towel. This is embarrassing."

"Imagine how we feel," I said. "Maybe next time you'll wanna consider taking a look in the mirror before you answer the door, right? Not all of us are as impressed as Vee here with your assets."

The eyelids of both Twins rolled up like someone had just yanked up the shades as they glared at Vee with a look that let me know a really scary light had just been switched on inside their heads.

"Surely you're not…"

"…*that* Vee…?"

"The one from the…"

Vee's only answer was to rev up that purring sound she did so well, before stroking #1 inside the thigh, right next to his…

"That just might get you half a towel, sweet. Even though I can see that won't be enough to cover up such a big, thick critter like yourself, hey?"

By now, pretty much everyone in attendance was snickering and pointing. Seemed like the only ones not having any fun were the Twins. For some reason, #1 singled me out for a cold stare.

"I don't remember her being with you the last time."

"Yeah. And I don't remember you being butt naked the last time either. Time passes, things change. Now why don't you guys hush up for a minute while my friend Cluck fills you in on a few things."

Cluck gave me a quick confused look, probably 'cause I called him 'my friend', but then he got back into character real quick as his eyes rolled back and forth from one twin to the other.

151

"This really needn't take long at all, you know. There are just a few slightly irritating developments that seem to have presented themselves since last we met, and since these particular developments do appear to not only involve you but our planned excursion to Earth then we felt it might be wise to address these issues up close and personal. So to speak."

They say that twins can sometimes communicate with each other without even saying a word, and I got the distinct feeling I was witnessing one of those communications at that very moment, watching the two of them watching Cluck, their eyes real hard and cold, but neither one uttering so much as a word. I could tell there was something they were sharing, something they knew that they didn't want us to know, but they weren't quite ready to share just yet.

"The problem we have," said Cluck, who I could tell was having a bit too much fun with this as he clasped his hands behind his back and started to pace slowly back and forth in front of his captive audience, "is that it appears our departure date has somehow been leaked to certain outside parties that we had not cleared for inclusion. One might wonder how such a thing could have happened. And why."

The Twins made some uncomfortable, reflexive movements to cover themselves up again, but they kept looking straight ahead.

"Suffice it to say that we are fairly certain of the *how,* and the *who too,* for that matter. But what is causing me a rather uncomfortable amount of consternation is the element of *why,* don't you see. Because I just cannot fathom the reason anyone might have to pass along such information to the authorities, particularly if that someone – or perhaps let's say those identical *someones* – had no idea why this trip was being made or why it might be important. In other words, what would be the benefit? And what might be the incentive, do you think?"

Right then, Vee, who had stepped a few paces back to give Cluck room to move and maneuver, stepped forward again to within thigh-stroking distance of the Twins. Both of them leaned backward away from her as far as they could without falling off of their stools.

"Towel, boys?" she said, leaning forward just enough to expose some appetizing cleavage.

Twin # 1 started to answer, but then #2 elbowed him hard in the ribs. Twin #1 gave his brother an embarrassed look, then cleared his throat as he looked away from Vee's treats.

"You *suuuuurrre?*" she said, leaning forward just a bit more, "because it does appear to me that although you fellas may be Twins, one of you two has a bit more rise in his little occasion, if you know what I mean…?"

I think it was the 'little' part of the occasion that really set #1 off, hollering about how could she call his occasion little, and didn't she just refer to them as a pair of thick twins, and on and on as Vee just stood there with a mild grin on her face, and I knew she had to be wondering why this was so much easier than she'd thought it would be. Then she winked, spun around on her heel, and gave them both a lesson in the rhythm of departure I'm sure they will never forget. And judging by the appreciative grunts coming from Beardy, I suspect he carried those images with him in a safe and happy place for quite a while too. As for Cluck, I gotta give it to him, he stayed focused on the business at hand.

"You can bring those towels back with you, Vee my dearest. I do believe our two friends are in a bit more of a cooperative mood. Am I correct in that assumption?"

Twin # 2 gave his brother a look that could have melted diamonds, then called him a few choice names that I had to file away for future use. But after that the two of them nodded.

"Fine," they said.

Cluck's smile lit up like it had been plugged in.

"Fine it is then!" he announced.

"But the chickens have to leave," said #2. "We're not spilling our guts in front of those freak birds of yours. Despite appearances, we're still pretty civilized."

If it hadn't been for Beardy's quick reflexes, Butch would have stomped both Twins into the ground right then and there without even ruffling a tail feather. All those birds stayed pretty revved up, which was why they'd wound up outcasts in the first place. But Butch was the worst of them by far. That chicken was close to dangerous.

"You sissy boys want civilized? Huh? 'Cause I'll give you civilized right here and now, you got me? Do you? I'll…"

Beardy shook Butch. *Hard.* Then he smacked the back of his head.

"Timing, dude," he said, sounding more calm than I'd ever heard Beardy sound. "Timing is everything. We need these clowns right now. So bottle it up and save it for when we can put that temper to some serious use, right? So easy. *Eeeeeeasy."*

Gradually, Butch's chest heaves subsided from huffing and puffing back to normal breathing level. A few minutes later and all the chickens had been cleared out, mumbling protests under their breath the whole way. Once we heard the door close, the four of us remaining – me, Vee, Cluck and Beardy – pulled up four chairs right in front of our hosts. By now they had their towels and, though I wouldn't exactly call them relaxed, they did appear a bit more loose, which worked in our favor. That combined with the fact that these guys really weren't that bright.

"*Sooooooo…*" said Cluck, raising an eyebrow.

"First of all, we're not confessing to *anything*. We're not crazy. But there are some things we could probably help you with," said #2, followed by a sharp nod from #1. I was getting the distinct impression that #1 was the flunky in this equation.

"Right," he barked.

"Oh absolutely right, I'm inclined to agree," said Cluck. "For example, I believe you can help us right away with moving up our planned departure date. Once we have that squared away then we can proceed to the other items."

"Move it up to when?" asked #2.

"It will have to be tomorrow morning, I'm afraid. First shuttle."

"Excuse me *what?*"

"I'm sorry, I didn't realize we were sitting quite so far apart. I said that me and my colleagues must be on the first shuttle departing for Earth in the morning."

"Oh wait a damned…"

"I am quite sorry again but no, I'm afraid we cannot wait. If someone or someones had not felt compelled to leak our planned departure date to various and sundry outside parties that had no need to know, then suffice it to say we would not be having this discussion. But seeing as how this is indeed exactly what did transpire, then we unfortunately were left with no other workable options except to depart as soon as

155

possible. We all stayed up practically all night packing our belongings in a rush and it really was quite a trying ordeal. But we are survivors and adaptors. I must say this is what we do quite well. So. Are we understood?"

"Look, I know we're the go-to guys for last-minute transportation around here, especially when it has to be kept off the books, but there's only so many miracles in a day, all right? I mean…"

Cluck looked at his watch, grinned like a maniac, then shoved his scrawny branch of a wrist in front of #2's face.

"Do you see the time? It does appear to me that we are only minutes away from entering into a brand new day. *Time for another miracle!*"

So this level of back-and-forth went back and forth for a few more minutes, I think mainly because Cluck loved listening to himself talk these guys into a really painful corner. Even I had to admit it was quite a work of art, and I'm not exactly what you'd call a connoisseur. But when it was all said and done, the Twins had managed to see the light and Cluck had extracted the promise that whatever else might not be on that shuttle in the morning, all of us most certainly would be. Then we moved on to the part I really wanted to hear about, namely how the Gerruh had found out about our plans to get off the planet.

"To be honest? I don't have the slightest idea how they found out, and I'm serious about that. We never talked to the Gerruh because we like to live. And anybody who talks to the Gerruh directly, except for a few Way Higher Ups, usually doesn't have a lot of time left on his dance card, if you know what I mean."

"I do indeed," said Cluck. "So then the question becomes, exactly who was it that you *did* tell? And, of course, why? Since, well, we specifically told you not to tell anyone and all of that."

Twin #2 put his fist to his mouth and cleared his throat, making a sound like a small rodent could have been caught in there, then looked away. He slumped a bit, and was back to having a hard time getting comfortable.

"Yeah…about that…"

"Yes. *About that.*"

"Right. Well…we got this call not too long after you guys left. Call was from the Travel Bureau. They always call once a week to check on our log of who's going where and when. Mostly they don't care, except when it comes to Earth travel, which makes sense because of all the illegal trafficking and all that. Seems like no matter how hard the officials clamp down, they can't clamp down hard enough, you know? Because…"

"Yes. Moving right along, then?"

"Oh. Right. So, well, the call comes in, and I take it. They ask me this and then they ask me that, like they normally do, so I'm not focusing in real hard because everything seems routine at first. My mind is kinda roaming in other places. But then whoever it was on the other end of the line asks me if we'd had any unusual visitors recently. So right then my mind stops roaming to those other places I was telling you about. Because this here, this was not a routine question. I ask the guy – it was a guy – unusual like what? Specifics is what I need."

"Certainly so."

"Absolutely. So he doesn't say anything for awhile, and I'm starting to think maybe he'd hung up and I just didn't hear the click, but then he repeats it again, like he thinks I'm dense or something. 'Unusual, meaning the opposite of usual. That's what I mean by unusual,' is what the guy says. Which is why I called him an asshole. Which I'm

pretty sure is why he started threatening to pull our license if I didn't give him what he

needed to know. So then I back up a bit because without the license we're through, and I

tell him I'm not trying to be that difficult I just need something to go on. Something more

than 'unusual', which could fit just about half the folks on this rock, you know?"

Cluck chuckled.

"Quite true. Go on."

"Sure. So then he asks me if I know who killed Johnny Beardy, and I tell him last

I heard was somebody found his body face-down dead in a mayonnaise sandwich, but

then his body disappeared or something. Whatever was in the Screamer. Said I didn't

know any more about it than anyone else. I promise you guys I did not let on that I knew

anything different. But then this guy's voice comes back at me, and for some strange

reason I'm starting to get the feeling he sees me at the same time he's talking to me. Just

a chill I got, and my twin can tell you when I get a chill it's something to take notice of.

And right after I got that chill? That's when he asks me if I have any idea why a dead

rock star would want to book a trip to Earth."

"Whoa. *Dude!* Hold the fuck up. *What?"*

Johnny had gone from leaning way back in his chair, looking around the room

like he didn't much give a damn what the guy was saying, to leaning forward all the way

up in front of #2's face. Cluck grabbed Beardy and pulled him back.

"Kindly let the man finish. He has information we may need prior to our

departure."

"But did you hear what he…?"

"I'm sitting right here, so yes. But you're obviously not dead, so I hardly think it matters right now. There are more urgent…"

"More urgent my ass, man! Because *nobody* except you guys are even supposed to know I'm still around, and if *that* cover's blown, then…"

"*Shhh!*" Cluck says to Beardy, looking seriously pissed, then he looks back at #2 and says, "So what you're telling me is somebody, quite likely a somebody at the highest of levels, has somehow managed to come into possession of rather sensitive information regarding our little exploit and you are unshakably certain that you are *not* in possession of any knowledge related to how this particular somebody may have stumbled upon this information. Correct?"

Twin #2 had a look forming on his face like a kid gets when he's tryin to solve this really tough math problem in front of the whole class.

"Uh…yeah. Something along those lines, yeah. What you said. So anyway, that exchange right there kinda let me know that maybe this whole thing might be above my pay grade, you know?"

"Meaning…?"

"Meaning it could maybe get me and my brother in the kinda trouble that we might not be able to get out of."

"Ah. I see. So you were scared, then?"

Twin #2 started nodding like one of those bobble-head dolls.

"Oh yeah. *Oh yeah.* And I don't mind saying it either. Normally we're not the kind to scare easy, but sometimes you damned sure *better* be scared, and you need to recognize those times when they show up. This was one of those times, believe me, and

159

that's why - just being honest here – that's why I decided to put me and my brother's general health and well being above your travel plans, OK? Whoever that was on the other end of that line knew how to make it plain without saying it straight out that not answering those questions would be the last mistake I'd ever get a chance to make, and that's all the encouragement I needed. So if you guys want your money back then..."

"Oh my dear no! Why ever would we want our money back when you're going to have us on the first transport leaving tomorrow morning as we just discussed? No, I am one who believes that a deal is a deal, and our deal has been sealed. I simply would like to know if you recall whether there was an indication this terrifying voice you encountered happened to betray any particular knowledge about the *nature* of our trip? After all, if they know how to bring the dead back to life then it would not particularly surprise me if they knew a few other things as well."

"Knew how to bring the dead back to...? Oh. Oh! Right. Good one. And no, I'm pretty sure not. For what it's worth, I didn't give any long answers, meaning I didn't spill any more than I had to."

"Quite right. So then when he asked you why you thought a dead rock star might want to book a trip to Earth, you said...?"

"I said damned if I know is what I said, and that's the truth. Told him I didn't ask my clients questions about why they were going where they were going I just collected the money plain and simple. Just business."

"Thought you said you didn't give any long answers."

"You think that's long?"

Cluck shrugged.

"Some might say. But then who's to say, hmm?"

Twin #2 shrugged in response with this pathetic-lookin grin.

"Right? Who's to say."

Cluck asked him a few more questions but from that point forward the interrogation routine was pretty much through. We got all we were gonna get outta the guy, and we'd gotten a lot of what we needed, so wasn't any need to push much harder on this thing. A few hours later we were all asleep on the floor.

Next morning somebody's shakin my shoulder hard, sayin my name over and over again right in my ear. It was Beardy, which I thought was strange. Plus his wasn't the kinda voice anyone like me would ever want to wake up to.

The first few sounds I made didn't resemble any known language, but eventually I stumbled my way into coherent.

"Whathefuhhhh…??"

"Dude, I think you're gonna wanna see this. If you ain't woke yet, seriously, this right here is gonna make you sit up straight like somebody shoved a pole up…"

"WHOA."

"Look at this man, *look at this.* See what it says? Man, this is not good, all right?"

When my eyes finally focused I saw the thick letters of a Screamer headline shoved right up to the tip of my nose, which was kind of annoying.

"Beardy?"

"Yeah, dude. What?"

"You want me to read this headline, right?"

"Too close?"

I just let the glare tell him the rest. He pulled the paper back a few inches, and then I saw what…damn. This really *wasn't* good.

"Where'd you get this?"

"Is that really the first question you wanna be askin' me, man? Do you see what it says?"

"Oh, you mean about me and Vee being wanted fugitives and there being some kind of reward for any information leading to our apprehension? Or was there another headline up there you were referring to?"

"Right. So then you see why the part about where you askin me about *where I got this* might not be…:

"*Where the hell did you get this?*"

"Wow. You're persistent, I'll give you that. Probably comes in handy for a detective, right?"

"Pretty much."

"Right. So like I pretty much got this from the Twins over there. Twin #2 if you wanna get specific. Guess they subscribe or something, which is kinda wild 'cause I really didn't peg them for the reading type, you know?"

Both Twins, who were sitting at the table nearby eating whatever they ate for breakfast, turned around and gave Beardy an evil eye that would have scared…well…no one.

"Oh, and you're Shakespeare?" said Twin #1.

"Good one," said #2.

"You know Shakespeare?" I asked.

Now the evil eye was on me, which was like being tickled by a pesty little kid.

"Perhaps the more pertinent line of inquiry here might be what this rather distressing development portends for the rest of us," asked Cluck, without even letting his eyes wander from the bowl of cereal in front of him. Frankly I was surprised he trusted the food.

"What it portends? Seriously? Well if you're really worried about what it all *portends* then I suggest you *pretend* like you really care what this *portends* for all of us instead of just you and yours."

Cluck turned down the sides of his mouth like he was mimicking a sad clown.

"Oh that does *hurt* me so. I *do* care, I *do!* Now please answer the question."

"Simple. It doesn't *portend* anything for you that it doesn't *portend* for me and Vee."

"Cute. Which is?"

"Nothing good, since we're all together in this thing, all for one and one for all. I'm pretty sure about that one. But since we're leaving outta here in the next few hours then I don't suppose that matters much because whatever they got planned we won't be here to receive it."

Cluck's mock frown turned itself upside down, but his eyes were cold. His next question was directed at the Twins, but he kept glaring at me and Vee.

"I'm sure our agreed-upon arrangements are still firmly in place, correct, my friends?"

"Oh yeah!" said Twin #1.

"For sure!" said Twin #2.

"Well then. I guess we'd better prepare to be on our way, hadn't we?"

The earth transport, which was docked all alone at a gate far away from the rest of the fairly crowded hub for intraplanetary transport ships, was one of those super-sized double-decker outfits with several large compartments on the bottom level usually set aside for staff and storage. We were herded into one of those compartments through a separate entrance after everyone else had been boarded. The early morning light outside was fairly dim, which meant anyone glancing in our direction from the passenger windows as we hustled our way onboard might be curious about what they were seeing, but they wouldn't be able to say for sure what they were seeing, so we were pretty much covered.

Once inside the compartment, which I could tell was normally used for food storage, I noticed there were only two small windows to see out of, each of them fitted with a sliding cover, both of them closed. I managed to nab a seat next to one of them. As the engines revved up, I decided to unfasten the little latch and take a look since it might be my last view of home for quite some time.

What I saw nearly made my insides turn to jelly. For the life of me I couldn't figure out how in the world they had found us. And if they could find us here, would we *ever* be able to get away? I decided to try the fake bravado approach and wave goodbye with a smile and a tip of my hat.

The Gerruh, who were staring directly at my window, winked and waved right back. They didn't bother smiling. They didn't have to. And they never wore hats.

Chapter 11

It had been a long time since my last trip to Earth, or the Mother Rock, as some of us liked to call it. Never would have been a Planet 10 if there hadn't been some Earthlings to build it. Or colonize it. Whatever it was they did. Anyway it kinda brought me up short when I realized my last visit had been more than 20 years ago. I was just a little critter stompin my dad's last nerve asking him what was this and what was that on our way to whatever business it was he had come there to do. Didn't take me long to figure out that everything I saw was either a 'shuttup' or a 'hushdammit'. One time I asked him was he sure the tall sculpture I had just asked about was a 'shuttup' because it looked an awful lot like a 'hushdammit'. I never saw that backhand coming, and I never questioned his labeling preferences again.

Anyway that's what was goin thru my head as I looked out the window on our way to making a landing. I probably should have been focusing on what it was we were supposed to be doing here and how me and Vee were gonna navigate this whole tricky deal, but sometimes it helps to back away from the abyss and put your mind on better days. At least that seems to work for me most times.

But once my teeth registered that bone rattling impact of the ship actually landing on hard ground, it was pretty much all I needed to shock me back into the here and now. I looked over at Vee to gauge how she might have been feeling, and she gripped my hand real tight. Tried to smile, but wasn't havin a whole lot of success. I could relate.

"So what's the plan now that we're here?" I asked Cluck, who was seated on the other side of the compartment whistling something out of tune and enjoyin the hell out of it. Beardy was squinting his eyes and biting his bottom lip, which meant he wasn't exactly getting the same joy out of the occasion.

"Quite simple really," he said after he finished the last tortured verse of thank-God-it's-over. "We catch a ride to Justice and then we commence production."

"Justice? Where's Justice? And where are we right now?"

"Right now we are in the city of Denver, in the state of Colorado. Exquisitely beautiful and scenic location if scenery is the sort of thing that appeals to you, but far too large and populous a location for us to begin our operation. Also, since we might as well accept the fact that we are, in a sense, entering the drug trade and do plan to take it over with a far superior product, we must be mindful of the threat posed by too much competition too early. Never bite off more than you can chew as they say, so we shall begin chewing on a little Justice and then, when we are ready, step up to the much larger and more appetizing plate of Denver. From there? As far and wide as the wondrous and joyful addiction of MayoMadd can take us, my good friend."

"Wow. Sounds great," said Vee, her voice flat as a board. "My first trip to Earth, and this is what I have to look forward to."

Cluck smiled, but not really.

"My lady Vee, I do seem to recall your presence was neither required nor requested for this particular journey. As a matter of fact, I seem to remember not that long ago when you showed up at our abode in the company of your friend here practically begging…"

"I was *not begging,* hey?"

"Begging your pardon, madam, but you most certainly were. Why? Because that's the way I remember it, and my memory is the only one that matters now. My house my rules, are we clear?"

This time it was my turn to squeeze Vee's hand because I knew the woman's temper. Never did know the meaning of caution. If Vee had something to say, she usually said it; didn't matter what it was needed saying or who it was needed saying to. Which was an admirable trait for the most part except that in this particular case it could get us admirably dead, or at least admirably in a whole lotta pain. I wasn't in the mood for either one. Plus, until we figured something out, this really was Cluck's house and Cluck's rules.

All of a sudden Vee turned on the charm, like going from night to day in a finger snap.

"Of *course* we're clear, sweetheart. Of *course* we are. Why wouldn't we be? And by the way this really is a *maaaaarvelous* house you have here, even if those pesky rules are a bit stuffy. But we girls do know how to adapt, hey? We've grown quite professional at it. *All because of wonderful male creatures like you!"*

Cluck wasn't stupid, he knew the game she was playing, but being a master game player himself I think he kinda got off on it. Might even have turned the ugly little nerd on.

"Well now. Then from one professional to another, let me extend my sincerest appreciation for your efforts, dear heart. And with that behind us, let me say before we disembark that we should probably tend to a rather obvious bit of pressing business, namely what to do about helping our chicken friends blend in with that wonderful scenic extravaganza that is Denver."

The chickens started mumbling amongst themselves, but as usual they let Butch be their spokeschicken.

"Uhh, what the hell you talkin' about boss?"

"Oh come now, Butch. It's because of what these heathens did to you and your brethren all those years ago, and *why* they did it, that explains the sum total of why we undertook this mission in the first place, correct? These Earth snobs mistreated you, spat on you, jeered at you, and why? Because they couldn't control you. And why couldn't they control you? Because they created you to serve them, but instead you stood up to them. You were made half chicken, half man, but contrary to their twisted design you turned out more man than chicken *and they hate you for it.* Make no mistake, my friends, this is naked, cold-blooded revenge and nothing more. Except that it will be *fun.*"

"Wow. OK. Revenge. Absolutely. But uhh…what the hell you talkin' about blendin' in?"

Cluck rolled his eyes in frustration, probably because he was expecting applause after that little speech.

"Good Lord, Butch, for how long will you persist in being this dense? Plain and simple, since that seems to be what works best for you, we can't have you and the others mingling amongst the Earthlings looking, well, looking like *yourselves,* if you understand my meaning. Our immediate goal is not to draw much attention as we set our plan in motion, and the presence of huge man-looking chickens strolling about doesn't accomplish much toward that end. *Now* are you somewhat more clear on the task at hand?"

I could see Butch was pissed at the condescending tone, but he held it in. If that remark had come from anybody else I'm pretty sure they would have been spending the next few months in traction, but Cluck was commander so he got a pass – for now. Still, it was the first time I had seen Cluck snap ugly like that to any one of his feathery cohorts, and that got me to wondering if something else we didn't know about might be pushing pressure on those stressed-out little brain cells of his.

"Yeah, OK, I'm more clear," said Butch, his voice tight and hard, matching the expression on his face. "And I got a suggestion."

Cluck raised one eyebrow in response.

"Out with it then. We don't have much more time."

"Right. So I'm thinking maybe the best way we blend in, at least for tonight, is Halloween."

"I'm sorry, *what?*"

"Look outside, boss. I mean, it's dark out there, right? And I looked at the calendar and there's no doubt about it; tonight is that day they call Halloween down here, and the kids love it, remember? Even some of the adults get into it in a kinky kinda way. Everybody running around in costumes all happy to be anybody but themselves. They love that kinda stuff down here. I figure that gives us the perfect cover for now until we figure something out for later."

Cluck's expression changed as he realized Butch was onto something.

"I confess I truly hate to admit it, but you just may have come up with the solution. As a matter of fact, I believe it just may work marvelously. As for the days to come, there is a considerably less fun approach we may have to consider, at least for awhile."

"What's that?"

"Please keep in mind that you're really going to hate this, but I don't believe there is any other way."

"What way?"

"The Bureau. You check in. Just like all the other critters."

Butch glared at Cluck like he was ready to strangle him. Cluck even took a step back, and that wasn't something I'd seen before. Then he looked around at the other chickens, who, as if on cue, were giving Cluck the exact same look. The silence in the room felt thick and heavy.

"No Bureau, Cluck? You understand? No Bureau. *Ever.*"

Cluck cleared his throat.

"Certainly I understand your reservations, Butch. Contrary to what you may believe, I have not totally forgotten from whence we all came. I was there remember? It was the accumulated pain of it all that is what gave birth to our little family, wouldn't you say? Still, I simply do not believe at this point, for the sake of the mission and its importance, that we can afford the luxury of taking anything off the…"

"No Bureau," all the chickens chanted in unison, their expressions even more murderous.

Cluck looked around the room and did some quick calculations, most having to do with the art of self-preservation. After a moment he smiled, then shrugged his shoulders.

"But then there is always more than one way, correct? Absolutely. And we will find it, I assure you. Now, with that settled I believe it is time for us to depart."

****

The so-called disguise wound up being pretty basic for the sake of time, but it worked. Beardy was dispatched to a nearby clothing store that was just about to close and he bought a bunch of identical dark sunglasses, trench coats, black pants and black hats. The chickens were all pretty much the same size – extra large in the chest - so the shopping came easy. As for the huge webbed feet, we all agreed no one would pay much attention to that on Halloween night, but after that we'd have to work something else up. Cross that bridge when we came to it.

Later that night after we'd left the ship we were wandering around downtown in the 16th Street Mall to kill time until our ride arrived to take us to the bus station where we were scheduled to catch the early morning bus to Justice. The ride, somebody named Fred who was gonna be driving an old yellow school bus, was supposed to meet us near the train station around nine, which gave us all about 90 minutes to waste however we saw fit.

Since Justice wasn't exactly a tourist destination there were only three scheduled departures per week that made the nearly 4-hour trip into the mountains, and from what we were told they were hardly ever even close to full. Taking a plane to Aspen, which was nearby, was an option but then not really. The risk of attracting way too much attention was obvious, especially when the destination was the home of all the Beautiful People and the Rich and Famous for No Particular Reason. Riding the bus we'd just be coasting along with some other misfit freaks who didn't wanna be bothered. Just like us.

So there we all were, a bunch of huge chickens in trench coats, a poorly dressed geek, two edgy critters and an ex-rock star all huddled up together in the center of the mall looking around at everything like it was our first time ever on Planet Earth. Why we didn't think to maybe split up and wander around aimlessly in smaller groups eludes me, but when the pale kid with waist-length dread locks riding a skateboard screeched to a halt next to Butch, it was obviously too late to come up with a sensible plan. Within a minute or two there were another five raggedy little board-ridin munchkins all swerving back and forth in front of us, their juvenile grins making a mockery of who they thought they were screwing with. Because if they had actually known they would have ridden those little steel wheels just as fast and far away from us as they could have possibly gotten, not giving a damn who they had to run over in the process.

But they had no idea, we couldn't let on, and so there we were; held hostage in the middle of the 16th Street Mall in Denver on Halloween night by a group of mangy skateboarders, in full view of at least a hundred fully amused witnesses who seemed to think maybe this was all a scripted part of the evening's entertainment.

"Hey man," said dreadlocks, "those have got to be about the stupidest costumes I've ever seen."

"Totally unoriginal, dude," said another, whizzing by.

"Your mother too cheap to get you guys some real Halloween costumes? 'Cause…"

Butch started to make a lunge, but Beardy grabbed him by the arm.

"Not the time, man, not the time. Just remember, we got somethin' for 'em."

Butch actually grinned, then relaxed.

"*Yeah,*" he said, sounding as if he'd just inhaled a healthy hit of good dope.

Dreadlocks must have overheard what Beardy said 'cause he got an odd expression on his face, like he was nervous but didn't want it to let on. He stopped swirling around on the concrete and pulled up in front of the ex-rocker.

"Yo, whadda you mean by that, man?" he asked.

Beardy put on a grin that he must have perfected from all those years as a bonafide star dealing with pimple-faced kids trying to score autographs.

"What do I mean by *what.* Dude?"

"What you just said! You said you had somethin' for us. What?"

Beardy kept his grin plastered on his face like it was coin-operated and still had minutes left over. He glanced over at Butch and asked him if he had any idea what the kid was talking about. Butch, catching on, shook his head real slow, his eyes staying focused on the kid.

"Not a clue, pal. Not a clue. Must be hearin things or something, ya think?"

Beardy nodded.

"Could be, yeah. But that would be sad. Young kid like this, and already hearin things, you know? Wow. Yeah, that would be truly sad."

Dreadlocks started to say something else, but then it was like all of a sudden the image of nearly a dozen stocky chickens with sunglasses staring him down, fronted by a long-haired smiling maniac just might suggest something could be wrong with this picture – even on Halloween night. Slowly the same message started to seep through the rest of the skateboard posse like a slow-acting virus.

"Hey, you know Halloween is a holiday, man, not a way of life, dude."

I had to admit that was a good one, and I'm sure for a second there I probably looked a whole lot less threatening than I meant to, although I was looking threatening to keep the kids at a distance for the sake of their own lives and enjoyment thereof. Same with Vee. The rest of the crew looked that way because they wanted to commit an act of mass slaughter right there in the street. Except for Cluck, who was starting to giggle. Apparently I wasn't the only one who appreciated some good wit now and then.

"Well played, young man! Oh yes, well played indeed. I suspect unfortunately that the appearance of intelligent commentary is not a frequent occurrence in your dialogue, particularly that shared with the rather dim bulbs you have chosen to surround yourself with, but if there is even a sliver of a chance that this admirable witticism is evidence of functioning gray matter between those jug ears of yours, I strongly encourage you to follow the light, my child. *Follow the light.*"

One of dreadlocks' riding buddies who was about the size of a teenage buffalo with a face to match and eyes noticeably devoid of even a spark of intelligence capable of creating wit, frowned noticeably as he screeched to a halt beside his pal.

"Yo, what's he talkin about, man? What's he sayin'?"

At this, Cluck broke out laughing at a volume that attracted more attention than I think was intended. But stupidity on display to Cluck was something like a football you see abandoned in the park; you kinda have to kick it around for a moment or two.

"Pre*cisely!* My point exactly!" he yelped, his hands clapping together like a circus seal.

"Huh?" said Dumbo, to the obvious embarrassment of Dreadlocks, who tried too late to put a mask on the expression that gave him away.

"Oh this is *priceless,* wouldn't you say? My new young friend?"

Dreadlocks got heated.

"I am *not* your damned friend, man, all right? You and your whole packa morons are way too fuckin weird, and I'm outta here. C'mon guys."

"Going in search of easier prey, eh? Well. I don't blame you. After all, you do have your dim-witted buddies to consider, correct? Not much fun when you're the only one who gets the joke, is it?"

The look on Dumbo's face was almost painful to look at. He knew what was being said wasn't complimentary, but you could see he didn't know why. As for Dreadlocks, the look on his face was cold and hateful enough to start a new ice age. Without saying another word, he shoved off on his board down the mall, followed quickly by his raggedy, clueless gang. Dumbo was the last to follow, his slow-witted eyes focused on Cluck, not quite sure of what was happening.

"C.J.! *Come on,* man! Leave those jerk mother fuckers alone, dude!"

C.J. nodded, backing away slowly at first, before he turned and sped off after the pack.

Cluck watched them go, and I noticed he almost looked sad, like a game he was playing had just been switched off.

"And that, my friends, is why we must bring MayoMadd to these poor, lost, masses, wouldn't you agree?"

"Oh hell yeah, dude," said Beardy. "Can't wait to get those little maggots strung out and droolin.'"

The chicken posse loudly grumbled their agreement with their deranged leader.

Vee and I exchanged glances, Cluck's statement coming like a kick-in-the-gut reminder of why we had attached ourselves to this little expedition. As critters who had experienced more frequent contact with Earth folks than either one of us would have preferred, neither one of us was what you would call fond of their kind. True, they had pretty much created Planet 10's civilization and the whole surrounding system, and Planet 10 was the only home Vee and I had ever known. But I also knew the reasons why they had created it in the first place, namely to keep the distance between our kind and theirs. We have stuff they need just like they have stuff we need, which set up the whole basis for trade. But business is one thing and socializing is something else altogether.

Saying all that to say critters like me and Vee have been used to the smart-assed quips and finger-pointing ever since we became aware of their existence. Folks think they're better than critters and that's just the way it is. But that doesn't mean I want to see all the little folks wind up dead – or hooked on some drug where they might as well be. I never hated them like that, and neither did Vee; we just always did our best to restrict our contact with them to the bare minimum. But Cluck and his crew had a whole other feeling about the matter. They'd been carrying around that hatred of theirs for so long it had almost become like a living, breathing thing to them that had to be fed. They really were a sick bunch.

****

About 15 minutes before it was time for us to rendezvous with this Fred guy, we all started to make our way toward the Union Train station where we were supposed to make the meet. When we got close I looked around trying to see if I could scope the yellow bus, but he apparently hadn't gotten there yet. For some reason Vee and I were holding hands the whole walk down, not so much a lover's thing as it was a support group of two in the midst of the madness. The only way either one of us was gonna make it through with this crowd of wackbrains was to stick together and keep an eye out for sanity.

The bus showed up about a half hour late, but still in enough time to get us to the station. Fred was pretty much like I imagined him to be; a runt of a guy who looked to be in his 50s with just enough scraps of gray hair on his small balloon head to be able to say he still had some. Thick, rectangular black plastic-rimmed glasses of the sort that you buy one get one free from just about any optical shop that assumes most self-respecting individuals wouldn't want to be caught dead in a set of specs like that. But what any optical shop didn't know about folks like Fred was that the term 'self-respecting' held little or no meaning. Fred was one of those mole humans who only came up from underground when required, then burrowed his way back into the darkness once his topside business was through. He didn't utter not one word the whole way to the bus station, and once we were there he just yanked the bar that opened the door and waited for all of us to depart before pulling away. Never looked at any of us when we got on the bus, never looked at us when we stepped off.

"Dude's a little weird, wouldn't you say?" said Beardy, as we stood there in front of the bus terminal watching Fred speed away. He honestly seemed upset by this.

"Dude, define weird," I replied, then went inside the terminal to wait for our way out of town.

"Yeah, I guess you do have a point there," he said. "Yeah, I guess you do."

We had another hour or so to kill before the coach pulled in to take us to Justice. Not surprisingly, it wasn't quite nice and shiny like the ones headed to more desirable locations. In fact, we probably would have been just as comfortable making the trek through the mountains with mole man Fred, but by this time I didn't figure I was in much of a position to be making too many quibbles. Vee and I both had to keep our concentration focused on the stuff that really mattered. Like locating the proper-sized big-assed monkey wrench to throw into this operation to screw it up good and permanent, and then figuring out a way to get back home – after figuring out a way to convince the home critters that we should no longer be declared wanted criminals.

The bus driver for Justice could have been Fred's twin brother, separated at birth. One of those guys who looked like he'd never seen a sunny day in his life, never heard a kid laugh, never heard a woman moan in just that right way. Just counting the days until he received his expiration notice from the Grim Reaper so he could move on to whatever other hell he figured was waiting for him in the next life. Maybe being a wanted criminal on Planet 10 wasn't so bad after all.

Once we all got settled on the bus – there were only about five other folks headed to Justice, and they all looked like they'd just woken up from the same bad dream – Vee nestled her head on my shoulder and was sound asleep snoring within minutes. The fact that she was my friend and was probably one of the sexiest critters I had ever laid eyes on was pretty much the only reason I put up with her snoring. I also knew she was gonna call me a liar when I told her about that damned snoring soon as she woke up, just like she always did, but that was OK too. Vee was Vee, and when you're that fine you do get special privileges in life. At least you do from critters like me.

By the time she woke up we were only a couple hours outside Justice, which was a pretty admirable feat considering the extreme discomfort level provided by the transportation. She sat up, eyes at half mast, then stretched like a cat with long arms before asking me where we were as she sleepily observed the scenery sliding by outside the window.

"Earth, darlin'," I said. "We're on Earth."

That response from me got the desired response from her, namely a quick glare designed to cut me down like a scythe. Now I knew she was fully awake.

"Vid makes a funny, hey? How cute. Now would you mind please…"

"We're about two hours outside of Justice, or something like that. A lot closer than when you first started snoring, that's for damned sure. Glad you liked the funny by the way. I worked really hard on that one."

She wanted to kill me right then, I know she did. Kinda got me hot, to tell you the truth. But then just thinking about the raspy sound of her voice got me hot, or thinking about her in those tiny little skirts she always liked to wear, or thinking about …well…just thinking about her.

"I don't snore," she said.

"No, you're right, you don't. Because what you do makes snoring sound like a baby's slumber. Vee, I'm tellin you trucks make less noise goin thru tunnels. Sad, but true, sweetheart. Got nothing to do with how I feel about you, but you know we've always said that honesty…"

"Oh you want honesty, dearest? Is that what you want, because…"

"Children, please. Enough with the infantile sexual foreplay. The adults on the bus are trying to enjoy a little relaxation before we arrive at our location," said Cluck, who was seated across the aisle from us. Just hearing that voice was enough to remind us both, in case we'd forgotten just that quick, that we weren't among friends. Which meant we couldn't afford to be goofing around as if we were.

"You're the boss, Cluck. We live to obey."

Vee smirked, then sat herself up straight and shifted her gaze back out the window. I don't think she took her eyes off the road again until we made it to Justice.

****

Justice, Colorado was an ugly little town. Period. Really wasn't much more to say about it than that. Used to be a mining town back once upon a time, but once the mining dried up then Justice dried up right along with it. Just coming into town I could see that half the houses were boarded up, and the rest probably should have been. It was after 3 o'clock in the morning, and not many small towns look their best at that time of the day, but there wasn't much of an excuse for this. Judging by the near suffocating darkness, I don't know if there were more than a handful of working street lights in the whole place. Even the so-called bus station where we dragged ourselves out of the so-called bus wasn't much more than a run-down shanty with a few broken benches tossed out front, lit up by a sick-looking light post that kept sputtering and stuttering like those light bulbs you always see in cheap horror movies. The 'station' itself was pitch black inside and closed, and pretty soon it was just us rejects standing there in what I guess was supposed to be downtown Justice, looking just as stupid and out of place as we did in Denver. I don't know what happened to the few other passengers that were on the bus; it was like they just faded away.

"Like I said earlier, Cluck, you're the boss of this here outfit, pal. So maybe you have an idea of what we do next in this dump?"

"What's next is that phone booth over there," he said, pointing to one not more than 30 feet away, planted in the ground all alone and far away from the station like whoever put it there was making a statement of some sort. Not sure what statement exactly, but something that was probably important in the larger scheme of things in Justice.

"You folks stay here while I go make my call," he said.

"Dude, you think we're gonna run off somewhere?" said Beardy.

Cluck made a frowny face, then tilted his head to the side like a sad clown which, come to think of it, was kinda how I pictured Cluck most times.

"Beardy scared? HMMMMMM?"

"No, but you best believe Beardy gonna…"

"Going to *what,* exactly?" said Cluck.

Beardy looked away and shrugged, mashing his lips together tight.

"Nothin' man. Just go ahead and make your damned call so we can get outta here, all right?"

Cluck let the silence hang for awhile, which made everyone a little edgy because we didn't know what might be coming next. Then he flipped the switch and on came the megawatt smile, crooked teeth and all.

"Certainly! I'm sure we're all tired and need a little rest."

After some affirmative grumbling in the ranks, Cluck ambled over to the phone and made his call. I'm sure it would have been easier with a cell phone, but none of us lived here and there weren't any cell phones on Planet 10. Even if there were I doubt they'd do us much good all the way down here.

A few minutes later Cluck comes back to tell us that he's made contact – some guy named Haley – and that he has directions to Haley's place.

"So nobody's comin' to pick us up?" asked Beardy, startin to get pissed all over again, apparently not caring about the near-miss confrontation he'd almost had a few moments ago. "Man, it's just after 3 in the mornin', Cluck! You see any cabs around this dump? How we supposed to get there?"

Cluck grinned.

"This is a very small town, Mr. Beardy, in case you hadn't noticed. In very small towns nothing is very far away. So dry your tears, dear child. I promise you the walk will not be long. Who knows, our host may even have hot cocoa and cookies waiting for us upon our arrival? Wouldn't that be nice? Wouldn't that improve your mood? *Hot cocoa and cookies for Beardy!*"

The way he said 'hot cocoa and cookies for Beardy!' was kinda like how you might say 'I'm about to shove a handful of razors down your throat and make you swallow!' The look on Beardy's face made it plain he probably wouldn't be voicing much more dissent that evening.

And Cluck was true to his crooked little word about things in small towns being relatively close together. The whole trip on foot didn't take us much longer than about 10 minutes, and we didn't see not one human being or any other moving thing the whole time. Maybe somebody already had their justice in Justice and nobody lived to tell the tale.

Except for Haley. Haley's house was a small, squat piece of a place looked like it was made out of a bunch of big stones held together by cement and mud. One window in the front next to a well-barricaded door, and the drapes were drawn tight. A dim light was showing through, so I was guessing that was Haley waiting up for us. Cluck knocked on the door real light, then stepped back kinda quick like he thought maybe something was about to blow. Then came the sound of chains and locks rattling, and that went on for awhile which made me wonder how many folks this guy was worried about.

When the door opened at first, I thought it must have opened itself because nobody was standing there – until I looked down. Haley was what the more politically incorrect Earth types would call a midget. I single out the humans here because we critters don't have any midgets in the ranks. Every one of us is pretty close to the same height. But this guy was definitely *not* the same height as most other humans. His hair, what he had left of it, was hangin down to his shoulders and grey. He wore thick glasses that made his eyes look like a bug-eyed fish in a bowl. And he didn't look like he'd smiled since birth.

"Haley! My good friend! So glad you're awake at this hour!"

"So why wouldn't I be awake? Didn't you just call me?"

Cluck leaned back and laughed out loud like this was the funniest thing he'd ever heard. Since it wasn't the funniest thing me or Vee had ever heard, we just stared down at the guy, trying to make up our minds about him. He glared back up at us, not giving any indication he planned on letting us in.

"Who are *they*?" he asked, pointing right at me and Vee like he was identifying us out of a lineup.

Cluck didn't miss a beat.

"Who, *them?* Oh they're *fiiiiiine*, Haley, and what's more they'll be useful. Trust me on this. You know I would never do anything to put our little thing at risk. After all this planning that we've done? All this time and effort we've invested? *Haley.* I thought for sure you knew me better than that by now."

"I never fuckin met you 'til tonite, so I don't know what your talkin about I should know you better. And I don't like the way these two are lookin *down* at me. They're really lookin *down* at me and I don't like it!"

It wasn't often you saw Cluck looking nervous, but if it wasn't so dark outside I'd almost swear the man was close to breakin out in a sweat. This obviously wasn't going quite as smoothly as planned.

"Well, perhaps we haven't met in person, you and I, but we have certainly shared an abundance of correspondence leading up to this moment, and …"

"What you just say?"

"I said…nevermind. It's really not important. Certainly not as important as all of our plans, wouldn't you agree? All the money we stand to make as partners in this venture? And on behalf of my good friends Vid and Vee here, I'm sure they will agree when I say they never intended any disrespect whatsoever. None. I can assure you."

"I wanna hear *them* say it."

The strange thing about this, and there were a whole bunch of strange things about this encounter in just the first two minutes, was that here we were accompanied by a posse of giant chickens wearing trench coats and dark glasses, but *we* were the ones that made this runt uncomfortable. Sometimes life really doesn't make any sense at all.

Cluck looked over at me and Vee, his eyes practically beggin us to play our role in this joke.

OK fine. For now.

"Haley, is it?" I asked, not wanting to start this whole thing off wrong by screwing up his name straight out the gate. But the little gnome wasn't no help at all. He just kept staring up at me with those two bugged-out fish eyes of his.

"OK, right. Well then I'm just gonna assume I'm saying this right since it's how I heard Cluck say it. OK? 'Cause I definitely don't wanna say anything else that might piss you off. Vee either, but I guess she can speak for herself in a few. Matter of fact I know she can, but anyway, just sayin. Look, I'm sorry, all right? If I was looking at you with any kind of disrespect or anything like that. Never my intention. Cluck says you're the man down here, and I figure he oughta know, so that's good enough for me. No disrespect, all right? My apologies. Vee...?"

Vee offered Haley the hobbit half a grin, but it was a sexy half grin. Then I heard a purr startin to rev up in the back of her throat, so right then I knew we were gonna be all right. Once Vee got into purr mode, there weren't too many males of any species who stood much of a chance.

Then she leans over, just enough to give the hobbit a glimpse of somethin – a couple somethins actually – that he'd probably never been that close to in his whole sad little excuse for a life. She even stroked the top of his head.

"Listen to me hon, OK? I think you can look at me and tell I'm just not that kind, all right?"

"What *kind?*"

"Oh sweetheart I think you know. The kind that would be stupid enough to say the wrong thing to the wrong man, and one look is all I need to know you're the wrong man to say the wrong thing to, am I right?"

The gnome just stared, but I was getting the sense she'd worn him down a bit with just those few words of conversation.

"OK, you don't have to say anything. That's OK. In fact, that's the way it should be, hey? Because you're the one in charge here, and the one in charge doesn't need to do the explaining. It's us needs to do the explaining. I get it, dear. I do. But just so's you know; me and Vid? We're not the ones you need to be worried about. We're not. If we were any kind of a problem or a threat, do you really think Cluck would have wasted his time dragging us halfway across the galaxy? Seriously? I mean there really are better ways to dispose of a problem, trust me. And besides, maybe you two guys haven't met in person before, but I'm thinking surely you know enough about the man by now - however you know him - to know he wouldn't do anything to put money at risk, hmmm? I mean all you have to do is think about it."

"Oh and this is about so *very much more* than the simple allure of cash, as you and I have discussed," said Cluck, acting all dramatic. "There is a very real principle at stake here. A debt must be paid, and we have come to do whatever must be done to collect on that debt in full."

Unbelievably, Haley chuckled. He didn't crack even the trace of a smile, but I distinctly heard him chuckle.

"Principle at stake," he muttered, as he stood aside and motioned impatiently for us to step inside. "Ain't that about some bullshit."

"Beg your pardon?" asked Cluck, looking highly offended.

"You heard me. You ain't deaf. Because the one thing you all need to understand about me starting right here and now tonite is I don't give a shit about *none* of it except the money. That's the way it is with pretty much any reputable drug dealer you're likely to run into down here on Earth. But I guess up there in that rarefied air you kids breathe on Planet 10 these kinda things involve *scruples* and *principles* and what all else. Just so long as I get my end when it's all said and done, and there ain't no funny stuff, then you boys can defend all the damned principles you like, hear? Knock yourself out. Just so long as Haley gets paid, Haley don't give a shit. Now let's get on downstairs so I can familiarize you fellas with the setup."

Given the trouble he had with those big words Cluck was throwing out a minute ago, I was kinda surprised to see Haley break out with the scruples and the principles, but then the more I thought about it the more I kinda figured he was probably testing us all out. Which, considering the business we called ourselves being in, was probably a fairly routine sorta deal.

The difference between downstairs and upstairs in the Haley household was enough to give a critter whiplash. Upstairs looked pretty much like what you'd expect a single guy's place to look like, especially a single guy looked like Haley. Boring as hell. An old TV up against the wall in the livingroom, blaring some show he probably hadn't even been watching, and a well-worn sofa propped up opposite the TV behind a glass coffee table. A few old magazines scattered around the floor. Couple half empty coffee cups on the table. Lazy, lonely gnome's paradise.

Wasn't nothing lazy about downstairs, which didn't even look like it could possibly belong to the same house, let alone the same human being. For starters it was way too big, far bigger than the entire house upstairs. Imagine a block of sugar placed on top of a slice of bread, and now you're getting the dimensions. Plus the whole place looked like it had been molded out of aluminum and steel, and it was spotless. All kinds of different beakers, vials, measuring cups, and a whole bunch of other instruments I couldn't begin to imagine what they were for. Lotta funny-lookin' machines with lights on the sides that blinked non-stop.

Just who the hell was this guy anyway?

"Anybody else here besides you?" I asked. "I mean, this is a helluva lotta space for just one person, isn't it?"

Cluck gave me a furious look, like I'd just asked the Pope the color of his underwear, but I didn't see where it was written I was supposed to sit still and be quiet over in somebody's corner. Especially not with what I was lookin at.

Haley stopped in his tracks and turned around. The rest of us had been following behind like a herd of sheep, so we all stopped too. On a dime.

"Do you *see* anybody else skipping around here keeping me company, bright eyes? 'Cause if you do you be sure to point 'em out so I can get myself some target practice in."

"So then I'm taking that as a 'no', right?"

About 10 seconds passed where you could have heard a rat pissing on cotton – across the street. Felt like the whole room suddenly held its breath.

"You know, you may think you're qualified to be a damned comedian, but what you think ain't what it is. Just think about that for a moment."

I started to say something else smart-assed, but then decided to just nod. No need in pushin my luck. Seeing I wasn't gonna take the bait to enter a fight I couldn't win, Haley chuckled again, then shook his head and turned back around.

"We might as well start the tour over here," he said, pointing to a huge steel vat on the far side of the room that was easily big enough to boil an entire human being standing up. A bunch of hoses were attached to one side of the vat, and there was some sort of gauge attached to the top of all the hoses. I had absolutely no clue about what I was lookin at.

For the next hour or more Haley held court all by himself explaining his entire operation. After spelling out the function of nearly every single instrument he had down there, because he figured we all might need to know this for some reason, then he spelled out his dos and don'ts of the lab. With all the detail he was layin down I could pretty much guarantee there would be a good number of screw-ups early on until everybody started to internalize the drill. No way were we memorizing all of that in one night, and since he couldn't afford to write all those procedures down for obvious reasons then, well, there you were.

"Any questions?" he asked, once he was finally through and standing in front of us with his scrawny little arms folded over his chest.

Beardy eased his hand up, like a scared 3rd grader in the principal's office.

"Well, *yeah*, dude. I mean, like, how are we supposed to cram all that stuff in our head in just one shot? We're gonna go over this a few more times before we get started, right?"

Haley gave Cluck a look, and it was enough of a look that Cluck had to look down at his feet and not look up again for awhile.

"We cook our first trial batch of the MayoMadd day after tomorrow. In the morning. Early. Make sure everything's clickin like it should, get rid of all the glitches. And when I say early in the morning I mean 3 am on the money. Ain't nobody out on the streets at 3 am, and ain't hardly no cops snoopin around. Makes it easier to get things done without any hassle. No knocks on the door. More relaxed. We work 'til 7, then we eat, then we get some rest until around 1. That's when my nephew's gonna come by and pick up our little batch for a trial run out on the streets – provided everything goes like it should and the batch is ready. And unless you clowns are too dumb to follow some simple instructions, I don't see why that would be a problem. Any questions you got that can't wait, you ask 'em tomorrow."

"Haley I can assure you everything will go smoothly as planned. I told you I would be bringing a professional crew, and you will see I was telling you the truth," said Cluck, looking like he was about to get down on bended knee.

I really could not figure why Cluck felt like he had to kiss this guy's ass. I never did like Cluck much, but I at least had some measure of respect for him like I did for most crooks I dealt with who were good at what they did and followed some sort of code. But this waggy tail thing was starting to make me wrinkle my nose at the smell. I suspect I wasn't the only one in the room with these kinda thoughts, and I wasn't just talkin about Vee.

"You can assure me of that, eh? Yeah all right. Well I guess the proof is in the pudding on that one. We'll see what's what when the time comes. In the meantime let's just tend to business. There's a room farther back for all you guys to crash. Get used to spending most of your time in the basement because I don't need you raising a whole lotta questions outside, which is exactly what's gonna happen if a motley lookin' crew like yours suddenly shows up in a little town like Justice. They'll be onto us in no time. So I hope ain't nobody claustrophobic or whatever."

Beardy suddenly looked worried, like he was about to break out in a major sweat.

"Whoa, dude, are you sayin'…"

I wouldn't have believed it if I hadn't seen it, but Cluck literally clamped his hand over Beardy's mouth. Hard. Like he was tryin to smother the kid. Vee and I looked at each other tryin to figure what the hell.

"That will be sufficient for now, Haley. No problem at all. Good night."

****

Two days later we were all in the basement watchin Haley give us more instructions, this time on how the trial batch was gonna be made. Beardy was still lookin a shade green from bein inside too long, but Cluck kept insisting he was just fine. Personally, I figured Beardy was the one member of the bunch that we could let out for a stroll now and again since he was about the closest lookin thing to normal by Earth standards that we had. I said as much to Cluck later on out of earshot of everyone else, and he indicated maybe he thought I was right. I knew I was right. I also knew that eventually either Haley was gonna have to accept the fact that no way were we all gonna be his prisoners – and Cluck too – because otherwise there was gonna be one hell of a mutiny. What was the point of being successful illegal drug entrepreneurs if the only reward you got was being held against your will in some wacko's basement making more illegal drugs and watching TV?

Anyway, once Haley was through with the first part of Illegal Drug Manufacturing 101, he asked if anybody had any questions. Deciding I'd already put my foot in it enough not to matter at this point, I spoke up again and suggested we'd all probably do better just learning by example and following along. Haley acted like maybe I'd uttered an intelligence of some sort, probably by accident, but then began cranking up his machines and commenced to manufacturing what would be the first batch of MayoMadd ever manufactured on Plant Earth.

Gee. History in the making.

I should mention that the smell was the unholiest odor my nostrils had ever encountered in my entire life, and all of us were wearing masks that I thought were supposed to offer at least some protection. I would try to describe it, but even imagining what volume of rotted waste and bodily leftovers it would take to create this head-blowin stench would only make me sicker. I'm not sure if God has any connection to Planet 10 so most of the critters up there don't have any relationship with prayer, but since I'm told the common mythology down here involves some sort of Super Being who can hear your every thought and stays on call, I figured maybe it was time to give it a try. Anything to deliver me from these damned fumes.

But then, about an hour later, just when I swore I could take it no longer and was steeling myself for my big chance to launch a one-man flamethrower suicide attack on Haley and the entire setup, the smell switched on a dime from unbearable to roses, cinnamon, and cream. Swear to God. The change was so quick I'm surprised everyone in the room didn't fall over. I wanted to rip off my mask and breathe as deep as I could, and was about to do just that when Shorty Almighty caught my intent and wagged his finger in my direction while shaking his head real slow. He was grinning. What made me think he was the only one with a mask that actually worked the way it was supposed to?

"Am I the only one?" I asked, looking around the room at everyone else. "I mean, damn. You guys can't...?"

"Dude, you ain't alone. Trust me on that one."

Vee squeezed my hand, then moved her little finger around inside my palm in a real obscene kinda way that nobody else could see but that made my rocket pop up for launch so hard I thought my zipper was gonna scream for reinforcements. Then she leaned over and put her full lips to my ear and whispered, "If it wasn't for this crowd, I would make you pop and squirt like a ripe fruit right here right now, Missster Vid. And oh, I do believe you would enjoy it sooooo much…."

Jesus. Yes, the time had come for prayer.

I wanted to say, "Who are you and what have you done with my Vee?", but what came out instead was, "The hell with the crowd, baby doll. I bet they like to watch anyway, and I'm game to give 'em a show they'll never forget. I'm gonna part those luscious sweet…"

"This is wonderfully entertaining indeed, but I do wonder whether the two of you are aware we can hear every word you happen to be exchanging at this current time? But, please, do carry on. I find myself plunging deeply into a realm of vicarious thrills and spills from which I would prefer never to return, all thanks to your wonderful exchange. Whatever you do, *please* do not cease on our account."

I remember smiling, but that's about it. And Vee isn't talking.

CHAPTER 12

Two days later we were all sitting downstairs in a circle of chairs. The first trial batch of MayoMadd was done and Haley had called a strategy meeting for 2 p.m., so there we all were glancing back and forth at each other after nearly 20 minutes of waiting for Haley to finish whatever it was he was doing with all those charts and graphs on the other side of the room. We were getting antsy but nobody wanted to say anything because, as much as nobody wanted to admit it, that little midget gangster had everybody freaked.

Then, finally, at around 2:45 Haley ambles over and sits down so hard I'm surprised he didn't fracture his butt. He looked around the room from one face to the next like he was expecting one of us to start the meeting. I figured what the hell.

"So I'm guessing the question now is what are we supposed to do with this stuff, right?"

Haley squinted at me, shook his head, then gave Cluck a disapproving glare.

"And you're seriously tellin' me that on all of Planet 10, this is the best talent you could find? Either you got way too few crooks up there to choose from, or you need to do a whole lot better at choosin. One or the other."

"Well, perhaps…"

"Skip it, Cluster Fuck. We got considerably more pressing things to deal with right now, and time ain't our friend. We just go with what we got. Anything screws up? You know what happens, because I'm getting mine, rain or shine."

195

"Well, perhaps…"

Haley took two quick steps toward Cluck, who flinched, then turned his head to the side and cupped his ear upward in Cluck's direction like he couldn't quite make out what just got said.

"I'm sorry, what was that? You said something worth sayin did you?"

"…perhaps…"

"*WHAT?*"

"Nothing."

"That's better. So listen up guys, 'cause this is what's gonna happen over the next few days. We got our product ready to go, so now this little piggy goes to market."

Butch cocked his head to the side with a huge question on his face.

"What a piggy got to do with all this?"

Beardy barked out a laugh.

"Dude. It's a nursery rhyme. C'mon, you never heard…?"

"Never heard *what?* Some dumb-assed story about a pig goin' to a market? Look, where I come from…"

"SHUT UP."

And that's exactly what everybody did because, like I said, Haley may have looked like a runt, a short runt at that, but there was something about the way he carried himself that was very un-runt like. Kept us all on edge.

"Jesus Christ! *Really?* I swear, if I had any choice at all…? I mean *any damned choice at all.* But money talks which means we got to make this

MayoMadd do the walk if we all wanna get paid, so like I was startin to say before all of that whatever, we gotta get this stuff out in the street for a trial run. Gotta put some trainin wheels on this here package to give us an idea what we're workin with. My nephew Ronnie been dealin ever since he fell on his head crawlin outta the crib. He knows the crowd and the lay of the land as good as anyone out there, so we're gonna let him float a few samples with a few members of his little experimental pharmaceutical posse, and if they give it the thumbs-up then we move it up a step to Civic Park. That's where all the local heads hang out, and from what little whispers I been hearing there's a lotta dissatisfaction with the local produce, if you get what I'm sayin. Way too weak is the word, and I suspect that's because we're up here in the hills light years away from the major market, which means our stuff gets stomped on a bunch before it reaches our mountain folk clientele. That's a sad story for them, but it's all roses for our side. MayoMadd's gonna hit like a *bomb,* you hear me?"

Cluck smiled wide, in full snaggletooth glory.

"Indeed we do, Haley. Yes we do indeed!"

The rest of us weren't looking quite so enthusiastic as Cluck was sounding, although a couple of the chickens managed a weak grin, probably a reflex for self-preservation. Haley picked up on the cool reception – how could he not? – but he pushed past it like it wasn't anything for him to worry about. He was probably right.

****

The next day, close to midnight, was when the knock came on the door. Me, Beardy and Cluck were upstairs with Haley watchin some cop show passing the time 'til Ronnie showed up. Vee could have come upstairs too, but she said she wanted to stay in the basement, which I figured was kinda strange but I'm sure she had her reasons. She always did.

Haley looked through the peephole, chuckled, then undid his four security locks and chains and yanked open the door.

"Hey, punk! Get your narrow ass in here. Business is a- tickin'."

"Why you always say that, Uncle?" came a whiny, nasal voice. I couldn't quite see the body that was attached to it just yet.

"Because I like it and I feel like it, now what did I just say?"

"Oh. Yeah. Right."

What stepped into the room was pretty much what I expected would be stepping into the room based on that voice; a raggedy, teenaged wreck stuffed into a pair of torn, filthy jeans, a ripped t-shirt with a wide-open and screaming blood-filled mouth sketched across the front, and unlaced black boots – one with red laces, the other white. The hair on top of the kid's pear-shaped head looked like it had been assaulted by a windstorm.

But the eyes were the two things that didn't look like they belonged. There was way too much intelligence going on behind those dark little orbs for this kid to just be written off as some kinda aimless stoner. He paid a lot more attention to what was goin on around him than he let on, which I guess was good for the business he was in. Probably had a lot to do with why he was still alive and in possession of all his body parts.

After Haley locked the door up tight all over again, he reached up to clamp his arm around the kid's narrow shoulders and dragged him over to make introductions. Throughout the entire uncomfortable process Ronnie barely muttered a word and never smiled, extended his hand, or offered any other form of greeting. This was obviously something to be endured – by both sides - and that was as far as it went. Then we all headed to the basement for Ronnie to get a look at the product.

Once he did, the reaction was underwhelming to say the least.

"I dunno, man. It kinda looks a little too much like some of the other stuff that's out there. Could be a problem, you know?"

Beardy's face screwed up like a paper bag being balled up inside somebody's angry fist..

"Dude, what difference does it make if it looks kinda like this or kinda like that? Once they take a taste? *That* will remove all doubt. No question about that one, right Cluck?"

Cluck opened his mouth like he was about to say something, but then his eyes locked with Haley's and his trap snapped shut so hard I'm surprised he didn't break any teeth. Beardy caught the exchange, then went kinda pale.

"Yo, I didn't mean any disrespect to your nephew or anything liked that, all right? I'm just sayin it seems to me…"

"I dunno, man. I just dunno."

"OK. But..."

"You deaf, rock star? My nephew says he don't know."

Beardy bit his lip, and it was probably a good thing because what I'm guessing was about to pass those lips would not have resulted in a healthy outcome.

Ronnie's intense expression, which was focused somewhere between me and Vee (she came over to sit right next to me soon as we were back in the basement) didn't change a bit throughout. Matter of fact he acted like nothing had even transpired, like he hadn't heard a thing.

"You're calling it MayoMadd, right? Yeah. That's cool. Kid's'll like that. But you're gonna have to do something else with it to make it stand out a little bit you know? Yo, these are *kids,* remember? *Kids.* Kids like toys. They like the bright and shiny. And if it's a girl then she likes cute. I'm talkin about the new customers here, the ones you wanna trap, right? Once you got 'em and they're good and gone then it really doesn't matter 'cause a junkie doesn't give a shit. But early on, you gotta have the hook. I mean, I *know* the high is the hook on the back end, but you gotta have that way of getting 'em in the door first."

Haley grabbed Ronnie by the shoulder and shook him hard, then surveyed the room beaming with this look of pride as if he'd raised the kid himself. Hell, who wouldn't be proud of having such a smart kid grow up to be such a smart drug dealer? Like I said, he may have looked at first glance like just a another scruffy goof, but those eyes could tell anyone who was paying attention that this was someone to pay attention to.

"Yo, that *does* make some pretty good sense, man," said Beardy, letting me know he was beginning to peep the kid's potential as well.

"Indeed it does!" said Cluck, still playing the role of the suckup.

"So then how do we do this?" I asked. "I admit, like Beardy says, Ronnie has a good point here. But what can we do to a little pill to make it sexy? If that's even the right word…"

I wasn't quite prepared for Ronnie to grin. It actually made him look closer to a normal teenager.

"Sexy. Yeah. *Yeah!* That's cool, and that's definitely the right word. And it's easy, all right? Doesn't have to be anything complex. Simple is good. Simple is *best*. Like, OK, how about instead of just making it into a bunch of little white pills, like aspirin or something? How about making the pills blue, and then shaping them like stars? Huh? See? Yeah, *little blue stars that take you to the stars!"*

Ronnie's eyes weren't just glittering, they were actually *crackling,* like Fourth of July pinwheels. In that short span of time he had transformed from extremely uncomfortable and awkward teen to a kid possessed. But I had to admire the logic in what he was saying, even if it was twisted and being employed for all the wrong reasons. I nodded and grinned, thinking just maybe I had been around this criminal element a bit too long.

"So is that something we could do?" I asked. "Making the pills into stars, I mean."

Cluck's head swiveled in my direction, his face wearing a mocking smile.

"*Well* now. *This,* I must confess, is a remarkably unexpected contribution, coming as it does from the cheap seats?"

To my surprise, it was Haley who came to my defense. His eyes had gone cold.

"Sometimes I just don't get you, Cluster Fuck. I mean, why would you wanna degrade your own people like that when the man is obviously tryin to participate in making us all a whole lotta money?"

"Yeah, I was kinda thinkin the same thing, man," said Ronnie, casting a critical glance at Cluck, who was shrinking right before our eyes at a rapid rate.

"Only kidding…" he said, his voice sounding like it was disappearing even as he phrased those two little words.

"Huh," said Haley, then commenced to ignoring him altogether.

"The answer is yeah, we can do that. Easy. It's a cookie cutter thing, you understand? Making pills into shapes ain't no big deal. Didn't you ever pop Flintstone vitamins as a kid?"

"Flintstone…?"

"Oh. Damn. My bad. Nevermind. Anyway, all you need to know is the answer is 'yeah'."

"Got it. Soooo…"

"Sooooo *what?*"

"So is this what we're gonna do, then? The star thing?"

"Well only if you approve, pal. You do approve don't you?"

"Oh yeah! Sure. Why not."

I could feel Vee stiffen up, but she knew better than to even sneak a glance in my direction. We had to play this thing out, and the more convincing we were, the better our chances.

"Fuckin splendid. So Ronnie, you heard the man, right? He approves, which I think is a wonderful thing. So then I guess that means we get to work on making us some little blue stars, starting today, and then I'd say we'll have you a good test run batch ready for pickup in a couple days. Sound good?"

Ronnie nodded. He was back to looking like the fish outta water little punkster that had first come through the door.

"Yeah, Unk. Whatever, man. I'll be ready."

****

Three days later the knock came at the door again around 2 in the afternoon. The package of stars was on a small table just inside the door wrapped inside two layers of Ziploc plastic inside a plain brown paper bag. As usual around that time of day, we were upstairs watching some TV, but not really watching a thing. Boredom was becoming the norm, and that wasn't good.

Haley popped up, opened the door, then grabbed the bag off the table and handed the package off to Ronnie with a few mumbled words and a couple of nods. Then he slammed the door and came back to slump on the couch. I looked over at him, then thought better of asking any questions, but he must have read my intent and decided to indulge me.

"Kid's headed over to the park right now for the test run. Already got a few prospects lined up just from the hype he was able to drum up in these past couple days alone. Ronnie always was real good at marketing. Probably coulda done real good on the legit side on Wall Street or one of those places, but then again, who the hell says they're any more legit than me and Ronnie, right? I mean you hear me what I'm sayin' right?"

Beardy took the last swig of beer from the bottle, then confirmed Haley's analysis with a grunt followed by a burp.

"Hell yeah I'm right," replied Haley, before drifting back off into TV watcher's oblivion.

Three more days go by – pretty slowly if you ask me – before that knock comes on the door one more time. Only this time I noticed it was kinda frantic, which had me a little bit worried, like maybe the cops were on the way and he was trying to get some shelter before they caught up to him. My heart started to race. Haley musta had the same suspicion because he didn't move to the door quick as he normally did when he knew it was Ronnie. Matter of fact, he glanced over at me and Cluck like he was trying to get a quick read on what he ought to do. Cluck and I looked at each other. Haley cursed under his breath, then made for the door.

"Whatever it is, it is," he said.

But once Ronnie was inside, the look on his face told us right away that this had nothing to do with bad news. Haley actually had to calm him down before he could get it all out, but once he did…

"*Dudes.* I mean, this shit you got? These stars? Man, I'm *tellin'* you. You don't know what you got here. I mean, you shoulda *seen...*"

Haley started bouncing up and down on the balls of his feet like a little kid waiting for Santa to come down the chimney.

"So just to be clear, what you're sayin here is that..."

"What I'm *sayin* is that I think these kids would be willing to kill somebody to get this stuff, including members of their own family, OK? That's what I'm sayin. Look, every single kid who tried the stars, and I mean *every single one*, was ready on the spot to switch up from whatever high they were on to get on board with this right here. And we're even talkin committed junkies who been hooked on one thing or another for years. Most of them don't switch to a whole other high too quick if at all, but they gave it a shot on my go-ahead 'cause they know me, right? And once they did? BAM! New customer. Just like that, man. *Just like that.*"

Vee and I glanced at one another, not having to say a word knowing what this meant for our situation. Then we both plastered on our smiles and gave a thumbs up.

"Looks like things are going our way," I said.

"Dude, you have no fuckin idea. You guys gotta get to work, and I mean quick."

Several days later, when Haley decided we were running a bit low on provisions due to the fact that the frig was damned near empty of anything even remotely edible, he assigned me and Vee to go to the store and pick up whatever was needed. When I asked him for a shopping list he just shoved a crumpled 100-dollar bill in my hand and said he didn't have time to worry about that. Just bring back the change if there was any. Tosses me the keys to the Jeep he says is out back, which I then hand over to Vee. She's the better driver.

"You've driven Earth vehicles before, right?" I asked, as we stood in the driveway looking over the black, somewhat rusted vehicle parked inside the rundown shack that passed for a garage. Vee nodded slowly.

"It's been awhile, but I'm pretty sure I remember enough about them to get us to the store and back without putting our lives too much at risk, Misssster Vid."

"Wow. Say my name again, babe. You know what that does to me."

"Right now the only thing I wanna turn on is this Jeep, so get in and hang on."

"Oh! We're talkin dirty now. Daddy like."

"If daddy doesn't get his wide behind in that passenger seat inside the next 10 seconds he's going to be be talking dirty to himself in the driveway, hear?"

"But, alas, no sense of humor. OK, let's go. Killjoy."

One thing we both knew we had to get a lot of was eggs – as in 15 to 20 dozen, because eggs were a critical ingredient in MayoMadd. If it hadn't been for the need for eggs, Butch and all his freak chicken pals would never have been born, and the whole sordid story that followed behind what happened to them as a result would never have been written. But it all did happen, and now here Vee and I were pushing a squeaky cart down the aisles of the local grocery store – located

20 miles away in the next town over - trying to decide whether it even made sense to opt for a healthy diet or to just grab whatever quick junk food we came across until the basket was full. We ended up stocking up on a bit of both, and were glad to be done.

So there we were standing in line waiting to check out, minding our own business and not paying much attention to much of anything until we both got the same chill sensation at the same time. It's the feeling you get when you know you're under intense surveillance. Prior to those internal alarms goin off I think each of us had drifted off into our own little private universe trying to sort through the dilemma we found ourselves in, but then suddenly we found ourselves getting yanked back to the here and now, and looking around us to see more than a handful of folk staring at us as if we were a couple dinosaurs just came down from the mountaintop. Which, come to think of it, is exactly what we were to a lot of these folks. Hell, way the hell up here most of them probably hadn't even seen a black person except on TV, so when a couple of critters come walkin into a store with gills, well...I can only imagine.

What I really, really wanted to do right then was to raise my hand, palm out, and ask them to take us to their leader. I mean, you have no idea how bad I wanted to do that. But for one thing, I'm pretty sure Vee would have cut me deep right on the spot in full public view. Second, it didn't look to me like these folk were acquainted with the concept of humor. They all looked incurably tired, and not particularly healthy. Not like they were sickly or anything, but kinda like how you'd imagine folks would look who spent most of their spare time watching TV or sittin on the porch looking across the street at their neighbors sitting on the front porch looking back at them. I don't imagine there was any such thing as a gym within three or four hours of the place, and it was obvious nobody took advantage of any opportunity to do any hiking.

Right now, they were exercising their eyeballs staring at the two of us. Even the cashiers. I decided to smile and wave, kind of like a Miss Universe coming down the runway. OK, maybe that's the wrong image, but you get the idea. So did Vee, and she started doing the same thing. Guess we both figured this was the best we could do for public relations.

"Morning folks," I said. "Nice store you got here."

"Verrrry nice," piped in Vee. "Yes! Verrrrry nice."

We kept waving for what felt like an absurdly long time until the cashier handling the checkout line we happened to be in spoke up. She looked to be in her upper teen years, and therefore wasn't quite yet suffering from the same level of incurable tiredness as the older crowd, but she was well on her way. Already her doughy body was taking on the dimensions of a bored housewife-in-training.

"You guys don't live here," she said, more as an accusation than an observation. Then came the mumbling and the rumbling from the rest of the crowd, accompanied by the nodding of heads. This wasn't good.

"No. We don't. But we sure would like to, though! I mean look at how beautiful it is here, right?"

Now the stares were shifting from uncomfortably curious to a bit more hostile. Obviously I'd said the wrong thing when it came to integration. Critters and aliens hand-in-hand for a better world as not what this crowd had in mind. Change tactics.

"But! Unfortunately my wife and I here have to keep moving on. Miles to go before we sleep. Miles and miles and miles. Yep. Lonnnnng way to go. So we're just gonna pay for our few items here and then just be on our way, OK? Yep. That's what we're gonna do."

An old guy, hunched over with a long gray and white beard, spoke up from behind us.

"Looks to me like you two have a bit more than what you call a *few* items, don't you? Christ, look at all them eggs. What's with all them eggs? Why so many eggs?"

What I wanted to ask this little old bastard was since when did buying a lot of eggs become a crime in this town. Way I saw it, we were contributing mightily to the local economy, which needed all the mighty contributions it could get from what I could see. But what I actually said was "Oh we're not buying just for us, buddy…"

"Not yer buddy."

"Right. We're not buying just for us, friend."

"Friend either."

"OK. We're not buying just for us. Simple. How's that?"

"Who you buyin for needs all them eggs?"

Now they were startin to get a bit too damned nosy. I knew we were outnumbered, but this was gonna have to stop. What Vee said next let me know she felt the same way. She was smiling wide when she said it, but that was just the cover.

"I'm sorry, what is your name sir?"

'Sir' didn't say anything for what felt like forever, but Vee just kept smiling and staring hard right into him, letting him – and everybody else in the store – know she wasn't backing down. And since they didn't know what to expect from a couple of critters with gills, the fear factor gave us a bit of a leg up. At least temporarily.

"Bob," he muttered.

Vee's smile stretched a little wider, and even I had to grin. Round One goes to the lady.

"Bob. All right, Bob. We don't want any trouble here, and I'm sure you know that because…"

"I don't know…"

"*Shhhhhhhhh.* Bob. Calm down. Just callllllllmmm down, OK? No trouble here. We're just a couple visitors passing through your town picking up some groceries. That's all. Now, you asked why we have so many eggs, would that be correct?"

Bob nodded briskly.

"Right. OK, Bob, well I suppose that's a fair question. But first let me ask you one thing, if that's OK."

"S'pose."

"OK, what's that I see in your basket, Bob? That looks like a pair of ...stockings? I didn't know you could buy stockings at a grocery store, but that's great. So, you wear stockings do you, Bob?"

I had to bite my lip to keep from screaming with laughter. Not so with Bob, whose craggly face was flushing fire red, like one of those Looney Tunes cartoon characters when they start to levitate and the smoke belches out of their ears. Come to think of it, Bob himself looked kind of like a cartoon character.

"Them damned stockings ain't for me!" he exploded. A few snickers could be heard from some of the other customers. Involuntary snickers I'm sure.

"Bob! What did I say about staying calm, dear? OK? This isn't a fight, here. Just asking, not judging. Never judging. Because we're the outsiders, right? So how can we judge? But just asking then, if those stockings aren't for you, then who might they be for, hey?"

Bob starts to sputter. Someone else remarked that they hadn't even noticed the stockings until then. Gee, that *was* kinda strange, huh? Said another.

"For my wife!" said Bob.

Vee nodded enthusiastically.

"Oh! OK then. Well..."

"Wife...?" said the cashier. "Bob, everybody knows you ain't got a wife. Far as I know you never even had a girlfriend. That's right, isn't it Ellie?"

The cashier at the next aisle over nodded her head, one of her eyebrows arched in curiosity.

"Yep. No girlfriend I ever heard of."

I figured Bob was scheduled to have his head blow up within the next few minutes. Vee picked up on that too, so she jumped in.

"OK folks, hey, like I said, I'm not here to judge what Bob does with his stockings that he likes to buy for other people. *Not my concern*, you know? I was just trying to help my new friend Bob understand that sometimes you might not want everybody else to know all of your business, and that there's nothing wrong with that. Right Bob?"

Bob was still too pissed off to mutter anything vaguely coherent, but at least his face wasn't looking quite so much like an angry red tomato anymore. Make that a shriveled up angry red tomato.

"Wonderful! I'll take that as a yes. And with that, if you good folks wouldn't mind, my husband and I would just like to pay for our goods and be on our way, never to bother you again!"

"What? You don't like us?"

Something was seriously wrong with these folks. Seriously.

On the ride back home, I suggested we swing by that park where Haley's nephew had supposedly done his initial distribution of MayoMadd.

"What for?" asked Vee.

"Because I wanna see for myself, that's what for. Ronnie says the kids are going nuts over this stuff, which is making me sick thinking whatever part we may be playing in this whole thing, and, well, I just wanna see for myself."

"Should we stop off somewhere and buy a whip for you to flog yourself with? Would that be helpful?"

"You're a regular comedienne, Vee. You really are."

"Listen, it's not that I don't understand where you're coming from, Vid, because I do. It's the same place I'm coming from. We're on the same side. But do you really think it's going to make anything that much better for us if we beat ourselves up over this? Don't you think it might be better to keep focused on how are we going to disrupt this whole thing? And then still manage to stay alive?"

Vee was making a good point, and it was hard to argue if you were interested in being rational and making sense. But right then those two qualities weren't real high on my list of priorities. I just wanted to see our brand new junkies.

"Point taken and considered. Now if I remember what he said, we'll run right into it if we take a right up here at the next light, isn't that right?"

Vee slumped back into the driver's seat, then sighed real deep. I almost felt guilty, but for some reason this was important to me and I felt an unquenchable need to follow through.

"Left," she said.

"Huh?"

"It's left. You have to make a left. Not a right."

"Oh…well…OK, then."

The road that led to the park went from paved to dirt about three or four minutes into the drive. Not long after that was when we both saw the little shrimp of a kid doing cartwheels down the side of the road while trying to rap at the top of his lungs. No doubt about it; this was one of ours. Unlike most of the drugs out there, MayoMadd wasn't the type of substance that had you drooling, or wanting to lock yourself up in a crowded dirty room with a bunch more drooling idiots. MayoMadd was the sensation of stomping on your joystick like it was a gas pedal, taking you from zero to hero inside of two eye blinks. That was pretty much the way it worked for the kids back on Planet 10 back in the day when Vee was out there slingin, and that's the way it apparently worked on humans too, most likely because we weren't all that different from one another except for the gills.

So anyway there he goes, cartwheeling by my side of the window just as free and easy as you please. Vee stopped the car, then looked over at me.

"What do you want to do?" she asked.

Stupidly, not knowing what else to do, I shrugged. Vee could have reamed me out right then, but she was my friend, and friends were patient when the situation required.

"*Vid.* Do we go after him? Or do we keep going until we get to this park?"

I took a deep breath, rubbed my eyes hard with both thumbs.

"We go on to the park. I have to see this."

Vee stared at me for a long moment, I guess giving me the chance to rethink my decision, but I was holding firm. I had to see this. I had to see what could happen. Vee sighed, nodded, then pulled back out into the road. Several minutes later there we were.

The park should have been a beautiful spot, and it had everything needed to make it that kind of place where a family would want to come with the kids and just lay back. Lots of tall trees, open green spaces, park benches, and even a couple of baseball diamonds. Not too far off in the distance I could see a small creek trickling through. It was as beautiful a location as you could ask for…except for those kids. I guess to a degree I knew MayoMadd couldn't be held responsible for all of this because these kids had been hanging out here doing whatever long before we showed up. That's why Ronnie knew to bring the stuff here for the trial run. Still, as we pulled into the parking lot to observe the show, I had a strong suspicion that however bad it may have been before, there wasn't much comparison to what was about to touch down. This town had no idea what was headed their way – or why. The fact that this was all about revenge for a tribe of angry freak chickens who had been the victims of human prejudice was all a bit too much to absorb on a nice summer day.

And so Vee and I just sat there, letting the time tick away as we watched the circus of geeked up kids running, jumping, bouncing off each other, off the trees, off of whatever, like insanely happy maniacs who couldn't control their ecstasy. And it seemed like the longer we stayed, wondering how long they could keep this up before passing out from exhaustion, the more amped up they got. It was the craziest thing. Got me to thinking maybe with a few alterations this stuff could be a good thing for energy rejuvenation, but then I had to smack myself for even thinking anything legitimate about this crap. Somehow, some kinda way, we had to stop this.

"Seen enough?" asked Vee, after we'd been sitting there close to an hour.

"For now," I said.

Once we got back to the house, the mood inside was not far removed from all that warped joy Vee and I had witnessed at the park. The fact that we (why do I keep saying *we?*) could be sitting on a multi-million dollar drug empire was beginning to seep into everybody's cranium, and the result was mass delirium. Everybody was calculating the size of their individual mansions before the first dollar had even made an appearance. After Haley locked the door behind us, he even helped carry the groceries into the kitchen, which had me wondering if maybe he'd been sampling some of the product himself.

"So you lovebirds found it OK, eh?" he asked.

Vee and I looked at one another, then back at Haley.

"Lovebirds…?"

Haley's grin would have given the devil the creeps.

"Oh. OK. Sure. I get it. Your secret's safe with me, kids."

He laughed hard, then started yanking stuff out of the bags.

"So what do we have here?" he asked.

I shrugged.

"We didn't know what you wanted really, 'cause you didn't tell us. So we just got some things we thought would work. If you need something else we can always go back. Although probably not to that same store."

That got Haley's attention, as his demeanor took a hard left from a rare happy and relaxed back to viciously suspicious.

"Problems? You guys had problems at a damn *grocery store?"*

"Hey, nothing major, all right? Calm down! Nobody's comin after us or filing any sorta report. But you mighta noticed Vee and I don't exactly fit in with the local wildlife, OK? And the local wildlife don't take too kindly to those things what don't fit in. Upsets the natural order of things, I guess. Anyway, we had to spend a little extra time smoothing some feathers is all. And I don't think it would be a good idea for either one of us to make a repeat performance there anytime soon. Matter of fact, it might be a good idea to send somebody else out next time. Somebody like maybe Beardy."

"And you think *Beardy* is good at fitting in?"

"Hey, I hear where you're coming from. But Beardy doesn't have gills, OK? You get what I'm sayin?"

Haley glared at us a little longer, then his grin returned as he resumed emptying the grocery bags onto the table.

"You give this thing we got here about another three-four months? Ain't gonna matter one damned bit what those hillbillies are thinkin or *not* thinkin about your gills, hear? 'Cause this thing takes off like I know it will and we're gonna have enough cash to buy up every town inside a hundred-mile radius. We're about to be so damned rich the only thing we won't be able to afford is giving a damn 'cause we'll be doing whatever the fuck we wanna do. And that's a guarantee."

By then the others had followed us into the kitchen and were nodding their heads, even clapping. I'm guessing Haley anticipated our response would be just as delirious as everybody else, and that's probably how we shoulda played it, but maybe it was the scene at the park that put both me and Vee in somewhat of an anti-celebratory mood. Vee in particular.

"Listen, maybe we should slow down a bit with this whole thing, you know? Take some time to get our bearings and all that. Make sure we're not missing anything...?"

You coulda heard a cotton ball drop onto a cotton ball floor. Everybody in the room except me was lookin at Vee like she had just grown a full set of very unwelcome appendages from her head. Haley especially.

"And what it is you think maybe we might have missed, Sweet Pea..? You're saying you think maybe we didn't do our proper homework on this thing? Or, to be more specific, sounds like you're saying it was...*me*...who dropped that ball. Am I reading your concern accurately there, sugarplum?"

Under normal circumstances, Vee would have castrated any man who talked to her like that, and she'd be yawning while she did it. Vee is not the kinda female critter you wanna be talkin down to for any reason whatsoever. But seeing as how this was far from your normal circumstance, Vee wisely adapted and swallowed her reflex whole.

"Well...and I mean this with respect...but no. That wasn't what I was meaning to say at all, Haley. I am well aware that you have been planning this for quite some time, and meticulously so..."

The mention of a big word got Deep Cluck's attention, plus a crooked-tooth grin of approval.

"Well spoken, my dear. Well spoken indeed," he said.

"Thank you."

"Don't mention it."

"And don't fuckin interrupt," said Haley with a cockeyed glare.

"Sorry…" mumbled Cluck.

"So anyway, Sugarplum, you were sayin'…?"

"Yes…I was saying that it was not my intention to suggest that you had not been taking care of business in any way. Quite the contrary. All I was trying to suggest is that we all take a minute to think about the full scope of what it is we're moving into here because this is a really big deal, hey? I mean, introducing a drug from another planet into an Earth population, especially a bunch of unsuspecting kids..? I know they already like to get high so it's not like we're poisoning innocents or anything like that…"

"Poisoning..? *Poisoning???* Is that really the word you wanna use here? Are you seriously calling our product *poison?* You know, that word 'poison' does have somewhat negative connotations that I am not entirely comfortable with. You comfortable with those negative connotations, Butch?"

"I *hate* negative conno…I *hate* those things."

"How about you, Cluck?"

"I have always viewed them as rather pesky, this is true."

"And *you,* Vid. Where are you in all this, seeing as how Sugarplum here is such a close friend of yours and all."

We were getting in deeper by the nanosecond, so I figured my only play at this point was to come on strong and butt heads. Either it would work or we'd be dead, but I knew for sure that if I played the weakling kiss-his-royal-highness-ass card then we'd be worse than dead. Haley was a Grade AAA thug, and thugs were a breed I was quite familiar with.

"What I think is you all heard the lady the first damn time. That's what I think. Anything else?"

It got so silent I think I could hear everybody's heartbeat, or maybe everybody's heart was beatin so loud because everybody figured somebody nearby was about to eat dirt real quick. Haley's eyes looked kinda like pinwheels, sparks 'n all, as he took a few casual steps to where I was standing. I could smell his breath, which was beyond foul, and he was smiling the smile of a complete lunatic. I was familiar with that too, and not in a good way.

"Is there anything else?"

"Just askin."

"Oh. *Just askin.* OK *Just Askin,* perhaps maybe you wanna be tellin me…"

"Only perhaps maybe I don't."

"Vid, don't…"

"It's OK, Vee. I got th…"

The problem with short guys is that, when you get into a fight with them, especially if they know how to fight, they have quick and direct access to various parts of the anatomy that can make any opponent wither up like a weed in gasoline. Which was pretty much what I did, considering that my nuts felt like, well, what nuts feel like when they've been dealt a full-on direct hit upper cut. Vee rushed over, but wasn't much she could do for crushed nuts except to look sympathetic and rub my arm. It must have been five minutes before I could even talk or sit up. But when I did, I looked up from where I was sitting and noticed Haley's eyes were no longer like pinwheels. I grinned.

"I guess if I was short that's probably where I woulda aimed too. Nice shot."

For a long moment me and Haley just stared at each other, then he started to chuckle and shake his head. Cluck, who was standing behind him to his left, was looking both pissed and confused, and I knew the reason for both. Butch was just looking confused.

"Yeah, it was a nice shot, wasn't it? So unless there's *anything else,* why don't you raise your sorry ass up off that floor so we all can get back to work. Oh, that is, unless the Missus over here is still worried that the help may be in over their heads in this operation. So are you still worried sweet pea, or are you gonna leave the worryin to us professionals?"

Vee's face eased into a smile that gave me the chills. And if Haley knew Vee like I knew her, he wouldn't have been feeling too comfortable either.

"I'll leave the worrying wherever you tell me to, doll."

Then she winked and stood up real fast. I'm pretty sure he didn't mean to, but Haley took a step back. Vee noticed and smiled even wider.

Chapter 13

As Vee swiveled those hips away, looking far more calm than either one of us had a right to given our current situation, I took another good look at Butch and changed my mind about something. That look on his face wasn't confusion at all. Naw. Not one bit. That look on Butch's face was pure unadulterated rage, and it was way out of proportion to the circumstances. I guess I could understand him being a bit pissed that we managed to escape with all our limbs after standing up up to Haley like we did, but no way did that explain the burn in his eyes as he watched Vee disappear down the stairs.

Then again, if you knew what I knew about Butch and how he came up you probably wouldn't be so surprised at all that anger he keeps bottled up inside like a mixture of vinegar and hot chili peppers gone bad and no release valve in sight. Yeah, just think on that image for a moment…

What I know about Butch I pieced together from different places, but mostly from Deep Cluck during those occasional times when he was in the mood to actually ramble on imitating a decent conversation instead of always attaching those pretty little knives to every word he utters. Sometimes it would just be flat out boring at the Haley compound, and since Haley had done a pretty effective job of cutting Cluck down to size just for the fun of it and to let him know who was boss, Cluck seemed more disposed of late to share bits and pieces of his past, the most interesting parts of which were associated with his beloved chickens.

So anyway it seems Butch's story wasn't that much different from most of the freak birds in that he had no idea who his parents were because he didn't actually have any parents per se. All of the chickens like Butch, the mutants, were manufactured by some engineered combination of human and chicken DNA, which was made to work by some brilliantly screwed up process that is way above my pay grade to understand. Suffice to say that when all was said and done, each and every chicken was born an orphan. And an unwanted orphan at that. No hope of adoption, no hope of affection. No hope period. The only function of the mutants was to produce those gigantic specialized eggs for The Collective, which was responsible for producing the drug that was then shipped up to Planet 10 to keep junior critters quiet during their formative years. And that was that. Not much to look forward to each and every day of a life.

But if the chickens had been poor dumb animals like their purebred cousins that were actual honest-to-God *chickens,* then the whole sorry deal may have worked out somehow. Because they would have been too sorry and stupid to complain. But as Butch grew older and began to figure things out, it became harder and harder for him to keep everything inside. For one thing, he simply had to get an answer for why, when it came to regular chickens, one had to be a female to lay an egg. But with the mutants, males could produce eggs just fine. Matter of fact, there *were* no female mutant chickens. And the males could actually produce larger, more potent eggs at a rate three times faster than normal chickens.

But then how were they producing these eggs, if there were no female mutant chickens to get it on with? Why were those dumb-assed feathered idiot cousins of theirs allowed to have all the fun to produce an inferior egg, but somehow Butch and those like Butch had been endowed with some messed up biological trait enabling them to manufacture an egg without the need for copulation? The mutants were producing eggs by *getting it on with themselves!* Sure it was efficient, but really? Whose idea was this anyway?

So since none of the other mutant brethren seemed to have an answer for this, Butch decided to ask one of the humans the next time one of them visited the giant cages (they looked like prison camps) to extract the eggs. And that right there was Butch's first major miscalculation since, up to that point, the humans had no idea that the mutants could actually talk. And not talk like a parrot or some other mimic, but actually express ideas and opinions. Opinions such as, "Why are there no female mutant chickens? What the hell is up with that? Why weren't we engineered to get it on like everybody else?"

Well, see, overseers can feel good about being overseers when those they oversee are understood to be too dumb to *not* be overseen. But what happens when the lie breaks loose? It's kinda like that saying I heard from somewhere that always cracked me up; "Ain't no fun when the rabbit's got the gun."

Except that it's tons of fun for the rabbit I imagine, and would have been just as much fun for Butch and his mutant brethren - provided they had access to a gun. But since they didn't even have one good working slingshot between them then, well, there was a bit of a problem. At least that's the way Butch remembers it...

Let me back up. OK, every day around the same time - twice a day, actually - the same red-headed freckle-faced kid would enter the compound pushing a wheelbarrow in front of him containing all the slop for the chickens. The wheelbarrow was old and squeaky so they could always hear the kid was on his way long before he made it to the front gate, which meant they had time to interrupt whatever they had been up to at the time and get back to looking like normal everyday extra-large half-human chickens. Only this one particular day came along when he figured he just couldn't keep his silence any longer. Somebody had to speak up. He wasn't necessarily the brightest of the bunch, but he was likely the most fearless, which was why the other chickens kept trying to talk him out of it once he told them what he planned to do.

"You guys are cowards, all right? I mean they're just human, that's it. Nothin special. Hell, *we're* the ones special, right? I bet one-on-one any one of us could probably beat the pants off this stupid-lookin kid and his daddy too. Take a look at yourselves guys! We ain't small. Not by a longshot."

"We might not be small, but being big doesn't mean a damned thing out here if you don't have somethin to back it up with, and they ain't stupid enough to store their weapons in here are they?"

"Maybe not, but we don't need weapons to ask questions do we?"

"We just might, Butch. Think about it; the kid gets scared, runs to tell his dad, then…."

"Look, sooner or later this day has to come. That is unless you all are happy sittin and shittin eggs all day for the rest of your lives; and not even getting any female chickies to scratch that itch, if you catch my meaning."

"Butch, we don't even know what a female chickie looks like 'cause they didn't make any, so what…?"

"My point stands, guys. We gotta speak up sooner or later, and I'm all for sooner. I just can't keep doing this."

And Butch was true to his word. The next time the kid showed up, whistling all outta tune, Butch waited until he was through tossing the food into the cages then stood up and walked over to the edge of his cage and calls him by name. The kid's hand was on the door getting ready to push it open and head back outside when he hears himself being called by a chicken. So you can imagine what was going through his mind. Something along the lines of whether somebody upped the dosage on his favorite pharmaceutical.

"Joey. Somethin' I wanna ask you."

The kid doesn't wanna believe it, but he's already too scared to take another step so he just stands there with his hand on the door. He doesn't turn around. Butch grins. Some of the other chickens start to chuckle. After all it *is* pretty funny.

"Jooooooeeeeee…c'mon kid. Talk to me. I don't bite. Besides, even if I did, I'm on the other side of the cage so what can I do?"

Pretty soon Joey takes a deep breath and turns around, eyes wide as saucers. Butch is standing there looking back at him just as calm as can be, beckoning Joey closer with one finger.

"Somethin I wanna ask you."

But Butch never got the chance to ask the kid a thing because the kid screamed at the top of his lungs then bolted out the door like he'd been shot out of a cannon, screaming the whole way.

"Damn," said Butch. "I really didn't see him taking it like that."

"Really? And how *did* you imagine a human kid reacting when a chicken starts talking to him straight outta the blue with no warning? No, seriously, I'm curious; how did you see that playing out?"

That was Fred, who had always been a bit of a smartass, so Butch ignored him. Or tried to. Fred, like most irritating folks - or chickens, in this instance - usually have that rare gift of making themselves very hard to ignore, even when you're trying your best.

"So what do we do now?" asked Vince, who was usually one of the more thoughtful of the bunch.

Butch shook his head. Fred spoke up.

"Well, the first thing we need to do is to familiarize ourselves with the phrase 'fast food' because I suspect that's what we're all going to be here pretty soon thanks to Mr. Revolutionary over there. Didn't we try to tell him not to do this guys? I mean didn't we? But nooooo! Butch figures he has the right to get us all in trouble because *he* can't take it anymore. I mean, did any of us get a vote on this? Huh? Did we? I'm asking did we..."

"Oh for cryin out loud just shut up Fred, OK? Please? Yeah, OK, so maybe we didn't have a full-out discussion on this thing, but does it really matter now? We are where we are so let's deal with that because chirpin about how Butch should have taken a poll before doing what he did isn't gonna help us figure a way out of this."

"So I'm guessing that means you've thought this all through then, Vince? You're the McNugget with the master plan?"

"I got a plan."

"Huh? Who's that?"

Each chicken was in his own cage, and the way the cages were lined up, stretching all the way from one end of the compound to the other, which was about 50 feet long, meant that not all the chickens could see one another that easy, even though the cages were made out of open mesh. The chickens that knew each other the best (in this particular compound, because there were five compounds containing 20 mutant chickens each) were the ones kept in the cages closest to one another, the exception being those chickens like Butch who were always making a lot of noise and spouting off. But Pete, who was stuck in the cage at the farthest end, hardly ever said a word to the point where most of the others prractically forgot he even existed.

Until now.

"It's Pete."

"*Pete?*" asked Vince. "Down at the end?"

There was the sound of a throat being cleared, then "Yeah. Pete."

Fred groaned.

"Surely we're not going to listen to this silent little gnome from…"

"I'm not a gnome. I'm Pete. And I have a plan. Does anybody else have a plan?"

Silence.

"OK so here's my plan, and it's simple too. So we pretty much know the kid's gonna bring his dad back here, right? Because that's what a kid would do after a traumatic event like that."

"Traumatic event? You sneak off to college when none of us was lookin'?"

"I'm just sayin that's what a kid would do. *Any* kid. A kid's gonna run and tell the parents, and then the parents are probably gonna laugh him off. But even if they do they're probably gonna come back to check just to satisfy the kid, and because the kid is so worked up. Which means they could be on their way back here any minute."

Fred groaned again.

"At which point we become fast food. I believe I already covered that point."

"Not if we don't talk we're not."

"And that's your grand plan?"

"Do you have a plan?"

"That's not the point!"

"I believe it is. And all we have to do is sit here like the dumb chickens we're supposed to be and don't give any sign that we understand a word they're sayin when they start trying to quiz us or trip us up or whatever. And that means you especially Butch, because he's gonna be comin to you first."

"Got it," said Butch.

Now Fred was the one who couldn't take any more.

"Are you *serious?* Is anybody else actually accepting this as our strategy for survival?"

"Well, I just heard the house door open and close, so I figure you've got about a minute to come up with an alternative, Fred," said Vince.

Silence. Except for the sound of approaching footsteps.

"So it's settled then," said Vince. "Everybody knows what to do?"

The chickens mumbled their assent, even Fred. Rule of the pack.

"Hey Pete?"

"Yeah."

"Thanks."

"Yeah."

****

Pete's plan worked like a charm, but it almost didn't, mainly because it worked like a charm. What I'm saying is it was all any of them could do to keep from bustin out laughing looking at the expression on that Joey kid's face when he came creepin back into the compound, peepin out from behind his dad who wasn't that much bigger than he was, but who was a hell of a lot meaner.

"Now tell me again what it is you think you saw Joey, and this time calm down and tell me like a man. None of that high-pitched whimpering and yelping you were just doing in front of your mother, getting her all worried. You're my only son, and I'll be damned if the one son I do have turns out to be some kinda sissy boy. You're not gonna let me down like that are ya? And get your butt from behind me! See, that's what I'm talkin about! You gotta cut that out!"

So the kid comes easing around the side of his dad, all the time his eyes locked on Butch, who winked at him when dad wasn't looking. The kid jumped, and his dad swatted him upside the head.

"Dammit! What did I just say?"

"But *Dad!* That chicken, the one who was talkin to me earlier, he just winked at me!"

The kid's father squeezed his eyes shut then balled up his fists, and for a minute there it looked like he might beat the kid senseless right there in the chicken shack, but instead he just started mumbling.

"I swear you have got to be the *dumbest*...OK, point him out, Joey. This amaaaaazing talking chicken that you say you were having this fascinating conversation with. Point him out to me *right now.*"

Joey took several unsteady steps forward toward Butch's cage, then raised a trembling finger, pointing it in his direction. Butch squawked, then kicked around some dirt with his feet, doing an A-1 imitation of those idiot cousins of ours.

"That's the one, dad. That one right there. The one that just squawked. Only he didn't squawk when I was here before. He walked right up to the edge of the cage and said there was something he wanted to ask me."

"Is that so? You're saying that chicken right there actually told you he had a question to ask you?"

"Dad I swear! And he called me by name too. He said - and he said it just like this - he said *Jooooooooeeeeeee*. Just like that, Dad. It was really spooky."

"A chicken. Spooky."

"Well it was!"

"And there's nothing about your story you wanna change? Because if this chicken doesn't talk before we leave here, then believe you me you're gonna be doing more than talking when I get you back to the house, and don't think your mother's gonna be able to save you this time either. Are we clear?"

For awhile there it looked like Joey might change his mind, and you could see what few working gears he had in that little red head of his head rattling around trying to compute if sticking to his story was worth the risk of what he knew he was in for if Butch didn't perform. But in the end Joey even stood himself up straight when he announced that he knew what he saw. Kid might not have been too bright, but he did have some guts. His dad nodded, then shrugged. He took a long hard look at Butch before approaching the cage.

"So you're the one," he said.

Butch didn't say a word.

"The one who's got my kid all spooked thinking you can talk instead of squawk."

Butch cocked his head to the side and squawked. Dad chuckled, but he was still in a foul mood.

"You know I oughta light you up just because the kid *thinks* it's you, you know that? 'Cause otherwise I wouldn't be wasting my time down here right now actually talking to a damned freak of a chicken when I could be finishing up my meal back at the house."

If Dad had made the serious mistake of opening up that cage to make good on his threat, there's a good chance he wouldn't have come back out in one piece, which meant the Great Poultry Uprising probably would have gotten started right there right then. But as luck (if that's what you wanna call it) would have it, he made a few more smart-assed comments then made the wise decision and left, dragging his kid Joey by the ear, who was squealing all the way still trying to convince his Dad that Butch could talk. Once they heard the door close, every chicken in the compound fell out laughin. It was one of those rare good days to be a mutant.

But it was definitely a rare day. Conditions in the compound didn't get any better, and in fact they got worse. The slop they were feeding the chickens was bad enough to begin with, but over the next month or so it turned into something really disgusting, and close to inedible. Matter of fact it *would* have been inedible if it weren't for the conditions. But all that time Butch kept on working out his plan of liberation, working on every chicken that would listen convincing them that the only thing standing between life in the compund forever and being a chicken sandwich was an uprising. They had to raise hell loud enough to get respect.

"You know one thing I still don't get is why they think it's OK to treat us worse than they treat the regular chickens, dumb as they are, when we got so much more on the ball? I mean, we can think, we can talk, we got ideas. We're *half-human* for cryin out loud. I mean, we could really be a benefit to these folks, you know? A hell of a lot more than just cranking out these eggs all the damned time. And why they need us for the eggs anyway? Isn't that what the regular chickens are for?"

It was the most Pete had said at one time since they had been stuck in the compound, and he was making a lot of sense.

"As for the eggs, I think they're using ours for something else altogether. They definitely ain't for breakfast in the morning, I know that," said Butch.

"For what then?"

"Something evil. I'm sure of it. But what you said about being a benefit to them? Why would you say that after what they've done to us? Why would you even want that?"

"I'm just sayin is all. It doesn't make sense the way they treat us. It's like they don't even wanna know what we can do. They're not even givin us a chance."

"Yeah. And they never will. You oughta know that by now, Pete. You ought know that. Which is why I'm saying something needs to be done, and we gotta do it soon or else we lose that window."

"Oh well we *certainly* wouldn't want to lose a window."

"Shut up, Fred. If anyone ever deserved to be a chicken sandwich it's you."

Fred didn't say anything else for the rest of the day. The rest of the crew started listening to Butch. Eventually Fred did too. What choice did he have?

****

What came to be known as The Great Poultry Uprising began on that day the humans (at least the ones calling themselves Christians) refer to as Easter Sunday, which was two months after Butch spoke his first few words to Joey. The chickens had spent a lot of time deciding which day would make the biggest statement, and they finally decided on Easter because that was the day when that guy they call Jesus escaped this cave he was trapped in by rolling aside some huge rock and then heading on up to Heaven. The point being that Jesus wasn't about letting anyone keep him cooped up anywhere, not even after he was dead. The guy was serious about freedom, and so were the chickens. By rising up and demanding their freedom on the same day Jesus rose up from the dead, the chickens figured the humans would have to pay serious attention to their movement. And that was the key thing the chickens were going for was to be taken seriously by the humans. If not as equals, then at least as a class above those idiot cousins of theirs who did nothing but lay eggs and peck in the dirt all day long.

Day 1 of the pre-revolution began when Joey entered the compound like usual, his memories of a talking Butch having apparently buried themselves somewhere deep into a locked closet inside his memory where they could never be heard from again. And that denial strategy may have worked just fine if Butch hadn't said "Hey Joey" and then waved to him with a smile on Easter Sunday morning. Joey's eyes popped open again like saucers, just like last time, and his face flushed red. He started muttering and stuttering like a village idiot, which he kinda was.

"D-d-d-dad says you ch-ch-ch-chickens can't talk."

Butch nodded his agreement.

"You know what? Your dad's right, Joey. Chickens *can't* talk. They *can't*. And those dumb-assed birds you got down the road peckin and scratchin are chickens. *We*, on the other hand, aren't exactly chickens, are we Joey? I mean look at us; you gotta admit we look a whole lot different than your standard cluck, right? I mean, we got the feet, and the beak is close enough, I guess, but when's the last time you saw a chicken with arms like these? And do these feathers look right to you? *Do they?*"

"D-d-d-daaaad says...."

Butch slammed his fist against the wire mesh, causing the whole cage to shake.

"Quit that damned stuttering! You may not be the brightest bulb around, and neither am I, but you're smart enough to know we don't look like any chickens you've ever seen! Now isn't that right? C'mon Joey! You've been around chickens all your life, and then here we come. I mean, if we're just chickens, then why don't they let us mix with the other chickens? What's the deal with that? And how come those chickens you got down the road get to have hens? Huh? Why is that? How did we end up so screwed up, Joey? *How?*"

Joey dropped the barrel full of chicken slop and took off out of the compound, which was according to plan.

"Don't forget to bring your daddy back here! I got a few words for him!" shouted Butch.

Sure enough, Joey comes back to the compound with his mad-as-hell dad in tow, this time swearing to beat the kid senseless - while Joey's mother pleaded and begged on Joey's behalf.

"Please, Homer! You know Joey's not that bright. He doesn't mean anything, and he always does his chores. It's just that sometimes…"

"It's just that sometimes he cries like a little girl and says the chickens are being mean to him, right? Is that about right?"

The mother started to respond, and by that time they were all inside the compound. Talk about your dysfunctional family.

"So your name's Homer, is it?" asked Butch, who was leaning comfortably up against the wire mesh, his feet crossed at the ankles.

Silence never sounded so loud. Homer's mouth was open so wide it could have been a tunnel. All three of them - father, mother, and dimwit son - looked like they were frozen in place.

"I'm sorry, I don't think I got your name, m'am? 'Course we all know Joey 'cause he brings us that lovely slop you wanna feed us each and every day, but I don't think we've ever had the pleasure of seeing your lovely face up in the place. Have we guys?"

"Nope, not in here," said Vince.

"Thankfully. No we have not," said Fred.

"Nope," said Pete.

Butch nodded.

"Yeah, that's what I thought. Soooo…?"

"Hannah," she blurted. "It's…Han…"

"Hannah! Stop talkin to the chickens!"

"But Homer…"

"RIGHT NOW dammit! You hear what I say? Ain't no tellin what they're up to."

"What we're *up to?* But Homer, ain't nobody here but us chickens. I mean, how…? Because isn't that why you were about to bounce young Joey there off the walls was because he was trying to convince you these dumb clucks could actually talk? So how could we possibly be up to anything?"

Butch could see a thick vein on the side of Homer's head starting to throb so hard it looked like it might burst any minute. The thought of that made his grin stretch a little wider.

"How long have you been like this? What happened to you? Something had to…"

"*You* happened to us, Homer. And you know it. What, you think we had a say in making ourselves like this? Seriously? You know better than that, Homer, and you had to know there were gonna be some dues to pay sooner or later. Well, sooner *and* later are both here starin you dead in the face, buddy."

"Just tell me what it is you want. That's all I need to know so we can be done with this once and for all."

"So we can be done with this once and for all, eh? Because after all this is such an inconvenience for *you,* right, Homer? We're the ones making life hard for *you,* have I got that right?"

"C'mon, Butch. Don't get all emotional with him. This is about business, remember? Just fill him in on the demands."

Butch was already hyperventilating, but what Vince said managed to calm him down just a bit.

"Yeah, Vince. You're right. Business. So Homer, you asked what it is we want? Simple question with a simple answer. What we want is our freedom. No more layin eggs all day, at least not without some sort of…you know…something in return."

"What he means is we won't be laying any more eggs without a mutually agreed-upon contract that protects our interests as well as yours."

Butch grinned, then pointed a thumb in Vince's direction.

"You can tell he's the smart one, right? But yeah. What he said."

Homer's glare went from Butch to Vince, then back to Butch again. His wife and kid were hugged up against each other right by the door, which they kept open.

"Freedom," muttered Homer, sounding like he wasn't quite sure what the word implied.

"Simple question? Simple answer. I think simple is always better, right? Makes things easier for everyone."

"Sometimes it does, sometimes it doesn't. So now, this freedom you've got in mind; does this mean I'm supposed to just open the cages on all 100 of you freaks and just let you roam the countryside as you wish? Just because you asked me for freedom? Is that how this is supposed to work?"

"Homer, honey, maybe…"

"Shut the hell up, Hannah. I'll handle this."

"Because you're the big man in charge, right, Homer? That would be why your wife and kid are so scared of you?"

"Business, Butch. Business," said Vince.

"Right. Back to business. Because, after all, your family business is none of mine."

"Glad you realize that."

"So here's where we stand; I understand you got a business to run here, and business expenses and all that. That business being me and my friends here. So I don't expect you to just walk away from all that money we must be bringing in for you without some resistance. That's why my associate Vince brought up the idea of a contract that we can all agree on. You get your quota of eggs for whatever it is you use them for, and we get out of these cages. Roaming privileges."

"And just how far is it you think I'm supposed to let you roam? You have any idea what the neighbors would think if they saw you guys walking around, talking, actin like normal folks? Lookin like the freaks you are? They'd shoot you on sight, friend."

This was something none of the chickens had planned on, namely that they were a kept secret. There being so many of them, and the size of them, how in the hell could they have been a secret all this time? And more importantly, *why?*

"So you're tellin us nobody else even knows we exist?"

"You got it, bub. Well, nobody from around here. There's definitely some other folks who know about you, namely the ones who made you, but they ain't exactly what you would call locals."

"So then…"

"Let me see if I can take a stab at this," said Vince.

Butch nodded, looking noticeably shaken up.

"Obviously we're part of some rather large experiment, and obviously we're making somebody somewhere - in addition to you - a lot of money. That being the case, it seems to me that there is likely to be some motivation in paying some attention to our demands since, without us, your never ending supply of super duper eggs comes to an end rather abruptly."

"Is that right? So is that a threat? You guys don't get your freedom and we don't get our eggs? Is that how you wanna play this?"

"I wouldn't consider this a game so 'play' isn't necessarily a word I would use. But yes, I think you've got the general idea of what we're proposing."

Homer nodded.

"Hmmm. OK. No freedom. No eggs. No eggs. No freedom. Yeah, OK, I can *kinda* see where that makes some sense? Where that's fair? Except I'm kinda left wondering what use we have for you guys once you stop making the eggs, see? Because that's really the only reason you guys were even thought of or invented is for those eggs. So uhh..no eggs? No reason to keep you guys alive. Think about it anyway. I'll be back for your answer a little later. Hannah? Junior? Let's go and let these chatty chickens put their heads together."

And that, as they say, is the straw that broke the camel's back. Except that in this case it was the chicken's back. And they all agreed they had come too far at this point to back down. They had crossed a line, and chances were pretty strong their days were numbered anyway now that Homer knew what it was he was dealing with. It was safe to say things could only get a hell of a lot worse unless they made a move. So when Homer came back later, as promised, to get his answer, Butch lied and said he understood the predicament they were in and guessed they were stuck with it.

"Don't none of us like it one damned bit, but it is what it is," said Butch, glaring hard at Homer to convince him of how pissed off he was.

Homer chuckled.

"It is what it is indeed, pal. Glad you guys saw the light."

"Don't know if it was a light, but we saw somethin' all right,"

"Well good for you. Joey will be back in the morning, and this time with some real special gruel I think you fellas will like a lot. Kind of as a celebration that we were able to come to this agreement. Among equals."

At that Homer broke out laughing as he left the compound, laughing all the way back to his house. Once Butch heard the door slam shut, he grinned.

"What's got you smiling, Butch?" asked Vince.

"Realizing that just might be the last time that asshole ever laughs in his life."

"I see. Well that would do it all right."

****

For the next 10 days all seemed normal, at least to Homer and his family. Joey went out to feed the chickens, the chickens ate, the chickens produced their eggs, and that was that.

The 11th day was Easter, and that's when all hell broke loose.

It started when Joey entered the compound for his normal visit. By now he had gotten somewhat accustomed to chatting with the chickens, although he still wasn't completely comfortable with it. But as Homer said, at least he didn't "run out of the door screaming like a little sissy girl anymore." Now he would just stand there for a moment or two after dispensing the slop and smile and nod like some sort of toy doll as Butch - or sometimes Vince- would chat him up about things like school, homework, what sports he liked to play.

So when Joey showed up on Easter Sunday morning, he was actually whistling a little tune as he came through the door. His hair was combed neat and he looked somewhat more spruced up than usual.

"Hey guys," he said.

"Wow. You look pretty good there, kid. Takin out one of the neighborhood girls for a ride or what?"

Joey's face turned red as he flashed an aw-shucks grin. He shrugged his shoulders while looking down at his feet.

"Me? Naw. I told you before girls don't like me much. Besides, my dad would never let me go on a date. Too many chores and things to do around the house. Anyway, today's Easter. That's kinda why I'm all dressed up."

"Easter? Today's Easter? Well you know I completely forgot about that, Joey. Sure did. Say, any of you guys remember it was Easter?"

They all shook their heads.

"Hmm. Guess maybe that day doesn't mean quite the same thing to us as it does to you folks. But it looks like you're planning on enjoying yourself, eh? So what all do you have planned for this Easter anyway? And one I've always wanted to know; what's up with the rabbit?"

"Oh we always go to church on Easter Sunday. That's what everybody around here does. It's a pretty big deal I guess. As for the rabbit, I dunno. Never really understood that myself. Guess you'd think with all the eggs we'd be paying more attention to the chickens, but then maybe it's because those rabbits are so cute and everything. Everybody loves rabbits."

"Right. I understand. Everybody loves rabbits."

Joey's eyes opened wide, suddenly realizing what he had just said.

"Hey, no, wait a minute. I didn't mean…I mean chickens…that's what I meant when I said chickens should be getting the attention because…"

Butch raised both his arms, palms down, then lowered them slowly, letting Joey know he needed to calm down.

"Joey Joey Joey, *shhhhhhh*. No harm done, OK? Not even a problem. I just need you to come over here a minute because I need to ask you something."

"Well…but can't you ask me from over there? I mean why…?"

"You're not scared of me are you Joey? I'm just a chicken like your dad said, and I know you're no sissy boy the way he's always trying to tell you you are. Naw, not you, Joey. Besides, what it is I wanna ask is kinda between you and me. One-on-one. This isn't anything these other birds need to hear. This is personal, you know?"

"Personal?"

"Yep, pretty much. It's definitely not anything I can talk with your dad about, or your mother. And well, I hate to say it, but I'm afraid these chickens might laugh at me if they heard what it is I'm about to tell you."

"But why would they laugh at you? I thought they were your friends."

"I know you're not aware of this Joey, but chickens can really be cruel, man. You just wouldn't believe. I think maybe it comes from us being cooped up all the time. But listen, I really can't say too much more until you come on over. Won't take long, that I can promise you."

Butch was true to his word about it not taking long. Soon as Joey got about a foot away from Butch's cage he sorta leaned in, maybe figuring that made it safer somehow. It didn't. What Joey didn't know was that Butch had been working hard, like every day, twisting and pulling on the wires on the front of his cage. But not the whole front, just a small section about a foot in diameter, located the height of his shoulder. Once Joey leaned in close enough, Butch punched his fist through the wire and grabbed Joey by the throat. Shook him hard.

"First thing you need to know? I'm not gonna kill you. I'm not human like that. But if you don't do as you're told, I promise I'm gonna hurt you real bad. You understand that?"

Joey croaked a 'yes'.

"You believe me?"

Joey croaked another 'yes'.

"Good boy. Now open up this cage first, and then we're gonna go down the rows and open every last one. Got it?"

Joey choked and gasped for a few moments after Butch let him go, then shook his head slowly.

"But I don't have the keys though! My dad…"

"Joey, Joey, Joey. Turn around."

Joey turned around.

"Now look straight ahead and tell me what you see hanging on that wall. Right beside the door you just came in."

"I don't…wait…wow! But dad always said…I mean why would he lie to me like that?"

"Kinda tells you something about your dad doesn't it? So go grab 'em, then come back here and start letting us out."

Joey said 'OK' and headed over to where the keys were hanging from the wall, but just as he was almost there a revelation came to him.

"Hey, wait a minute. Why should I let you guys out? You don't even have your hand around my…"

But just then he felt a familiar choking feeling squeezing tight against his larynx.

"Your throat? *This* throat?"

Joey croaked a 'yes'.

"I think I told you before that I'm not the brightest bulb in the barn. But I'm not the dimmest either. I'm not stupid, Joey. But you kinda are. Now grab those keys and do like I said."

When Joey had unlocked the last cage, and 100 mutant chickens were standing outside their cages for the first time in their lives, still not quite sure whether this freedom thing was such a good idea, Butch told Joey to step inside that last cage. Joey gave Butch an incredulous and disbelieving look. Those eyes wide open all over again.

"But..."

"Don't worry, kid. Somebody will be back to let you out when it's time. We're not gonna let you die in here. Like I said, I'm not human like that. But right now, we got some serious chicken business to take care of. Time for a little justice, with some payback thrown in."

****

The uprising began with a friendly knock on Homer's door. Only Homer didn't answer. Hannah did, and what she saw made her scream at the top of her lungs before passing out.

"Damn. What do we do now?" asked George, whose cage had been located five stalls down from Butch.

"We go in and we wait for Homer. And we drag her back inside with us so she doesn't cause us any trouble."

"But why are we waiting for Homer?" asked George.

"Because we need Homer to present our case to the community."

"The way he is, you really think he's gonna do that for us?"

"Not to do us any favors he's not. Don't worry, I have a plan."

George looked down at Hannah's crumpled body, lying half in the house, half on the outside porch.

246

"Damned sure hope it works," he said.

"Yeah, me too," said Butch.

And maybe if Homer had been just a little further away from home when Hannah had screamed, or maybe if the window on his truck had been rolled up and he had been playing the radio loud like he usually did, then everything could have gone according to plan. At least up to the point where the chickens got to present their case to the community using Homer as ambassador.

But the radio hadn't been playing loud, the window was rolled down, and Homer wasn't so far away that he couldn't hear his wife's terrified scream. He started to turn back around, but then realized he might need backup. After all, he had no idea who or what was waiting for him back at the homestead. So he pulled over to the side of the road, pulled out his cellphone, and started making calls.

An hour later, three cars, two vans, and a pickup truck were following Homer back toward home. But then, as Homer's truck rounded the bend in the road, the one he always complained about because you could never see what was coming around in the other direction or how fast it was coming, his truck came to a screeching halt. His buddy Elmer, who was in the truck right behind Homer's, almost rear-ended him and exited his vehicle, waving his arms around, to tell him so. But then, as he got right up alongside the driver side window, he saw what Homer was looking at in the distance.

"Holy shit," he muttered. "*Holy shit.*"

"So I guess you're seeing this, huh Elmer?"

"I'm not sure if I am or not. You mind tellin me what the hell it is I'm seein'? 'Cause what I think I'm seein' I'm pretty sure I'm not believin. What I think I'm seein looks like one of those movie of the week type shows I used to watch all the time when I was a kid. The ones that used to come on the sci-fi channel…"

"Not a movie, Elmer."

"Then what…?"

"Elmer I'm not even supposed to…"

"We're way past 'supposed to' here, Homer. Because those …whatever the hell they are down there walking around on your farm? *They* aren't even supposed to exist, you get me? Now you and I both know everybody's back there looking at you and me right now and watching and knowing something ain't right. And soon as they come around this corner they're gonna see for themselves just how not right this is. So I think maybe you'd better start explaining something to me and quick."

So Homer explained. And once he finished explaining then he and Elmer instructed the other vehicles to all turn around and to meet them at JJ's bar in town where he would explain it all over again to everyone. And then they would decide what to do, because it was obvious that they were going to need a lot more backup than what they had right then.

"Maybe you should call home. Just to see what happens. Who answers," said Elmer.

Homer nodded, took out his phone and dialed. Waited. His face warped into a mask of anger.

"Put him on the line, Hannah."

The conversation, such as it was, was brief. Somebody asked what did the chickens want. Homer said it didn't matter what they wanted. All that mattered was that they had to be put down. And as soon as the reinforcements arrived, that's what was going to happen.

****

"Butch, it's 2 o'clock in the morning and we haven't heard a word since you talked to Homer for about a minute all those hours ago. I don't think it's a good idea for us to just sit around here like this. It's like we're waiting to get ourselves killed or something."

"Thanks for the cheerful support, Vince. But I don't see what other options we have but to wait it out. Did you see about the kid? Joey?"

"Yeah. Brought him inside and took him to the basement like you said. Gave him something to eat. He's tied up, but not so it'll hurt, or at least not too bad."

Butch nodded his approval, then started to say something else when all of a sudden they heard what sounded like an explosion. Seconds later two of the chickens that had been standing guard outside half ran, half stumbled through the door yelling that the compound had just blown up and was on fire.

"They just blew up our home!" one of them screamed, after which Butch grabbed him 'round the neck and shook him hard.

"What you just said right there? That's a big part of our problem."

""What? That they blew up our home? But they…"

"That's not our damned home you idiot! That's a CAGE! Are you so damned stupid you don't even know the DIFFERENCE??"

"Well…I mean.. I guess when you put it like that…"

"How else…"

"LISTEN UP ALL YOU CHICKENS. WHAT YOU JUST SAW IS ONLY THE BEGINNING. YOU HAVE ABOUT TWO MINUTES TO DECIDE WHETHER TO DO THE SENSIBLE THING AND COME OUT OF THAT HOUSE –AND FROM WHEREVER ELSE YOU'RE HIDING OUT - OR ELSE."

Butch stormed outside onto the porch, glaring and squinting in the direction of the bullhorn-assisted voice, but seeing only the darkness. And the flaming compound.

"Or else *what?*" he yelled. "I'm not surprised to see you burn down the compound, not that I give a damn. None of us do. But are you so loony you're willing to burn down your own house with your wife and child inside?"

He heard some whispers, what sounded like some brief arguing, and then:

"TWO MINUTES. AND COUNTING."

"So your own family doesn't mean a thing to you, Homer? I know you don't mind slapping them around and yelling at them sometimes, but do you really want them dead? Matter of fact, let me go get your wife and bring her out here. I think this might be something she'd wanna hear for herself. Because I'm thinking she might have a slightly different opinion about how you're going about this whole thing."

Butch stood there for a full ten seconds expecting some sort of response, or at least an acknowledgment of some sort that a human life may be in danger. But all he got was silence.

"All right then. I'm going inside. When I come back out I'll have your…"

What Butch heard sounded not quite like a scream, but more like what a scream might sound like heard underwater from someone being choked to death. It was an unnerving gurgling sound, and it only lasted several moments. Then came the brief hollow sound of something being thrown his direction. Then came the thud as it landed at the foot of the stairs leading up to the porch.

"It" was the head of Pete, the quiet chicken from the end of the row. The one who had the plan to…

It was Pete's head.

"ONE MINUTE."

All Butch could do was stare. He didn't know how to move. This was way past what he had expected, which just showed how little he knew about the humans. Vince, realizing the risk Butch was in just standing there with his mouth open, ran outside and grabbed him. Yanked him back in the house.

"You can be shocked later, Butch. No time for that now. We have to figure out what we're going to do, because I think we see right now just how crazy these people are."

"But *Pete?* Why would they…*Pete…?* Pete would never hurt *any*body! *Ever!* What kind of…"

"Later for that Butch! By my count we've got about 30 seconds to make a move, and from where I sit there's only one move to make and that's the hell out of here."

"But how.."

"Everybody! Right now! Turn off all the lights. *All* of them. Right now. Porch lights, kitchen, everywhere. No time for questions! Do it!"

The chickens inside the house, all except for Butch and Vince, quickly scattered to carry out the order. An understanding look came across Butch's face. Slowly he started to nod.

"I think I get it," he said. "Good call."

"I think it's the only call," said Vince. "It's gonna be a risk, and some of us aren't gonna make it. But if we don't do this then *none* of us are gonna make it. We've got to try. So you ready?"

The last houselight went off. Everything was shrouded in darkness.

"Ready."

****

Moments before the shots started firing, the chickens bolted out of a basement backdoor. Running right alongside the chickens just as fast as they could were Joey and Hannah. Butch couldn't help but notice what a strange image it was that Homer's own family felt safer running out the back door of their own home with a pack of mutant chickens than they did staying close to home and yelling out that they were OK. Or even tellling the shooters which direction the chickens were running.

But right now everybody was simply running for their lives.

It didn't take long for the shooters to figure out what had happened and cut to the chase, but it was long enough for a fair number of the chickens to escape into the nearby woods, where they holed up plotting strategy for the next two days. For some reason no one came looking for them. But those that didn't make it to the woods, which was more than half, were mowed down in a hail of bullets and then later butchered. The next morning it looked as if nothing at all had taken place. Not even so much as a feather was left behind as evidence. And those who participated in the hunt never spoke of it to outsiders, and rarely spoke of it to each other ever again.

As for Joey and Hannah, they crept back home from the woods several hours after they heard the final gunshot ring out. Homer didn't make it home until two days later, acting as if he had just run out to the store for some groceries.

Three months later the remaining chickens encountered one of the strangest yet most wonderful human beings they could never haver conceived of. Soon after meeting and adopting his new family of mutant chickens he would begin to refer to himself as Deep Cluck.

Their lives would never be the same.

Chapter 14

It was around 3 in the afternoon the day after Haley had clubbed me in the nuts when Ronnie showed up. By then my nuts were back to feeling normal again and everybody acted mostly as if nothing much out of the ordinary had transpired. Or at least they were trying to act that way. Haley had decided for whatever reason that it would be a good idea for me and Vee to ride along with his nephew when he started recruiting workers to help with the distribution. It wasn't like Ronnie needed babysitting since he had to be one of the most motivated drug dealers I'd ever seen so I wasn't quite sure what our function was supposed to be. But at that point I really wasn't interested in asking too many more questions of Haley or getting my nuts rerouted into my stomach again.

"So you guys about ready?" asked Ronnie, who was standing just inside the door looking all fidgity like he'd been drinking way too much caffeine.

"Yeah," Vee and I said at the same time. I think we were just anxious to get out of that house, even if it was to ride around with an overzealous drug dealer.

Ronnie drove a rundown rust-red pickup truck, which I figured at first was kinda strange given all the money he was making with the drugs, but then I figured maybe he was actually pretty clever. At least he knew enough not to draw too much attention to himself.

"So where we headed, sunshine?" I asked, once we'd been on the road a few minutes. "The park?"

Ronnie snorted.

"The park? Why in the hell would I recruit a buncha junkies to help me distribute junk? That sound like an intelligent plan to you, man?"

I shrugged, feeling more than a little stupid.

"Guess not, no."

"Guess not. No."

"No need to be a smartass, kid,"

"Yo, since I'm the one gonna be in charge of this crew I think maybe…"

I gave him *the look;* the one that says, 'I ain't the one'. He picked up on the message rather quickly I gotta say.

"I think maybe there's no need to be a smartass," I said, tapping him on the shoulder for some emphasis. Then I looked in the rearview mirror at Vee, who was grinning. She always did like it when I put on my tough guy routine. "And you're not Haley."

"Look, today hasn't been that cool, OK? So I'm sorry if I snapped at you like that, man. Seriously. No hard feelings, right?"

I winked, then patted him on the back.

"Right. No hard feelings at all, kid. Just remember we're all on the same team. We all just want this thing to work so we can all get paid."

Ronnie threw me a sideways glance like he wasn't quite sure how to take what I'd just said. I started to say something to maybe clarify, knowing that anything I said suspicious, which could be just about anything after that last incident with Haley, would get reported back. But then I thought about it and figured best to let it lie. The more attention I drew to anything, the likelihood was it would only get worse.

"So ummm, where we goin'?" asked Vee, who knew me well enough to pick up on what I was feelin without even having to ask.

Ronnie looked in the rearview, then back at me, then back at Vee. I didn't see what it was but she did something that made the kid relax, which made me relax. Vee was gifted when it came to putting males at ease, even when they were males of a whole different species. Then again, humans and critters were actually more like second cousins, so I guess we were close enough.

"See a coupla guys I know is all. But not from around here. We got about a two-hour drive ahead of us."

"Why so far?" I asked.

"Because we don't need anyone from around here knowing what we're putting together. This place is way too small a pond to be fishin' in for the kinda fish we need, if you know what I'm sayin'"

I nodded.

"Yeah, I guess that's pretty smart."

"Yeah, well I guess I'm a pretty smart guy."

There was a moment there when it felt kinda tense, me not knowing if he was trying to be a smartass again. But then he looked over at me and I could see everything was all right. At least for that moment. We both laughed.

"Guess you are at that, kid. I guess you are at that."

****

It was close to two hours later when we pulled up at the end of a long dirt road in front of a small, worn-out tan trailer in the middle of a clearing in some woods. The thought did occur to me that maybe Ronnie had brought us out here for another reason altogether, but then I braced myself and put the thought outta my head. Too many movies.

Ronnie reached across my lap to open the glove compartment, reached inside and pulled out an elaborate-looking pipe that could have been carved out of pure ivory. With all the money this kid had pulled in as a dealer it wouldn't surprise me. He reached in again and pulled out a small pouch containing some rather powerful-smelling weed. He raised the pipe in my direction, offering to share, but I shook my head with a smile.

"I'm fine. You go ahead though. That stuff doesn't agree with us critters real good."

He chuckled.

"That right, Miss?" he asked, looking at Vee in the rear mirror with this mischievous look on his face.

"Now does Vid look like the kinda man who would pass up on a good time if he had a choice? Really now, does he?"

Ronnie made a show of looking me over real close, then chuckled again. He shook his head.

"Point taken, Miss."

"Vee."

"Huh?"

"If we're going to be doing all this work together, then I think it's all right that you call a lady by her first name, hey?"

Ronnie cut his eyes in a way that would signal to any species anywhere what thought had just tip-toed across his mind.

"Hey," he said, his voice shifting into seductive gear. Or at least the closest thing he had to it. Vee winked, then shifted her gaze out the window toward the trailer.

"So I'm guessing this guy doesn't get much company, am I right?"

Ronnie took a deep hit off his pipe, held it in long enough to let me know he was no novice at this, then exhaled in a slow smooth stream before answering.

"Valdez? Company? Man, the farther this dude is from human contact the better. Not a bad guy, not dangerous or anything. But just, well, *peculiar.*"

Once Ronnie had finished the last toke on his nutritional supplement, he tossed the pipe back into the glove compartment and we all got out and headed toward the trailer. There was a crumbling three-step walkup to the door, but before we'd even made it that far a siren alarm began to screech and a small light tower rose up from the top of the trailer, blasting what appeared to be a compact version of the sun directly in our faces.

"*Yeeeeooowww!!!*" said Ronnie, raising his forearm to shield his eyes.

"Hey!" said Vee.

"Hey *Ronnie!* I thought you said this guy was just peculiar! This guy is fuckin…"

Then everything stopped. As if it had never happened. The door to the trailer opened, and out steps this huge dark-skinned guy wearing some kinda greasy blue sweatshirt with the sleeves cut off, and black running shorts. He looked like a walking oak tree with a big smile. The ground shook like jello when those massive feet of his stomped down. Right away he put himself in this spread-legged stance like some kinda warrior you only see on TV, then looked up at the sky, closed his eyes, and let rip the loudest yell I'd ever heard in life. If there were any animals nearby I'm certain that cleared them out. Either that or deafened them on the spot. My ears were ringin' for five minutes after he got through.

Then, once the last echo of that shout disappeared, Valdez walked right up to us and snatched the whole crew into a big, vice-grip group hug. Nobody could breathe until he finally put us down. More like planted us into the ground.

"Hey, you guys like Beethoven?" he asked, that big smile still shining through.

"Who?" asked Vee, trying politely to smile back.

"Oh yeah, I forgot to tell you guys…"

"Tell us what, Ronnie?" I said.

Right away Valdez gets this twisted-up look on his face letting us all know he can't quite believe what it is he just heard. Me being the highly cultured-type critter that I am, naturally I had heard of this guy Beethoven, but long-dead classical music heroes from Earth, generally speaking, were not on the priority list of things taught to most critters during their formative years. Generally speaking? We didn't give much of a damn about that kinda thing.

Valdez stomped his disbelief into the ground like a pissed-off elephant, making me feel kinda sorry for the ground. Nothing should be forced to absorb that kind of abuse.

"*WHOOOOOO???*"

Sounded like a damn foghorn. Vid gently put her hair back in place, then looked up at Mount Valdez and batted her eyes as she bumped her hip into his side. *Damn* that girl was good.

"Honey you're gonna have to forgive me for not knowing your friend, hey? I'm just a girl critter, and, well, we're just not always so up on that kinda stuff, you know? It's not that we don't care about it because I just know this Beethoven guy has got to be something super special but we're just kinda dingy that way. Soooo…friends?"

Valdez was watching Vee the whole time she was free-forming this 'I'm just a dumb chick' response, and I wasn't so sure he was buyin it. When she finished, he just stood there staring at her for a pretty long, uncomfortable moment strokin his chin with both eyes at half mast. They never blinked. Not once. I had to hand it to Vee, though. The girl didn't flinch. She kept her flirty little smile locked in place, and even dropped her eyes to half mast to match his.

Then, as if he was breaking out of a deep freeze, Valdez threw back his head and roared a laugh that by all rights should have peeled the bark from all surrounding trees and any other victimized vegetation. He put one ham-sized hand on her shoulder, then leaned in close. The next words that came out of his mouth were actually delivered at semi-normal volume.

"I know you're not that ditzy, OK? I know what I gotta look like to you guys 'cause I know how I look and sound to most folks. But I ain't that. But it don't matter 'cause I like you. I can see you got some quick thinking skills and that's a good thing. Lets me know Ronnie didn't bring any dummies out here *like he's done before* and that's a good thing. So y'all come on inside and I'll play you some Beethoven while we conduct business."

Then he turned around and started up the few steps into his trailer. But when he got to the top step he turned around and raised his forefinger up in the air, signaling he was about to make a very important pronouncement.

"Beethoven? Perhaps the most important classical composer ever. I know not everyone agrees with that but they don't have to. Wikipedia says that "He was also a pivotal figure in the transition from the 18th century musical classicism to 19th century romanticism , and his influence on subsequent generations of composers was profound." OK, c'mon in.

Vee and I looked at each other.

"Wiki *what?"*

"I wouldn't worry about it," said Ronnie, who was picking up the rear. "Not really why we're here is it?"

****

Just like Vee wasn't hardly anybody's ditzy chick - and anybody who called themselves knowin her at all knew that above all else - Valdez wasn't anybody's definition of a pea-brained, trailer trash country bumpkin either. Once you got past the obsession with Beethoven and some of his other quirks, the guy was strictly business. The tone of his voice even changed. Before two hours was up Valdez had lined up what he said was the perfect crew for Ronnie and his uncle, and he provided a list complete with bios, references, the whole shebang. We all thanked him, said our goodbyes, and left in considerably less dramatic fashion than our bells and whistles arrival.

Once we got back I convinced Haley that me and Vee could be trusted to take the van for a gas run. I'm not so sure a great amount of trust was involved, but I guess he figured how much harm could we do going to and from the gas station which wasn't more than about a 15-minute drive each way. But it was long enough for me and Vee to re-assess our situation and how we were gonna handle it. Seemed like we had been part of this whole crew for so long now that we were running the risk of starting to think more like them and less like who we really were and lose sight of what it was we were really trying to do.

"So what now?" asked Vee once we'd turned the corner, already reading my mind about why I'd suggested the gas run.

"We need to get this figured out doll, and we need to do it quick before we get ourselves drawn in too deep."

Vee's eyebrow raised, and I already knew what she was gonna say.

"Doll? I think that just maybe we may be a little bit past that point already. Maybe even a lotta bit. You know? Just saying. I mean, we just came back from meeting with the man who put together Ronnie and Haley's drug running street team, hey? How much deeper are we supposed to get before we reach *too* deep?"

"OK, OK. I hear you. And I know we've been on this ride a long time, but it's not like it was what we chose, right? I mean not exactly anyway. Hell, I'm a detective and you're a page-scratcher for cryin out loud! Lending a hand to interplanetary drug dealers is not what we do, am I right? We did what we had to do to keep our heads attached to our mainframes, but that doesn't mean we signed on for a tour of duty with the dark side, babe. It just means digging our way outta this is gonna be a little harder and take a little longer than maybe we originally thought."

Vee didn't say anything for awhile, and I didn't push it. Matter of fact she didn't say anything until we pulled up to the gas station. She sighed, and for some reason that made me ache a bit inside.

"OK you're right, Vid, but where does that get us? We're thousands and thousands of miles away from home traveling around with a crew full of fully-certified Fruit Loops, and the Fruit Loop in charge doesn't trust us anymore because he thinks we're up to something, which we are. So what are we supposed to do? *What's the plan, Vid?*"

****

It was all I could do to keep from laughin' which, under current circumstances, could have resulted in severely negative consequences for my health. For some reason the sight of Haley sittin there at the head of the table in this king-sized ornate wooden chair he musta picked up from some store where they sold used props from gangster movies was more than I could take. But I knew there would likely be consequences if I broke out laughing in the middle of a staff meeting, especially seeing as how I wasn't exactly on anybody's good side right now except Vee's, and she was starting to have questions.

So instead, I just bit my lip and looked down at the table throughout the whole ordeal, pretending to be deep in thought about what was being said, namely who was going to be in charge of the various parts of the operation. Not surprisingly, Haley was over everything, meaning each and every decision about everything had to go through him. Deep Cluck was appointed First Lieutnant under Haley, which came as something of a surprise since I thought it might have been Ronnie. Keeping it in the family and all that. Then again, it was probably a smart move to avoid the nepotism thing, especially if he wanted to keep the loyalty of the chickens on board, Butch in particular. That bond between Cluck and his birds was tight, and Haley knew it, which meant he had to keep that relationship to his advantage. Plus Haley probably wanted to stroke Cluck a bit in light of the fact that he'd pretty much been shoving him around at will ever since we all first showed up at his place. Cluck was strange but he was the farthest thing from stupid and if there was one thing I'd learned from him it was that he could hold onto a grudge like a dying man to a life raft, and that was a grudge even a thug like Haley didn't want to be saddled with.

Anyway, Cluck was obviously feeling good about the position, looking around the table at everyone with this snaggle-tooth grin and nodding. Butch got a chance to stick out his feathered chest too when Haley named him overseer of the chicken contingent, which would coordinate with Ronnie as part of the distribution operation. I knew part of that was him being able to be so closely involved with actually getting the drugs direct to the kids, which was the revenge he'd been waiting for.

Then, finally, Vee and I were saved for last. Both of us were seated at the far end of the table from Haley so all eyes from the head chair all down the side shifted in our direction, and they didn't look all that friendly. Except for Haley, who was wearing a smile that would have made a shark whimper.

"SO. What are we gonna do with you two, right? Don't wanna leave you two lovebirds out of the fun, now do we?"

"Wouldn't be very Christian, no."

Haley leaned forward, the look in those burning little eyes of his completely contradicting that smile.

"Wouldn't be *what?*"

"Just saying it wouldn't be the nice thing to do. And I know you're a nice guy."

Haley wasn't stupid either, which meant he knew exactly how I meant what I said, but he chose to let it roll off his back as he started to chuckle. After all, he was in the driver's seat and he knew it. Or driver's chair, I guess. At his queue, the rest of the table started to chuckle and nod too.

"Yeah. I am. You know everybody says that about me, and it's a mystery 'cause myself? I've never seen me that way. But then I guess sometimes other folks can see things in you that you just don't see in yourself, isn't that right?"

"Strange how that works."

"Yeah. Isn't it. So here's the deal; I've been thinking about this a lot, and talking to some of the guys about how you and sweetie fit into all this, and it wasn't easy because you guys are, well, *unusual.*"

You say that like it's a bad thing."

"Not at all! Far be it from me to offend. I'm simply sayin you two bring a slightly different flavor to what we've got going here, which means I have to sort of adjust the recipe."

"So you're a chef now?"

"Careful. Your joke quota is running low."

"Apologies."

"So like I was sayin, I've been givin this some thought, and it seems to me the best way for you guys to contribute to the cause is by neutralizin threats."

Vee raised an eyebrow, started to lean forward, but then thought better of it. I already knew what she was thinkin 'cause I was thinkin the same thing.

"Neutra…? I'm sorry, but if I could just ask what kind of threats you think me and Vid could possibly help you…"

"Not quite feelin up to the task sweetheart? Is that what I'm sensin here?"

Vee cleared her throat.

"Well…it's just…"

"How about you, spud? You afraid you might be shootin blanks?"

I grinned.

"Naw. My barrel's always full-loaded. I just think what my friend here may be worried about is…"

Vee cut me a look, and she was right. I shoulda known better. She picked up where I left off.

"What I was starting to say? Is that it seems to me the best way to run an operation is to take advantage of everybody's strengths, am I right? So what is it about the two of us that makes you think heavy-duty security work is what we're best at? Do either one of us really look like the types to scare anybody off?"

Haley leaned back in his chair with his eyes at half-mast, I guess tryin to look like he was giving what Vee had just said some deep thought. But that tiny bit of a grin I caught let me know he'd already made up his mind and he was just havin fun. Fun for him, not for us. Which further let me know that what he really had in mind didn't have much at all to do with security. My guess is he was counting on us not doin our new jobs right. Easiest way to get rid of us without gettin his own hands dirty. Just send us out in front of the wolves, let the wolves do what what wolves do, and close the gate behind him.

You gotta admire a guy who puts that kinda care into a plan, even if it's a plan for murder.

Chapter 15

Vee and I were sittin on the porch watchin the crew pack up the van full of all the required gear, both of us feelin like a coupla hourglasses without a whole lotta salt left on the top side of the glass. We had offered to help with the packing, but Haley had said we should just take it easy and think about how we were gonna prepare for our new roles in the organization. Then he laughed.

Me not being the kind of person who can 'relax' in this kind of rather uncomfortable situation, I decided to take myself a walk around the block - a few blocks actually - to clear my head and see if maybe some grand strategy might plant itself inside my skull that would give me and Vee more time above ground. Vee wanted to come with me, and normally I would have been more than happy to have some company - especially her company - but this was a stroll I needed to take alone. Haley was preoccupied and didn't seem to care so I set off down the street of small brick bungalows, hands in my pockets, intent on taking my time.

The distance between me and Haley's operation, even if it was temporary, was starting to feel good - to the point where if it hadn't been for Vee I might have considered making this a much longer and more permanent walk than originally planned for - but then this deep black, smooth, shiny vehicle that looked like a cock on wheels pulls up alongside me with the engine murmurin like a whisper. Tinted windows on all sides. Heart startin to race, and wonderin who this might be to suddenly take such an interest in my wanderings around the neighborhood, I was flippin through options quick in my head when one of the windows eased itself down and the vehicle came to a stop. I came to a

268

stop too. Being the talkative type, and always figuring it best to take control of the situation, I decided to engage in a little preemptive conversation before whoever it was stuck their head out the window.

Only when that head *did* stick out the window, my words got choked up in my throat like what happens when a kid tries to eat and swallow too much too soon.

"How...?"

The smile - I seemed to be getting smiled at by all the wrong sorta folks recently - was enough to lower the temperature a good 20 degrees. Teeth that small and that sharp didn't belong inside a smile. It was a contradiction in terms, plus it was just plain wrong. Like a lollypop made out of barbed wire and nails.

"Well at least he didn't ask *who.*"

That voice didn't belong to the head recently poked out of the window, but to whoever was doin the driving behind the wheel. I stooped down slowly to get a look and saw a near exact replica of who was eyeing me from the passenger seat.

The Gerruh.

"How in the...?"

"Did we find you?"

I nodded, trying to stand myself up straight again but not completely succeeding.

They both laughed in unison.

"We are Gerruh."

"Oh. Right."

Another laugh in stereo, which creeped me out. Hell, the *Gerruh* creeped me out. With that paper-white skin and those dead black eyes they made the Mafia look like overanxious do-gooders. I still remember seeing them on the runway just as we were pulling away from Planet 10, and how calm they seemed. I should have known then that somebody's days were numbered. But somehow it just didn't seem right that those abbreviated days would belong to me. After all wasn't I supposed to be one of the good guys?

Damn. Talk about answering your own question.

"So am I gonna have enough time to find out why you're gonna take me out, or you guys runnin' on a tight schedule?"

The Gerruh in the passenger seat, who was closest to me, looked back at his twin, then back at me again with what looked like it could have been a frown. Last thing I wanted to do was make these guys mad, but then if they were here to kill me then I don't guess it would have made that much of a difference.

"Take you *out?* Whatever gave you that idea?"

"Whatever gave…? Guys, c'mon. I mean this is what you do for a living, right? It's what you do. Everybody knows that. Though I didn't know you could take out contracts all the way down here on Earth. I always thought you worked for more local type concerns."

"We do. But sometimes those local concerns have far-reaching interests that need to be protected."

"Yes. Local is quite a bit bigger these days than what it used to be," piped in Gerruh #2.

"Apparently so," I said. "So then. If you're not here to kill me then what? Ice cream?"

They both just stared.

"No," they said in unison.

"We are here to make you an offer."

"The kind of offer I'm expected to accept, right?"

"That would be the idea, yes. You should know that we are aware of your activities - yours and your lady friend - since the two of you arrived here with Deep Cluck and his crew. We have been monitoring your activities with a considerable amount of interest and..."

"Whoa, whoa. Wait a doggoned minute. You guys don't think we're actually a part of this whole operartion do you? Because if you do you've got the wrong..."

"Actually we believe we have the right."

"But..."

"Because we already know you're not part of Deep Cluck's crew. Or Haley and Ronnie's. We know all that. Which makes the two of you considerably more interesting to the people we represent back on Planet 10."

"Interesting how?"

"Information. Inside information to be exact."

"On the operation."

"Exactly"

"So me and Vee would be, like, spying for you guys. On an interplanetary drug operation."

"Exactly again."

"But we could get hurt."

They both grinned.

****

Once I got back from what was supposed to have been a nice relaxing walk to clear my head, I don't guess I was lookin all that relaxed. Especially not to someone who knew me as well as Vee. She'd been waitin for me on those porch steps the whole time, and once she saw me draggin back down the street she came to meet me. Picking up on the stress once she got close, she glanced back over her shoulder to make sure nobody was within listening distance then picked up her pace just enough not to attract attention.

"What?" she said, starting to reach out and grab my hand, then pulling it back on second thought.

I shook my head.

"Later."

"Now."

By now you should already know what my chances were of winning that particular showdown.

"Don't look surprised whatever you do when I tell you with this smile on my face that the Gerruh have been following us and they know what we're up to and we now have to give them the inside dope on this whole operation. There. Now you see why I said 'later'? Turn around and smile for the nice people, Vee."

"Oh my God…"

"Smile Vee."

****

Once the van was loaded all the way up, Ronnie asked me to ride with him to pick up our initial crew of dealers that Valdez had hooked us - I mean them - up with. It wasn't exactly the kind of trip I would have volunteered for under normal circumstances, but seeing as how much things had changed just within the past hour I figured this might just prove to be a twisted sort of blessing giving me a closer look at how things were shaping up and it would also give me some meat to feed the twin beasts -the Gerruh - who now had me dancin to a completely unfamiliar tune, namely a tune that wasn't mine. All these years workin' as a detective I had pretty much gotten in the habit of bein in control of my own movements, but I was being forced to learn how to adjust to a whole other way of doing things if I wanted to survive. Plus this wasn't just for me it was for Vee's sake as well. No way was I havin anything goin wrong with her on my conscience.

"So where we supposed to rendezvous with these new dealers of yours?" I asked, once we were about 20 minutes out. Ronnie didn't answer right off, so I looked over at him and noticed a plug in his ear. If his taste in music was as bad as his taste in attire, I could only guess at what those tunes were doing to his head. I tapped him on the knee.

""*Hey.*"

"Huh? What?"

"Where we goin, spud?"

"Like I told you, to pick up the crew."

"Right, but where is that? They all waitin for you at one main spot or..."

"You got somewhere to be, man?"

I felt like smackin the kid right then, but I knew this would have been the worst possible time. So I decided to put his smackdown on layaway for a time when I could really enjoy it.

"Your show, kid. I'm just along for the ride at Your Majesty's request."

"They're not all in one place, all right? I mean how stupid would that be? No, we have to make a few stops and it's gonna take awhile. Now. Anything else?"

I shook my head.

"Nope. Think I'll just enjoy the scenery."

Actually the scenery wasn't bad to look at with all the trees and whatnot. Had kind of a calming effect, or at least as calm as anybody can be knowing their days might be numbered. The first stop we made took us about an hour to get there, and it was way back in the woods in a spot that reminded me of where Valdez stayed. Trailer and all. I guess maybe it made sense that some of the folks he knew might be backwoods hermits like himself. Except that once we met the kid it was obvious he was nobody's hermit, and probably wasn't even from around these parts. Even though I was a little out of my element being this far away from Planet 10, a detective still knows what a detective knows. Plus it didn't take a detective to figure out that a mountain hermit wouldn't likely be wearing fake gold snakeskin boots with snakeskin pants to match. Unlike Valdez he was pretty small, with these hard gray eyes. Maybe it's just me, but something about that outfit and that look just didn't quite fit in the hills.

"You're Rusty?" asked Ronnie, once the kid had gotten himself situated in the back seat. The kid nodded quick, not botherin to look at either one of us. Folded his hands, which had a few scars on them.

"I'm Ronnie. This is Vid."

Rusty grunted, then gave me a sideways glance.

"You're a critter," he said.

"I've been called worse."

"Hmph."

"Right."

And with that pleasant introduction, we were off to our next appointment. Before the day was through we'd made five stops total, and each stop was a surprise. On our way back to Haley's, where everybody was gonna spend the night before heading out for Denver the next day, I was convinced this had to be the biggest collection of misfits I had ever seen. Not only that, but if I told the Gerruh who Haley and Ronnie had picked to be their top ground team picks, they never would have believed me. They'd swear I was tryin to pull some sort of joke. So now here I was once again stuck up to my gills in unsolvable problems in need of a solution.

Somebody somewhere was leading my life, a better life, and I wanted it back.

****

That next afternoon we were back in Denver, sitting on a couple of concrete benches in Sundial Park, waiting for some locals to show up to discuss some sort of business arrangement. They were late, which didn't come as much of a shock. Not because they were thugs, but because Haley and Ronnie's crew were the newbies on the block so they didn't have a whole lot of pull yet. At least not in Denver. They might have been the big deal in Justice, but Denver wasn't anybody's idea of a small mountain town. It wasn't New York, but it wasn't Podunk, Idaho either.

It was 3 o'clock, and the meeting had been scheduled for 2:30. Me, Haley, Ronnie, and Deep Cluck were the meetup team, although I wouldn't exactly say I was honestly a part of the team. The real reason I was there was because Haley didn't want to leave me unsupervised for too long a time here in Denver. Figured it was easier to keep me close. He may have been right. As for Johnnie Beardy I'm guessing he figured him to be a little too wild and unpredictable. Butch was left behind because he stood out too much and would draw too much attention, plus recently he was wearin his anger at the humans everywhere we went and that wasn't the vibe was needed at this meeting. Vee? No girls allowed, even though she was smarter than all of them shaken up and stirred. Well, except for Deep Cluck.

"So what's the deal, Uncle?" asked Ronnie. "They can't tell time or what?"

Haley lit a cigarette, inhaled deep, then grumbled.

"They tell time just fine, nephew. They just don't know who they're dealin with yet, that's all. But they will. Soon as our stuff hits these streets they'll all be bowin down."

"Either that or usin you guys as target practice," I said.

"What's *that* supposed to mean?"

I shrugged my shoulders.

"Just sayin it could go either way, right? This whole thing gets too big too fast and you start makin all the money, you don't think all the dealers around here are gonna roll out the thank you rug, do you? That's money out of their piggy banks, and they're not gonna like it. Just sayin."

Haley took another long drag on his cigarette, then squinted his eyes real tight as he looked at me.

"I guess maybe that's why I put you and Vee in charge of neutralizin threats, right? You see anybody staplin a target to any one of our backs, I expect you guys to get that handled, hear?"

No doubt about it. He didn't want the blood on his hands directly, or on the hands of any of his crew, but he was settin me and Vee up for an execution just as pretty as a couple of shooting gallery ducks. Why in the hell else would he assign a pair like us to conduct security for an interplanetary drug cartel? I mean *really?*

"Sure thing, Haley. You know we got your back."

I smiled. Haley didn't.

It was about 20 minutes later when the locals rolled up, and I must say they knew how to play it smart. No big fancy cars, no poundin music, none of that. No flash at all. Just three plain cars that pulled up quiet one behind the other. Seeing as how we weren't exactly holding this meeting on the bad side of the tracks, I figure they knew any of the wrong sort of attention was likely to get reported in a hurry. And unlike what happens on the wrong side of the tracks - Planet 10 same as Earth - the law actually answers the phone in neighborhoods like this.

But once they all stepped out of the cars - and there were more than a few of them - anybody who took more than a second or third look would have figured fairly quick that these guys did not just happen to be in the neighborhood, and they weren't here to mow anybody's lawn. The guy who everybody else was following looked like a beefed-up fire hydrant with legs. He wore wraparound shades and had a long, ugly purple half-moon scar carved into the side of his left cheek. He walked slow and easy, like someone who knew he didn't have to rush to anywhere he was going because all clocks wherever he went were set to his schedule.

I knew the type.

His posse, or whatever, followed about two steps behind, I'm guessing in rough order of rank. Nobody else was wearing shades, so I guess Fire Hydrant Guy was the only one with sensitive eyes. He walked straight over to Haley. Nodded.

"Rodeo."

"Haley."

"Good to meet you Haley. My apologies for the delay. We had a little problem we had to get squared away. Held us up."

"Nothin too serious I hope."

"Nothin we couldn't handle. And nothin for you or us to worry about. It's all good. So I got the word from Valdez you guys were maybe needing some sort of cover or protection for a minute while you get your thing set up? That right?"

"Yup. I'm thinkin a month. Maybe two…? Ronnie? One or two?"

"Two probably. Just to be safe. 'Til we get the feel of things a little better."

"This your nephew?"

"Yeah."

"Been hearin good things about you, nephew. Been hearin good things about alla y'all. Valdez is my guy and we go way back. Damned near to crib days and all like that. So if he put in the word for you then I don't need to run no more checks. Just need to get the details of our arrangement settled so we can move ahead on this thing.

"Sounds like a plan," said Haley.

****

Where the meeting took place was at a spot located near the midpoint of the western side of the park bordering Albion. Parked on that same street, about 50 yards away near the intersection of Albion and 1st, was a beat-up red car that had pulled into that spot several minutes after Rodeo and his crew rolled in. The driver of the car made sure to park behind a much larger vehicle which partially hid him from view, or at least made him less likely to draw attention. Besides, from what Detective Bobby Soames ('Soamy to his friends on the squad) knew about Rodeo, he wasn't likely to be carrying out any major business today that could possibly draw the wrong sort of attention. Rodeo hadn't gotten to where he was at the top of the Slime of the Earth food chain by being stupid; he'd been in the game practically since he took his first steps and his father, "Big Rodeo", started showing little junior the ropes. Soamy had taken a strong interest in the Rodeo family business ever since Junior took over operatons from Pops nearly a decade ago. Primarily because it was Soamy who had put Big Rodeo away for life. For him, to lock down the son would be a sort of closure to what for him had been an obsession to the point where it sometimes got raised eyebrows at work and caused the occasional friction at home - and not the good sexual kind. But the tension at home rarely lasted too long because Soamy's wife of 15 years knew what she was getting into when she'd married a cop, and when that cop's father was murdered by Big Rodeo (never proven) two years later she knew it was something that would haunt their entire family for the rest of their lives.

And so Soames sat patiently in the car, cop-issue magnifying lenses inserted into his otherwise normal-looking eyeglasses, staring at the activity taking place in the park. All of Rodeo's people he recognized, and they would have recognized him with a quickness if he had chosen to make his presence known. But instead he just sat there, letting everything unfold, confident that sooner or later what was wrong with this picture would become clear. He watched as Rodeo extended his hand to Haley, but although he didn't know who Haley was - yet - he was far more interested in the character in the trenchcoat standing several steps back and to the left looking noticeably uncomfortable and out of place.

"Now what in the hell would a critter be doing in the middle of all this…?"

****

Two days later I'm sittin in a small booth in a cheap diner on Colfax Avenue waitin for the Gerruh to show up. I decided to bring Vee with me this time, even though I was certain the Gerruh wouldn't be too appreciative of the extra company. Frankly I didn't care whether they appreciated it or not. Me and Vee were connected in this thing, and I needed her backup dealing with these guys. It was never a good idea to deal with a couple as dangerous as the Gerruh all on your own, not if you could help it.

"So this is their version of crocka?" Vee was askin, her face all twisted up in disgust as she held a cup of coffee in front of her lips.

"You don't like?"

"*Vid.* This stuff is *horrible.*"

I shrugged my shoulders.

"Yeah, well. Just remember that what they call coffee isn't their version of crocka, it's the other way around. What we call crocka is our version of coffee. We came later, remember?"

"Really? You'd never know it by drinking this sewage. If they're supposed to be so superior, you'd think they would at least have mastered how to concoct a superior warm beverage wouldn't you?"

I shrugged my shoulders again.

"I gave up tryin to figure out the humans long ago, Vee. It's done miracles for my peace of mind."

Vee rolled her eyes before forcing herself to take another sip.

"So if you don't like the stuff then why in the..?"

"Am I drinking it? Fair question. Because I have a highly addictive personality, dear. Which means even though this stuff tastes like week-old dishwater, it's still close enough to satisfy the craving, hey?"

"Really?"

"No. But like I said, I have an addictive personality. It's what our kind does. We punish ourselves."

"That really is a shame, doll."

"Yeah, well."

I started to offer some more consolation when Vee's eyes grew noticeably wider. She was the one facing the door, so it was easy enough to guess what had prompted the change in demeanor. And I really should have been the one facing the door.

"They're here?"

Vee nodded, taking a deep, quick breath to pull herself together. Not much rattled Vee, but the Gerruh could make a shark whimper. I turned around and caught their attention. Motioned them over. They both gave a disapproving look at Vee, then looked around the room before making their move to join us. Once at the table they asked me to sit on the same side of the table as Vee. Talk about separation anxiety.

"Fine," I said.

"Our understanding was that our dealings would be with you and you alone. I don't recall us approving the addition of another member to our arrangement."

"Yeah. And I don't recall being told I needed your approval. For anything. Vee and I have been in this thing since the beginning, something which the two of you already know. And you know she's good at what she does. If we're gonna make this work then we're gonna need her to be a part of it. It's that simple."

"Nothing is ever that simple, I'm afraid."

Maybe it was the stress of being caught between a drug-dealing psychopath and a pair of ice-cold enforcers that made me just not care about the danger they posed to my general well-being. Because it certainly wasn't that the Gerruh were any less dangerous today than they were the day I bumped into them on my walk, or when I saw them on the runway back on Planet 10, signaling that they weren't through with me yet.

I leaned forward.

"Sure it is."

I felt Vee kick me hard under the table, letting me know she thought I might be losing my grip. But I didn't blink for nearly the entire minute when none of us was sayin a word. I knew it wasn't so much that I had included Vee that was causing the friction, but that I hadn't asked permission. And I also knew that if I started asking permission, down on my knees like some kind of street corner beggar, then I'd never be off those knees again. I had to let them know I knew.

"So what can you tell us?" they said in unison.

Mission accomplished.

I wasn't stupid enough to tell them everything I knew because if I did then there wasn't much reason to keep either me or Vee around. We were only as valuable as our information, and whoever had hired the Gerruh to come after us (I still didn't know for sure who was behind this thing, although I had some good ideas) weren't much interested in what happened to us once they had what they wanted. So I told them a few things about Haley, that some initial contacts had been made here in Denver but that I wasn't close enough to Haley or Ronnie to get too many more details, which wasn't far from the truth. Once I was done neither one of them said anything for awhile, just staring at me hard with those dead black eyes. Finally the one on the left cleared his throat, then reached across the table to put his rather large, cold hand on top of mine. He squeezed, and I grimaced. The guy definitely wasn't weak.

"The next time we meet? Whatever it is you have decided to withhold you will withhold no longer, is that understood? You and your companion came all the way to Earth from Planet 10, where you both were doing fairly well in your respective careers, to spend time with the likes of Deep Cluck, Haley, and a group of mutant chickens? A celebrated page scratcher and a detective? No detective work is required to sense that something is slightly out of place here, wouldn't you agree?"

He squeezed tighter, and I grunted. This had just crossed the line from discomfort to rather intense pain.

"Yeah, sure. I would agree."

He released my hand slowly, then the two of them pushed away from the table.

"I'm glad. Until the next time. And please keep in mind that we already know why you are here. We just need the details. Inside information, as we explained in our previous meeting. We need to know why MayoMadd, why now, and why *here.*"

"Wait a minute. You mean you already know about...?"

"We're very good at what we do. The next time we meet please do not disappoint us. That would not be pleasant for anyone involved."

"Yeah. I'm sure."

Once they were gone, Vee and I didn't say anything for a few moments. Didn't need to.

"How's your hand?" she asked finally.

I shrugged.

"Not bad I guess. Guy's got a grip could crush a rock though. Wasn't expecting that."

"Don't think either one of us were expecting a lot of things we've had to deal with recently."

"Oh you do have that right, sweet Vee."

She smiled, then reached over and caressed my hand.

"What are we gonna do, Mister Vid? Seems like the Gerruh have us in a bit of a vice."

"Yeah well. What something seems like and what it is ain't always one and the same, you know?"

"Plan?"

"Workin on it."

"Yeah well, you better…"

"Work fast? Yeah. I know. And it's percolatin, trust me. For instance, I'm thinkin this could turn out to be the one chance we've been lookin for if we play it right. I haven't got it all worked out in my head just yet, but the general idea is we use the Gerruh just like they're tryin to use us. We make them a part of our plan when they think we're a part of theirs."

Vee raised an eyebrow.

"And how does that work?"

"What is it that Gerruh said before they left? *I'm very good at what I do.*"

Chapter 16

From all indications during those first few weeks, it looked like the MayoMadd operation was running pretty smooth. Haley and Ronnie were both relaxed and smiling a lot, and Deep Cluck and Butch both were obviously taking a lotta joy out of watching more and more kids getting hooked on the stuff. For them, I'm sure nothing tasted as good as revenge, and it was a taste that was just as addictive to them as MayoMadd was to their client/victims. The more doped up kids they saw, the more they wanted to see. I admit I didn't have much love for Earth kids, or grownups either for that matter. The way they all looked at us critters like we were somethin stuck to the bottom of their shoes made it kinda hard to feel anything remotely resembling compassion. But even with all that ugly history I didn't think they deserved the storm that was comin, and neither did Vee.

But for now, as Vee and I drove around the city with Haley and Ronnnie checking out the five primary distribution sites, there wasn't a whole lot we could do about it. We had to bide our time. And we had to become really good at acting.

"Hey, check it out!" said Ronnie, pointin out the van window at three kids bouncing around doing frantic handstands and somersaults in the middle of the street, not even seeming to notice the cars swerving and honking. It was eerie.

"Looks like a few of our happy-assed customers!" said Haley, as he took one of his hands off the wheel so he and his nephew could slap palms.

"Wow. That's great, huh? Yeah, nothin like success…"

Haley shot me a quick glance through the rear view and I knew he had picked up something in my voice.

"What?"

Haley grinned, and I had to wonder which one of us was better at acting.

****

Soames was tailing three cars back, not too close but just close enough. When he passed by the park bench he shook his head and muttered angrily to himself. He was well-acquainted with junkies, which meant he was equally well-acquainted with whatever substances happened to be launching them into a fool's paradise at any particular time and how it made them react. Most of the drugs stayed the same, but every so often a new strain would show up, usually just a stronger (or weaker) version of whatever was already out there. Sometimes it turned out to be a combination cocktail mix, and those were the bombs that usually lit up the streets for a good long while. And then, very rarely, there would come along something altogether new. And that's when things got scary.

Whatever had a hold on these kids was something else altogether. He made a quick call to headquarters to get the situation handled while he kept following the crew. He could not afford to lose them.

Soames had been around the block more times than most, and he recognized a threat when he saw one. His gut told him this was worse than just a threat. This was a promise, and if this promise was kept then God only knew what was in store…

****

When we reached the final distribution spot, which was a broken down apartment building not too far from downtown, Haley decided he wanted to take a look up close and personal, which meant parking the van and going inside. The two pitbull-lookin guys at the front door gave Ronnie and Haley a brief look then motioned all of us through the door. Me and Vee got the most oddball glances, I think because we were critters, but other than that it didn't seem like anybody was paying us that much attention. From what I could see pretty much everyone was involved with the selling, which made me wonder where the customers were located. The only ones out front were the security, and when we drove up from the back side I didn't see much activity back there either. I decided to ask Ronnie, who told me they were all stashed in another building down the street 'for appearances'.

"Appearances..?"

"Yeah. As in it doesn't look real good having a line of junkies down the block waiting for product, you know? Kinda draws attention. Better not to even have them near."

"What are the guys doin out on the street that you got to have your customers makin housecalls?"

Ronnie shook his head.

"We still got the street runners. That's why we made that run to meet up with Valdez. But this keeps things close and keeps our costs down on personnel. Plus, long as these kids keep seekin us out as hard as they are, no need for us to run all over the place, you know?"

"But doesn't this make for a great big target for the cops? I mean sooner or later word's bound to get out what this is all about, right?"

Ronnie grinned.

"But we're not doing anything illegal. At least not yet. Ain't no laws on the books sayin a man can't make a profit selling hopped up mayonnaise. Not on Earth there ain't."

"Holy…"

"*Right.*"

"But then you just said about appearances…"

"Just because it ain't illegal now don't mean it's gonna stay that way, which is why we wanna keep this thing contained for as long as we can. 'Cause soon as word gets out the whole games changes. Plus look at who we're workin with. Rodeo and his gang for protection. Valdez' guys. The product may not be illegal yet but the network we're dealing with is somethin else again, and that right there is enough to draw the kind of attention we don't need."

And then, as if on cue, there was a sudden explosion of shoutin and thumpin comin from somewhere upstairs. All of us looked up at the ceiling at the same time.

"Aw shit, not *again,*" I heard somebody say.

"What the hell you mean *again?*" said Haley, his eyes darting around to see who had just spoken up. It was a teenage kid looked to be about 16 wearing a Broncos baseball cap and an orange T shirt and sweatpants. Skinny as a rail.

"Man, these new guys from outta town they don't mix real good with the local crew. Not sure what the beef is all about, but this keeps up somethin bad's gonna happen. Folks need to be together on this thing, you know? Just sayin."

Haley grunted.

"Yeah. Just sayin."

"What you thinkin' uncle?"

"I'm thinkin we better get our asses upstairs and see what the hell this is about and squash it before it winds up puttin a squeeze on the business. Confusion is never good for business."

"I'd say that's true. OK let's go."

Me and Vee followed along behind as Ronnie and Haley started jumpin up the steps two at a time. Once we got upstairs it was clear we might have gotten there just in time. One of Ronnie's guys - I recognized him as one of the first we had rounded up when I was on the ride-along - had one of the locals in a tight headlock and was rammin his knee up into the guy's face repeatedly, quick and hard, and he was smilin like this was some sort of entertainment. When he looked up from his activities and saw Haley and Ronnie headed his way he smiled wider and nodded.

"Hey what's up? Just tryin to straighten this fool out 'cause he think..."

That was when Haley swung a pole upside his head which, not too surprisingly, made him loosen his vice grip around the other guy's neck. I didn't even know Haley had a pole. Anyway the guy in the headlock slumped to the floor like a bag of clothes. But what *was* surprising is that the guy Haley clocked with the pole just rubbed the back of his head as if Haley had swung on him with a loaf of bread.

"Dude, you didn't even let me tell you what this was about, right?"

Haley took a step back, I'm guessing caught off guard that this guy was still standing, let alone carrying on a conversation. But Ronnie didn't look all that surprised as he squeezed his uncle's shoulder.

"I got this," he said.

"But how in the hell…"

"He's different that way. No way you coulda known."

"Yeah. No shit nephew."

"So you're Clay, right?" asked Ronnie, takin a wary step closer toward the guy, who was still rubbing his head and looked to be growing angrier on slow boil.

"Hey man, *he didn't even let me tell my side.*"

"OK, so I'm askin now all right? What's your side in all this? Talk."

The guy glared at Haley a few more moments, and I was sensing this wasn't the best possible situation as a crowd was starting to gather around us - and we were the ones outnumbered.

"Talk *quick,*" said Ronnie who was noticing the same development.

Turns out the whole thing had somethin to do with some chick who the local guy said was his but who Clay said came onto him which was why he acted naturally and took her in some back room to take care of some business. Local guy walked in on it and freaked out. Girl suddenly starts screamin that she was forced into it. Also turns out this wasn't the first time one of Valdez' recruits helped himself to the local scenery.

I looked over at Vee, who was smirkin and gave me a wink. Then she shifted her attention to Clay and the local guy, who was still lying in a heap on the floor.

"Looks like you boys follow the same head no matter where you're from, hey? Critter or natural born. Such a shame, really."

You could feel the tension start to ease out of the room like air whistling slowly out of a balloon. The tart in question, who was standing up against the wall not too far away with her arms folded across a rather healthy chest, smiled in appreciation. Nodded. Vee nodded back.

I'll say it again, *the girl is good.* Even Haley and Ronnie looked relieved.

"I got no say so over the locals," said Haley. "But so help me if I have to walk in on anything like this ever again with one of ours? You don't wanna know."

Clay frowned.

"Hey, but what if it wasn't our fault, man? I mean like…"

"Apparently I didn't make myself clear enough. You clowns are here to work. For us. That means nothin gets in the way of that work 'cause that's what you're gettin paid to do. Something finds a way to get between you and that work? You find a way to get rid of it, and I mean without makin a mess. I don't care where you lubricate your joint, hear? Not my concern. But the minute your joint lubricatin activities starts to cost me money…?"

This time it was Clay's turn to take a step back.

"Yeah, OK. I understand."

"I knew that you would."

****

The Gerruh, both of them sittin across from us with their hands folded neatly on top of the table, were smilin. The sun was shinin bright and hard outside the diner, but I felt cold all inside.

"Well now. This does appear to be a happier occasion than last we met, am I right?" said the Gerruh on the right.

"Hope so," I said.

He smiled a little wider, exposing a few of his serrated choppers. I felt colder still.

"The last time we were here I said that we needed better intel. From what you've told me so far, it sounds like you did get the message. Makes our job much easier when folks get the message the first time, and for that we are both very appreciative."

"Yeah well. Makin the two of you appreciative and whatnot is what makes our day. Really does."

"Hmm. Yes. Well. So then to review; what you're telling us is that there may be some trouble in paradise, is that right?"

"Not quite sure you would want to define that as paradise exactly," said Vee.

"I'm sure. But the point remains the same, correct? This team that has been put together does not appear to be functioning as one big happy family. Some cracks in the surface. And you have attached some names to a few of those cracks, which is helpful indeed. Our employer will be quite pleased."

"Good for him. Her. Whoever. So how long do we have to keep this up, guys? You know eventually we both would like to get back home. Clear our names. Get back to our lives before all this."

"We sympathize," said the other Gerruh. "Truly we do. However I am sure you understand that what you are currently caught up in - involuntarily we know - is something quite big that could pose a threat not only to certain interests that our employer maintains here on the Mother Planet but also back on Planet 10. Madame Vee, if anyone is familiar with what that threat could be, I believe that person would be you."

"I'm not sure what you mean…"

"Oh we think that you are," the two said in unison.

Vee didn't look helpless often, but the look she gave me just then was, well, *helpless*. She had no idea how they had managed to dig up that part of her background dating back to her MayoMadd days, and neither did I. Then again, if anybody could dig up useful dirt on somebody - before planting them in that dirt - it would be the Gerruh.

"I believe your memory is coming back to you, is that correct? Bits and pieces of those early days when you had to leave daddy behind for … certain reasons..?"

Vee's mouth was gaping like a fish out of water, which was pretty much how I felt right then. After a few hoarse attempts she tried to speak, but the Gerruh on the left put one long, bone-white finger to his lips while wagging another in silent warning.

"*Shhhhhh.*"

Vee could only nod.

"By now you should know we're not here to hurt you. Not yet anyway. We just need information, and you two are the only ones who can provide us with that information, so you will have to do. So keep up the good work! And once we get what we need and our employers are satisfied, then I guess we'll just see what happens next, won't we?"

"Say what do you need all this intel for anyway?" I asked. "I mean, if you already know what it's about, and with the resources I'm guessing you have, can't you just shut it down whenever you feel like? Why do you have to wait 'til we report back with this info?"

"Who says we want to shut it down?" said Gerruh on the left.

"But wait, you just said it poses a threat to…"

"Then again, who says we don't?" said the other.

"Oh. So it's like that."

"Keeps life interesting don't you think?"

"Yours maybe. Me? I can do without that kinda interesting."

"Indeed."

Chapter 17

So as it turns out that kid named Clay never did quite absorb the message Haley was trying to impart, or at least not in the way that Haley was expecting that he would. A few weeks after Clay roughed up that local for getting mad when Clay couldn't stop jumping his girlfriend's bones, the kid was at it again, only this time with some overanxious customer who had developed a rather serious addiction for the MayoMadd. Every time he saw Clay he would run up to him beggin him for a free sample that he kept swearin wasn't for him but for some anonymous customer he was tryin to get hooked on Clay's behalf - so that Clay could give him more free samples.

Knowing that he was already treading water - deep water - because of his last screwup, Clay kept his temper on a leash for at least a week which, from what I was hearin, had to be some kinda record for the kid. But Clay wasn't getting any gold medals for new records and this client apparently got on his nerves to the point where he just beat the guy down in broad daylight in the middle of the street something brutal, then left him there for some poor traumatized neighborhood girl to come drag away before he got run over.

Of course, our luck being what it was, this particular local happened to be related to who else but Rodeo, the same local who was being paid to provide Haley's operation with protection. I don't know how we were supposed to know that Rodeo's cousin was a MayoMadd junkie, but that didn't change the fact that Clay's beatdown of this particular junkie was bound to have some blowback that none of us needed. The unneeded attention we were bound to get from the police and Rodeo's reaction were the two most obvious

296

parts, but there was also the impact this could have on the business, because this kinda violence this soon could easily scare off the customers, not to mention make the neighborhood folk more willing to look the other way instead of looking out for the operation whenever trouble showed up.

And I can't believe I'm sittin here analyzin the risks to a MayoMadd drug operation like I got a stake in this thing somehow. I really have been around this operation way too damned long.

****

It wasn't the first time Soames had encountered witnesses too scared to talk about what they'd seen. Matter of fact it was way more common in a neighborhood like this to run into the wall of silence than it was in an area like Sundial Park where cops were considered friends and hardly anybody ever had to worry about anyone like Rodeo or his crew stomping a member of their family into the ground.

Still, Soames would never have made detective if he didn't know how to grow contacts, the kind who came through when he needed them. So when he knocked on the door of Harrietta Forster, the young girl who had witnessed Clay beating up that junkie in the middle of the street and who had (against all common sense) felt compelled to drag the man to safety, it was the girl's mother who answered. The look of sheer terror in her large brown eyes as she looked past Soames up and down the street let Soames know that the odds of him getting much information at all weren't good, but he still had to try.

"Mrs. Forster? I'm..."

"Who told you about this? *Who told YOU?"*

"M'am, I can understand why you might be..."

"She's 16 years old, Detective Soames. *She's just 16 years old!* Still don't have enough sense not to know when to leave things alone. She's still got a good heart, even in a neighborhood like this, and that's what's gonna get her killed if YOU don't get us both killed first by showing up here like this. Do you have any idea the danger you're putting us in?"

"M'am the only way I..."

"Listen, I've heard good things about you and that's fine. But you ain't superman, and you just can't...I'm sorry. You gotta go."

And with that she slammed the door. Hard.

"Shit."

****

"So I don't guess I have to tell you guys this puts kind of a wrinkle in our arrangement, right? I'm assuming we can just move on past that part to where we discuss what it is you plan to do to make this thing right."

First of all, this had to be the first time I ever heard a gangster like Rodeo use a word like 'wrinkle' in that context. Almost sounded dainty, which was definitely without a doubt a serious contrast to how the boy looked. A lot of words came to mind when you saw someone like Rodeo, but 'dainty' would not be on that list. Which is why I had to work hard to keep myself from laughin out loud as I leaned back against the trunk of a tall tree behind Haley and Ronnie, who were seated at that same concrete bench across from Rodeo and a couple of his top guys in Sundial Park where we first met not that long ago. Haley, being the pro-active sort, had called the meeting -after chewing out Ronnie for not doing a better job of vetting Valdez's picks - so that everything could get smoothed out ASAP. Haley didn't give a damn about the beatup cousin, but how it affected his business was a major concern.

"Yeah, sure. Look, we're all professionals here, right?"

"That's what I was told."

Haley bit his lip, then tried to laugh it off.

"Right. That's funny. OK look, I wouldn't have reached out to you soon as I did if I didn't want this thing handled and handled right. Obviously this isn't the way we like to make an entrance. Causes problems for everybody and I realize that. But you should also realize that you're not completely off the hook on this thing."

"Oh?"

"Your cousin. What was his name?"

"We called him Sally."

"Really?"

Rodeo's face tightened up, and now I really had to work to keep from laughing.

"Interesting. OK, Sally. That's fine. The point here is that your cousin *Sally* was an addict and somewhat of a pain in the ass is what I'm told. A simple heads-up might have gone a long way toward preventing this whole thing."

"Heads-up about him being an addict or heads-up about him being an asshole?"

Haley grinned.

"Not much either one of us can do about him being an asshole, right? But if we'd known to look out for him as being one of yours, protected so to speak, then I can tell you for sure he never woulda been touched. And from this point forward I'm tellin you nothing like this will ever happen again. Not with one of yours, and not with *any* of the customers. What's bad for business is bad for all of us, agreed?"

After awhile Rodeo nodded, extended his hand.

"Agreed."

"Oh, and by the way?"

Rodeo raised an eyebrow, wondering what could be coming next.

"Does the name 'Soames' mean anything to you? As in Detective Bobby Soames from the Denver Police Department?"

Rodeo's eyes caught fire as his grip tightened around Haley's hand. But Haley just grinned.

"Easy, chief. Easy. We're on the same side in this thing, remember? Just a little heads-up from one of my people that he was doing some nosing around the neighborhood the other day asking questions about that beatdown. He didn't get nothin though. Looks like you got your duckies in line. Still, might wanna keep an eye on him, right?"

Rodeo leaned back, slowly regaining his composure.

"I shoulda killed that bastard years ago."

"Hmmm..."

****

It wasn't more than 10 minutes later when we were at a filling station, stocking up as much on junk food as we were on gas. Seeing a copy of the local paper near the checkout counter, Vee decided to grab herself a copy. Being a page scratcher I guess it was automatic for her to pick up a paper wherever she saw one, see how someone else was covering the news. While I was payin for a couple candy bars and some other health food she opened up her purchase and started half-whisperin under her breath as she scanned over the articles.

"Well?" I asked. "Anything interesting?"

She shook her head.

"Not really. Either it's a slow news day or this is just a pretty boring little...*whoa...*"

"Whoa? Whaddya mean *whoa?*"

"I mean take a look at this. Right here. Top left. That guy took one heck of a hit from the linebacker, hey? I mean look at him, Vid, *look at him.*"

When you know someone as well as Vee and I knew each other, you can send signals and decrypt signals back and forth without even havin to give the other fair warning. Somethin about the pitch of the voice, or a shift in body language lets the other know that what just got said wasn't really what just got said at all.

"Didn't know you were a big football fan," I said, while lookin over to where her finger was pointing. "Let me take a look at ..."

"Really somethin, hey?"

Yes. It was. Because back there on page 8, near the middle of the page, was a small story about some kid who was beaten to a pulp in one of Denver's tougher neighborhoods and then actually left out in the middle of the street.

"If my daughter hadn't dragged him back to the curb he would have gotten run over. Can you imagine that?" someone named Marjorie Forster was quoted as saying, who happened to be the mother of 16-year-old Harrietta Forster, the kid who dragged Rodeo's drug addict pain-in-the-ass cousin to safety.

" 'That's what this neighborhood is coming to now, and I just want to know when somebody is going to do something about it. How do you think this is going to affect my daughter now, huh? You think she hasn't seen enough out here already? And now there's this new stuff they got out here that's got all these kids just crazy. They say it's better than anything else. Mayo something I think it's called. I don't really know and don't want to know. And don't want my daughter to know. I just try to keep to myself and protect my kids, but sometimes a mother can't even do that, you know?' "

"Police Chief Hanson agrees. 'Things have always been tough in that part of town and we've always done our best to keep it safe. Perhaps we need to do more. But it's true that activity seems to have picked up noticeably and we're going to find out why. It's our job to protect all of our citizens, not just some of them. As for this new drug, this Mayo-whatever, I don't really have any comment on that at this time until we get more information. To be honest I'm not even sure it's anything new at all. Not to accuse anyone of not telling the truth, just saying it's our job to sort out the facts and get to the bottom of what's really going on. We've had these scares before where folks thought a new dangerous drug had hit the streets when it was just a tweak on an old formula, so it pays to be careful before jumping to conclusions."

Oh this wasn't good. No, this wasn't good at *all*.

****

What Vee did next she didn't tell me for nearly a month, but I can understand why she did it. I didn't at first, you can be sure of that, but then, when I thought about it, it made all the sense in the world.

Vee had always been a daddy's girl, plus she was the only child. Even though she had pretty much lost all direct contact with her folks ever since the day she had to leave Very Very sector for the part she played in using her dad's discovery to create MayoMadd and liberate the local youngsters from a life of enforced silence imposed by a sick society of adults who believed kids should be seen and not heard (*phew*), she was still able to reach out to him when she needed him through some kind of back channel hookup the old man had devised. I had no idea such a hookup -whatever it was - could function on Earth too, but apparently so. The man hadn't been known as one of the smartest scientists on the planet for nothing.

Anyway, Vee, like most daddy's girls, knows there's only one place to turn when things get a bit too hairy and you need some advice on how to unravel it all. After first explaining to him what she was doing on Earth in the first place, and convincing him not to believe whatever it was he might have been told about why she had left her job as one of the most respected page scratchers in Vivacious 5 sector - and actually all of Planet 10 - he gave her some advice that I'm pretty sure came as more of a surprise to her when she first heard it than it was to me when she passed it along.

"He told me to reach out to a couple of my friends on the Daily Screamer. The ones I was sure I could trust."

"Come again?"

At the time she was breaking the news to me we were sitting in that same coffee shop where we'd been meeting the Gerruh.

"OK, I know it sounds kinda crazy but…"

"Good. At least you do know that."

"You need to listen to me, Vid."

Something about the tone in her voice set me back a bit. I nodded.

"Yeah. OK. I'm listening. But first let me ask you just one question?"

She sighed.

"OK never mind," I said, knowing what the whole female sighing routine usually meant.

"No, go ahead. Ask. Let's get this out of the way."

"Fine. So how do you know that these journalist friends of yours on the Screamer who you used to know you can trust are friends you can still trust? I mean, a whole lot of time has passed since we bolted the planet and this whole time they haven't heard not one word from you, Vee. Which means more time for anybody else to be dropping them poison pills telling them anything they want about why you really disappeared, and how do they know what to believe?"

"Because they're page scratchers, Vid. They're professionals. Questioning everything they hear is part of who they are. It's how they're wired, hey? It's how *I'm* wired, all right?"

"Exactly. So then why wouldn't they question *you?*"

"Because they're also my friends, Vid. And I trust them. And I'm sure they trust me."

"*Were* your friends, Vee. You may have been able to trust them before, but how do you know whether that trust still makes sense?"

"You and I are friends, right Vid?"

"What...? Of course we're...what are you..."

"And we trust each other, right? Always have?"

"Vee you know..."

"Good. So if you didn't see me for three months, and you weren't sure where I'd disappeared to, and then some folks who you don't even know, or don't know as well as you do me, come up to you and start telling you I left to become a hooker in some far away place, are you telling me you'd believe them? Just because you hadn't seen or heard from me in awhile?"

I really hated it when she used her brain like that. It just wasn't fair. Not fair at all.

"No, Vee. If somebody told me you'd decided to sell your body for cash then I probably wouldn't believe them."

"*Probably?*"

"Well, I mean, look at you doll, right? It's not like you don't have the goods."

I grinned because I just couldn't help myself sometimes. Vee just shook her head.

"There really isn't any hope for you, Vid. You know that right?"

"Please proceed."

"Look, you and I both know we have to do *something* about all this that's going on. We just can't...we just can't *sit here* doing *nothing*. I know we got kinda trapped into coming along on this ride, but Vid! What these guys are doing, hey? I'm not a big fan of these little Earthling purebreds any more than any critter, but getting their kids hooked on

MayoMadd just because of what happened to some steroid chicken freaks years ago? It shouldn't have happened and they have a right to be pissed off, but not this. Not this..."

"Vee, sweetheart, why you gettin all worked up with me? You're preachin to the choir here. I know what's wrong when I see it, believe me, and this is all kinds of wrong. But you also got to remember what kinda position we're stuck in here. I mean with the Gerruh. We got Haley and his crew all suspicious of us on one side, and then the Gerruh pushin us from the other side sayin we have to feed them info on the operation from the inside *or else.* And anybody who knows anything about the Gerruh knows what that *or else* means with them."

Vee leaned forward across the table and squeezed my wrist. She was givin me one of those intense looks I hadn't seen in quite awhile.

"So then let me tell you my plan."

"I thought you just said it was to contact your trustworthy friends at the paper."

"And then what?"

"That's what I wanted to know, Vee. Because I'm still not seeing what they can do for us, even if they're still your fans. We're on Earth. They're all the way back on Planet 10."

"Yeah, they're all the way back on Planet 10, but you know my paper gets read by a lot of folks right here on Earth. Plus ...."

"Wait a minute. Are you talking about..."

"You just may be catchin on, Vid. Yes. I'm saying I give them the story about the whole operation as seen from the two of us who have been on the inside for all this time. This would be the biggest story the Screamer's ever seen, and you don't have to be all that smart of a page scratcher to figure that one out."

"But what about the Gerruh? How are they gonna react when they see a story in Planet 10's biggest paper spilling the guts on everything that was supposed to go to them?"

"We put them in the story."

"Say *what?*"

"Think about it Vid. It's the best way to cut their little hitman nuts off.."

"Whoa! When did you start talkin like…"

"I'm sorry, was that over the top?"

"More like too far down."

"Point taken. Anyway, here's what I'm saying; by putting the Gerruh in the story and saying they're the ones on the trail of what's going on here, that puts them in a really tight spot, right? Because even though everybody knows about the Gerruh and what they do, which is why everybody's so scared of them, part of the reason why everybody's so scared is that nobody even speaks about them out loud hardly ever. It's like that movie where those kids say the name in a mirror three times and then the boogieman shows up and chops their heads off."

"That's not quite how the movie went, but point taken."

"It's been awhile since I've seen the movie, OK?"

"Go on with what you were sayin."

"I'm saying once that story comes out and people see where we're working undercover with the Gerruh to bring down this interplanetary drug ring, we're protected. Kinda."

"Yeah, well it's the 'kinda' that's got me worried, right? Because we're *not* workin undercover with the Gerruh."

"Doesn't matter. Once it's in the paper it's the truth. That's the way it works. And once it becomes the truth then the lid is blown on this whole thing, which means we become heroes, the Gerruh have to leave us alone, and we can go back home where everybody will love and adore us. Forever and ever."

"You've been dippin into that MayoMadd haven't you?"

Chapter 18

Several days later the two of us were back in that same diner with the Gerruh starin at us across the table, hands folded all polite, grinnin like a couple of sharks about to tell a joke. And the joke's on you.

"So we got your message. I'm assuming this means you have something for us? Something a little more substantial than before? Because this is why we're smiling."

I raised an eyebrow.

"You're smiling? Wow."

Vee kicked me under the table. Hard enough that I had to muster up all my manliness not to let a tear slide down my face and into my coffee. Crocka was better, by the way. *A lot* better.

"Yes," said Vee, soundin all perky. "Yes we do."

Both Gerruhs unfolded their hands, turning them palms up. Chalk white on both sides, which still freaked me out. They tilted their heads to the left at the same time, grins a little wider.

"By all means," they said.

"We've decided to tell you everything. Top to bottom."

"Really? And what might be the reason for that? Did you suddenly discover how everything worked overnight after only getting glimpses before? And then you decided to rush rush rush and tell us all about it? Is that what happened?"

"You're both still smilin, so I'm guessing this is humor, right? And don't kick me any more Vee. It hurts."

Instead, she reached over, grabbed my wrist, and squeezed gently. Her smile didn't crack and she never took her eyes off the Gerruh. Which was good because they looked like they hadn't been fed in awhile.

"Fair enough question, I suppose."

"I thought so."

"And here's your answer; what's in the past doesn't matter. You boys wanted information about the operation because that's what your employers sent you here to get. We're the ones that have that information. So I'm proposing a deal."

"Is that so? We don't normally make deals, as I'm sure you're well aware."

"Yes. And I'm sure you're both well aware these are not normal circumstances, meaning if we all did what we normally do then we all lose. I'm assuming your employers want this info about the operation because they want it shut down, is that right?"

"Whatever communication that transpires between us and our employer…"

"Is off limits. I figured as much. Nevertheless I'm going to take a leap of faith here and assume that I am right. Because there would be no other reason for whoever it is employing the likes of you to get this information from us. That is, unless your employer is thinking about getting into the business himself…?"

Silence. The grins faded away.

"Phew! So I'll take that as a no. Which means we have a common interest, which is bringing an end to this entire MayoMadd operation. It's no good for Earth, and it's not good for Planet 10 either.."

The grins returned, wide enough to expose a few serrated teeth.

"You're proposing partnership. With us. Do you know…?"

"Yes I do. And we are not asking for any compensation or whatever else. Just that if we succeed in stopping this thing then we get our good names back. We can go back home."

The Gerruh looked at one another for a long moment, and I got the feeling they were somehow communicating without letting us in on the contents of that communication. When they returned their attention to us their black eyes were burning hot, but not like they were angry. To be honest I wasn't quite sure *what* it meant.

"We believe this particular situation may warrant an exception to our standard procedure. We are willing to make this deal, but only on what you might call a daily renewal basis."

"In other words, if you find out we're screwin up then the deal is dead and so are we," I said.

"I would say that is a fairly accurate portrayal of our position. So are we partners then? Let's shake on it!"

"Ummmm…let's not. Let's just agree to be partners and call this meeting to a close. Whaddya say?"

They both smiled. Kind of.

****

Several days later, after Vee and I had finished running some makework errands for Haley (because he still had too many suspicions to give us any real responsibility

311

anymore except to responsibly stay out of their way), Vee managed to contact her friends at the Screamer using the same device she used to reach out to her father. As I suspected, they had been hearing quite a few stories and were no longer sure of what to believe. Absence doesn't always make the heart grow fonder. Absence is just absence, and where there's an empty space you can rest assured somebody somewhere is figuring out a way to fill it.

Still, to Vee's credit, they were willing to hear her out. Once she was done explaining everything that had happened I could hear one voice say that they would call her back within an hour after they'd had a chance to talk some more about it, but then another voice cut in, high-pitched and kind of screechy, telling whoever had just finished speaking that to wait on a story like this was "crazy".

"Didn't you just hear what she said, man? Vee's life is in danger right now. *Right now.* The clock is ticking here folks, and not just on this story but on Vee herself."

"Well let's not get dramatic here, OK? Because I think…"

"Dramatic? *Dramatic?!!* Did you not hear the word 'Gerruh' ? Huh? Do you know what that means? And MayoMadd? And drug dealers? And those angry as hell mutant chickens looking for revenge? Man, I don't even think it's *possible* to overdramatize this situation! We need to move on this right *now.* We need to grab the editor and let him know what's…"

"Wait wait wait. I mean, I like a good story as well as anyone else, but we haven't even confirmed any of this yet. For all we know this may not be the whole story, or maybe it's been exaggerated. I'm just saying…"

"You were here when Vee was the biggest star on the Screamer, right? Just like that Bob Woodee…"

"Woodward."

"Right. Woodward. Just like that Bob Woodward purebred back on Earth. Well Vee was like that here before she left, and it hasn't been that long she's been gone, all right? Are you seriously saying we can't trust her now because she's in trouble? Really?"

"You know that's not what I'm saying! I've always trusted Vee's reporting and you know that better than anyone. But you and I both know that if Vee were in this same situation don't you think she would want to make sure everything was legit before we went to press with something this hot? Because all it takes is one wrong piece of information to blow all of us out of a job and destroy the Screamer's credibility. You know I'm right."

Vee was squirming and grimacing, which wasn't like her at all. This was really painful for her.

"OK listen guys, I'm sorry I bothered you with this. And you're right. If it had been me sitting where you are right now I'm sure I would have been just as professional as you're being right now. Unfortunately I don't know how to give you all the verification you're going to need in time for it to make any difference with what's going on down here, so maybe I should just…"

"Vee?"

'Yes."

"Stop yourself right there."

"No, really. I don't want to cause any…"

"I said *stop.*"

Vee put her face in her hands and slowly started to shake her head. I was glad none of those on the other end of the line could see her right now.

"OK this is what we're going to do. Or rather what *I'm* going to do. I can't speak for anyone else in the room so I'll just speak for myself and say that I'm going in to see Ven, the top editor, as soon as we hang up from this call and see what he thinks. Any of you who want to come with me are free to do so. But that's where I'm going because this can't wait. Will that work for you Vee?"

"Sure. That would be great," she said, sounding way more tired than she should.

"Good. And if we get the thumbs up from Ven then we're rolling. If not then, well, we'll just take it from there. I refuse to give up on this thing. But first let's start with Ven because,. Well, you know him, right Vee? Hasn't he always been pretty fair about things with you? I mean we all know he has his ways, but I'm saying just in general."

"Yeah. Ven's good. I never had any problem trusting his judgment."

"Sounds like a plan then. You'll be hearing from me real soon one way or the other."

"Thanks."

Soon as Vee hung up I had to ask "Who the hell was *that?* Geez, talk about your take-charge personality type. He just took the ball and ran with it."

Vee chuckled, which was a good sound to hear.

"That was Vord, and yeah he's always been like that. Sometimes it's a good thing, sometimes not so much. But in this instance I think it's going to be a good thing."

****

314

Sometimes a critter can speak too soon, and when Vee said Vord's take-charge take-no-prisoners personality was gonna be a good thing I thought she might be right at the time. After all, the guy pretty much single-handedly changed the entire direction of the conversation. If it hadn't been for him the two of us might have been left sitting out in the cold trying to figure out how to play our next hand with no cards. So the guy deserves his propers.

But three days later was already shaping up to be a less than joyful occasion when Vee got into a heated conversation with Ronnie over what she was supposed to be doing at the time. More and more, I was noticing whenever Haley wasn't around Ronnie would start stickin his chest out and just givin orders to be givin orders because he was Haley's nephew and he thought that gave him permission. Except it didn't. Even the other members of the crew who were on considerably better terms with Haley and Ronnie than the two of us had been were getting irritated with Ronnie's behavior. I heard Butch tell one of the other chickens he thought it was because he was tryin to look good in front of the Denver crew, actin like he had more power and say-so than he really had. But since nobody had the guts to bring it up with Haley directly then Ronnie just got worse.

So we're outside the main distribution site, a small group of folks standing scattered around and Ronnie is lightin into Vee tellin her she ought to be doin more of this and less of that and I'm about to step in when Vee gives me *the look* so I step back. Then Vee turns the tables and starts cuttin little Ronnie up like she's slicin a carrot, and she's smilin the whole time which only makes it worse because nothin hurts a man more than a woman cuttin him down to size with a smile. I saw Ronnie startin to step toward her which made me reconsider my willingness to let Vee fight her own battles when, at the worst possible time, her phone rings. Ronnie gets this strange look on his face and cocks his head to one side, while the bystanders all focus on Vee with a serious intensity because, well, who would be calling Vee here on Earth, right?

I was asking myself that same question, but then it came to me...

Oh. Shit.

The phone rang twice more and Vee is standing there semi-frozen trying to act like nothing at all unusual is going on when in fact if nothing unusual was going on she wouldn't look like the proverbial deer in the headlights.

The phone rang again.

"You gonna get that? I don't think it's for us."

"What? Oh...."

"Yeah. Oh."

Another ring.

"Hello...?"

"....."

"Uh huh. Well I'm not quite sure how you got this number but..."

"..."

"Oh right. I see. Well I guess then....listen, can you maybe call me back at another time? I'm kind of in the middle..."

"..."

"Oh. Sure. Well I guess that makes sense. OK then, I guess go ahead and read me what it says..."

Not quite a minute later Vee clicks off the phone, then looks around at all of us lookin at her. I could almost hear the gears rattling inside her head, practically catching fire, tryin to spin her way out of this one. I hated feelin this helpless, but there wasn't a damned thing I could do.

"So was that Mommie checking to make sure you were eating your vegetables?"

I guess now it was Ronnie's turn to smile as he started slicin. But then Vee smiled back, lookin way more confident than she had any logical right to be.

"I always eat my veggies, Ronnie. Bet you don't though. So no, it wasn't Mommie. It was a cable. Sent to my line."

"Really? A cable? Well since there's no need for anyone to cable you from anywhere on Earth, I'm guessing that cable probably was forwarded from Planet 10, would that be right?"

"Not that it's any of your business, Ronnie, but yes."

"As long as you're working for me and my uncle? Then you getting cables from Planet 10 would be my business, sweet. Believe that. Especially since nobody else from your crew seems to be getting these cables except you. I wonder why that is? Especially since I wasn't aware anyone on Planet 10 knew you were down here on Earth?"

"If you ever got a cable from Planet 10, Ronnie, then you would know that cables get forwarded to your phone. They don't track where the phone is unless there's a reason, like maybe if the keystones suspected I was running drugs or something terrible like that. But of course nobody thinks that so my cable just shows up wherever I happen to be and I answer it. Technology, hey?"

"So what did it say?"

"The cable? The one that was meant for me? None of your business I'm afraid."

"Didn't I just tell you..."

"You can tell me anything you like, Ronnie. And you can play grownup all you like. But that doesn't make it so."

For obvious reasons I thought Vee had pushed her luck too far, and so had some of the other bystanders who all took several steps back so as not to wind up collateral damage from whatever was likely about to happen. Except that it didn't happen. Instead, Ronnie just glared at Vee for a good long time, I guess evaluating the pluses and minuses in his head of what he wanted to do to Vee right at that moment, then said "Fuck it" and announced he would just take it up with his Uncle Haley. That wasn't necessarily a better option for us, except that it bought us a little bit of time to figure out what to do before all hell broke loose.

Later, when Vee and I had some time alone, she confirmed what I had already guessed, namely that the cable had come from the Screamer. The story was a go from the editor, which was fine except why in the hell they figured it made sense to reach out to Vee via cable knowing what we were involved in made no sense to me whatsoever.

****

That night when Haley finally showed up from wherever he had been - Ronnie was usually the only one to know what Haley was up to - Ronnie made a big production out of what had happened, making it sound like she had gotten a personal phone call from the President or somethin crazy like that. All we could do was sit on the sofa, listen, and watch Haley's reactions to what his nephew was telling him. And those reactions weren't very encouraging.

"All I'm asking, Unc, is who could it be, right? I mean all the way down here? And she's tryin to spin some story to me like I'm an idiot about how cables just automatically get transferred to anyone's phone line. Yeah sure, maybe if it was coming from Pueblo. But *Planet 10???* Unc, *c'monnnn.*"

The whole time they were standing there in the kitchen doorway talking like we weren't even there not more than 10 feet away, except when Haley would give us these increasingly enraged and nervous looks over his shoulder.

"And she wouldn't tell you who it was?"

"Not even a hint. Just kept reminding me I wasn't the one in charge and she didn't have to do what I said."

"Yeah. Well she's right."

I could see from Ronnie's expression he didn't quite see that one coming.

"Unc….? C'mon, man. At least not in front of *them,* all right? This is family business, man. And whatever else you get pissed off at me about, you know you can trust me and you know I take care of the business. Always have."

Haley nodded slow, then clapped a hand on his nephew's shoulder before turning around to face the two of us full-on.

"So you guys keepin secrets? Is that what this is now?"

"Haley, this isn't meant as any kind of disrespect to you. But even if you don't believe us, I mean, are you seriously telling us we're supposed to tell your nephew the name, rank and serial number of everyone who calls us on our own phones?"

"Oh, so you're getting calls from Planet 10 too?

"I was just sayin…"

"I didn't think so. Shut the hell up. So who was that on the line, sweetness? This isn't Ronnie askin you anymore. This is me. And I'm thinkin maybe you should answer."

"Sure. OK," said Vee. "It was my dad."

Ronnie almost jumped out of his pants.

"What? WHAT?? Are you fuckin…"

Haley grinned, but there was still some nervousness behind it.

"Calm down Ronnie. You ain't helpin."

"Her *dad?* There is no damned *way,* Unc! Ask her why would she ask her dad how did he get that number, huh? If it was her dad then *how come she had to ask him how did he get that number?"*

"Hmm. Good question, don't you think, Vee? At least I think it's a good question."

"My dad and I aren't that close. What can I say? Guess he got it from one of my friends. Whoever it was gave him that number will have some explaining to do once I get back."

"You mean *if* you get back, sweetie. Which isn't looking good around now."

Vee bit her lip.

"Good answer, doll. Good answer. And next time you talk to your daddy give him my best. Or even better, let me talk to him why don't you? I'd love to meet the old man. Understand he's kind of the reason we're all about to be so rich."

Vee just stared.

"Right," said Haley. "Right…"

****

Over the next few days it was obvious just how paranoid Haley was. Or maybe he just had a really good set of antennae and knew when the walls were starting to cave in. First it looked like he was planning a quick trip back to Justice to shut down production, at least for awhile, until he had a better handle about what was going on. But then, after talkin to Butch and Cluck, he changed his mind. Later he called Johnny who was still back in Justice with a couple others looking out for the lab and overseeing production. All three of them were emphatic that the operation couldn't be shut down. They had been waitin a lifetime to get their revenge and when you want blood that bad, there wasn't much could get in the way of it. For the most part they were as intimidated by Haley as everyone else, but when it came to whether or not they would get their chance for payback, Haley was just a roadbump. Nobody was getting in the way of that.

"Simply put, it is of the utmost imperative that the children of these so-called purebloods be made to pay for their crimes against our kind. Naturally I am looking forward to the rather healthy financial remuneration to be coming our way from these otherwise shady endeavours, but first and foremost it is about..."

"All RIGHT! Jesus. All right. Whatever you say, Cluck, just please stop talkin like that or you're gonna make me kill you."

Cluck sniffed indignantly.

"If you have difficulty with my particular and peculiar..."

"Cluck, I swear if you don't..."

"Fine. Fine. Just remember the chickens."

Chapter 19

"How much time do you figure we have, Vid? I mean really?"

Vee wasn't one to sound worried all that often, but what we were facing was somethin to be worried about, and she was feeling the pinch. We both were.

"Not a lot, doll. Not a lot. But if we put the time we do have to some good use them I'm figuring we got a shot at surviving this thing. Just as long as we get that shot."

We were taking a much-needed walk around the block to try and sort through some strategy. Just a few days ago me and Vee taking this same walk was something we probably would have had to clear, but now Haley and Ronnie both figured whatever it was we were up to meant they could spend their time better pumping up the operation than trying to keep us under lockdown. Matter of fact when I overheard Ronnie question his uncle the other day about our back and forth, wondering if maybe that already tight leash should be tightened some more, Haley just said "That horse is already out the barn, kid. What we gotta do is make sure our thing is tight before this whole thing comes down on our heads."

It's not that any of them ever really trusted us that much, not Deep Cluck, not Butch, not Johnny Beardy, and definitely not any of the crew from Justice. Vee and I were always looked at as a kind of weak link, but a link they needed nevertheless. And a link they wanted to keep an eye on. But now that little thread of trust that had been more or less keeping us above ground was worn all the way through and the sound of that ticking clock had the two of us more on edge than we were accustomed to being. We'd both been in some tight spots before, but nothing like this.

"So then I say we run for it," said Vee. "Fast as we can while that door is still open."

"Run for it where, Vee? We got noplace to go. At least not until that story runs in the Screamer. Right now anywhere we go too far from here we get caught. Don't think Haley doesn't have a reach that goes way outside Colorado and just because he isn't bothering to monitor our trips around the block or to the diner or wherever doesn't mean he's just gonna sit still while we catch the first thing smokin for someplace way out in another time zone. And we definitely can't sneak back to Planet 10. So for now? We're stuck here. We gotta deal with the reality of that right there."

Vee muttered some choice curse words under her breath, then stopped. I kept walking for a few more steps then turned around.

"You still think we can take off running to safety? You still believe that?"

"Well *what* then, Vid? Are we going to just sit here and hope nothing happens before the Screamer decides to publish? You and I we've got targets on our backs, hey? And that's not the kind of fashion statement I want to make."

"Let's walk."

Huh?"

"For two critters on Earth with targets on their backs, standing in place talking on the sidewalk isn't the best. Let's keep walking."

"Fine."

"So here's what I suggest; I suggest we get ourselves ready for the confrontation we got coming from Haley, because we both know it's coming and probably sooner rather than later. That last little dustup we had wasn't the full deal. They're gonna want another powwow, and this time it's gonna be us versus everyone else. And when that day comes they're gonna think they're holding all the chips, that we've outlived our usefulness and that is when we tell them that the Gerruh are in town sniffin around. Soon as we play that card, I guarantee you the weight on our side of the scale starts to get real heavy and that's what gives us some bargaining room."

"Just by us telling them the Gerruh are snooping around? You think that's enough?"

"No. Not by itself. But when I tell them I may be the only option to throw the Gerruh off our scent then I think it definitely gets more interesting."

****

In my next life I'm plannin on bein a prophet.

Three days after our little walk-around-the-block strategy meeting is when everything started to go down pretty much as I predicted. I knew Vee was impressed, but she was also kinda ticked off and wasn't gonna show it.

So here's what happened; we were all back in Justice because that's where Haley and Ronnie needed to be to ramp up production. I knew it was also where they figured was the best place to have this showdown away from the eyes and ears of the Denver crew, because letting Denver overhear Haley's suspicions about us could have been a deal-breaker all the way around. So Vee and I are sitting there back on the couch in that cramped up little house, minding our own business and watching/not really watching TV because nobody wanted us doing anything else and nobody was talkin to us much. Or at all, really. Then, straight outta the blue, Haley hollers downstairs telling anyone and everyone who's down there to get their asses upstairs because there's a meeting about to happen.

"Here we go…" I said to Vee, almost in a whisper. "Remember the plan."

She nodded quick.

Once everyone was upstairs, Haley launches into his attack right away, and not just at us. He also starts jumpin all over Deep Cluck for bringing us along and sayin he shoulda left us for dead back on Planet 10. Deep Cluck starts tryin to explain why that wasn't an option, besides which there was no way he could have known anything was wrong back then, but Haley just shouted him down. That's when Butch jumped in attackin Haley and telling him he'd better not jump on Deep Cluck like that and he didn't give a damn who Haley thought he was because "I'll stomp you so deep in this ground they'll have to sweep you up."

Just when I was starting to think they might all self destruct before even getting to me and Vee was when Ronnie, surprisingly enough, got the runaway train back on track. He *reeeeally* didn't like us anymore, and he was determined we were going to get punished one way or another.

"Ronnie's right," said Haley. "We can't let ourselves get distracted on this thing. We don't have the time, thanks mostly to what these two have been up to recently. So I don't guess I need to rehash everything because we all know, or at least have a good idea, of what they're doin. They're tryin to shut us down, and they're workin with somebody back on Planet 10 to do it. We may have needed them before, or at least thought we did because I'm not even remembering why or what it was they brought to the table we couldn't do for ourselves, but anyway we damned sure don't need them anymore. They got to go."

I raised my hand.

"You can put that hand back down, junior. This thing's already been decided."

"So then you know the Gerruh are here then, right?"

Just mentioning the word was enough to bring a chill into the room. A low rumble of nervous murmurs started to percolate. Haley took a step back, almost like he was expecting them to break down the door right then.

"Here? Here like where? Why they here?"

I shrugged my shoulders.

"Not real sure, but I'm guessing somebody tipped them off about the MayoMadd. But seeing as how me and Vee are about to get exterminated up in here and that's already been decided then that's not really our problem anymore, is it? But I'd say it's definitely something that's gonna keep you clowns up late nights."

Haley and Ronnie exchanged glances. I grinned. Then I saw Butch and some of the other chickens standing together with Johnny Beardy and Deep Cluck. They all had their arms folded and didn't look worried in the least. How they looked was pissed. Pissed that something might be about to get in the way of their revenge.

"Maybe he's lyin," said Ronnie, sounding not quite convinced. "Besides, how would he know if the Gerruh are here? Not unless…"

I grinned wider.

"Yeah, unless *what,* Ronnie?"

"Jesus. You guys been workin with the *Gerruh??* But the Gerruh don't work with *nobody.* How in the...."

"Let's just say me and Vee here are your best bet of getting them off your trail, all right? You want them outta the picture - and mind you I'm not promising anything - but if you got any shot at all of getting them outta the picture so you can go back to business as usual, then it's us. Otherwise this whole thing's about to come crashin dowen, and I don't mean a long time from now either."

I don't know who it was came up with that phrase 'it was so quiet you could hear a rat pissin on cotton', but I'm tellin you it was the most beautiful sound I'd heard in awhile. It was the sound of survival.

Ours.

****

Three days later Vee and I are sittin at a booth in the back of a beat up little Justice bar. Come to think of it, it may have been the only bar in Justice, which was hard to figure since you figure anybody stuck in a rut like Justice would want as many excuses to drink as they could possibly find.

Sitting across from us, hands folded just as calm as always, were the Gerruh.

"Our first meeting as partners. This is quite an occasion," said the one sitting on the outside.

"Yeah, I'm thinkin we shoulda got some party favors or somethin like that. Sorry."

They both shrugged. Smiled.

Vee and I exchanged glances, then focused back on our guests.

"So. Here's where things stand as of today; production is getting ramped up double time. That's why we're back here in beautiful Justice, Colorado."

"And why the need to ramp things up, as you say? What could possibly have them spooked?"

"From what I heard they got wind of a possible raid, so they're kinda stockin up for the winter, if you know what I mean."

They both raised their eyebrows, and I could see the question marks hovering over their heads.

"Right. OK, what I mean is they're takin precautions, all right? Makin sure they have enough product to last them through whatever storm might be headed their way, and they're gettin it done quick."

"Hmmm. And where do you suppose they got wind of this raid you're talking about? Who else even knows enough about their operation to be raiding them? Aside from us, that is."

"That's a very good question, and I promise to get back to you with an answer just as soon as I can. Because we're partners and that's what partners do, right? In the meantime, my advice is you guys move in for the shutdown tomorrow before they have a chance to wrap this thing up. That way you guys get what you want, we get what we want, and everybody goes home happy. Nice, huh?"

"Indeed it is," said the one sitting on the inside closer to the wall. "Perhaps a bit too nice."

The other one didn't say a word. Just looked at me, then at Vee, then back at me again with those black, shark eyes.

"No such thing as too nice," I said.

****

The Gerruh decided they couldn't wait, which was kind of what I was hoping for. I knew they didn't trust us, and that our arrangement was just an arrangement of convenience. We were the only avenue to what the Gerruh needed so they had to work with us and they had to give us some of our terms. But they weren't about to just accept anything we told them as the truth. If we said it was raining outside, one of them was bound to step outside to make sure it was wet.

So that same night after we had our little meeting in the bar, the Gerruh headed over to the house to make their raid, probably thinking that since we told them to wait until tomorrow that might be some kinda trick to give the crew more time to leave.

Except that they had already left. Haley's gang hadn't wasted any time moving everything to an abandoned house three blocks away. It was pretty impressive how they managed to move everything so quick. Then again, when you saw how much junk they left behind maybe it wasn't such an amazing feat after all. Either way, Vee and I agreed that we weren't gonna find a better time to make our escape. Haley's crew was all caught up getting everything back online, and for them time really was money. And now that the Gerruh had figured out they'd been had by a couple of critters, it was only a matter of time - and not much time - before they tracked us down and reminded us of all the reasons why everybody was so scared of them. Although they still most likely wouldn't have killed us because they still didn't know where the operation had moved to. But if we had given them the crew's new location then they wouldn't have had much more use for us anyway and they would have killed us for sure, so it was a gamble we had to play for time. We needed to make our move and then hold tight until the Screamer ran that story.

But just before we disappeared we thought we'd leave Haley's gang a little something to remember us by. I got a neighborhood kid to drop it inside the mail slot of the front door at their new operation site. The note said:

Hi!

You may have noticed by now that we're gone. I'm sure you don't miss us, and the feeling is mutual. But just so we're clear, we're still in touch with the Gerruh, and the Gerruh kinda know your new address. That probably says it all, right?

You kids take care of yourselves. And best of luck with improving the world through better chemistry.

"But that's an abandoned house, mister. Why you wanna leave a message for somebody at an abandoned house?"

"You want the dollar or don't you?"

"I want five."

"What? Kid all I'm askin you to do is put a note on a door, not build the door to put it on. What the hell's wrong with you?"

"You want that note posted or not, mister?"

****

Two days later Vee gets the call from her father telling her the story just broke in the Screamer about the MayoMadd operation and how the Gerruh were named specifically as being involved in trying to "chop the head off the snake". Everybody knew about the Gerruh, how they were hired to 'take care' of certain situations by whoever had the resources to put them on the payroll, but it was the first time ever that the Gerruh had been publicly connected with anything at all. The Gerruh didn't just live in the shadows, they *were* the damn shadows. That was how they operated and how they got things done. It was also a big part of why everybody's heartbeat sped up whenever they were mentioned. They were the original mystery. Nobody even knew for sure where they had come from, whether it was Earth or whether they were some mutant form of critter. There were no records.

So when the Screamer made the decision to run a headline story using a disappeared star reporter as a source to finger Planet 10s two most dangerous individuals as being involved in trying to shut down an illegal drug operation on Earth? Yeah, well. Pretty big stuff. Which was why Vee's father was so sure the story would get picked up in a matter of days down here on the Mother Rock, as I liked to call it sometimes. Not to mention all the online chatter sites that were bound to eat this kinda story up like candy. After she finished telling me what he'd said, and then showing me a copy he had managed to wire through to her device, we were both feelin a little cocky. It was hard not to feel that way when you knew you had the Gerruh's nuts in your hand and you were about to squeeze real hard.

That afternoon we were right back at that ugly little Justice bar, at the same booth, sitting across from the Gerruh. They were reading the Screamer story, and they didn't look quite so calm as they had the last time we'd met. This really did feel good.

"Pretty good read, huh?" I asked. "Man, those reporters on the Screamer are top notch, don't you think? Kinda like that New York Times they got down here. The way they do that investigating and all that stuff. Pretty amazing I'd say, and you know…"

"You used our names."

"Huh? Where?"

"In the story. You used our names. We are never named."

"Oh wait. You mean both you guys are named Gerruh? Really? I always thought that was kinda like the name of your species or something like that. Didn't wanna ask though. That would have been rude. Anyway, that's why I - we - didn't think we had given them your names because we thought, well, like I said. But wow. Real sorry about that. Anything we can do to make it up to you?"

They both leaned across the table, shoving Vee's device toward us real slow.

"Where is the new location?"

"Except for that, I should have said. Sorry. That's the one thing…"

His hand felt like a cold vice clamped around my neck. Clamped a lot harder than how I thought we had them by the balls. At least at that moment. Vee started to jump to my rescue - don't know what the hell she thought she was gonna do - but the other Gerruh shot her a look that made her rethink the meaning of loyalty to one's friends.

"It doesn't take long, in case you were wondering. My hands are very strong."

I couldn't speak a word so I just wheezed to indicate that yes, I would agree he was very strong.

"What you two have done has put our arrangement with our client at risk, and that is not acceptable. You understand that?"

I wheezed again.

"Good."

He threw me back against the back of the booth. I hacked and choked for about a minute.

"Hey! Everything all right over there? I don't want any trouble in this place, OK guys?"

Both Gerruh turned to look at the bartender, a short stubby little guy with a face full of graying whickers, and soon as he got a glance at those eyes he backed up. His bravado shrunk like a you-know-what in ice cold water.

"Just try not to break anything, OK? The owner he don't like that kinda stuff."

"We won't be long," said the one who had nearly choked me to death.

"Not long at all," said the other.

The bartender nodded, then scooted away into a back room. The rest of the place was empty. The Gerruh refocused their attention on me. My neck hurt like hell, but the fact that I wasn't dead let me know we still had them in a tight spot. They needed to know where the new site was, and we were the only ones who could give them that information.

"I'll tell you this much. It's closer than you think, but far enough."

"Maybe I didn't make myself.."

"Clear? Sure you did. Because I'm still here. And the only way the two of us stay breathin is you don't find what you're lookin for until we're out of range. So yeah, we're very clear."

"There is no such thing as out of range, Mr. Vid. Not with us."

"That's what I hear, so I guess we'll see. But if you guys are such good investigators then you shouldn't have any trouble finding the place, right?"

"Perhaps. So then why don't I go look while my partner stays here?"

"Because he's not your partner he's your brother, and because the two of you have never been seen apart - *ever* - which tells me something."

The silence was hurting my eardrums, and it lasted a long time.

"I'm sure you're aware this is not over between us," he said.

"Gives me something to look forward to."

Chapter 20

But the story never did break big down here like it did back on Planet 10, which was not what we had been planning for, to say the least. It never made the 'feed', which was where all the stories that mattered were run on a constant flashing loop. There were a few alternative weeklies that picked it up, and the Weekly World News ate it up, which I guess shouldn't have been all that surprising since their long history of trafficking in the ridiculous hadn't changed since Jesus was in diapers. But that was about as much coverage as we got. To say we were shocked, amazed, surprised, or whatever ???!!$#@@#?!! word you can come up with related to those sorts of emotions still would fall short of what it was Vee and I were actually feeling as the days passed by and it began to dawn on us the situation we were in. The only coverage we got on TV was reported like some kind of amusing joke by a substitute anchor near the end of the program as she practically guffawed right into the screen about how ludicrous this whole thing was.

What she said exactly was this:

"OK, we're about out of time here folks, but just before we sign off and go to national news there's a little story that appears to be making quite a few big waves back on Planet 10. So big in fact that the Daily Screamer, Planet 10's largest and most respected news site, ran this story as a *banner*. So then what is this story? Well, the story is that (she starts chuckling here) a group of genetically engineered mutant chickens teamed up with rock star Johnny Beardy, a character named Deep Cluck, and a gang of local drug dealers to distribute a drug called MayoMadd to Earth kids. Apparently this was supposed to be some sort of revenge payback plot hatched by the chickens and Deep Cluck for how the chickens were mistreated when they were created here on Earth years ago as an experiment gone wrong.

"Are you with me so far? OK, well apparently the whole base of MayoMadd operations is right here in Colorado! But not to worry, because the notorious Gerruh twins are apparently on the case to shut the operation down, aided by an intrepid reporter and a gumshoe detective from Planet 10's Vivacious 5 sector. The only problem with the story? Well, actually there are a few. Johnny Beardy was found dead **several months ago by that same reporter and detective,** the mutant chicken experiment was terminated years ago along with all the mutant chickens, and if this new drug hitting the streets of Denver was some part of a plot to take over Planet Earth by getting kids hooked on it then Police Chief Hanson would like to know why this is all news to him. Good question! Let's listen in again in what he had to say at this press conference earlier today:

"I understand people are scared, and like I've said before I'm not denying there's a real serious drug problem in certain areas of this city. But so far our investigations just haven't turned up any evidence that this is anything different than what we've already seen. And so far it's not spreading beyond those boundaries so at least it's contained."

"Oh well. Fun story though, right? That crazy Screamer. You never know with those guys sometimes. And now for the national news where we discuss what's *really* going on in the world, right Bob?"

I'm willing to trade anyone else's life for mine right about now.

337

Deep Cluck, Beardy, and Butch had been watching that same news report back in Justice and they were fuming. For Deep Cluck and Butch especially it was like going back in time to a set of memories that held nothing but pain and anger. To the time that had taught them all they needed to know about rage; the rage that had come to shape and define them for the rest of their lives. Once upon a time they had been the perpetual punchline. They had been laughed at and scorned with no way out.

Those days were done.

"They think we're a damned joke," said Butch. "*A damned joke. This joke was never* supposed to be on *us,* guys. "

Deep Cluck nodded slowly, but said nothing.

Beardy cleared his throat.

"OK, listen, here's how I see this, and you dudes can tell me if I'm wrong, right? Look, it's nothin' against those other guys, Haley and Ronnie and them, all right? They're not that bad I guess. But I don't think we have the same perceptive here, you know?"

Deep Cluck winced.

"Objective."

"Huh?"

"I do believe the word you intended to employ was 'objective', dear boy. It is not quite possible for us to either have or not have the same '*perceptive*'. It is, however, and I would agree wholeheartedly by the way, entirely possible and even likely that we do not indeed share the same *objective* with our new friends."

"Wow. Dude, I'm sorry. I'm a rock star, not a grammar king."

"It's the thought that counts. And while we are on the subject of thinking, and possibly re-thinking our current situation, I do think we all three of us need to recall the original reason and motivation, the original *objective* as it were, for why we signed on to this MayoMadd operation in the first place. Was it for the money?"

"Hell no!" said Butch.

"What, then?"

Butch and Beardy shared a heated glance, then answered Deep Cluck in unison:

"Revenge."

****

"Haley? Ronnie? We need to talk."

The two had been on a supply run and were noticeably edgy due to the recent turn of events. Haley, who was edgy all the time, was particularly annoyed by the more forceful tone he picked up in Deep Cluck's voice. And what was it with the way the three of them were standing there all together with their arms folded like that? What the hell was going on?

"Yeah, well. We probably do. About a lotta things. But now ain't the best time for that Cluck. We got things to do, and we got a tight schedule to do it in, so…"

"Excuse me but we happen to agree that now is the perfect time. If you don't mind my saying so, of course."

Nothing in Cluck's voice implied that he cared even the slightest bit of a damn whether Haley minded or not.

"Oh? So then the three of you are in agreement on this thing? *Really* now. Well then you should have said that in the beginning, because naturally if the three members of the Planet 10 brain trust are in agreement on a thing then that thing, well, that thing obviously must be extremely important. Wouldn't you say so Ronnie?"

Ronnie chuckled, then lit a cigarette.

"Whatever you say, Uncle."

"Uh-huh. Right. So then let's hear it fellas. What is this thing that now is such a perfect time for? Spit it out so we can all get back to work. Time is money, and money's being wasted here."

"It was never about the money," grumbled Butch.

"Yo, not that we have anything against…*oooff!"*

Without a word of warning Deep Cluck had jabbed an extremely pointed elbow directly into Beardy's rib cage, and he had done so with considerable force.

"Hey man, what the…?"

"I believe what my colleagues are attempting to convey is that although money is fine - it does make the world go 'round and 'round after all - it was never the primary motivation in this particular instance. The production of MayoMadd is merely a jig in the saw of a much larger puzzle we consider a much higher calling."

"Say *what?"*

"Dude, you ever hear of a rock group called the Beatles?"

"The *who?*"

"Beardy, perhaps I should be the one to…"

"They were huge back in the 20th century. I know that's a while back, but still most folks…OK. Anyway. They had this song, right? It went kinda like this…"

"I don't fuckin' believe this," said Ronnie, as Beardy started to hum and then to sing:

"Talkin' 'bout a revolution…"

Deep Cluck smiled, then listened appreciatively. Once Beardy was through, he began to lay out the plan as Haley and Ronnie stood there trying to figure out exactly what had just happened.

"What we will need is reinforcements from back home. Lots of them."

"Reinforcements?"

****

Soames didn't spend a lot of time at home. He was a workaholic. His wife, Patty, knew

this about him when she'd married him but it didn't bother her. Much. The two had

known each other since kindergarten, and the one thing she knew about her husband that

mattered most was that he had been a good kid, the kind who always jumped in whenever

other kids picked on the weaklings, and who had grown up to be the same kind of man.

So whenever he got wrapped up in a case that sent him to that other 'place' inside himself,

she had learned how to adjust.

He was a good man.

As she stood leaning against the bedroom doorway, watching him stare at the TV with an

intensity that was almost frightening, Patty reminded herself of that. Then, as if he had

been listening in on her thoughts, Soames suddenly looked over at her and smiled. Patted

the empty spot on the bed next to him, then motioned for her to come over.

"So what's this you're watching on the news?" she asked, seeing what she considered a

factory-issue attractive TV anchor laughing in an airhead cutesy sort of way about

whatever news she was reporting. Then Police Chief Hanson appeared on the screen.

"I understand people are scared, and like I've said before I'm not denying there's

a real serious drug problem in certain areas of this city. But so far our

investigations just haven't turned up any evidence that this is anything different

than what we've already seen. And so far it's not spreading beyond those

boundaries so at least it's contained."

"*Contained..?*" mumbled Soames, his voice almost sorrowful, seeming to forget his wife was in the room just that quick.

"Jesus Christ, I don't even believe this."

"Honey I don't...I don't know what you mean. What is it he said?"

Soames reached over and gently squeezed his wife's wrist, then began to stroke the back of her hand almost absent-mindedly.

"Bobby what is it? What's wrong?"

"That man is the Chief of Police, Patty. The Chief of Police. And he has no idea what's about to land on his doorstep."

****

Vee and I should have been aboard a transport headed home where everybody would welcome us as big celebrities who put the brakes to the MayoMadd plot to enslave Earth kids. Instead, we were somewhere far out on eastbound I-70 at a gas station with no idea where we we were headed and even less of an idea where we would end up. Our one big shot to set things right meant that the local rags had to take the Screamer seriously and recognize what kinda threat they were facing. I knew the purebreds always liked to have a few laughs at our expense and always figured we were a few steps too far down the evolutionary ladder to share the pedastal with them and their kind, but usually we still had enough of a mutual respect or whatever where they would listen if they knew it was

343

something big. Our story wouldn't have been the first time their news media ran a scoop from the Screamer, not including all the times they just flat out stole the Screamer's stuff and called it their own. But still, Vee said it wasn't anything new to run a Screamer piece down here, and some would even put it up front.

"And none of those stories were as big as the one I practically hand-delivered to those bastards," she said, standing next to me stretching her legs as I pumped the gas. "*None* of them. This would have been the biggest scoop they ever ran, even bigger than most of the stuff they come up with on their own. This is a huge story Vid!"

I nodded, staring at the nozzle and wondering how much longer we should keep driving this stolen car.

"Yeah. It is. You know that, and I know that. So then why doesn't anyone down here even care? I mean they're acting like this whole thing is something we just made up. If they think the Screamer would do somethin that unethical like print an imaginary scandal as front page news then why did they ever trust them enough to take stories from them in the first place? Does that make sense to you? I mean…forget it. Let me finish pumpin and then I gotta take a piss. This crap is taking up entirely too much space between my ears right now."

Once I got done taking care of my business (I was pleasantly surprised at how clean they kept their stalls) I flushed, dried my hands with a paper towel because I hated those hot air machines, then reached to pull open the door when I heard this small knock. The men's room door was located around the side of the building not quite in plain view so I figured maybe whoever this was hadn't seen me step inside.

"Occupied, but I'm comin out right now," I said.

No answer, which shouldn't have been a big deal but for some reason it bothered me.

"I said I'm comin out right now, OK? Just hang on."

I heard a hoarse cough, then somethin that sounded like a shoe scrapin back and forth on the ground.

"Um yeah. Cool. No rush, man."

"Uh-huh. OK. Good. Comin out."

When I stepped outside, I noticed the kid was built small and kinda reminded me of a bird that hadn't eaten in awhile. A bird with long dark brown hair and a dirty green army jacket wearing red sneakers. He tossed his hair out of his eyes then looked up at me with a nervous kinda smile. He was holdin somethin in his right hand, a small packet…wait a minute…I recognize…

"Hey you're a critter right? Yeah, that's cool. Real cool."

"What? Oh, yeah. I'm a critter. You're real observant. So what's that you have in your hand, kid?"

The smile stretched wider as his eyes did a quick survey to make sure nobody else was standing near. Then he leaned in close.

"You know they're sayin on the news that this shit ain't real man, that it don't even *exist*. But once you try it?"

He shook his head back and forth real slow, adding emphasis to what he was about to say.

"Dude."